The Fall of the Saudeleurs

The Legends of Ḷainjin

Book Four

The Fall of the Saudeleurs

The Legends of Ḷainjin

Book Four

A novel of historic literary fiction by Gerald R. Knight
Follow the story at GeraldRKnight.com

IGUANA

Published by Iguana Books
720 Bathurst Street, Suite 303
Toronto, ON M5S 2R4

Publisher: Cheryl Hawley
Editor: Shelley Egan
Cover design: Jonathan Relph
Front cover image: "Canoe Models" by Herbert Kawainui Kane, with permission from Herbert K. Kane, LLC.
Back cover image: Erika Bisbocci

ISBN 978-1-77180-635-0 (paperback)
ISBN 978-1-77180-636-7 (epub)

This is an original print edition of *The Fall of the Saudeleurs: The Legends of Ļainjin.*

"Knowledge of the past gives us a rudder to navigate the present."

— Herbert Kawainui Kane

The escape

"Your father … is Nahn … Sapwe! Your father … is Nahn … Sapwe."[1] Chanting to himself, Ijokelekel[2] dog-paddled across the canal as best he could with a lime tucked between the thumb and forefinger of each hand. Now and again, he eyed the tops of the walls towering around him to assure himself that watchmen weren't looking, then turned a furtive glance back with what may have appeared a taunting smirk to his pursuer, Lañinpo,[3] whose out-of-breath silhouette stood boxed by the stone-walled entrance of Pahn Kadira.[4] At first, he'd been worried that Lañinpo would follow. Now he was elated because the foolish foreign bully hadn't dived and used his long, lanky arms to propel himself to quickly capture him.

Of course, that changed instantaneously once Ijokelekel reached Lañinpo's outrigger canoe, anchored among others at Kelepwei,[5] and arrogantly drew his small, skinny body out of the water to board the vessel. He heard the other's plunge as he carelessly discarded the bright green limes, which rolled toward the lip of the deck, and untied the boat from its stern anchor. Then he scampered to the other end to release the bow line. Struggling with Lañinpo's gigantic paddle and straddling the foredeck, Ijokelekel managed to nudge the large *proa*[6] backward into the sheltered

---

[1] Pohnpeian spirit of thunder; he cracked the megalithic basaltic crystals from the cliffs with his voice.

[2] Ļainjin's son with Lipanmai.

[3] A name: "heavy weather requiring the striking of sails." A Seeker; Rojak's brother.

[4] The man-made islet of the Saudeleur.

[5] A man-made islet across from Pahn Kadira used to house visitors.

[6] An outrigger canoe rigged with a sail.

water of the canal, then rush back abaft. Straining with all his might, he turned and paddled the craft, too large for him to maneuver properly, just fast enough to beat his pursuer to the oncoming breeze at the islet's corner of stacked *takai.*[7]

The foreigner's proa was much like the one Paratak[8] had taught him to sail, only bigger. "Sail boom heavier," he thought, striving to hoist its halyard as quickly as possible while at the same time anxiously watching Lañinpo — but half the man he once was, people said — endeavor to close the gap.

"No! Wait! Let me explain." Lañinpo pleaded from a distance in Pohnpeian, treading water and panting as he spoke. "No one will hurt you! No one wanted to…" he muttered, losing his breath.

"*Liet*,"[9] the boy shouted back. "*Liet*! *Liet*! My father is Nahn Sapwe, and you are a filthy *liet*!" With that, despite Lañinpo's continuing entreaties and then warnings that he had "no place to go," he sheeted in and swiftly headed off across the reef. The morning tide was outgoing. He headed toward the passageway through the west-most wall, built of the same megalithic, multisided stones his ancestors had used to build their village on the reef.

He spoke to his mother's spirit. "He says I have no place to go, Mother, but my father goes everywhere! Does he not?"

"Always remember you have a *pali*[10] who, one day, will come back and teach you everything." She had informed him of this nearly every day. "They call him Pako.[11] You must offer him a lime and tell him you are the son of Nahn Sapwe." He reminded himself of her words, gathering the limes and quickly placing them safely below.

---

[7] Pohnpeian for "stones"; essentially the same as the Kajin Rālik word "dekā." The hexagonal basaltic crystals used to construct the pre-historic city of Nahn Madol upon a reef flat off the eastern shore of Pohnpei. These megalithic crystals date back to the volcanic origin of the island.

[8] Ļainjin's Pohnpeian friend and the father of Likōkkāļọk's daughter, Erwina.

[9] Pohnpeian for "cannibal" or "cannibal peoples."

[10] Pohnpeian for "palu." "Traditional navigator" in the languages of what are now the Western Caroline Islands of the Federated States of Micronesia.

[11] Shark. Ļainjin's nickname: "man shark." Aka Ļōpako.

"Mother, I don't have to wait for the pali to come. Paratak knows where his island lies. He has taught me the direction over the swells that roll beneath the waves. I know the direction, Mother. I'll sail to the pali now and learn everything."

Then he looked back and saw the hated cannibal swimming down the channel between Kelepwei's high, magically stacked walls of enormous takai toward Idedh,[12] and he felt his throat droop at the thought that Lañinpo might take Paratak's canoe and sail after him.

He had helmed his Uncle Paratak's canoe out into the ocean many times through the western break in the otherwise impenetrable stone walls that protected his father's temple. He had been told to call Paratak "uncle" though he was not. This time, he was alone but waved at the watchmen atop the west wall anyway. "I am the son of Nahn Sapwe," he shouted up at them, as was his wont.

The man on the right laughed. "Ijokelekel, you are a sand crab."

"You better scamper back to your hole before you're eaten by a bird or a fish," said the one to his left.

"It's rude to call a man by his name, but no mind," he thought, thankful they had apparently not seen him steal the canoe. Soon they would hear that his mother had been killed by the ugly little creature that Lañinpo called "brother" and be sorry they hadn't treated the son of Nahn Sapwe with more respect. He smirked at the thought that the Saudeleur[13] would no doubt reprimand them for not preventing him from sailing off in his favorite cannibal's canoe. One day, he would return as a man with a fleet of loyal followers to cure the ills of these unbelievers, and his name would remain silent on their lips like a herbal tea too hot to sip.

Ijokelekel cupped one hand around his lips and *woo*ed up at them. They each responded good-naturedly with a short, soft blast from their conch shells.

By the time he had heard Lañinpo's warning blast from Paratak's conch and the watchmen had blasted their response, he was halfway to the blue-water drop-off at the little southern lagoon. That tiny gulf of blue water, like

---

[12] One of many man-made islets on the reef off the coast of eastern Pohnpei.

[13] The highest titled one of Nahn Madol. The ruler of Pohnpei.

the much larger northern one that harbored the stone village, allowed them to sail directly into the ocean. This allowed them to enter the deep water without having to overcome the dangerous edge of the reef that spanned the distance between. All along that reef's edge, he could see and hear swells breaking scarily into white water. Ijokelekel hoped he was tricking Lañinpo into thinking he was headed for the mangrove swamps to the south. There were lots of hiding places there. He wanted Lañinpo to chase him through the same route he had taken. If he headed through the north lagoon, the older man might cut him off before he escaped into the western horizon.

Luckily, Lañinpo wouldn't see him flip his sail and head north, because the enormous south walls of the village would block his vantage until he cleared the west-most one.

Ijokelekel needed to head into the wind. If he kept upwind of him, Lañinpo would never catch him. How many times had he listened to Paratak say his craft was no good sailing into the wind? He said the pali had the proa made that way to prevent his return to Lae. Paratak had told him he'd freed himself from the enchantment of their chief's niece there. She had enticed him with her magic, but he was sad for his beautiful daughter, whom he missed terribly. Lañinpo's boat, on the other hand, was Ijokelekel's best chance to sail to this pali.

Once safely at sea, it was time to shunt his sail. He released his sheet, scooted to the bow, unsecured the forestay, untied the thing Paratak called the *bal*[14] from its seat, and lifted it back onto the foredeck. He had done this often for Paratak, but this sail was heaver. He tried to scoot the *bal* down the foredeck, but as the boat turned and the mast went vertical, it raised the *bal* of its own accord. And as the canoe's direction was swung by the wind's invisible hand, he had to scramble to guide it over the canoe's yoke and down to the opposite end.

Successful beyond his expectations, he adjusted the mast's stays, drew his sheet, and guided the boat as close to the oncoming wind as possible. Shortly thereafter, he saw Lañinpo emerge from the western break in the wall. He surprised Ijokelekel by flipping his sail with incredible quickness. His

---

[14] The foot beneath the clew of the lateen sail where its vertical gaff and horizontal yard join.

intention, apparently, was to cut across the reef diagonally and brave the breaking swells that rolled onto the reef's edge.

This was a turn of events Ijokelekel hadn't expected. "He'll be sailing faster on his reach run and might just be able to cut us off," he thought, still speaking to his mother's spirit. "Maybe we should have headed into the swamps after all? No, those breaking swells should slow him down even if he is somehow successful in overcoming them." With that, he breathed in deeply and then pretentiously exhaled as strongly as possible — as though he were Nahn Sapwe himself — to do what he could to blow the waves even harder down onto the reef separating them. Such were his tactics, to sail as closely as possible into the wind and pretend to command the sea by such means. Then, when he saw Lañinpo cross over the edge of the white-water drop-off into the deep blue depths and effortlessly lunge his craft over, among, and between the crashing swells, he took solace that they had slowed him down just enough to allow him, in his more eastward position, to slip ahead of Lañinpo's anticipated point of closure.

As fate would have it, that was exactly what happened. Lañinpo closed in on him just shy of his stern and began to audibly curse Paratak's craft for its lack of cut into the wind. Then, perhaps trying to distract Ijokelekel from his course, Lañinpo raised his voice and attempted to negotiate with him from his wake. "Lipanmai's[15] death was an accident. She fell on the temple steps and broke her neck."

"The little *akebu*[16] pushed her. I know he did!"

"He only wanted to touch her. When you become a man, you will understand."

"He wanted to eat her! I heard him tell you that!"

"That was a joke. Where the little akebu comes from, men joke about such things, but they only eat their enemies!"

"Was it a joke when you ate Kielua?"[17] Ijokelekel asked, continuing to concentrate on his course.

---

[15] Ijokelekel's mother; a Pohnpeian name meaning "woman under the breadfruit tree."

[16] Komba word for a lineage leader who served as the priest or "forbidden man" of Lāpio cult worship and practiced the medicinal and magical arts.

[17] The man who failed to deliver his stone as agreed and was sacrificially eaten.

"That's the new law. He caught himself up in a bad trade. The Saudeleur had to punish him to maintain the law."

"The new law is bad. The Saudeleur is too young and unwise, and the little akebu should go back where he came from. Everyone says so. Paratak says so. My mother said so!"

"Well, that's the law now that Nahn Samohl[18] is dead."

"Dead, they say, by the Saudeleur's own neglect and disregard for our religion. The pali challenged the Saudeleur's unjust laws, overcame them, and lived to tell about it. I sail to find him! Paratak has shown me the way, and you can't follow. The next time you see me, I'll be a man. I'll grow to know everything," argued the determined boy.

Lañinpo was the one who now appeared to be worried about the widening gap between his bow and the boy's stern. Ijokelekel wondered whether he was about to plunge into the sea and try to swim the gap.

"I wouldn't try, *liet*! Your craft will turn away, and I will turn off wind and leave you alone out here without a float. You can't catch me, and you know it!" As the swell raised one boat in its wake and then the other, Ijokelekel imagined that the words he spit onto the light breeze were spears aimed at the ears of his pursuer.

"What are you to eat?" Lañinpo shouted into the breeze, apparently discarding the thought of putting his life in danger and returning to negotiation. "Didn't Paratak teach you to take food and water to sea? Have you ever gone a day without drinking?"

These words cut into Ijokelekel's throat like a shell knife. Paratak had never stopped talking about the need to take food and water to sea. In all the excitement, it had slipped his mind. "Don't panic! He's trying to get you distracted again," Ijokelekel told himself, noticing that the other canoe had crept closer. He doubled his concentration on steering as close as possible to the wind while contemplating the new view of his predicament that Lañinpo's words had awakened. "You are a pali too. You must have left plenty of food and water aboard your boat. I'll take my chances."

"I may have something, but not nearly enough to get you halfway there," Lañinpo said. "You're a little fool who is about to learn a big lesson! The sea

---

[18] The sacred eel used to arbitrate disputes between trading partners.

will swallow you like a leaf blown from a tree. How does the saying go? Like an inchworm crawling upon the sea."

"Thank you. I'll take my chances. Better than being eaten by cannibals."

"A boy knows nothing about the law and why it is so." Still holding his tiller with one hand, Lañinpo reached below to fetch Paratak's netted water shells.[19]

Ijokelekel watched him load them all onto the outrigger deck, twist their leaders into a single knot, and then — surprisingly — slide the lot of them into the sea. "Why did you do that?" he called back.

"Because even a misguided insect like yourself deserves a fighting chance. If your lot is to find your pali, tell him that I saved your life!" And with those final words, Lañinpo turned his craft from the wind and headed back toward the reef from whence he had come.

Surprisingly, the water shells had popped up on the surface, and Ijokelekel could see them floating over the shallow crests as they passed. He at once released his sheet and heaved to in the light breeze, watching his former pursuer sailing away without a glance back at him. So, before he lost sight of the precious gift, he flipped sail, came about, and snatched them from the sea. He unplugged one of the emptier ones and sipped to assure himself the water was still sweet. Then he glanced at the retreating figure, there between him and the island of his birth, and wondered why one pali was so good and the other so bad.

From an early age, some would laugh when he announced he was the son of Nahn Sapwe. Especially so the jealous children. "Your father was probably the Saudeleur himself! He got drunk one night and poked your mother from behind as she climbed the temple steps. When he woke, he forgot all about it and will never recognize who you are."

"That is ridiculous!" his mother had assured him. "Nahn Sapwe is your father. I am his mistress, and he rewarded my efforts by giving me you! Have I not kept his fire burning?" She never allowed his fire to die, and that was the obvious proof she told the truth.

Ijokelekel liked talking to his mother like this. Her voice ran as clear through his memory as the water splashing from the eaves onto the coral

[19] Mature coconut shells, their meat hollowed out by tiny crabs, filled with water and their mouths stuffed tight with a plug.

stones outside the window they had shared. Her presence gave him the strength to flip sail once again, and then again at regular intervals, tacking eastward like Paratak had taught him. She gave him strength to turn away from the mountains that lingered behind, the rain clouds filling its deep valleys, the white waterfalls streaking down its cliffs. She inspired strength to head back toward the sea, stretched sparkling in the afternoon sun before him — she, the sea, ever so silently whispering her promise of a better future into his ears. He faced her breeze as though listening to the ever so quiet sound of an empty shell. He would learn soon enough, as any seaman knows, that her promise is more like that of a fickle lover. Her charisma doesn't hold true like that of a mother expectantly remaining ashore but is subject to her erratic flux, torment, and distress. Surely, she was tempting him, even now, out into the midst of her domain with her most pleasant face, most revealing skirts, and her sweetest and most benign breath, lulling him to complacency with the elegant sway of his sail as it danced over one gentle wave after another. Not that Paratak hadn't cautioned Ijokelekel by telling his story of tortuous drift along the course now set before him, but this wasn't the time of the dangerous big winds. Nor was it the time of the long wind that daily whipped the sea into such mountainous swells — which crashed onto the island's barrier and fringing reefs — that no boat could cross them.

"No, this was the good time in between, so why would Paratak's tale apply?" Ijokelekel thought. The sea's docile draft cooled the sweat from his body, and he removed another plug from another water shell, taking a sip and gazing out at the sparsely clouded, bright blue horizon.

Some referred to Paratak as a pali for having crossed the sea and returned to tell of his adventures. Paratak loved him but was quick to admit he was ill prepared to teach Ijokelekel all the skills he would need for the voyage they had mused about. Paratak liked to show him the fishing skills he had learned from his father and the trolling skills the man called Pako had taught him. However, Paratak was known as a fair-weather fisher. He would wait till the weather turned just right before taking him out, and he had crafted nearly every experience at sea for his pleasure.

Therefore, despite his teacher's warnings, Ijokelekel lacked fear spurred from discomfort. He lacked attentiveness to the sea's moody temperament, the respect she expected and required. Yet his faith in himself would allow him to set all such thoughts aside — the shame he should feel for stealing another man's canoe and leaving a legacy of wrongdoing behind as well as the concern that he was setting off on an ill-conceived journey with a poorly drawn plan and much risk to his life. Lañinpo would have known this, of course, which was why he had offered him water, and so would Paratak, which was probably why Ijokelekel had hastened off with his canoe in pursuit. Deep down, Ijokelekel knew his mother would scold and warn him that he might be making a mistake. That was why he kept reminding himself who his father was and why he knew he would protect him in the end. Did his thunder not rule the sea? Did the earth not cringe at his booming voice? Did the takai not fall at his command?

Still, out into the great ocean he crept like the proverbial worm, a nothing telling himself he was truly something and would prove it so. He sailed. He looked back. He sailed on until the sun began to set behind and the seabirds seemed to squawk down at him as though to inquire why he was sailing away from his nest with no moon to guide him.

"I don't need the moon," he said aloud. "Liṃanṃan[20] will be my guide." He remembered the night Paratak had told him that the pali called Pako had been taken by the most beautiful star in the sky.

"I don't think it's so beautiful! Why didn't he take that one?" Ijokelekel had argued, pointing behind them to the much brighter evening star called Maalal.[21] "I would take her!"

"Then you would get but a brief kiss before she disappeared into the night to who knows where? Watch her," Paratak had proposed as they paddled out to the barrier reef to fish.

Ijokelekel had looked back as the star slowly abandoned him even before they had begun to bait their hooks — as though she had chased after a sliver of moon as it ducked behind the mountains and out of sight.

"Liṃanṃan is the only star among them all that doesn't move," Paratak had told him. "Yes, there are many brighter. Some are red. Some are blue.

---

[20] Irooj's daughter; Ḷainjin's chosen one. A name: "woman beautiful." "Li": the female prefix; "ṃanṃan": "very beautiful." The north star, Polaris.
[21] Evening star; Venus (evenings only).

She is pale white and very dainty. Sometimes her light is hidden by clouds that cover the horizon, but she is the one light in the sky that never, ever moves! You will be lucky to find a woman half as dependable!"

On other occasions, Ijokelekel would ask Paratak, "So, where is Lae?"

"Lae, I'm told, is an exceedingly small atoll. It's the only one I've seen, but I'm told that many are out there, like pendants on two necklaces stretching far beyond the entire length of the horizon from north to south. But there is one problem. There is much ocean between them."

"Point to it!"

"Okay, this is what the pali taught me. Only he taught me backward from Lae. First, you face Liṃanṃan and point your … left hand toward her. Now put your right hand out, pointing perpendicular to your left, and swing your left arm halfway to your right. Cut the distance in half, like you're cutting a wedge of, say, breadfruit. Now cut the wedge in half again with your left hand. Okay, that is your wedge of life. Sail into that wedge and you live. Lae is just inside the northern limit of that wedge. It took me four days. But I saw clouds and then the mountains. There are no mountains in Rālik[22] or Ratak.[23] You watch for birds at sunrise, flying away from land, and at sunset, they return toward it. The secret is to feel the swells beneath you. There are waves that come from whichever direction the wind blows, and then there are swells. Pako says they come from each quadrant and sometimes cancel each other out. The swell he taught me to ride is the big one that comes from the east. He taught me to disregard the waves and follow the swells. I crossed them one after the other, like rolling hills, at the perfect angle he taught me. To get to Lae, you need to know what I did and then perform it properly in reverse."

Those directions — including the exact cut of his bow over the swells that underlie the waves, keeping Liṃanṃan at her point of reference and the corresponding cut of his sail to the wind, depending on its direction — were the entirety of his instructions for this voyage. That, and his certainty

[22] The western chain of atolls of what is now known as the Republic of the Marshall Islands.

[23] The eastern chain of atolls of what is now known as the Republic of the Marshall Islands.

that his father, Nahn Sapwe, wouldn't let him die out there. His father had inspired his mission because surely, he wanted him to take up where his mother had left off. She had wanted him to return one day to avenge her death and lead his people against the Saudeleur who, under the little akebu's influence, had brought the shame of cannibalism down upon them all.

Nevertheless, once the sun had set behind the horizon and the light from the stars was glittering upon the sea around him, Ijokelekel felt a glimpse of doubt. How was he to sail the night through without sleep?

He struggled to stay awake. He began to doze a bit now and then. Before he realized what was happening, he awakened to the abrupt sound of his rigging as it crashed down across his outrigger platform, leaving him distraught. He had allowed his sail to backwind. That was that, and all he could think to do was to crawl into the very narrow hull, wrap himself in Lañinpo's mat, and sleep. His sleep was no good and neither were his dreams, interrupted as they were by the incessant, sometimes violent rocking of his stolen craft. He rose at dawn to view the mess on deck. Draped over the outrigger booms and deck — like a cover over a pile of dried copra — lay Lañinpo's beautifully plaited pandanus sail. The sail's head propped over the outrigger float and pointed down into the sea. The leech end of its boom was propped up by the two upward-slanting outrigger booms at an awkward angle well above the waves, its telltale feathers still fluttering horizontal in the breeze.

"What a mess," he thought, quickly retreating into his rocking shell like a hermit crab would when disturbed and tossed into a basket of bait to await its uncertain fate. What was he to do now? He knew too well that the mast was too heavy for him to lift by himself. It wasn't as though this hadn't happened before, but Paratak had always used his strength to put things right again.

So, he slept late, mostly because he had slept poorly. He had become dizzy below and thrown up the last of his mother's cooking. Now, he found himself burrowing through the canoe in search of food. He found one net of sun-dried bananas and another of sun-dried breadfruit wedges. The food was moldy. Lañinpo should have discarded it before the last moon. He started washing a piece but stopped himself once he remembered he had no water to spare. He ate his morning meal despite the mold and lay back, discouraged by his circumstance. He knew other children lacked his ability to solve problems, and he often searched for opportunities to surpass them — especially the ones who teased him. He saw them laughing at him now, and this spurred him to show them he wouldn't fail. After some thought and much intermittent observation, he cautiously concluded he must stop crouching like a hermit crab in his shell and scramble to save his life.

He sat for a while, observing the situation. The trick would be *not* to try to do what he had seen Paratak do. Not to struggle with everything at once, because he wasn't strong enough to do that. He must work creatively and replace brute force with deliberation. First, he needed to free the sail. All lines supporting the mast ran through the masthead. None of these lines would have broken, so none should have tangled, leaving no reason to detach them. But he had to release the halyard that secured the yard and slide the yard down the prone mast — gathering the wet sail as best he could in the process. He crawled across the outrigger platform beneath the sail, following the mast until he reached the cleat that secured the halyard and untied it. From this angle, he could see the yard loosen from the masthead as the waves washed over the submerged head of the sail.

Unfortunately, there was no line to pull the yard down from the masthead. In its proper raised position, the yard would naturally fall from the weight of the sail once its halyard had been released. He crawled back to the hull, found a line below, sank down into the sea, swam out to the masthead, and tied the line to the yard about a third of the way down from its tip, where the masthead and the yard had joined. Though the sail was wet and heavy, he pulled its yard from the stern deck all the way to the sail's horizontal boom. The pocket of the sail now closed, its triangle halved, he climbed out on the outriggers and bundled up the heavy, wet sail as best he could. After much struggle, he maneuvered it, with halyard still attached, into the water to lee of the hull.

Now the mast was lying across the outriggers all the way to the float supporting them. His biggest problem was that, with all lines attached, the mast was too heavy for him to simply grab hold of and step, as he had seen Paratak do many times. The trick would be to somehow lever the end into its place at the yoke of the vessel and pull it upright, using the wet sail in the water as a counterweight. Its butt end rose nearly to his knees as it teetered over the outrigger platform. He pulled on the halyard. The masthead rose a bit, but the butt of the mast just slid backward, further out of place. He could see that it would eventually slide into the water stern of the outrigger deck. Somehow, he needed to secure the butt of the mast to prevent it from sliding away from its seat at the yoke.

He ducked below, brought up Lañinpo's sleeping mat and marlinspike, and chuckled to himself as he began prying holes between the strips of tightly plaited material a few hand's lengths from each corner. His idea was to fashion the mat into a sort of cradle to trap the butt of the mast and prevent it from slipping backward as he raised the masthead. When he pulled on the halyard now, it lifted the masthead, but the butt of the mast remained cradled and secured. And after a few more tugs, it levered itself down onto the outrigger platform close to the yoke, where it normally stood. In this way, he was able to raise the mast — which was already secured by its forward and rear stays, and the heavy line to the *kubaak*[24] — to its normal position using the halyard attached to the floating sail as the counterweight. He had to periodically loosen the lines to the mat's upward corners as he pulled the mast vertical. Once it was upright, he could slide and then lift the mast butt a short distance to its normal seat at the yoke.

Once all four lines secured to the mast were taut and, therefore, immovable, the yard began to rise from the sea and catch in the breeze. At that point, Ijokelekel moved forward, secured the *bal* to its place at the bow, and then resumed raising the yard until the entire sail flapped wet and heavy in the breeze. Then he sheeted in, and his craft moved forward as before, no worse for the mishap.

So it was that the sand crab showed his detractors he could think through the mechanics of his predicament and continue his journey toward whatever destiny the sea, in its capriciousness, would afford him. Lesson learned, he would henceforth heave to, lower, and prop his sail before he slept. Unfortunately, he would find other mistakes more difficult to rectify. As the days passed, Lañinpo's warning that his water would last but half his

---

[24] Outrigger float.

journey reverberated through his thoughts. More so as his lips began to crack in the dehydrating breeze and persistent glare of the benevolent yet merciless sun.

Grey clouds occasionally appeared on the otherwise brilliant horizon from day to day, but even when they passed overhead — with Lañinpo's sail dropped and funneled — what rain he collected was brackish from the sail's previous bath in the sea. So, like the sand crab the watchmen had accused him of being, he learned to hide himself below during most of the bright half of the day. Then he'd scamper about during the other half, under the cold light of the moon's quickly setting crescent or the night sky's more slowly revolving and incredibly distant glow. Finally, all food was gone and, still far from land, his trolling lure struck not, and his strength dwindled. Most evenings, he could hardly raise his halyard. Eventually, after several more days, his fate — as Lañinpo had foreseen — was to drift like an insect on a leaf, waiting in silent desperation for the sea to snuff its life with one erratic splash.

* * *

Yet somewhere out there, in the great expanse of ocean south of his position, silently crept a powerful current of water like a deep river in the sea, a broad ocean eddy that flowed contrary to the prevailing swells. Rālik Islanders called it *kāleptak.*[25] As its name implies, it flows from west to east. Sometimes the stream sways northward and sometimes the opposite, depending on the season. The weather surrounding this stream is characterized by violent thunderstorms and intermittent doldrums.

Somewhere out there was a vast stretch of calm with virtually no horizontal breeze, only one that slowly rose skyward from its smooth, reflective face. A breeze often felt only by those flocks of birds brave or hungry enough to venture forth onto its calm, fiery surface in an audacious search of food. Somewhere, predictably there amid this calm, a dark storm

---

[25] Swell that "slaps from the west"; the countercurrent of the Intertropical Convergence Zone, which periodically streams through the islands just north and south of the equator.

brewed as this warmed air rose above the clouds, where only the biggest of birds were known to fly. There, high in the cool sky, the rising warm air turned heavy with rain, reversed direction, and came tumbling back down to form a perpetual core of cold, wet air. Then, like water rushing down a well, the core began to spin. It formed rotating arms of force that began to swirl and accelerate as the cycle grew in intensity, eventually whirling off erratically like an insatiable monster randomly gobbling up the still, warm surface of the calm around it.

Somewhat to the north — and west of Ijokelekel's position, sadly — Ļainjin[26] was fishing in the Lae lagoon when he first observed the storm rising in the southeast. It had been calm from first light with that bright red, early morning glow in the east that presaged what was to come. So, though he wanted to take advantage of the calm lagoon waters, he knew not to paddle too far away from the northernmost islet that was his home. He had been drifting around his favorite fishing spot — a large sunken reef, tear shaped, that gradually rose from the bottom of the lagoon three hundred or so paddles to the south and west from his islet's shore. He knew from first sight of the rising clouds that he should head back, but the fish were nibbling at his bait.

As his bait dangled, he gently jerked it up and then lowered it again in a motion the islanders called *worik*, after the up and down motion of the sexual act. He laughed to himself as he often did, remembering that first night when Liṃanṃan's sister had tried to coax him to enter her. Had that been a test? He often wondered what Liṃanṃan's reaction would have been had he done so. Joļọk[27] was still part of their household, and still the flirt she always had been despite having chosen a man from Ujae and given birth to two beautiful children. The memory of that first night had always remained an enticing joke between them.

He snagged one last fish. By then, the storm had risen so far above the horizon that prudence got the better of him, and he began paddling home. The storm approached with such speed that its first gusts swept the surface

---

[26] Tarmālu's son, left behind shortly after birth when she led her fleet to sea in the face of a typhoon; Liṃanṃan's chosen one and Kāmeto's father.
[27] Liṃanṃan's sister; aka Lijoļọk.

of the lagoon and billowed short, hand-high crests that slapped against his hull as he paddled his canoe's last lengths to shore. In the face of the storm, his fellow islanders were scrambling to gather mats of fish that had been drying in the sun and flat sheets of *jāānkun*,[28] yet to be rolled. Several men left that work to others and scrambled to lay down coconut-frond rollers between shore and boat house. His daughter Kāmeto[29] came for his fish but failed to untie the basket Ḷainjin had secured beneath his outrigger platform. Joḷọk hurried downshore, glancing furtively at the approaching storm and smiling knowingly at Ḷainjin to acknowledge his well-timed return. She quickly helped Kāmeto untie the basket of fish and then grabbed one side. Her niece held the other, and they scurried the heavy load toward the cookhouse. Four men — one at each end of the canoe, one at the outrigger, and one lifting the platform behind him — nudged the canoe over the rollers and up the shore to its boat house. Then the four left him there and headed for better cover from the first stinging drops of horizontal rain that spewed from the mouth of the approaching dark clouds.

Energized as always by the storm, Ḷainjin peered out from below the eaves of the boat house at the rustling fronds of the coconut crowns, their trunks bent backward almost to the point of breaking then counterswaying just before the storm's second breath. He walked below the eave to expose himself to the pelting rain, letting the full force of the storm's cold fury enter his soul until he had absorbed enough. Laughing, he drifted to the inland end of his canoe, where the air was calmer and the rain didn't reach. He had purposefully drenched himself, counting one by one the storms he had suffered, remembering the strength each had imbued him with. Then, as always, he finally came to that fateful storm when his soul had intertwined with that of Liṃanṃan and the rest was… Well, exactly what his mother had promised.

Yet the words of Lipanmai were there carved into his throat as well: "I go with you. You stay with me." Yes, his life would have been different had he

---

[28] Sun-dried sheets of pandanus pulp rolled into a log and wrapped in a sheath of pandanus leaves.

[29] A name: "Fly the ocean"; Ḷainjin's daughter.

not purposefully passed Pohnpei[30] on his way home. But just then his thoughts were interrupted by Liṃanṃan herself. She had hurried through the storm to share this moment with him. She pressed her wet head deep into his chest, and he squeezed her bare, wet back with his still-muscular arms and rocked her to and fro as the waves had that first night they were alone together at sea.

[30] Currently one of the principal island groups that make up the Federated States of Micronesia, located in the Eastern Caroline Islands.

Another world

The squall had swept over Ijokelekel late in the afternoon as he slept, his sleep often interrupted by delirious thirst. The first wave of rain overwhelmed him, blowing cold into his blistered face and onto his feverish, fragile frame. His mouth bled at the corners as he instinctively cracked it wide to catch and quench what he could while rushing in a panic to partially hoist and prop open the bow corner of the lowered, hanging sail's booms. The chilly rain quickly rinsed the caked salt from his hair and immediately relieved the unbearable, incessant sting where it had worked itself into the crevices of his sun-breached skin. Soon he plunged the first of his many netted, empty coconut shells into the sail's fold as he struggled, shivering, to squat there amid the quickly emerging tumult breaking over the now-slippery deck. Filling them with one hand as he manipulated the fold, he felt the air bubbling against his palm from the mouth of each as he pressed them below the rainwater trapped toward the sail's clew corner.

With the rain came the wind, but then came the storm's waves. He continued to fill his shells until these waves began to break dangerously over his bow. Then he abandoned his task and took his position at the stern. The strong wind was now propelling the limp, partially opened sail forward into the oncoming and increasingly steep waves, and he needed pressure on the tiller to angle his bow over them. The storm proved a harsh rescue. He helmed there and held his own, one cold moment at a time, against the jerky violence of the sea. It challenged not only the boat's lashings but every muscle and each joint in his body. The direction of the wind and waves turned, unbeknownst to him, amid the black of the night. He felt caught in a nightmare, struggling to awake. He drank the rain from his open mouth. Then, after what seemed like an eternity of torture, when the worst of the wind had abated, the lightning finally flashed at him. His father's voice cracked just as abruptly, and he knew that had saved him — exactly as he had promised himself. Thereafter, as the waves abated, he wrapped himself in the satisfaction of this thought as he lay in the narrow hull below in total exhaustion, tottering back and forth, snug beneath damp mats that lined the floorboards of his perpetually teetering berth. His outrigger float abeam and his lowered, now-bundled sail propped to lee, the sea rocked him to sleep as he drifted on in the darkness, anticipating a new, more hopeful morrow.

Halfway through the night, he noticed the rocking subside. Later still, the sea's constant upheaval abated, and he felt a much calmer breeze change direction and invade the damp hull where he lay. He knew he should immediately take advantage, hoist his sail, and make way, yet his aching, sun-beaten body argued to rest and won. Sometime well before dawn, the rhythmical sounds of swells stumbling, seething, and repeatedly plunging — one beneath the next — began to penetrate his dreams and ever so pleasantly, gradually waken him. It was the sound of sand.

Curiosity drew him through the stern hatch into the cloudless — now moonless — sky of a new, star-strewn night. The air was clean, and the sight before him was worth all the thirst he had endured and the hunger and weakness still afflicting him. It killed his fears and quenched all the dire scenarios swirling about his imagination. From the sea's perspective, he supposed what he saw ahead, in the dim light of the silently creeping stream of stars above, was but a narrow islet of white sand impairing its forever-forward surge. It appeared to be capped with what looked to him like a narrow crest of brush without even a coconut tree to distinguish its outline. What he envisioned was a fateful refuge — a curious though obviously safe place to rest and escape from the ever-moving, abrupt reality that had traumatized him.

Surprisingly, the islet distinguished itself with an absence of reef flat, at least on its ocean side, where he would have expected waves to be crashing dangerously onto its edge. Instead, swells rolled right up to the beach and tumbled onto the sand of the islet's shore with a gentle thump of white water. It was as though the sea had wanted to swallow the islet up whole, but then finding it not to her liking, spit it up as it receded — only to return yet again to taste again, and ever again. He had never seen or heard of such a place, where the ocean could wash herself up and lick at a reefless shore. What was to stop her, in a fit of rage, from washing such a pile of sand back into the sea? Paratak had warned him about the dangerous reefs surrounding Lae. Clearly, he had drifted up someplace else. He could see the pale white sands of islets both north and south in the starlight. Then, in a mixture of joy and fear, he spotted the light of a fire on the next islet down the string.

There were corals below him. He saw them in the starlight as he took the helm, untied his oar, and turned his craft directly toward shore. The corals rose beneath him like the brush on a steep shore ahead as he paddled shoreward, beneath the cheeps and caws of night birds flapping out to their fishing grounds. Then he lost their melody in a rush of white water all around that, with some fright, propelled and lifted his craft high onto the beach. His feet rejoiced at the gleeful feel of sand siphoning between his toes as the surf receded and then returned, and each time, he nudged his craft landward by placing its outrigger platform flat on his shoulders and bent neck. Belatedly obsessed with an overabundance of caution, he took Lañinpo's trolling line and tied the partially beached craft to the sturdiest limb he could find amid the thin ridge of brush that overlaid this long and narrow sandpit he now welcomed as home.

Finally, he flopped down onto the beach high above the tide line, gazed out at the glistening sea he had crossed, and silently congratulated himself. His mother had accompanied him. Liṃanṃan had provided direction. His father had saved him. He had survived. Only the sea would know how lucky he had been. Finally, he removed Lañinpo's wet mat from the boat and laid it out on a bed of leafy tips torn from the brush behind him. Covering himself with half, he lay amid the comforting stench of guano and fell asleep, lulled by the sounds of the shore and comforted by the magnificence of the motionless sand below him.

In his hunger and exhaustion, Ijokelekel paid little attention to the morning sun and dug deep inside the fold of his mat, like a hermit crab protecting itself from its dehydrating glare. He felt like he needed to rest into the next night. Yet the new day brought him a second unexpected gift from the sea, by way of the sound and feel of a small, sandy foot gently brushing the outside fold of his mat. Surprised, he opened it to find a boy but a little older than he, with a bright green basket made of freshly plaited coconut leaves. Instantly, he sat up — with the startled look of a bird about to fly from its nest, he supposed. The boy jumped back reflexively but held his shy, confident smile. Ijokelekel realized the boy's father had probably sent him. He stood below them in the retreating tide, steadying their proa as the surf rushed in and out around him.

"*M̧ōn̄ā*."[31] The boy extended the basket of food again. His smile turned concerned as his eyes roamed over Ijokelekel's sun-injured body.

Because this word happened to be the same in both their languages, the communication gap about to begin was not yet apparent. "Eat" had filled Ijokelekel's thoughts for days, as though the mere thought could satisfy the pangs within. The impatient hunger pangs he'd felt on previous days had strangely quieted, though. Now, with a basket of food before him, having landed safely after so much trial, he suddenly found himself too proud to snatch and dig rapaciously into it. After all, he too had confidence. He was the son of Nahn Sapwe. No, he must demonstrate no desperation. He must summon his strength and appear too proud to show his hunger.

"*Kalahngan en komwi*,"[32] he replied, and immediately drew a questioning look from the boy who, up to that point, had no doubt assumed that Ijokelekel was one of his own.

His eyes immediately darted to Lañinpo's proa, which was obviously not foreign.

"*Ngehi sang Pohnpei*,"[33] Ijokelekel explained.

As the word for "I" happened to be nearly identical in both languages, and the pronunciation of the word "*sang*" was close to the Kajin Rālik word "*jen*,"[34] the confusion cleared, and the lad immediately shouted to his father that they had found a boy from Pohnpei! Then he politely plopped down on the sand before Ijokelekel.

---

[31] Kajin Rālik for "eat."

[32] Pohnpeian; "Kalahngan" means "thanks." "Komwi" means "honorific you."

[33] Pohnpeian for "I'm from Pohnpei."

[34] Kajin Rālik word for "from."

At this news, the father gave up steadying his canoe in the oncoming surf. Switching tactics, he nudged his proa as best he could up onto the sand below Lañinpo's much larger craft, which he fingered admiringly as he passed.

Did he approach out of curiosity or concern? Ijokelekel hadn't touched the basket the boy had set on the mat before him. He straightened his back as though he were the Saudeleur himself and assumed the noblest posture possible, given his just-awakened face, refusing to reveal any inkling that he didn't know where he was.

The father, not a large man himself, walked up to them, rattling off a string of unintelligible statements or questions, and then stood—somewhat perplexed, perhaps, that such a small boy had traveled such a great distance in such a large craft. He stared at Ijokelekel's sun-damaged face and body, then grabbed hold of his hand and coaxed him a few steps through a very narrow pathway over the brush-covered ridge to the other side of the narrow islet.

"Kwajalein,"[35] he said, wafting his open hand from left to right across the lagoon-filled horizon. Then he pointed to the exact spot on the next islet where Ijokelekel had seen fire the night before. That islet bent eastward, its lagoon shore exposed up to a point formed by a small gulf where the little man had raised a thatch house that was just barely visible from that distance. He mimed that Ijokelekel was to paddle over there as soon as the tide allowed him to launch. Then the kind man led him back and just as quickly left him to himself, instructing his son to follow.

The boy looked awkwardly back and forth between Ijokelekel and Lañinpo's canoe as though there was much that he wanted to ask but lacked words to do so. He ended up kicking Ijokelekel playfully in the foot and turning away. As they passed Lañinpo's vessel, his father spun around, took a step backward in the sand, and met Ijokelekel's eyes with a fatherly look of pride in a child who had completed a task much better than expected.

The boy hoisted sail, and they cut through the surf on the same tack from which they had come, so Ijokelekel assumed they would continue to troll for tuna along the ocean side of the next islet north. He felt good about their

---

[35] The largest atoll in the Rālik chain.

friendly visit except that he hadn't had the opportunity to tell them who he was. Hopefully, there would be time for that. Yes, he would take the little man up on his suggestion to join them on the next islet south. He had noticed two freshly husked coconuts in the basket, next to something baked in a leaf, and a large, recently cut slice of bloodred bonito. He sucked on the coconut until the boy and his father were well on their way, and only then did he allow himself to dig into the delicious meal like a greedy bird that quickly consumes any scrap of fish thrown its way.

His gullet filled quickly, so — deciding to save most for later — he piled leaves over his food and hung the basket from a branch. Too warm now to crawl back into its fold, he made a canopy of Lañinpo's mat by suspending it by the holes he had punched in its corners. He lay back on the branch tips and the sand and resumed his slumber. However, once the cool of the morning had dissipated, his sores began to ache, and he noticed that sand had ground its way into them as he slept. He instinctively felt a need to give his skin a good soaking so rose and crossed back to the other side of the islet. There, he found a reef pool close to shore and deep enough, given the low tide, to lie down and soak in the warm, salty water.

There was a mild stinging as he set himself down into the tepid shallow. He lay back with the top of his back and shoulders resting gingerly against the jagged dead coral and the stranded, sun-warmed water covering his body up to his neck. Intrigued, he looked out at the waves breaking at the white-water edge of the lagoon reef flat before him. Was this the atoll lagoon that Paratak had spoken of? He could see an islet to the north from the ocean side and an islet to the south from the lagoon side. Yet if this was a lagoon, where were the islets on the opposite side? Could it be that the lagoon was so large their distance was too far away to see? The tempo of the waves slapping at the edge of the broad reef flat was much more rapid than the slower lumbering sounds of the ocean swells tumbling onto the ocean shore behind him. Were these waves rippling toward him generated solely from the energy of that day's breeze? He thought so because their fetch seemed marked by a reef somewhere across a lagoon so large that he couldn't see its far side and so long that the islets to the south and north faded into the horizon. Surely, these waves were of a different origin than the swells outside the atoll's shelter that he had struggled with at sea over the past few days. They had grown larger and reflected a much greater energy, generated by the longer distance they traveled.

Paratak had described an atoll as a half shell floating precariously upon the surface of the sea, in constant threat of sinking below its surface. Not true. To Ijokelekel, this reef appeared as permanent as any other. Then, with a different explanation, he had said the lagoon depths were filled with coral-forested mountains and valleys as though they had somehow sunk below its surface. Ijokelekel was excited to explore this calm refuge. He marveled at the multitudinous shades of green reefs surrounded by bright blue water that no doubt reflected the sky above them. He associated these living corals with life as opposed to the more monotonous open ocean grey of the death he had but narrowly escaped.

A feeling of gratitude that he had somehow drifted upon such a refuge overcame him. Yes, he'd been struck by the stark differences between this unfamiliar environment and the one he had left. On his home island, beaches were somewhat rare because mangrove choked the shore. Here, white-sand beaches were everywhere. Instead of a series of narrow lagoons between barrier reefs and a gigantic, dark green island reaching through the clouds before him, there was this single, gigantic lagoon surrounded by flat coral islets and sand spits that sprouted numerous passages to the sea. How fortunate had he been to drift into this pleasant haven? He knew only that his father must have had a hand. Was Kwajalein the name the kind man had given this place? Where was Kwajalein in relation to Lae? Now, how was he to find out without revealing the secret that he was no pali and didn't know where he was? He lay back, crossed his arms over his forehead to shade his burnt face, and relaxed, thankfully accepting his fate and at one with the calm, warm water. Lae or no, he was certainly in no hurry to turn back into the harsh, ever-moving, weather-changing flux from which he had come.

By late afternoon, the incoming surf had begun to lift the oceanmost point of his hull, so he packed and readied to launch. Much earlier, he had acknowledged the two fishermen as he watched them return and troll diagonally from ocean to lagoon across a broad turquoise passageway that separated the two long and narrow banks of white sand that pointed each islet toward the other. The bare sandbank beach on the opposite islet appeared as lengthy as its green-topped, forested portion.

He launched Lañinpo's proa with much difficulty because the slope of the beach was so steep that his shoulders could barely reach the outrigger boom under the platform on its oceanmost side. It was easier to place his shoulders below the landward boom, face the islet, and nudge the craft into the surf by pushing his shoulders backward. Once launched, he had to lift himself up from the sea onto the stern and immediately battle with the cannibal's oversized paddle against the mighty surf that rushed in on him, threatening to wash the craft back onto the sand. He dug frantically on one side of the stern and then the other until finally, after much exertion, he reached the calm-water hills that swelled up over the coral gardens below before rolling in to break on the shore behind him. Ijokelekel caught his breath for a moment before hoisting sail and gliding off toward the passage. Curiously, the short sail across the entryway over submerged patches of coral into the lagoon to the little man's islet sapped his energy so much that he arrived relieved to no longer be on his own.

The woman on the beach had no doubt watched him approach and was well prepared with flower leis and a fresh kilt, no doubt previously made for her son. A broad-faced, husky woman of strong voice and helmsman-like temperament, she hung a lei around his neck as soon as his feet touched the shore. The father had prepared an anchor with line and assumed the responsibility of anchoring the craft a distance from his own before swimming ashore and joining hands with the other two as they sang and sang and circled him in a welcoming ceremony that was so silly he couldn't help but join in their laughter. Eventually, once he had absorbed the rhythm of their little dance, he accepted their invitation to join hands with them as they circled and danced and sat abruptly on the sand, then rose again to begin again. At the end of each song, she placed yet another lei about his neck and twisted his shoulders to and fro as though to encourage him to swagger with pride. They made him feel like, in this vast ocean, he had found his own harbor that had been prepared just for him. As one song ended and he expected to rest, unexpectedly, they would begin another that drove the feeling of being welcomed so deep it drove the pain from his past and made him wonder why he would ever leave them. Surely, were he not the son of Nahn Sapwe and had he no destiny to fulfill, they might have coaxed him to stay forever.

When the dancing and singing finally concluded, they skipped into their tiny home, where they placed so much food before him he couldn't eat but a quarter. The woman fussed over him so much she reminded him of his dear mother. Because she appeared to be in total control of her little household and mimed orders for him to follow, he could relax his mind from all the decision making that had gone before. What a comfort, he thought, to simply follow and obey and relinquish all the incessant decision making a man must carry out from day to day. If this was what following a woman was like, he was ready.

Their home was quite unlike any he had experienced before. Giant-clam shells to catch freshwater from the eaves surrounded the outside of the house. He recalled Paratak's brief description of atoll life: "No water!"

There were no takai, so the little house sat flat on a deck of beach stones, obviously brought to the site at some expense of time and effort. Pandanus-leaf thatch covered its lashed frame, with thatched walls right down to the bleached-coral beach stones that paved the living space. The whole area had a strong smell of dried fish. From the drying racks outside, Ijokelekel guessed that fish drying was their primary activity and the reason for isolating themselves on the weather-protected, cove-shaped islet. After he had eaten, the boy led him to a little shelter near a well. One of them had already drawn water to fill yet another giant-clam shell, and there was grated coconut for his bath. Alone again, he splashed the cool water sparingly onto his damaged skin and tried his best to cover his entire body with the soothing milk he had strained from the gratings to remove the ocean's salt from his skin.

He returned to the house much refreshed from his bath. She had laid out a freshly plaited sleeping mat beneath a lagoon-facing window where he could lie in the pleasant breeze and look out at the two proas anchored securely in the bay outside. Its far bank, made of dead coral reef, or shorehead, appeared as though it had been left exposed by some massive, ancient storm. The little anchorage, he would learn, was why this islet —

among so many others — had come to be planted and inhabited, even if only for part of the year. There was no sign of any stilt homes of the type described by Paratak. Ijokelekel would learn that this was but a seasonal home, used only during the wet time of the year because, during the dry season, their little well would turn too salty to sustain their presence. Yet the anchorage was important for overnight moorage for craft passing along this quarter of the atoll during any season.

Their stilt home, he was told, was on Kwajelein islet itself, a more substantial islet far in the distance. Before they allowed him to sleep, he listened to pleasant, unintelligible stories told by her man while she chanted softly and covered each of his sun sores with the waxy pulp of overripened *noni*,[36] the same nasty-tasting fruit his mother had always boiled and tried to get him to drink. He remembered her teaching him: it doesn't stink or turn watery or dry when it rots, and when kept out of the sun, it just melts into a blob of colorless, imperishable mush. Now he learned it was also useful to heal wounds.

This woman was treating him like her son. "Soon I must reveal who I am," he thought. "And she will be proud to have served the great spirit of thunder, who cracks the great takai from the face of the mountains with his clash and reaches out over the ocean to quell storms from the path of those he favors."

He slept the first of the nights — soon too many to count — with this friendly adopted family. Among them, he grew like a young taro plant in the mud with just the proper amount of sun and water. Over the following seasons, he and this woman called Lijāpe[37] came to treat each other like mother and son. He happily assisted her with her woman's work even as he learned the manly skills from the father, who was called Ḷōkijdik.[38] That was their word for "man rat," and it suited the nimble fellow, who could reach

---

[36] Fruit from *Morinda citrifolia*, a small tree prized throughout the islands for its medicinal properties; a tonic thought to promote health. Also called "nen."

[37] Literally, "woman container of breadfruit"; Ijokelekel's adopted mother. A jāpe is a wooden, trapezoid-shaped vessel carved from breadfruit wood and used to knead breadfruit.

[38] Ijokelekel's adopted father; literally, "man rat." Ḷō: the male prefix, used to emphasize respect.

the end of any limb, twist loose the largest of pandanus fruits, and then lug them energetically — two at a time — from one end of the islet to the other. Ijokelekel and their son, Jorailik,[39] who they called by the name of his deceased grandfather, learned over the seasons to treat each other like brothers. He followed the footsteps of this budding youth everywhere, as their prints on the shore seemed to grow larger with every step.

One bright afternoon, they hung the fresh kilts their mother had made for them in the last bushes at the islet's end. Then they went fishing for octopus along the lagoon side of the long white-sand beach. It extended toward the turquoise wilderness of coral that sank into the passageway that separated what was now his home islet and the one Ijokelekel had landed on so many seasons ago. They swam among the corals marveling at the large fish, some blue and some white. The white ones crunched the coral with their bird-like beaks and periodically pooped the residue, which streamed down to the bottom as little sandy flakes. "They must be the source of all this sand," he thought, watching the fish with blurry eyes as they grazed.

He and Jorailik were searching for the small, telltale mounds of loose pebbles the octopus used to cover their little caves from the *liele*,[40] which loved to bite off their arms. These silly mounds they would brush aside, and then they would agitate the little monsters out by repeatedly poking them with their narrow spears.

The two boys were about to emerge from the water, each with his quarry, when they noticed Limaalal[41] approaching along the lagoon shore. As they often did, she and her father, Lajalok, had stopped by on their way home from their small islet to the north, and their craft was anchored at some distance away, back at the cove. The little flirt had caught them naked beneath the water and was not about to let them easily off her hook. She walked right up to their new kilts and waved them in the air, daring the young men to approach.

Keeping his private parts submerged and out of sight, Ijokelekel followed Jorailik as he waded along the shore until they reached her point of ambush.

---

[39] Ijokelekel's adopted brother.

[40] Trigger fish.

[41] Literally, "woman evening star."

"Come ashore and show me that those coconuts have sprouted something substantial enough to report to the rest of the island girls." Her mat skirt covered her from her waist down past her knees, and her cute little breasts peeped at them above the fold like a second pair of eyes.

"Come on." She coaxed them like a mother calling her boys to shore. "*O-wa-tak-li*?"[42] Noticing their catch and laughing hysterically at her own joke, she brandished one of their puffy new kilts in each hand. "*O-wa-tak-li*," she repeated, having them right where she wanted and probably already bragging to herself about how her friends would laugh when she told them her tale.

The boys turned one to another, both crouched in the water, knees closed, hiding their private parts from Limaalal. The butt of each boy's spear rested on the bottom. Each point impaled a large octopus, its colors changing like clouds rushing beneath the sun on a windy day.

"Drop those kilts and run, or I'll throw this spear at you," retorted Jorailik, removing the *kweet*[43] and pretending to take aim at her.

She turned around, still brandishing the kilts, and sashayed her rear at him provocatively. At that, Jorailik hurled the wet, amorphous mass of droopy flesh. It struck her on the back and flopped off onto the sand. Laughing, she turned toward them, dropped the kilts, and took a few steps backward. "Now you've only got that spear to cover yourself with! Come on. *O-wa-tak-li*!"

Jorailik responded by slowly emerging from the water, allowing her to inspect what she might as she giggled and stepped backward in the sand.

Though Ijokelekel marveled at his brother's bravery, he took the opportunity to cover himself with his octopus until he reached his kilt and awkwardly, one-handedly, wrapped it around himself. By that time, she had triumphantly taken his brother's catch and retreated toward the cove down the shoreline from which she had come.

"He only wanted to touch her," he remembered Lañinpo saying. "When you become a man, you will understand." This girl, this time, had captured his attention. He couldn't take his eyes off her as she scampered down the

[42] These ancient words are a chant repeated in the fable of the giant octopus, the mother of Labibat. They translate roughly as "come east, or appear from west."
[43] Octopus.

shore, turning back to them now and again. He wished Jorailik had them chasing after her, but perhaps his brother could foresee that his mother was about to spoil all the fun.

The intriguing girl was about to suffer Lijāpe's verbal abuse as she ambled through the sand with a stick to confront her. She seldom missed an opportunity to take control of a situation and never refrained from standing up for her boys. She was still scolding Limaalal when they meandered up to deliver the second *kweet*. The girl, now squatting on the stony shoreline, was cleaning sand from Jorailik's catch. Lijāpe stood over her and berated her for teasing them, at the same time directing her to turn the octopuses' heads inside out and admonishing her to wash away every grain of sand caught in the membrane of the slippery, waist-high monsters.

"What type of girl rushes down the beach to view a boy's nakedness and spoil his catch as well?! I should beat you and spoil your blemishless back with this *kiden ta kiden*[44] stick! I'm sure your mother would thank me for it! If you were my daughter, you would be clearing every leaf from my sight as it fell every day until I saw that pretty face of yours lose its charm! Now go draw a bath for my sons, and hurry back here to beat their catch with this branch of *kiden*[45] until they're tender as fish," Lijāpe commanded. All four of them left the octopuses by the shore and walked toward the cookhouse.

"Lajalok, what kind of girl does something like that?" Lijāpe asked.

"She is very bold!" he said. "'Too bold,' we tell her — all the time. We've tried to teach her our customs, but she doesn't listen. Truth be told, we waited too long to have her. Now she's too grown, and we are too aged to handle her. She'll be tattooed in the next group, and after that, well..."

"Oh yes, I know," Lijāpe said. "My eldest son also, but he's coming right back here where I can make sure he chooses properly."

She was still moralizing with Lajalok as Ijokelekel followed his brother to the well for their bath. Limaalal filled the giant-clam shells with water from the well as Jorailik began husking the nuts for their baths.

---

[44] The words "Kiden, what's kiden?" are also part of the chant in the fable *Labibat*. A live branch of the soldierbush tree (*Tournefortia argentea*) is used to tenderize the octopus's otherwise tough flesh.

[45] Soldierbush tree: *Tournefortia argentea*.

"What a shouter your mother is. She makes me feel like a hand at sea." Limaalal said. "'Follow the customs! Don't have any fun!'"

"She's only pretending to be mad," said Jorailik. "Just the other day, she was teasing us, saying, 'I wonder when Lajalok will bring his daughter by. I could use her help with the *mokwaṇ*.'"[46]

"*Mokwaṇ*! I'll spit in her *mokwaṇ*. But you'd eat it just the same, wouldn't you? I bet you daydream about doing it to me all the time. I bet if I pooped in your hand, you'd lick it up like *mokwaṇ*." Limaalal addressed Jorailik again. "What are you laughing at? Open your mouth and let me spit inside."

She closed the distance between their faces, and for an instant, Jorailik looked at her like he was about to comply. Then he caught himself, laughed, and turned away, probably not knowing what to do or say. She might have caught him with the dreaming part. He mentioned her a lot when she was away.

Then Limaalal sat down on the grater, careful to tuck her skirts between her legs but showing her knees and parts of her thighs to their staring eyes. "What? I'm just doing what that helmswoman commanded." She spread her legs just a little more now that she had their undivided attention. "Bring me a coconut," she commanded, catching Ijokelekel looking for something between her bare thighs. She smiled at him flirtingly.

Ijokelekel grabbed a husked nut from his brother's pile, placed it on his forehead, and balanced it there as he walked over to her. Then he bent his head forward and dropped it toward her lap.

She caught it. "Very good, Ijokelekel. What a sense of balance you have. Did you see that, Jorailik?"

"He does that all the time. He could walk a coconut like that all the way to our mother by the lagoon."

Jorailik laughed. "Yes, he does that trick all the time. I don't know how he does it."

Ijokelekel proved it was no fluke by balancing another over to her.

---

[46] The atoll dwellers, especially the Marshall Islanders, cultivated numerous varieties of edible pandanus. Some had flavorful juice they sucked from the fibrous nodules. Other pulpier varieties were chewed like fibrous carrots or baked, and the pulp was subsequently scraped from the softened nodules. This mash, or mokwaṇ, was either dried into jāānkun or mixed with arrowroot starch and coconut milk and rebaked in a breadfruit leaf.

Limaalal was good and very quick at grating all the white coconut from the first half shells. With a teasing sparkle in her eyes, she began chanting again, opening her thighs all the wider and returning to the story of Labibat.

Kicking down coconut,
many falling,
grating, grating.
Kicking down coconut,
many falling,
grating, grating.
Too much than, too much than...

"You boys ready to drop kilts and wash those eager spears?" she asked provocatively. Her eyes now open wide, she stared at the bulge that was in danger of breaching Jorailik's kilt, then turned to Ijokelekel with a leaf full of gratings.

"Here Ijokelekel. You first. Go scrub that *kawko*."[47] She eyed the spot between his legs as if to see if it, too, was about to pop out between the fibers of his kilt. Giggling, she handed him a large leaf filled with the white, freshly grated coconut. "Be sure to clean under the foreskin," she teased, pretending now to be the mother of a small child.

She was jabbing at them both in retaliation for their mother's defensive heckling. Ijokelekel went behind the three-walled pandanus-leaf bathing stall and periodically watched Limaalal and Jorailik talking. She seemed to be opening her legs increasingly to his brother's gaze as she grated and spoke. Lañinpo's words "when you become a man" were still ringing in his ears. When she had completed her task and turned to go, his brother managed to back her up against the big kiden tree. There, they chortled a bit but spoke too softly to hear. Then he heard his mother, apparently approaching from the lagoon, screaming for her, and Limaalal scurried off to confront her.

"The coconut doesn't grate itself," Ijokelekel heard her argue back, sending a coquettish laugh back to his brother.

---

[47] The penis of a small boy; the term "child" is used until a boy dons a fiber kilt.

"Nonsense. Let my sons bathe in peace. You've seen too much of them already. I should pluck out those overeager eyes of yours and wash them in the lagoon!"

Jorailik stood beside the blind and politely asked if Ijokelekel had finished. He had and quickly tied his belt.

"I'm going to tickle her good," Jorailik said. "Do you want to watch? I'm going to poke her later, right there against that tree. We agreed. Here, look." He tore the pandanus leaves of the blind to make a hole he could see through to the tree. "I'm going to show you how you do it."

"Do what?"

"You know, *kabwebwe*!"[48] Jorailik tweaked his finger like a fishing pole. "She wants it. That's why she's always teasing us. She wants to get tickled so she can brag to her friends on Ennylabegan."[49]

Ijokelekel, feeling a lusty curiosity, turned to go.

Jorailik untied his belt. "After you eat, tell Mother you're going to the ocean side to check the current on the reef. Then wait here instead. If darkness comes and you haven't seen us, return to the house. Maybe she's all tease and no knees, but I doubt it!"

A little later, Ijokelekel went to the house to nap. Before falling asleep, he realized Limaalal had completely taken over his thoughts. He kept fantasizing about her sitting on the coconut grater, giving them peeks in her naughty way at the forbidden light skin of her inner thighs.

While eating their meal together in the cookhouse, the two families planned the next day's activities. The men would gather the pandanus fruits while the two women collected the firewood, leaves, and stones for the big oven needed to steam the fruit. Limaalal sat chastised yet defiant, with one leg tucked beneath her and the other covered but outstretched, her foot wagging like a telltale *ak*[50] feather tied to the leech of a sail. Ijokelekel couldn't keep his eyes off it. On two occasions, their eyes met, and both times, she poked an unchewed octopus arm through her lips then sucked it back quickly before the others could see. She had him captivated.

---

[48] Pole fishing.

[49] An islet of Kwajalein Atoll.

[50] The frigate bird: *Fregata magnificens*.

Toward evening, at his brother's continued insistence, Ijokelekel lied to his mother. He walked down the path to the ocean but doubled back and sat behind the bathing blind. What if his brother really didn't want her and was pulling a trick, sending her to him instead? What would he do? He had no experience at copulating. He waited a short while and then felt relief and a curious hankering for her when they arrived.

They got right to work disrobing skirts and kilt, and from the looks on their faces, they were excited by the sight of each other. They began touching each other's private parts. Hers burnished by a triangular thicket of black hair. His, not seen, must have stood straight up because she appeared to bend it down and start rubbing it right where she wanted between her legs. Then he went to work on her in earnest. He got her propped back against the tree with one leg wrapped around him and the heel of the previously wagging foot dug into the soft earth where the trunk reached out into the surrounding ground. Jorailik's arm moved as though he was repeatedly trying to snag a fish with a hand line. He seemed to be titillating her with his manhood. She maneuvered at the same time to catch it inside her and repeated the same words — "Stick it in!" — a little more insistently each time. He was obviously refusing to comply yet working all the faster, as though he was rubbing fire sticks that had begun to smoke. Her command to "stick it in" got so loud that Ijokelekel expected their mother to come running. Finally, Jorailik must have poked her good — more to shut her up than to please her, it seemed — because she immediately seemed to calm down even as he pressed her rear tight against the tree and their bodies gyrated in unison, wave after wave. Until suddenly he shuddered and groaned, and they maintained that very uncomfortable-looking position, each laughing at the other, until prudence apparently got the best of them, and she retreated toward the cookhouse.

Jorailik came at once and sat behind the blind. He had become enormously more important to Ijokelekel. He had always looked up to his brother, but this was something unexpected. Like when they had caught the giant, scraggly-toothed barracuda that he had grabbed by the gill just as the lure broke away from its mouth. Jorailik was brave and bold and everything Ijokelekel wanted to be.

"Did you see that? I rubbed her little *būtti*[51] until the lips that cover her well swelled and started spouting water all over the place. Did you hear her beg for it? I filled her up with so much seed her *jukkwe*[52] will be leaking the rest of the evening. That'll give her something to think about! Come on, I want you to get a second look at her. You'll see she's changed now that I have her flopping around like a bird with her flight feathers plucked."

Ijokelekel didn't notice much at first, except that Limaalal's back was scratched red here and there from being braced against the tree. Emboldened by what he had seen, he brushed some bark off the corner of her shoulder before entering the cookhouse to join the evening's storytelling. Then he was surprised when she sat next to him.

"You saw the whole thing, didn't you?" she whispered accusingly.

This embarrassed Ijokelekel, as he'd had no idea she knew he was there watching.

Calmly, like a seafarer in her boathouse, Lijāpe sat, commanding her element. A basket of freshly baked *mokwaņ* was being passed around, and she was ordering the men to try it.

Limaalal's father was busy telling Ļōkijdik a tale about something, but Ijokelekel was unable to concentrate on his words. His brother hadn't yet entered, and beside Limaalal, he felt isolated from the action around them. Suddenly, he became emboldened by the thought of what he had witnessed.

"Your back is all red where he ground you into the tree," he whispered proudly, as though he had been the one to do it to her. She scooted back against the slatted pandanus-root wall, her face flushed. Her defiance gone. There was no telltale foot wagging. She just sat there with a quite self-satisfied smirk that he couldn't help turning again to see. She responded each time by dropping her gaze to her lap and then darting her eyes back, perhaps daring him to recall what he had seen.

"You must feel all gushy inside. He claims he filled you up," he whispered, taking one of the baked, leaf-wrapped delicacies.

---

[51] Wart; projection from skin; slang for "clitoris."

[52] Sand clam; a bivalve; word used to refer to one's vagina.

"There's always room for more." She responded in a matter-of-fact manner, turning her head and untying the bun that held her hair twisted and piled upon her head, allowing it to flop, disheveled, onto her shoulders and back. It had the fragrance of freshly ground coconut. Ijokelekel wondered why she had done that if not to enthrall him, because his mother — on the other side of the cookhouse — was fanning a smoldering coconut shell in her fire. The smoke was starting to fill the air and was certain to foul the freshly washed smell of Limaalal's hair. So, he opened the window next to him and across from the other two.

The sight of her sitting there, covered in her mat skirt, both feet stretched out next to his now — and the thought of his brother's seed oozing out as she undulated one hip and then the other — began to bewitch him. Then, out of the corner of his eye, he saw her turn her head toward his ear so only he could hear.

"Jorailik wanted me to come straight to you behind the blind, but I said, 'Let him watch. You show him how to do it first.'"

"Looks like he showed us both," he responded, turning his head so only she could hear. Then his brother approached the open doorway and stood waiting for the smoke to clear before entering.

Her response was to smile coquettishly and then lower her eyes to her lap again. "Your brother was good, but the thought of getting it from a boy who's never done it before..." She darted a teasing glance at him. "Especially a hero like you. Wouldn't that be something to talk about?! All the other girls would have to have you too then." She spoke as though offering a bribe, looking directly at him now, nodding her head abruptly to confirm their pact.

As soon as the smoke broke into flame, his brother entered and Limaalal's father asked Ļōkijdik to tell a story.

The little man held up two fingers of his outstretched hand before the group, and all five of the others immediately quieted and turned their attention. "Two sisters," he exclaimed, as though answering a question none of them had asked. "The older takes the Irooj[53] of Wōjjā.[54] The younger

---

[53] Chief.

[54] Aka Woja Atoll; the easternmost islet of Aelōñļapļap Atoll.

takes an irooj of the west who has drifted up. Both sisters get pregnant at the same time, but the irooj from Eb[55] is anxious to go as soon as his proa is repaired and ready to sail.

"Before they part, those sisters say this of their expected children: 'If one is a girl and one is a boy, they'll end up loving each other and remain friends. And if both are girls, they'll be sisters and friends. But if both are boys, they'll be enemies and fight.'

"The younger sister bears a girl. On Wōjjā, her older sister bears a boy. One day, the older sister and her irooj take the boy to the ocean side for a bath. They place him in a large *jāpe*[56] and swim him up and down the reef in the calm tide. They're careless. The tide changes as they dive for clams, and the boy drifts away out of sight.

"He drifts westward to Eb and washes up on shore near the house of Irooj Rilik,[57] where his aunt recognizes him. He has the face of her sister in the east.

"So, she raises the boy as her own, but when he is older, he begins to long for his real mother on Wōjjā. The aunt tells her daughter, 'Take your brother to the island of my sister.' He follows her to the end of the island, but when they come to the edge of the shoreline, she stops. 'That water looks too deep to me.'

"That's when the boy launches his magic chant:

Bite coconut and
sow sand of Eb.

"She does as asked and waow! They fly like birds over the ocean, and they land on Wōjjā.

"When they arrive, all the boys are playing *kajjeor*.[58] The newcomer wants to play and asks a boy for his spear.

---

[55] Mythical cannibal isle far to the west.

[56] A wooden, trapezoid-shaped vessel carved from breadfruit wood and used to knead breadfruit; the constellation Delphinus, the dolphin.

[57] A mythical chief of the west side of the ocean.

[58] A boys' game, the objective of which is to ricochet a dried and somewhat flexible aerial-pandanus-root spear off the ground and into the air. The spear's throwing end is notched like an arrow.

"'Go play with the spear of your father' is the boy's lewd response. The newcomer asks another and another but gets the same reply. Finally, when he asks the youngest of the boys, that boy hands his over, so the newcomer launches his magic chant:

Kworlin, kworlin,
kwarlin, kwarlin.[59]
Fly farthest my
spear. Make proud
Papa Ļōetao.[60]
From sea atop tree
to vanish away.

"He throws his spear at the ground, and sure enough, it ricochets up over the palm trees and out of sight. It flies on into the village and puts out the eye of his mother.

"Waow! The irooj sharpens his adze. He commands that all the boys on the island come and stick their finger into the scar hole where her eye used to be. So, they come one by one and do as he insists. On and on they go till every lad has tried it.

"Then the irooj asks, 'Aren't there any other boys on this island?'

"They say, 'Only a couple of spent pandanus cores that washed up and have been sleeping here and there.'

"'Who?'

"'One little newcomer and his sister.'

"'Bring that boy here!'

"When the boy sticks his finger into the scar, it is a perfect fit. Waow! The irooj resumes sharpening his adze. He plans to cut the boy up. So, his sister begins to plait a mat for his grave, but her mother in Eb senses something has gone wrong. She turns herself into a bird and flies eastward to Wōjjā. She lands on top of their house and sings:

---

[59] A magic chant; no translation is available.

[60] A legendary trickster.

Sleepy, sleepy charm.
Sleep, sleepy charm.
Name your mother:
'Litijewa.'
Name your father:
'Ļōrikewa.'
Love, love, love.
In the face of love.

"At first, the irooj doesn't hear her song. He is perhaps too busy sharpening his adze and filling his ears with sounds of scraping stones.

Sleepy, sleepy charm.
Sleep, sleepy charm.
Name your mother:
'Litijewa.'
Name your father:
'Ļōrikewa.'
Love, love, love.
In the face of love.

"Her older sister is the first to hear. 'Wait!' she screams. 'Listen to what that bird is singing!'

"While the irooj stops to listen, she runs up to the little girl.

"'Girl, what were you two doing on Wōjjā?'

"'The boy wanted to see his real mother and father.'

"'And how are his mother and father called?'

"'Litijewa and Ļōrikewa.'

"She calls to the irooj, 'That is our son you are about to kill!'

"The irooj swings his adze and breaks it upon the stone. They cry and cry and cry.

"When they have finished, the boy says, 'Now you two tear your sleeping mat. You two keep half and I will take half. Break your drinking cup. Half for you two, half for me.' They do as he demands. He leaves and never returns to his true mother and father."

After a polite period of silence, Limaalal asked, "Where did he go?"

"Knowing her, she wants to chase after him!" quipped Lijāpe, laughing.

"No one knows," said Ḷōkijdik seriously.

"Well, he had to go somewhere!"

"It's a bedtime story," Lijāpe said. "By the end of the story, you're supposed to be too sleepy to ask questions."

"Maybe he went back to Eb," said Ḷōkijdik politely.

"So, where's that?" Limaalal asked.

"No one knows. Except a lot of stories end there. Maybe it's not a place at all. Maybe you must die to get there. All we know for sure is nobody ever comes back."

After his second coconut, Ijokelekel had to urinate. He walked down the strand above the cove, ducked behind a stand of *kōṇṇat*[61] bordering the lagoon, and relieved himself on the fist-sized stones that edged the anchorage. Returning, he met Limaalal on the other side.

"I have to pee too! Wait for me."

She disappeared behind the sprawling thicket of the heavily leafed, low-bending branches of the salt-tolerant tree. Ijokelekel picked up the flattest stone he could find and sent it skipping across the calm waters of the lagoon. He found another and another, and then a big rock splashed into the water in front of him, wetting his kilt. Limaalal had tossed it as she came back around.

As she strutted back toward him, she picked up a stone, skipped it across the water, then counted out loud. "*Juon, ruo, jilu.*[62] There, I beat you! Yours only skipped twice."

He searched until he found the flattest one yet and tossed it, but it took a high bounce off the surface and only skipped once.

She tried again. He noticed she had an odd way of tossing, but it skipped three times again. Then, as he straightened from picking up another, he felt her hand on his neck and her mouth against his ear.

---

[61] A short, sprawling tree that grows next to the shore; beach cabbage: *Scaevola taccada*; "naupaka" in Hawaiian.

[62] One, two, three.

"Don't feel bad. Most men can only do it twice. Some only once and then they're depleted."

He tossed as hard as he could, but the rock skipped just once again.

She addressed him facetiously by the name "Thunder" as she headed toward the cookhouse. "Ḷōjourur,[63] come stick your finger in my butt. Your mother needs to know if it's an exact fit."

"And what if it is?"

"Then that means you're destined to choose a girl from Kwajalein."

"I have a destiny that's much bigger than you can imagine. After all, I am the son of—"

"Nahn Sapwe," she joined in mockingly.

"One day, I will return to Pohnpei, punish the Saudeleur, and restore respect for my father's temple."

"You're too serious, Ijokelekel!" She turned to confront him. "Too much like your mother Lijāpe! Can't you just see her?" Limaalal changed her voice to imitate his mother. "Where have you been! And where's that bad girl! What's that I smell? Give me your hand." She grabbed his hand and held it to her nose, making a hilarious stinky face in the moonlight. They both laughed as they walked back toward the thatched cookhouse. The light of Lijāpe's fire flickered through the slatted walls.

"Don't forget I drifted up here. How did Father say it? 'Like a spent pandanus core,' and that woman took me in and planted me here. One day, my limbs will be strong and bear heavy fruit to feed many people."

"That's cute, but most girls would rather get a baby."

"My destiny is bigger than making babies. Soon I head back west to Lae, where a great pali waits to teach me all I need to know."

Suddenly, she stopped. "Wouldn't you like to spear me first?" She turned her face to his. "Poke me right now like an octopus," she dared. "I want to sit in there before your mother with the seed of both her sons all squishy inside me. *O-wa-tak-li*!"

There was an awkward moment as he hardened, wanting to take her up on her impromptu offer. He gazed at her in the faintest glimmer of light that reached them from the cookhouse fire, but alas, she

---

[63] Literally, "man thunder"; Ijokelekel's nickname.

must have felt the need to break the uncomfortable silence by returning to conversation.

"But you go sailing every day with Ḷōkijdik. He knows the sea, and they say he's a good teacher."

"Yes, but even he agrees that the best teachers are found along the back side of the ocean, and he has agreed to teach me how to get there. This pali I'm talking about is famous in Pohnpei. He has been everywhere. If there's such a place as Eb, he has been there and sailed back to prove it."

"You may get a lot of experience out there at sea. But if you're destined to go, let one of us cure you first. You're too full of it. You must sow your seed, or it will poison you. If not me, tell me. Which girl on Ennylabegan do you prefer? I'll arrange something."

He was embarrassed by her words. "Any of them. I might take them all."

He left her and entered the cookhouse. She stayed outside.

The jib in jowi

"Where is Limaalal?" asked Lijāpe.

"I saw her heading for the *kōņņat* bushes."

"That girl is naughty. I detect it in her eyes," said Lijāpe to Limaalal's father. "You must teach her."

"Teach me what?" Limaalal had entered the fire-lit cookhouse in the middle of Lijāpe's criticism. "I know how to process pandanus leaves, and I'm quick to plait them," she said respectfully. "When you need a basket, do I not plait one quickly? I don't even need to ask your precious boys to fetch me a coconut leaf. I'm perfectly capable of stripping one myself. Were you not wanting me to come and help you with the *mokwaņ*? Is that not because you know I'll collect more oven stones and baking leaves more quickly than you? The next time I stop here, fully clothed in new tattoos, will you not show me the respect I will have earned?"

Ijokelekel was a little shocked — though in hindsight, not surprised — to hear Limaalal stick up for herself before his mother. He would later learn that this was all about her lines and how she and her father planned to pay for them. She was bartering for a larger share of *mokwaņ*.

"Of course I will," Lijāpe said. "I never suggested you weren't a good worker, only that, once you wear your new lines, a little modesty will prove a good complement!"

"Sorry," Limaalal said. "I thought you might be suggesting I'm not good enough for your handsome son! It's my understanding that Ļōjorailik will be going to Āne-piñ[64] as well, so he'll shortly be strutting around in the skin

[64] An islet of Aelōñļapļap where tattooing was done.

of a man and pairing up with the newly tattooed women of Aelōñļapļap.[65] I was about to remind you that, in time, your son will be off tending the islands of someone else's mother. As you know, a strong tree will drop its seed where it may, and there's nothing we can do to prevent nature from taking its course. Unless, of course, you tie his foot to a *kōņņat* tree and treat him like a pet bird. If you need someone to tend your islet, since you have no daughter, you should have adopted a female heir instead of this…" At a momentary loss for words, she turned to Ijokelekel then laughed. "Thunderbolt!"

She said this in a polite but assertive tone, showing no lack of respect but seemingly insisting on such from Lijāpe. Perhaps taken aback, she met Limaalal's assertions with an awkward silence.

"I'm dying," the young woman continued, "to ask Ļōkijdik the details of how he was so modestly enticed off the reefs to plant and tend all these pandanus and coconut trees and work all your other strips of land elsewhere."

Chuckles by Ļōkijdik and Limaalal's father followed her words. They all knew he was unlikely to respond before the ears of his sons.

Now that Limaalal had placed words too true to be dwelled upon and seized leadership of the group, she redirected her eyes from Ijokelekel's adopted mother to him. As though kicking an *anidep*[66] his way, she asked, "Why don't you tell us a story from your islands?"

Ijokelekel's thoughts quickly turned to his mother and the stories she would tell him by her fire atop his father's temple in the courtyard of Pahn Kadira. Since childhood, he had learned not to tell stories of how he came about and who his father was. These stories had resulted in ridicule, teasing, and laughter on Pohnpei and polite silence among these Kwajalein Islanders. No, he would tell them her story of Jatokauai. It was his favorite except for the ending, which always came as a surprise. When questioned about the ending, his mother had always said, "That's just the way it's told." It haunted him nevertheless.

---

[65] Aka Ailinglaplap Atoll.

[66] A game in which a foot-sized cube of woven pandanus leaves is kicked back and forth within a circle by clapping participants.

The other five in the cookhouse had turned to him. None of them had ever thought to ask such a thing of him. They had asked, "Who is your mother?" "A fire tender at the temple." "Who is your father?" "The spirit of thunder." "What happened that you left in such a large canoe?" "I took it from one of the cannibals who killed her." Those sorts of things. Though they had undoubtedly noticed how quickly he had picked up their language, they probably thought he was uneducated because his mother was a mere fire tender. But that was just it. Because the tenders kept the Saudeleur's fires, they heard all the stories repeatedly. They were the ones who knew everything and were well respected for their knowledge by the commoners as well as the Saudeleurs themselves.

Without further thought, he introduced his story. "This is a story about a boy who was about my age when I landed here several seasons ago.

"His name was Jatokauai, and unlike the other boys who idled about, this boy liked the sea and went out fishing every chance he got. He and his mother lived on one of the islets of Nahn Madol[67] called Peilapalap. Of course, you have all heard about the great stone village of Nahn Madol…"

"You mean the one they built on the fringing reef from stones your father broke from the mountains, each one exactly the right shape and size?" Jorailik questioned his brother. "How could we not know it? You've told us that story a hundred times!"

"Okay," Ijokelekel continued, unaffected by his brother's sarcasm. He expected that. "First, you must understand that the Pohnpei lagoon, compared to yours, is inside out. Your lagoon is inside your fringing reef, but our lagoon lies between our island's fringing reef and a second barrier reef outside of that. Kwajalein has many passageways into the ocean, but we have fewer, and same as here, each has its own name. This story is about a passageway called Mueitenualiual."

Seeing them look at each other, perhaps bewildered by the word's many syllables, he tried to make a little joke of it. "As you know," he said, "we Pohnpeians like to use long names. No one bothers to steal a cumbersome name."

---

[67] A Pohnpeian village on the reef.

He succeeded in getting the group to laugh in agreement. Then, in a self-deprecating manner, he said, "Maalal, you might name your son Ijo, but you wouldn't think of naming him Ijokelekel, would you?"

"No, of course not." There was much laughter. "The tide would come in before I could remember how to say it!"

"Exactly. So, this passageway into the ocean is named after a large yellowfin tuna that the boy found there — stranded, somehow, by the retreated tide. This fish was so large that, had it taken his lure, it would surely have broken his line. It was so large he couldn't lift it into his canoe but had to tow it behind. He waited patiently for the tide to turn and then paddled the fish down the many canals to Peilapalap. After nightfall, he and his mother dragged it ashore and steamed it in their ground oven. After they'd eaten it up, they hid its bones amid the stone walls. This was because they were ashamed that they hadn't offered such a large fish as firstfruits to the Saudeleur, which is the custom there as well as here.

"Unfortunately, a dog named Aunimatakai passed by there one day and smelled the scent of the fish bones. I know you don't have these animals here, but they're like a porpoise with hair and four legs. They have big noses and go around smelling everything. Aunimatakai carried the fish skull to its master, the Saudeleur, who went into a rage and asked his attendants who among them had eaten such a thing. Eventually, the dog showed them where it had found the bone, and the boy admitted it was he. The ruler then assigned the boy a cruel task. He was to hunt up the *malpur* shell. This was an impossible task from the Saudeleur's point of view because such a shell had never been seen but only heard of. The history of Nahn Madol is ripe with examples of people being asked by the Saudeleurs to do impossible tasks. These people often banish themselves rather than face punishment upon their return, but not Jatokauai!

"He and his mother set off to look here and there for the proper medicine to create the magic necessary to accomplish this feat. Especially medicine to enable him to breathe like a fish under the water. Then Jatokauai left his mother, promising to return victorious, and entered the water at the place called Auankap. He swam down under the water until he met a gigantic fish called Itananjaralap, who asked Jatokauai what he was doing. He replied that he was the boy who the Saudeleur had commanded to bring back the *malpur* shell. Then Itananjaralap explained he was too old and blind and couldn't help him, but suggested he go on and ask Itananjaritik. It was he that gave Jatokauai the *malpur* shell and agreed to help him by returning him to Auankap. Then, with one breath, the fish sucked him into its belly, swam to that place, and stranded himself on the reef in the retreating tide.

"Word of a gigantic, stranded fish quickly spread to the greedy Saudeleur. Also to the boy's mother, who was expecting Jatokauai's return. When she reached the fish, she found a substantial number of people gathered there gazing at it. When she stepped forward, they scolded her and warned her not to approach the fish and damage it because it was the food of the Saudeleur and must not be dishonored. But others, recalling her son's task to retrieve the *malpur* shell, encouraged her to go ahead and inspect the fish. Perhaps she was simply curious. Perhaps she sensed that the fish had something to do with her son. At any rate, she took a spear from one of the men, went up to the mouth of the fish, and poked its gill. The fish opened its mouth and out came her son Jatokauai with the *malpur* shell in his hand. The people were astounded to see this, but even more astounded when the great fish flapped itself back into the water and swam away! Jatokauai and his mother went directly to meet the Saudeleur at Pahn Kadira and presented the shell. The great chief was excited to receive the thing that no one had ever seen. To this day, the shell remains in the village of Kitti in Onolan,[68] among the people of the Lipitan clan.

"As for the boy, he called together all the members of his family. He filled his mother's home with them, set fire to the house, and — under his direction — they all died with him on that day."

Even as he was telling the story, Ijokelekel felt the atmosphere of the little group change. He sensed he had bewildered them with his ability to relate such a story as though he had witnessed it happen. From the beginning, the little cookhouse had gone silent except for the occasional drop of a dried coconut shell into the hearth and the resultant crackling and hissing of his mother's fire.

---

[68] "Onolan" is Luelen's spelling; this region of Pohnpei is now known as "Onohnleng."

As expected, it was Limaalal who broke the silence sometime after he spoke. "I don't like the ending of your story."

With no hint of defensiveness, Ijokelekel reminded her that it wasn't his story. "I've never understood the ending either, but that is just the way it's told."

"One day, when you two are older, you'll understand," said his adopted father. "When a man completes a great task, he asks himself, 'What's left to accomplish?' If he has no answer, his story is over."

"One day, when I am older," said Ijokelekel, "I'll return to Pohnpei, fight the Saudeleur and all his attendants, and return the great stone village to the commoners whose forefathers lived and died building it."

Jorailik joined in. "And I'll accompany you on this adventure, my brother." He had heard Ijokelekel make this pledge many times before, after speaking of his mother's murder. But he had never understood how serious he was — or respected him enough to follow — until now.

"Enough of this courageous talk!" Lijāpe said. "We have *mokwaņ* to make, so we need our sleep. Tomorrow we rise early as we have much work to do. Limaalal, you and your father will sleep with us in the house. The boys will stop their talk of conquest and sleep here. Are you two listening to me?"

Yes, they'd heard her, but no, they didn't stop talking that night. Prior to that point, the direction in the brothers' relationship had always flowed toward the elder. He was the stronger. He was the one who understood the reefs, the passageways, the fishing methods, all the parts and lashings of the proa, and most important, the language that described it all. Now, like the turnabout of the tide, Ijokelekel felt the direction switch toward him. Now that he had told a story with no hesitation. No name, no place, no part forgotten. They must have thought, "How could such a story be told by a tattooless boy?" He had surprised them all, like the thunder they teased him about. He became known as a boy worth teaching — one who remembered. Truth be told, that story was but one of many he remembered from those formative nights curled in his mother's lap before his father's fire, and it wasn't the last he would tell them. He hadn't gained only the respect of his brother, but of his mother and father as well. Even Limaalal, the one he secretly coveted and wanted to learn to couple with, the one he kept continuously in the corner of his eye, would never speak to him with vulgarity again. She would stay one step behind rather than ahead. Yes, his story had turned the tide there as well. Likewise, he no longer had to question his mother or his father, because they were forever turning toward him with the answer even before he asked his question. They were no longer teaching the older with the younger listening in. That, too, had reversed, such that the older would practice his father's stories with the younger correcting as he continued.

Henceforth, his father was careful to explain every step of whatever endeavor they became engaged in. Ijokelekel learned the names of every passageway from the Kwajalein lagoon out into the sea and of every islet between. They taught him the names of every variety of pandanus, breadfruit, bush and tree, all the fish — as well as their characteristics and the fishing methods necessary to catch them — and all other sea life they gathered for their meals. Ḷōkijdik taught him how to slide the back of his hand against the very top of the coconut crab's cave, grab its torso, turn, and draw it — belly first — from its lair. And where to drop an octopus into a crevice in the reef at lowest tide to watch the lobsters rush out in fear of it. Best of all, Ḷōkijdik taught him what he knew of the sky, the tides, the sea, the wind, the waves it generated, and how they washed up on the shores around the atoll. Even better, Ijokelekel learned such things with such rapidity that, by the time the next wet season rolled around again and his brother was ready for tattooing, his father had decided to sponsor them both.

Tattooing was a skill much in demand and performed only for valuable exchange. Though Limaalal and her father came and went many times that wet season, as well as the one following, to assist in the *mokwaṇ* making, it was her share of the dried and packaged pulp, or *jāānkun*, that she was after. Both Ijokelekel and his brother grew their muscles cutting and carrying these enormous fruits, two at a time, to pile them high for Limaalal to break up and bake in her immense ground oven. Yet she kept *her* fruit, that overripe object of their desires, coyly tucked away from them now. Yes, she was keen at keeping them enthusiastic by periodically popping a knee through the slit between the dual mats of her ankle-length skirts or infrequently flashing a short or — if time permitted — prolonged view of the light skin of her inner thigh, so long as their mother was not looking. However, she was suddenly concerned that, if she got pregnant, she would have to get her lines marked locally in piecemeal fashion. She never tired of teasingly mentioning this to them. She wanted her lines drawn all at once at Āne-pin̄, as tradition required of an ambitious woman, so though she remained zealous about keeping them intrigued, she didn't offer herself — and boldly kept them yearning.

Apparently, the custom here differed from that on his home island. It was everyone's wish from youth to get tattooed by the best and most experienced artisans. What that meant for his adopted family was loading down a proa to its bulwarks with gifts gathered from Lijāpe's relatives on Kwajalein and setting off cross-ocean, southeast past Namu to Aelōn̄ļapļap. As described by Ļōkijdik, Rālik was a necklace made up of atoll pendants that stretched over a vast span of ocean from Enyu in the northwest to Ebon, far to the southeast. The season following, they heard that Limaalal and her parents had already arrived at Āne-pin̄ and that she was probably already in the recovery process. Lijāpe, despite Ļōkijdik's pleas to the contrary, had insisted she needed to accompany her boys to administer the proper medications that their new lines would require to heal properly and prevent scarring. So, he constructed a shelter for her on the lee platform of Lan̄inpo's proa, where she could maintain the privacy that she needed to retain her dignity before her sons.

Kwajalein's western perimeter, Ļōkijdik taught Ijokelekel, was shaped like the palm of his hand facing westward, ready to catch any craft like his that missed the much smaller targets of Lae or Ujae. Wayfarers often drifted up on their shores, and the islanders' habit was to adopt and care for them as they had him. Namu Atoll, he taught him, was the next pendant, a daylight sail to the southeast. That was where Ļōkijdik's ancestors had come from, but in recent history, the men of his clan had split off in a terrible dispute and sailed southeast to the next islet, Wōjjā.

"This is one of the principal islets of Aelōn̄ļapļap Atoll, and it's ruled by Taklur,[69] known as the Chief of Calm Waters. He agreed to shelter them,"

[69] Paramount chief of Wōjjā.

Ḷōkijdik said. Ḷōkijdik's own clan, he explained, now called Rilujien Naṃo,[70] remained fiercely loyal to Taklur for the open arms he had extended them. "Taklur's nemesis is Ḷañinni,[71] a minor chief who lives on the islet between Wōjjā and Āne-piñ. He hates the Rilujien Naṃo clan because of their loyalty to Taklur." Ḷañinni, he explained, had a rebellious streak. He considered Taklur weak and vulnerable. Apparently, a famous passage separated Ḷañinni's island and Āne-piñ, and Ḷañinni was known to show off his riotous nature by strutting along his shore before dawn with his string of chosen ones, beating their drums to irritate other irooj on the far side. Ḷōkijdik told him all this to prepare him for the *jib in jowi*,[72] the initiation his young clan members would be tested by to receive their lines.

Under the appointed moon, Ḷōkijdik and his family sailed at dawn one morning deep into the rainy season. On the windward side, the outrigger platform was covered over with matting to protect the valuable cargo. To port, riding just above the waves on the newly constructed leeward platform, sat Lijāpe, beneath her shelter. Ijokelekel and his brother hunched uncomfortably in between while Ḷōkijdik, with an aura of confidence, sat at the helm. Not surprisingly, they didn't stop at Namu that evening but passed it by.

That atoll was shaped like Kwajalein. Like a hand facing west, only that of a woman — shorter and much narrower. Most of its islets could be seen along the eastern edge of the narrow lagoon across the nearly islet-less western reef that they sailed close to during the moonlit portion of the night. Ḷōkijdik taught him that sailing along the western edge of each atoll was always the optimal course to the southeast. The eastern perimeter of each atoll absorbed the massive energy of the westward-flowing, short-period swell he called *buñtokrear*.[73] This left the western, mostly leeward side calm and frequented only by its rolling counterswell of a much longer period that he called *kāleptak*. They watched this swell gently surge up and break into white water along the lagoon's fringing reef. At high tide, where there were

---

[70] "Ri" currently translates as "people" but may originally have referred to bones. "Lujien Naṃo" means "those who lost from Namu."

[71] A name: "weather strong enough to blow coconuts from the trees."

[72] A rite or trial of passage that must be successfully completed for clan initiates to receive their tattoos.

[73] Swell that "falls from the east."

islets, it slopped up to shore and made its mark with a line of flotsam along its strand. Where there were no islets, it crashed against the reef at low tide and refracted back across the sea from which it had come. At high tide, the swell surged over the leeward perimeter of the shallow, light blue water and rolled gently across the dark lagoon beneath whatever wind-generated waves were there, eventually to find whatever leeward shores were there to slosh up on.

Ijokelekel came to realize there is nothing so spectacular as sailing along the leeward perimeter of a coral atoll. Ḷōkijdik had no doubt timed their trip in such a way that the moon was setting just as they completed their journey along Namu's western reef. They left its southern tip and headed on a course, still to the southeast, across the unfettered *buñtokrear* swells toward the northwest passageway of Aelōñḷapḷap. Per Ḷōkijdik, this was a distance equal to the length of the reef they had just passed. He warned them that these swells, of shorter period, would elevate over those of *kāleptak* as though they were no longer there. Then the swells would stream between the atolls, causing a current that would threaten to sweep the proas into an expanse of open ocean they were unprepared to endure.

However, not known for predicting weather, Ḷōkijdik admittedly had not planned for storm clouds erupting in the southwest and causing headwinds from the southeast that threatened to double the time to sail to Aelōñḷapḷap. As they were high into the stars of Jebrọ,[74] he assured them that there would be no gale they would have to surrender to. They sailed into the string of storms, holding each eastward tack for twice as long as the opposite tack to oppose the current that wanted to sweep them westward. The dark gusts and cold rain tried their determination, yet they didn't flinch during the long night. At dawn, they spied land ahead, and their spirits rose to meet it.

"Finally," said Jorailik. Then more softly so only Ijokelekel could hear, he added, "I can't take too much more of this cold! My breadfruit seeds have retreated so far I don't think they'll ever dangle again!"

---

[74] Aka Pleiades; constellation. Also, the youngest son of Ḷōktañūr, who allowed his mother to board his canoe. Jebrọ first appears just before dawn and disappears in the sunrise. Later in the season, he appears earlier in the night and thus higher in the sky.

"I feel like my spear has shrunk to something like that!" Ijokelekel laughed, putting his thumb to the first digit of his forefinger and holding it up for his brother to see.

"If we were all alone and Limaalal was sitting there with her thighs spread, I'd be embarrassed to show myself. I'd be asking 'Waow! Girl, when do you think this rain will stop?'"

"Mother," called Ļōkijdik. "Stop dreaming in there and show yourself!" Then, before she could answer, he looked at the boys with a laugh in his eyes, "It's noon and my clansmen are on the reef, waiting to carry you ashore."

"I was dreaming I was with a man whose proa was large enough for a shelter I could stretch out in. My back aches from curling into this snail's shell," complained Lijāpe from inside her little hut.

"Then come out and take the helm while I swim ashore to find a woman petite enough to fit."

"You wouldn't know what to do with her either." Lijāpe burst open the thatched flap door of her shelter and looked at the stunned boys, who had forgotten how close to them her ear was. "Now, no more talk of Limaalal or especially women from Aelōn̄ļapļap. Once your lines heal, we return to Kwajalein, where there will be plenty of girls to choose from. Remember, the most aggressive are the most desperate. Avoid them like *kallep*.[75] How can you find happiness living with an insect?"

As she continued to heckle the boys, they stole glancing snickers at each another and wished their father hadn't discharged her from her shelter. The clouds periodically splattered them with cold rain, and the wind kept lashing on the nose of the little vessel as they tacked back and forth toward their destination. However, Ļōkijdik pointed out that, on the favorable side, they were now in lee of the atoll's famous northeasternmost islet, Jeh. Though too far in the distance to see, its effect on the surface of the sea into which they now crept was palpable. As they sailed into the shelter of the atoll, *buñtokrear* ever so gradually gave way to the calming effect of its counterswell, and by late afternoon, they reached the shores of Wōjjā. Tired and unwilling to sail on to the northwest passage and back to beach his proa on the lagoon side as was customary, Ļōkijdik decided to ride the *kāleptak*

[75] Trap-jaw ant: *Odontomachus simillimus.*

swell over the now-flooded reef edge and beach his vessel on the ocean side of the piece of land that Irooj Taklur had given to his fellow clan members.

Ijokelekel, relieved at the prospect of completing his second cross-ocean journey, leaped off the bow to steady Ḷōkijdik's craft in the remnants of the lumbering swells that had sloshed over the reef's edge. These swells had gently surged them shoreward over reef rocks and all, finally washing them up to the flotsam-covered strand of the flooded beach. His shoulders shivered as he jumped down into the warm, waist-high water and held the buoyant, fearless vessel steady as it bobbed shoreward in the waves. As his feet sank into the turbulent sand, he pondered the time that had passed so rapidly since leaving Pohnpei and recommitted himself to his goal. That tattooed or no, he must soon seek out the great pali on Lae whom his mother had promised would teach him all he needed to know.

It was obvious to Ijokelekel that many more people lived on Pohnpei than, say, Ennylabegan, where they had stayed during the dry season. However, the Pohnpeians, as he remembered them, were spread out over a large and mountainous island while those on Ennylabegan were crowded together on a small islet. Yet neither place prepared him for what he was now experiencing, even before setting foot on Wōjjā's stone-lined pathways. More vessels sailing about at sea fishing amid the inclement weather than he ever would have imagined. Girls sauntering along shore, oiled shoulders glistening in the drizzle. Nicer homes than he had ever seen stationed along the ocean shore, with no trees uncultivated and no land left undeveloped. Wells, he would find, with water as fresh as the sky. The entire islet, from north to south, was uniformly populated from the ocean side to its crescent-shaped lagoon shores and would take an entire morning to circumvent.

Word of their vessel's arrival must have spread quickly because Ḷōkijdik's closest relatives had appeared by the time it took a band of his clansmen to nudge the loaded boat safely onto the strand. Despite the pleas of his mother, Ijokelekel stayed by Ḷōkijdik's canoe even after they had escorted the others off to shelter. Someone had left a shy boy to be his guide. Ijokelekel wanted to remove the sail and booms and take them with him. Struggling to untie the halyard, he felt the presence of someone who had approached from behind. Over his shoulder was a tall, thickly built young man with a friendly manner who grabbed hold of the two *rojak*,[76] heavy with wet sail between, and held them effortlessly while Ijokelekel untied the remainder of the lines.

"*Koṃṃool*,"[77] said Ijokelekel.

"For kindness's sake," responded the young man. "We can hang this in my uncle's boathouse. It's right over here." He swung the beams over his shoulder and started off down the strand.

The boathouse was indeed close, and it was the perfect place to shelter their sail. The canoe stored in the open dwelling sat dry from the rain, and there was plenty of room to place the sail's booms on its rafters and allow the halved sail to dangle and not drip on the vessel sheltered there. The small boy had offered his hand to escort Ijokelekel, but the young man leaned against his uncle's canoe as though he wanted to talk.

"So, what advice?" he asked.

Ijokelekel didn't have any idea what he was being asked so stood there dumbfounded, staring at the kindly looking giant before him.

"What advice for the jib in jowi?" he asked humbly.

Of course, Ḷōkijdik had told of this. One man from each clan must carry a husked coconut before a double line of assailants and survive their beating to successfully deliver the coconut to the presiding irooj at the line's end.

"If I fail, none of us will be allowed to receive our lines this season," the young man said with endearing sincerity. "Uncle says I should ask everyone in my group for advice."

How was Ijokelekel to politely respond? He had no skill at fighting and had never seen the jib in jowi performed. Ḷōkijdik had explained it as more a formality than a challenge, not as something likely to fail and all their work going for naught. He inspected the sensitive giant before him — surely a champion if he had ever seen one.

"Stay confident," he advised.

"I was very confident until I heard Ḷañinni and not Taklur will be the one who presides over my fate."

---

[76] The individual booms of the lateen sail. Vertical boom: rojak ṃaan; lateral boom: rojak kōrā.

[77] Thank you.

Ḷañinni's reputation was that of a treacherous bully. These concerning words were ruining his triumphant landing and expectations of a successful tattooing. Suddenly, Ijokelekel felt the urge to speak with Ḷōkijdik about this news. "What will they use to clobber you?" He had heard the explanation before but wanted to check its veracity.

"*Pap*."[78]

This response was what Ijokelekel had expected. When dried, the coconut frond hardens but becomes too light to have a harsh impact. When fresh — and heavy with water — it can deliver quite a wallop, but the water squishes out, the strands fray, and a second clubbing is much less impactful. "Well, what do the others advise?"

Showing confidence now, and pride, the muscular young man held his hand out as though holding an imaginary husked coconut. Tucking it under his armpit, he locked his other hand onto the opposite elbow with a fierce look of determination on his face. Then he began swaying his shoulders back and forth as though being pummeled on either side.

Never at a loss for élan, Ijokelekel declared him ready to champion their cause. "You have my confidence! When do we leave for Āne-piñ?"

"*Jekḷaj*."[79]

With that, Ijokelekel finally took the hand of his guide, who led him away in the rain. "What was the big man's name?" he asked the boy softly, as they walked through the village to where he would find his wearied family.

"Anitok!"[80] responded the boy, as though chastising him for not knowing the name of their champion.

---

[78] A coconut-leaf stem from the first leaflets after its base forward a few feet.

[79] The day after tomorrow.

[80] The one chosen by his clan to undergo the *jib in jowi* test by carrying the coconut through the lines of Ḷañinni's men.

Anitok is tested

The next morning began the final day for his fellow initiates and their families to prepare for an expected moon's cycle of tattooing. Proas rigged and carried to the shoreline. Tributes gathered and loaded, provisions prepared. Ḷōkijdik, having completed this preparation on Kwajalein, was free to fraternize with his clansmen. Anitok, with his champion status, had also prepared, but he showed up early to share their morning meal and then suggested Ijokelekel and his brother help him cut coconuts for his uncle, who was *aḷap*[81] of the *wāto*.[82]

The *aḷap* provided the adze. He was so old and bent over he couldn't look straight up and needed a stick to walk, but he knew every tree. He had to twist and point up sideways with his walking stick at the bunch he wanted cut — quite a trick, as he seemed to invariably select the perfect bunch. Ijokelekel was the first to scramble up the notches of the first trunk to its crown. He chopped through the stalk of the still-green bunch the *aḷap* had ordered felled. The adze was so sharp he cut it loose with but a few well-placed hacks. Likewise, the green stem of the bunch he pointed to next. Cut a bunch a moon too early and the shells — not yet hardened — within the green husks would smash upon impact, their water wasted. Thus, only two bunches were selected per tree. Ijokelekel had long ago learned to thump a nut with a snap of his forefinger to judge its ripeness and marveled that the *aḷap* was able to choose so well from below. Next, the *aḷap* directed him to fell a mature frond for a basket.

---

[81] A paramount landholder who manages land on behalf of an irooj; a lineage head.
[82] A tract of land from the ocean side to the lagoon side.

The first sound of falling nuts brought a few shy children to the spot where Anitok had set his sharpened hardwood stake, and even before Ijokelekel began his descent, he heard the familiar sound of the husks being speared and ripped apart by the boy's strong hands. Seeing the ease, quickness, and accuracy of his work, Ijokelekel quickly realized that this was his favorite task and probably the cause of the young man's admirable strength.

As he reached the ground, the *aḷap* requested his adze and began severing the fat-stem end of the large frond Ijokelekel had felled. He then hacked two V-shaped grooves of about an arm's length each into the midrib. This allowed him to strip away both sides of the leaf. Then, placing the stripped leaves face down on the ground, he began crisscrossing the leaflets, plaiting both halves together to fashion a heavy, hull-shaped basket with thick braids on either side to serve as handles. When he had finished, he unceremoniously tossed the crude basket toward Anitok, chanting, "*Enrā lale rārā.*"[83]

Catching a bit of breath, Ijokelekel watched Anitok place the freshly husked nuts into the *enrā* while Jorailik attacked the next tree. The mostly naked children scrambled to carry the heavy nuts, one at a time, to Anitok as he worked. The basket quickly filled with a pile of round, freshly husked nuts, each with a fibrous cap left on top to protect its soft mouth. On occasion, with a sneaky shift in his brow, Anitok would purposefully miscalculate the final motion, pierce a shell, and hand the leaking nut to one of the waiting children. This was always followed by a mumble from the old man and a chorus of laughter. In this way, they spent their day: climbing, husking, carrying, and listening to the *aḷap* launch his customary chants. At one point, the number of children gathered was twelve. This set the old man off on a story enactment, much to the delight of all.

The old man motioned for all to stop their work and enjoy their rest. "Who has been to Ailinginae?" None stepped forward.

At first, Ijokelekel thought this a stupid question. Surely none of these children had been anywhere.

"There are three atolls at the top end of the Rālik string: Rongerik, Rongelap, Ailinginae. Why do you think they call it Ailinginae?"

---

[83] A saying: "A basket to take care of those close to us."

"Because there's a lot of current there?" replied one of the children.

"*Wōt jeej*![84] Correct! And two women were there. One was young and one was old, and two islets — called Karwe and Jeḷā-eṇ — and a lot of current on the reef were between them. Why so much current? I'll tell you why. Because Rongelap sits on top of Ailinginae, and this causes a lot of current to build up between these two atolls."

"What were the two islets on the northern reef of Ailinginae again?"

"Karwe," answered one of the children.

"Jeḷā-eṇ," answered another.

"Correct! Now there is no passage between these two islets, so you might think, 'I'll just walk between them.' But nobody has ever made it. You want to know why?"

"Current?" answered one of the boys.

"Well, not at low tide. Something else. Something very sharp — *kapwor*!"[85]

This seemed to make sense to most of the children. Everyone knew that even the giant clams used for bathing have convex, sharp-edged protuberances along the sides that could cut a leg or foot if accidently bumped. The edges were like knives and often filed down for safety purposes.

"So, what happens when you try to walk on that reef?" he asked the children.

One of them answered tentatively, "You cut your foot?"

"*Wōt jeej*! Correct! Okay, I want everybody to form a line. Not you, Anitok. You're too tall. Everyone, put your left hand on the left shoulder of the child in front of you. Steady yourself and pick up your right ankle. Why would you do this? *Wōt jeej*, because you just stepped next to a *kapwor* and cut your foot! Now everyone take a single hop forward."

The children hopped without coordination. Some fell and giggled their way up again.

"That's good! Now another."

---

[84] The same as "jeej." An idiom used to express surprise that translates as "heck" or "darn it." Demonstrates more deliberation than "wōjjej."

[85] Giant clam: *Tridacna gigas*.

More coordinated this time, they hopped and laughed together. "Now another!"

They began to get the hang of the little dance.

"And that's how they hopped down the reef."

"Who?"

"Good! There's always one who wants a proper explanation. I'll start from the beginning. A young woman gives birth to a litter of twelve children, but because they have no father, they're born with only one leg, one arm, and one eye. But she raises them anyway, and when they get older, she makes them a net and tells them to go fishing. But guess who's watching?"

"The other woman!" answered one precocious child.

"*Wōt jeej*!! Correct! Likarwejoñ[86] is sitting in her kiden tree, watching and waiting for them to get halfway." He challenged the children. "Come on. You're not halfway yet!"

So, the children hopped along as directed by the old man with his walking stick, and then they broke up into laughter as before.

"Waow! She casts her magic chant."

The old man sang, casting his eyes sideways as though seeking inspiration, swaying his shoulders, and pitching his voice mysteriously.

They carry their net
to trap themselves!
Bunbunbun,[87] *they*
come along fishing.
Hop down reef.
Last of all come,
one called Stupid.
Come wave from sea,
wave from sea. Slap!
Cut up their legs for me!

---

[86] Legendary monster who lives in a kiden tree on Karwe, an islet of Ailinginae Atoll.
[87] "Bunbun" means to count; in the chant, the syllables are repeated for alliterative purposes.

"The tide comes in, the current sweeps them into the lagoon. The old woman Likarwejoñ ululates, swims, and eats the children up. When she finishes, she swims back to Karwe, sits in her kiden tree, and snickers a bit.

"So, the woman of Jeḷā-eṇ gets pregnant again, and she has twelve more children — no father. Same as before. One arm, one leg, and one eye. Only half-people, but she raises them anyway. When they get older, she makes another net and sends them off fishing. They wait until the tide is low and start hopping down that reef. Likarwejoñ sees them coming, and when they're halfway, she casts her magic chant.

They carry their net
to trap themselves!
Bunbunbun, they
come along fishing.
Hop down reef.
Last of all come,
one called Stupid.
Come wave from sea,
wave from sea. Slap!
Cut up their legs for me!

"Then, same as before, she ululates, swims, and eats them all up.

"On and on and then one day, that woman of Jeḷā-eṇ has twelve more sons, but the last one to come out is a real boy with two arms, two legs, and two eyes. His brothers call him Stupid because he looks funny, and they won't play with him. When their mother gives them a net to go fishing, they refuse to take him along. But never mind, he tails along behind and collects lobsters along the way. He connects them by facing their undersides together with the legs of one clutching the tail of the other. In this way, he makes a string of them trailing behind as he follows his brothers down the reef. Of course, when they're halfway, Likarwejoñ lets off her magic chant, and the current starts to wash them into the lagoon. So, the one called Stupid swims to his drowning brothers and tows them all — lobsters and brothers — to the shore of Karwe.

"When night falls, his brothers huddle together, and he builds a fire for them and starts to cook his lobsters.

Insect come!
Cry Likarwejoñ.
Insect you!
Spirit I.
I sing my magic oath. I
chant to the north. I
chant to the south. I
sing in this limb
of my kiden sit in.
I sit and ññūr[88] *and*
ññūr and ññūr and ññūr!
Throw us one lobster,
plus one of your brothers.

"The boys are so frightened they crawl upon one another like a ball of worms, but Stupid pays Likarwejoñ no mind and continues to build his fire.

Insect come!
Cry Likarwejoñ.
Insect you!
Spirit I.
I sing my magic oath. I
chant to the north. I
chant to the south. I
sing in this limb
of my kiden sit in.
I sit and ññūr and
ññūr and ññūr and ññūr!
Throw us one lobster,
plus one of your brothers.

---

[88] Growl.

"The one they called Stupid throws up one lobster for the greedy old monster to gobble. Then he throws up one red-hot rock, and she gobbles that too. Then goes 'Eh!' a bit and then groans a bit and dies.

"To this day" — the old man went on to state the moral of his story — "nobody has been able to make it from Jeḷā-eṇ to Karwe on that reef. Giant clams of all sizes are everywhere with no space between, and you know how sharp they are!"

With that, the *aḷap* wobbled toward another tree and pointed his walking stick up at another bunch of coconuts, and Ijokelekel scrambled up its trunk. He wasn't surprised when, later that afternoon, Anitok flopped, sweaty, before the *aḷap* and pleaded for his advice on the jib in jowi he was shortly to face. The *aḷap* was resting cross-legged at the time, having just plaited his third *enrā*.

The fragile old man had the same twinkle in his eyes that Ijokelekel had noticed from his first command. He no longer bothered to stuff rolls of pandanus leaves in his ears, and their stretched lobes flopped ringless against his jaws as he moved his head to speak. He appeared as cool as a coconut leaflet in the breeze. Not a drop of sweat crossed his brow. The tattoos across his slim shoulders, chest, and stomach presented the illusion his skin was bound by them. A comb of turtle shell that held his hair atop his head was his sole adornment other than a trochus-shell band around his wrist.

"Let me tell you something about Ḷañinni. He's currently the lowest of the chiefs, but he has designs. His uncle was a great chief who told me himself that that boy was out for himself. His favorite activity is collecting tribute from the atolls from south to north. Rather than passing it on to his uncle, he keeps most of it for himself and his followers. Now, you know what they say about Wōjjā?

Spread out your family mat
so to lay together
on island.
Taklur! Taklur!
Even water calm

upon our shore.
Know there is calm.
Only calm.

"Ḷañinni isn't a man who appreciates calm. He sails primarily in storms. He would rather swim than paddle or try to sail on a calm day. That's why they call him Ḷañinni — 'wind that makes the coconut tree bend.' He prefers motion to calm."

The *aḷap* turned now to Ijokelekel, who was obviously engrossed in his story. "When he's not storming between the atolls, he lives on Pikaajḷā. That's the islet next to Āne-piñ. A deep passage from ocean into lagoon runs between them. It's a wide passage, and the irooj who live on Āne-piñ feel safe there because there's a lot of current running at their doorstep. Yet their canoes lie in boathouses along the shore in case they have need to escape. But just to show them they're not safe on certain nights of slack tide, Ḷañinni and his men will swim the passage despite the sharks that frequent there and wake them up by asking for food or something. He can be very annoying and loves to impose on their generosity.

"You know, there's a custom never to walk or make noise between the shore and the home of the irooj. Well, when Ḷañinni sees that the wind is blowing from his side across the passage to theirs, he gathers his women. That's another story. He takes a lot of them. They gather their *aje*[89] — and his men, their conch shells — and they march up and down the shore on their side, making such a racket the irooj can't rest.

"That's Ḷañinni, and you boys of Rilujien Naṃo are in trouble this season. Ḷañinni sees your clan as Irooj Taklur's strongest support. The people love Taklur, and that makes Ḷañinni jealous. He must have a reason for wanting to preside over your jib in jowi. If he orders his men to prevent you from finishing your run, you're in for a beating, but you're a strong boy, so you should be all right." Those were the last words the crippled man spoke before energetically standing and again pointing his walking stick at another bunch of coconuts high up in yet another tree.

[89] An hourglass-shaped sharkskin drum carried by women when they accompany their men to a battle.

Anitok's honest face always reflected his sentiments. He appeared bashfully delighted at the elder's compliment, yet visibly troubled by the challenges he must soon overcome. That night, worried their trip would come to naught, Ijokelekel and his brother both fought restless sleeplessness. Before dawn, their father awakened them and took them as a crew around the south end of the island, crossing the reef there at high tide to reach the lagoon shores. Their mother would embark there, amid the rest of the fleet. They would sail with his clansmen as a group for Āne-piñ — though not without much delay. Each family struggled to pack and load their belongings and gifts even as the vessels they loaded were periodically dragged farther down the beach as the tide receded. Finally, by late morning, the small fleet of burdened-down proas sailed with the help of a pleasant breeze from the northeast. It was a damp yet cloudless rainy-season day, and the sun was nearly overhead and unshaded by their sails. As they proceeded toward their unseen destination, more islets came into sight along the atoll's northern and southern reefs. They sailed through several *wūnaak*,[90] one of which was composed primarily of rainbow runners that attacked their trolling lures and provided amply for their afternoon meals of breadfruit, paired with the coconuts Anitok had husked the day before.

When they first came into view, the flat, green islets of Pikaajļā and Āne-piñ appeared in the distance as one islet. As the fleet approached, the islets gradually revealed themselves: the shape of two feet next to each other, heels toward the ocean, their toes protruding lagoonward. The dark blue southernmost passageway ran between them, extending its mysterious, nearly black abyss inward like the ocean's tail twisting deep into the interior of the lagoon. The passageway was lined by submerged cliffs of multishaded blue corals that extended lagoonward on either side. Along its edges and on its shallow azure waters were many fishing vessels. Flocks of fisher birds swirled above the passageway's three openings into the lagoon, and any vessel traveling to Āne-piñ from within the western half of the atoll had to account for the various coral reefs that surrounded this dangerous cobweb of tide-swept corals.

---

[90] Flocks of seabirds diving for baitfish driven to the surface by tuna or other large fish.

The outflowing tide had nearly reached its ebb. Their fleet passed well lagoonward of these reefs and then tacked toward the sand beach of the Ānepiñ shoreline. It faced eastward all the way to its similarly hook-shaped opposite end, far onto the horizon. The women began beating their *aje* and ululating to announce their arrival.

The islanders had watched their approach, and their women were ready to ululate back and attack them with leis, flower-scented headbands, and freshly husked coconuts. Singing islanders of all ages soon covered the shore in typical *kaṃōḷo*[91] fashion to welcome the new arrivals. The singing would continue until the last of their gifts and belongings were stacked in piles within the large, open-sided *ṃōn kweiḷọk*[92] their clan members had been allowed to construct for themselves in years past. It would have to be rethatched prior to the various tattoo ceremonies that would take place in the coming days. These festivities continued into the evening as the islanders surrounded their group's meeting house, brought food, and performed little plays, interrupted by speeches from the various irooj or their representatives.

That next day, the sun rose upon the island's opposite end amid a cloudless sky and laid its path down the beach over a now-still lagoon. Gone was the night breeze that had wafted among them as they had slept on their mats after the various celebrations.

Ijokelekel turned to his brother on the mat next to him. He was concerned about the upcoming jib in jowi and needed a reprieve from this worry. "Did you see Limaalal last night?"

"No, did you?" responded his brother.

"No, nor her parents. I wonder if they left for Kwajalein."

"Wouldn't we have passed them as they sailed in the opposite direction?" Jorailik asked.

"Not if they passed by while we were tacking. I'm curious what she looks like with her new lines."

"More conceited than ever, I bet!"

"Well, she's got no more excuses!" Ijokelekel said.

---

[91] A newcomer celebration.

[92] A meeting house.

"That's true. We'll have to look for her tonight."

The other initiates, most sipping hot *nen*[93] tea from their coconut-shell cups, had already gravitated around Anitok to strengthen his spirit. They provided what encouragement they could, tossing around the coconut he planned to carry and inspecting each other's adornments. Each wore freshly cut pandanus leaves rolled into a cylinder and inserted just so in the holes of their extended ear lobes. Everyone wore a flower behind each ear, and most had hung an attractive necklace around their neck. Some wore a trochus armband. Others wore two.

A rumor had spread that Ļañinni and his men might not arrive by canoe but might swim the channel in the afternoon's slack tide instead. Ijokelekel wondered if his clansmen might appear too adorned for the occasion. Though they were expecting a pompous ceremony, he worried — from what he had heard about Ļañinni — that it might not end up being a normal "transaction-based" jib in jowi. Ļañinni's men were unlikely to be bribed by allowing the clan to pile gifts onto their boats, especially if they had all swum to the occasion. They would cut their *pap* at the island's end and would want to return before the outgoing tide. They would be anxious to return. They might even abstain from the usual puffing and speech making.

Anitok had chosen his coconut with the advice of his clan members. Under the circumstances, it was a very conservative choice. He didn't choose a nut with a rounded husk that would produce a large, round target but rather a long, skinny one cultivated to produce the long strands useful for *ekkwaļ*.[94] It would probably produce a small oval nut that would better fit into the grip of his hand yet, by the sound of the water inside, shouldn't prove to be embarrassingly small. Of course, the risk was that the shape of the nut would cause jeers from Ļañinni's men, but somehow, Anitok had said he didn't expect a silent, respectful event anyway. As the strong, humble man that he was, Anitok was unlikely to be offended by or cringe at any banter.

---

[93] Fruit from *Morinda citrifolia*, a small tree prized throughout the islands for its medicinal properties; a tonic thought to promote health. Also called "noni."

[94] Sennit; coir fiber line made from processed coconut-husk fibers.

He and the other initiates would have to be at the appointed place by noon, and sooner would be better. Ļañinni and his men were not likely to wait, nor would they likely participate in any festivities after the contest. The initiates and their families would walk the relatively short distance to the tip of the toe, where the absence of soil and exposure to the elements presented a large, sandy area. Uncultivated, it propagated few bushes and only a few hardy trees. As soon as the clan arrived, they saw that the rumors had not been completely true. There was already one large proa stranded farther down, on the broad, sandy shore, and several of Ļañinni's men were milling around the area where the jib in jowi would take place. The clan had brought no gifts other than the baskets of husked coconuts they carried with them. All did not seem right from the beginning.

Finally, when they heard the *aje* beat and ululations from Ļañinni's *du*[95] on the opposite shore, Ijokelekel followed the others around to the west side of the passageway to watch the men swim the dangerous and considerable distance across the dark blue channel. The tide was slack in the passageway. There was no need to speak of their bravery. All knew that these passageways between ocean and lagoon contained all manner of sea life, including sharks that might latch onto a foot or leg or whatever attracted the dumb brutes. The *du* was quite large, as many of Ļañinni's men had taken more than one woman. His men stroked in a disciplined line behind their leader as he swam.

The line swam slowly and deliberately and took a long while, as the passage was large enough for twenty or so proas to pass through at once. Slim and muscular all, the men emerged in single file, unadorned, their scraggly untrimmed beards dripping with sea, their long hair twisted into buns and secured with one or two stingray barbs. Their droopy working kilts of *atat*[96] contrasted immediately with the initiates' fine ceremonial kilts made of bleached pandanus and hibiscus bark. Their tall leader was unmistakable by the way he carried himself. He had only to glance

[95] Women beating drums and accompanying their loved ones to a battle or supporting their chant as they dance the jebwa.

[96] A plant with small, thin leaves; the stems of this plant, *Triumfetta procumbens*, were processed to make skirts and kilts.

downshore for his followers to untie the adzes at their belts and begin searching out the coconut fronds necessary to fashion into the clubs they would use to assail their victim. Ḷañinni, acknowledging no one and dripping seawater, walked across the sand to where his advance party was standing. After a brief discourse, he turned to inspect the crowd and found proud Anitok, standing unmistakably with his coconut and stake at hand.

With a brief downward swipe of his hand, Ḷañinni summoned the young hero to follow and, after judging the distance his men would need for their lines, appointed his place to stand. Anitok then stood alone as the last of Ḷañinni's men emerged from the channel and wandered off to cut and trim their coconut-frond clubs. Finally, the last of several tens of men lined up into two rows sufficiently separated to allow for mighty swings as the young man proceeded down the lines between them.

All eyes were then on Ḷañinni. He was a different sort of leader. No necklace, nor arm bands. No pandanus rolls hanging from his modestly stretched ear lobes. His kilt worn and scraggly. His face, also tattooed as a symbol of his status, made him stand out, but then there was that scar across his cheek, which made him appear vengeful. Other than that, it was the way he carried himself that marked him as a leader. He was a lanky man with an unpoised, swaggering yet deliberate manner about him that exuded a quiet physical strength no man dare challenge. Most shied from his piercing eye contact, and even his men turned their faces away as they spoke to him. His eyes toured the disparate crowd until they settled on the hero. He gave his commanding nod.

Anitok's mature coconut made intermittent crisp sounds as he pierced its dried husk again and yet again and twisted the hard nut from its encasement. The ceremonial silence surrounding this act then broke into jeers and recriminations from the two lines of oppressors, who were intent on striking it loose from beneath the armpit where he placed the nut and the clasped fist that would protect it. His free hand locked around the opposite elbow, and a shade of fierce determination crossed his face. With lips clenched, he began his run. Ḷañinni's men were careful not to strike his head, of course. Most ended up walloping one immense shoulder or the other though many tried to strike Anitok's legs out from under him. Some struck a second blow on his back as he passed. Others tried to land more strategic blows on his elbows. Others took aim at his shins. By the rules, should both knees touch the sand, the lines of men could disperse and pile onto him to wrench the coconut loose. Yet he fell not and cringed his way through the lines in such a way that all were certain he would reach their end in triumph. At that point, he began to move all the faster between the lines toward Ļañinni, who stood in his place a short distance from their end.

Then one of the men ahead of him fell to the ground behind the others. After a moment, he rose again and backed up, violently yanking on a line that had popped from beneath the sand, apparently held by another man on the opposite side. The line snared Anitok's feet and brought him tumbling down. What followed was a pathetic struggle whereby he attempted to roll himself forward against all odds but, alas, succumbed to the overpowering strength of his opponents until one emerged from the pile with the coconut and handed it to the chief.

Suddenly, all went quiet. The muddle was over. Strangely, there was no gloating from Ļañinni's group. No congratulations to the man who had recovered the coconut. No words of conciliation. The two conspirators dragged their line across the sand back toward their proa. The group of assailants returned to the shore from which they had emerged, each hurling his broken club into the passageway. The *pap* all appeared to veer lagoonward as they sank in the mild current. Nodding at each initiate, Ļañinni acknowledged the small, stunned group one by one. His eyes pierced those of Ijokelekel and accepted his anger. Then, without a word, he turned and headed toward his waiting men. Apparently, the longer he tarried, the more difficult the swim.

Ijokelekel alone got the urge to follow. He watched Ļañinni plunge into the passageway and head oceanward of the course toward his *du* on the opposite shore. Their ululations and drum beating instantly ensued. His men followed, each likewise heading oceanward of his mark to account for the turn in the tide that would stream around them as it poured, slowly at first, through the deep passage to refill the lagoon's shell from whence it had previously drained. By the time the last man entered the water, although each adopted the heading of the one preceding, their line didn't appear angled toward the ocean, but — due to the in-flowing current — straight across the channel toward the distant *du*, whose presence marked their destination. Their ululations seemed to invigorate the swimming. Their beat set the timing of the strokes.

Ijokelekel's clan members, perhaps stunned by the developments, found this sound hateful and derisive. To a soul, they had turned down the opposite shore along the lagoon side of the cape, where the intervening cultivated forest would absorb this eerie combination. He alone found the sound too compelling to resist, and he sat on the sand to watch and to listen and to contemplate this latest untenable turn of events.

A surprise for the defeated

Ijokelekel had hoped to appear as a tattooed man before the pali, ready to initiate his apprenticeship without further ado. Had he inadvertently tied himself to the wrong clan? Were his plans now ruined? Must he begin lineless under the tutelage of the pali? Then he recalled that, in his culture, lines were of no importance. His mother had said nothing about getting lines. The idea of waiting to get his lines had arisen later, probably from Lijāpe or Ļōkijdik.

As he turned these thoughts over and over, he couldn't help but notice a young woman who had playfully broken from her *du* and scampered down to the shore to where Ļañinni was about to emerge. She appeared to be throwing stones with an unusually familiar-looking underhand cast, as though attempting to skip them against the surface of the channel.

Was that Limaalal signaling to him? The distance was so great he couldn't be sure. He stood to better identify himself and watched her return to the *du*. She reemerged with two kilts in hand and stood apart, dancing and waving them as she had done the afternoon of her little octopus caper so long ago.

It was Maalal. She had proved it to him. He raised his arm to acknowledge her, and she responded by beckoning him with a downward whip of her hand. "What did she want," he wondered. Was he to get his proa and sail around these sprawling lagoonward reefs to retrieve her or take her to her parents? No, she seemed insistent that he come for her now. She wanted him to swim. Did she expect him to confront the great Ļañinni?

When the irooj appeared on shore, Limaalal was there to hand him one of the dry kilts. He accepted it, and they appeared to be discussing something. Both periodically turned to gaze across the water at him. Then Ḷañinni nodded at him more abruptly than he had previously and whipped his hand downward, casually beckoning him to cross the channel. Each of his followers was now beaching himself increasingly lagoonward of the one preceding, demonstrating clearly to Ijokelekel that the tide was having a progressively greater effect. He judged that the last in line was likely to surface at the islet's toe before the sprawling lagoonward reef that was about to be flooded by the incoming water pouring through the passage.

Caught up in the moment, Ijokelekel raised his arm to acknowledge the irooj's challenge, turning away as he did. He began pacing down the long shore of the channel toward the ocean until he reached a spot his instinct judged would provide the head start needed to cross in the incrementally shifting tide. Stepping into the water and removing his kilt, he held it up for all to see before tossing it. He would have to cross the current naked as a child at this point. Limaalal likewise held up the kilt she had been teasing him with to assure him she would be ready on the other side.

He sprang into the slowly flowing water, chanting "Your father … is Nahn … Sapwe! Your father … is Nahn … Sapwe" as he stroked. The chant was for courage, to overcome the many fears that surrounded him. There were sharks, of course, but they lived their own twisted paths that were unlikely to collide with his unless this current pushed him onto the sharp reefs beyond the passage and he cut his feet. "Current must always be respected," Ḷōkijdik was wont to say. "It could be used to add to or subtract from your time at sea." Ijokelekel feared what his mother would say when he returned the next day but then laughed as he had so many times before when Limaalal had taken his finger and put it to her nose. Most of all, he feared what he didn't know. Why was Ḷañinni summoning him? What ugly plan did he hold for him? What would he ask him to do? What might she ask him to do? Was he being foolish to comply?

He swam on like this, one pensive stroke after another. He felt the current only because the shore he was targeting kept slipping away faster than he could swim toward it. Finally, he was targeting the spot where Ḷañinni stood with Maalal. His arms and legs had tired some time ago. He watched the two grow smaller on the shore, and finally, the irooj began commanding his men. Then Ijokelekel watched them carry a paddling canoe down from the strand. He saw the island's end and realized they were planning to retrieve him. He was drifting into the lagoon, but at a lesser pace than their paddling with the current. Before long, he saw Limaalal above him, still teasing him with his new kilt. He summoned the last of his strength to pull himself up and lift a knee into the hull, and then she was wrapping him, but not before taking a good look and laughing with the men at his expense. The tide had beaten him. Forced him to abandon the heroic landing he had anticipated.

Now Limaalal informed him that she had taken Ļañinni and become one of several other women he slept with. This added to Ijokelekel's disappointment. "Risked my life for what?" he thought. All the others had babies and she was to be next, she told him. "Fantastic. Why did she summon me?" he wondered. She seemed happy, but he assumed she had made a mistake. What did her parents think? At least she wouldn't require him to fight Ļañinni. Had she told him who his father was?

"Do you like my lines?"

"Yes, they're beautiful. But why did you require me to swim over here?"

"To show you my lines — except, of course, the ones they tattooed over my *jukkwe.*" She giggled. "Only my new irooj gets to see those."

He couldn't help but look at her skeptically.

"And also, to make you wish you had taken me when you had the chance. There's nothing like lost opportunity to ignite jealousy, so I thought, 'Why not introject a little jealousy between the two of you?' It could work to your advantage, Ijokelekel."

So, had she risked his life just to show off to her new paramour and make him jealous? How could he have been so impulsive? What must Ļañinni think of him? How would he treat such a weak fool? The men were paddling against the growing current and were soon back to Pikaajļā, where they had started. Most of the men and their *du* had left, but the few remaining recommenced their ululations and drum beating as they disembarked. Ļañinni had waited and launched the first smile Ijokelekel had seen cross his otherwise taciturn face, and it was broad and welcoming. He quickly led the group up onto the strand toward his home, a large house of pole and thatch that sat high on stilts of coconut trunks. An active group of followers was carrying out what Ijokelekel expected were family chores in the accessible area beneath. There was also a large cookhouse, several boathouses, and separate bathing areas for Ḷañinni and his chosen ones — and another for everyone else. They escorted Ijokelekel to the latter, where he removed his fresh kilt and rinsed the salt from his body in privacy.

He returned to the house and accepted a place to sit next to one of the elders fashioning a piece of proa decking with a small adze. A young woman brought him a small coconut-leaf basket with two freshly husked coconuts just as Ḷañinni and Limaalal arrived from their bathhouse and climbed the ladder into the single entrance in the center of the floor above them. The latter clasped the halves of her skirts modestly as she climbed. The cluster of all ages beneath the home proved a bustle of activity. He wondered if these women were all Ḷañinni's, or were they his sisters or women of his followers? Their *aje* lay strewn about atop the many layers of pandanus mats covering the coral-pebble platform upon which they sat. Children of various ages scampered about, breaking off nodules of pandanus, chewing, and tossing them away. The women were busy in conversations as they plaited.

"How long has Limaalal been staying here on Pikaajḷā?" Ijokelekel asked the elder.

"Only a few days, but she's made quite a few trips up that ladder." He joked and laughed softly with twinkly eyes as he continued to hack gently at his project.

"Where are her parents?"

"They say they left for Kwajalein, mission completed."

"Do you have any idea why Ḷañinni would ask me to swim the passage and then climb up there without a word?"

"Wait a bit," suggested the elder. He hacked his adze on the edge of the board again in his ongoing attempt to square it.

Ijokelekel grabbed a coconut, tore off the fibrous cap left on top, discarded it into the basket, then opened the hole at its mouth with his fingernail. He brought the drink to his lips, tilted his head back, and sucked its thirst-quenching liquid as he had his mother's tit.

"There," said the elder, glancing up to their right. "Watch closely. They're no doubt being polite this time."

Ijokelekel noticed the floorboards moving above them.

"The last time she was up there midmorning, the whole house shook."

"I can imagine she's a bit like landing a barracuda. I know her from Kwajalein," said Ijokelekel.

"Then that explains why the irooj called you over here. Either the sharks eat you and you're out of his way, or he gets to demonstrate to his latest fire stick that he's not jealous. Either way, he comes out on top. That's the way he carries on. Most think he's a little crazy, but those like me who sit and watch carefully know there's always reason behind his behavior." Then more softly, "It also demonstrates how much control she has over him. He may be on top of her, but he's on his knees right now, begging her for more. She's blowing wind in his sail right now, but she can shut him down with a single word from her lips or a twitch of her nose. If she bears him a son, he'll snare the moon for her."

"Why a son?"

"Because he lost his first one, and the others have borne only daughters."

"What happened to his first son?"

The elder paused to take another deliberate hack at his plank then lowered his voice to a whisper. "An infant, really. He'd just reached his *keemem*[97] age. Lost at sea, and Ḷañinni blames himself."

"Why?" asked Ijokelekel.

"Ḷañinni and the boy's mother were tacking against a storm, there in the passageway. The tide was going out. They were busy shunting, and before they knew it, the boy was swallowed up by the sea."

"Why didn't they tie his ankle?"

"I'm sure he asks himself that question every day."

The elder picked up his bow, looped its bowstring around his stingray bit, and began drilling a hole in a corner of his plank. "What about you? I can tell from your accent that you're not from these islands."

"My mother is from Pohnpei."

"And your father?"

---

[97] The first birthday feast after the passing of two seasons or thirteen cycles of the moon.

"My father is Nahn Sapwe."

"Sounds like your father was a chief?"

"You could say that."

"What brings you to these islands?"

"I came to study with the great *rijeḷā*[98] on Lae. His name is…"

"Siss." The elder shushed him, then asked in a soft voice, "Ḷōpako?"[99]

"Yes, that's what they call him."

"Siss, I said!" The elder shut him up again for some mysterious reason, then whispered, "Pako is a taboo name around here."

"Why?"

"It's not even safe to talk about. And if you're smart, you'll stow that name below the prow of the canoe you came here in and leave it unsaid until you embark."

"But why?" Ijokelekel insisted.

"Okay, let's take a walk," the elder said, struggling to stand. "Hand me my walking stick. I need to get another bit from my house anyway. This one has lost its edge."

After a slow start, the old man picked up momentum and began pacing at a normal clip.

"The talk started the day they arrived," the elder began, as he led them over the stone-covered courtyard surrounding Ḷañinni's compound.

"Ḷōpako came here?"

"Last season," he answered, pointing ahead to a little hut he kept for himself.

"They came to tattoo his daughter, and a second daughter he had with their *lerooj*,[100] Likōkkāḷọk.[101] That woman is another story all by herself, I'll say that much."

"He brought two daughters at the same time? Strange, that's like me and my brother. Only we failed the jib in jowi today and can't continue."

---

[98] Literally, "bones that know"; navigator; captain; pali; palu.

[99] Aka Pako; Ḷainjin's nickname. Literally, "man shark." "Ḷō": the male prefix; "pako": "shark."

[100] Literally, "woman chief."

[101] Character introduced in *Man Shark*; Erwina's mother.

"Yes, I heard. Bad transaction that. Taklur takes all your tribute, but you boys go away without your lines. An embarrassment for everyone except Ļañinni, who — we suppose — wants to cause as much disruption between Taklur and his followers as possible."

"What's wrong with Taklur? He's known as a great chief, right?"

"Nothing, but a great chief makes a lesser, more ambitious chief jealous, right? Why do you think the old man agreed to let Ļañinni preside over the jib in jowi anyway?"

"Because he's an old man and has no throat to fight with his nephew?" proposed Ijokelekel.

When they arrived at the old man's hut, he opened the window flaps on two sides and asked Ijokelekel to open the other two. A cross breeze immediately began wafting through the little thatched shack.

"You sleep here all alone?"

"They send a grandchild now and again to stay with me and listen to my stories. I'm close to the irooj*'s* cookhouse, so we always get plenty to eat."

"Are you related to him?"

"My wife was his eldest aunt. She died a long time ago, but he continues taking care of me."

"Please continue. I want to hear the rest of this."

"As you should! Anyway, they arrived, the whole fleet of them, *lerooj* and all, in the middle of a terrible storm. So, right away Ļōpako crossed Ļañinni because that's a characteristic of his story. It's what Ļañinni is known for — his knowledge of the weather — but everyone starts talking about this new *rijeļā* from *kapin meto*,[102] so he feels mocked."

"So, Ļañinni gets jealous of Ļōpako, and that's why his name is a sore spot," said Ijokelekel.

"Yes, but that was just the start of it. The story goes on. Ļañinni decides he wants to take Pako's daughter. She is a perfect virgin and he goes crazy for her, but she spurns him bad — and publicly."

"All the more reason…"

"Ļañinni differs from the other irooj. He doesn't worry about following tradition. But he does care about his story and how people tell it. So, his next

[102] Literally, "back side of ocean"; the westernmost atolls of the Rālik Chain.

step is to ask her father. Ḷañinni claims he was willing to wait for her tattoos. He offers Pako an untold amount of tribute for her, but Pako refuses to overturn his daughter's decision."

"So, now he's dug an even deeper hole that he can't climb out of."

"It's said the other daughter was willing to take him, but first, he falls under the spell of her mother, Likōkkālọk. She is older than any woman he's ever chased here and makes sure their affair ends up on everyone's lips. Then they humiliate him more by embarking in the middle of another storm, and Likōkkālọk leaves word he's not man enough for her daughter either."

"No wonder…"

"Now you understand why nobody on this island ever mentions the names Pako or Likōkkālọk! Now let's get back before the irooj and your friend Limaalal get up from their mat. The irooj isn't one to sleep through a rainstorm."

"Rainstorm?"

The old man pointed his walking stick south to show Ijokelekel that the wind had shifted and was now breezing through the passageway. Then he said, "When they descend from their nest, you don't want them wondering where you've drifted off to. We don't want to have to explain, do we?"

"There's no way for them to know what we talked about," Ijokelekel said.

"Except by the look on your face. Your charm is your innocence, and that has faded from your countenance."

"You are a great teacher, old man," Ijokelekel said. He closed the window flaps before they left.

"Would that my grandchildren were good listeners like yourself."

When they returned to their spot below the irooj's pole house, Ijokelekel watched his elder friend drill several holes with his fire bow and stingray barb and hardwood handhold.

One of the plaiting women nearby joked with him. "I see you've attached yourself to the belly of our wise old shark. There's nothing he likes better than an attentive sucker fish. Be careful, though, or he'll lead you between the teeth of another."

Surprised, Ijokelekel and the old man glanced at one another, wondering whether she could have heard, but the elder closed his eyes and shook his head rapidly to the contrary.

Then one of the other women added, "Be careful, or he'll have you cutting and transporting mangrove for that cookhouse he has been asking for. He thinks if he cooks his own food, he won't be obligated to dig arrowroot for our dry-season meals."

"This is the way it goes every day," the elder said. "They jab at me, jab at me, waow! I tell them a story to shut them up. They won't come out and ask me because they avoid the obligation to bring me food. By the way, I dug so much *ṃakṃōk*[103] last season, they got tired of grinding it. You can ask the irooj himself, who had to complain, 'Look at all these baskets of arrowroot! You women must grind them before they dry up and all the old man's work is for naught.'" When he had finished, he closed his eyes and sort of half-smiled in a conceited way.

"That's the way he tells it, but when he closes his eyes like that, you know he's lying. Right, girls?"

But the children had already gathered round, and to prove his point, they were begging him for a story.

The elder snatched the group's attention by holding his forefingers wide.

"Two sisters," cried the quickest girl in the group.

"Two sisters from Eb," said another.

"How did you know?" the elder asked.

"Because your fingers are birds, and they fly in a circle."

"You mean like this?" He drew circles in the air above their heads. "They come as *kidid.*[104] What does a kidid look like?" he asked.

"They have skinny legs, and they walk along the shore catching small fish in shallow water," answered one of the children.

"Have you seen one lately?"

"I saw one yesterday!" cried a little boy.

"You did not!" the elder reprimanded him. "Tell him why, children."

"Because this is the rainy season. They only come when it's dry."

"That's correct, and they are very quick with their long beaks," continued the elder, darting his hand to catch a fish from the air. "They scrutinize

---

[103] Arrowroot; a nutritious starch processed from the rhizomes of the dryland, knee-high plant *Tacca leontopetaloides*.

[104] Wandering tattler: *Tringa incana*.

everything. Quick to fly away. One instant, they are fishing at the shore. The next, they're gone."

"Where do they go to? In the rainy season, I mean," asked one inquisitive boy.

"No one knows. Maybe they fly to Eb. This is the story of Abaratu, who was Irooj of Rongerik a long time ago. He is a handsome young man who has a bathing pool on the ocean side that fills with seawater at high tide and turns warm in the sun. The kidid come disguised as birds every night and land by the bath of the irooj to frustrate him. They come from Enewatak, singing,

Kidid flutter higher.
Day comes, so
throw away
flower lei.
Kidid you,
kidid I,
kidid fly ocean's secret path.
Sound of wave,
gentle wave.
'Cross east reef,
kidid did.
Fly high, circle low,
kidid did.
Fly high, circle low,
stir up water — waow!
Stir up water — waow!
Bath of Abaratu,
come and play. You
whirl 'round and 'round.
He comes soon so
let us go.
You and I.

"They change their sky and turn into beautiful women when they land, and they bathe with the coconut gratings mixed with flowers from the basket the irooj discarded the day before. Every morning, he carries his basket to the ocean side to take his bath but tosses it in disgust when he finds his pool murky from the women who preceded him. They have left two flower headbands behind.

"'Who was bathing in my pool?' he asks his women when he returns. No one knows. The tide comes in and sweeps the pool clean. Next day, same as before. Here they come from Enewatak, singing… Wait! Who wants to be a kidid?"

Several of the children pop up. The elder picks two girls with flower headbands and teaches them how to flutter their arms like kidid do. Then he resumes his chant as they pretend to fly around.

Kidid flutter higher.
Day comes, so
throw away
flower lei.
Kidid you,
kidid I,
kidid fly ocean's secret path.
Sound of wave,
gentle wave.
'Cross east reef,
kidid did.
Fly high, circle low,
kidid did.
Fly high, circle low,
stir up water — waow!
Stir up water — waow!
Bath of Abaratu,
come and play. You
whirl 'round and 'round.

He comes soon so
let us go.
You and I.

"Events turn the same as the day before. 'Who has been bathing in my pool?' No one knows. On and on like this, day after day, they come and spoil his bathing place. Until one morning, he gets up before dawn and makes his way to the pool under the light of a waning moon. Waow, there they are. Two beautiful women bathing in his pool, teasing him with their chant:

Kidid flutter higher.
Day comes, so
throw away
flower lei.
Kidid you,
kidid I,
kidid fly ocean's secret path.
Sound of wave,
gentle wave.
'Cross east reef,
kidid did.
Fly high, circle low,
kidid did.
Fly high, circle low,
stir up water — waow!
Stir up water — waow!
Bath of Abaratu,
come and play. You
Whirl 'round and 'round.
He comes soon so
let us go.
You and I.

"He grabs them and holds them to him.

"They cry,

Sun comes so
let us go!
Let us go!
Sun comes so
let us go!
Let us go!

"But he holds on to them until dawn and traps them in his human sky. He leads them to his house. Throws all the other women out and replaces them with these two. He takes good care of them. Now sisters everywhere love each other, but they rarely agree — and especially about men. The younger one grows to love him, but the older of the two wants to return to Eb. She hates Rongerik and his human sky. So, the younger pleads on her sister's behalf, and after a while, the irooj agrees to return them to Eb. He orders his proa made ready.

"Next morning, the three of them sail westward. Day in and day out, they head a little south of the setting sun, on and on — waow! When they get close to Eb, the older one starts to get excited. She feels her power coming back. She turns into a kidid and jumps from the top of the mast to the *kubaak* to the prow of the boat. The younger stays with the irooj in his sky, but the older flies off to Eb singing,

Blow wind over here,
blow wind over there.
Come wind, bring irooj.
We'll take.
Our vengeance cries out
ba-bake!

"Waow, people of Eb, chant out with her:

Come you over here,
come those over there.
Come all. Her irooj
we'll bake!

"When they arrive, the people of Eb are ready. They rush down and tear his canoe apart. They have him trapped in their sky now, with no way to return. Nothing to do but sit around and accept what will come. The younger sister protests. She doesn't want anybody eating his soul, but they decide to bake it anyway. They decide to do it when they celebrate the new moon, so he has only a few days to live.

"He goes down by the shore to sulk by the sea. That's when Jini, the proverbial sand crab, friend of all irooj, scampers up to cheer him.

Jini, Jini
makes home upon sand.
Dig and dance,
dig and dance,
dig and dance!

"'Don't worry,' he says to the irooj. 'I'll fix everything.'

"That night, and each night thereafter, Jini scampers up and down the shore while everyone sleeps. With the help of the tide, the crab carries every piece of the irooj's canoe and lashes them back together again. Each day, as the progress continues, the irooj goes down to the beach again and stares blankly toward his home in the east. The Eb Islanders assume he has no way to escape, so they leave him to his soul sickness. But every day, Jini scampers up to him, and gradually, the irooj's strength of soul returns.

Jini, Jini
makes home upon sand.
Dig and dance,
dig and dance,
dig and dance!

"Then, on the night of the new moon, everyone gathers for their ceremony on the ocean side, chanting,

Moon, you rise east.
Moon, you go west.
Always same way,
always err, err.

"Waow! They start one huge fire for Abaratu's oven. They plan to pile rocks on the fire all night and bury him beneath them at dawn, but not to fear, Jini has completed the reassembly of the irooj's canoe. That night, Abaratu and the younger sister from Eb proceed with their escape. They wait for the highest tide just before sunrise. They say good-bye to Jini and slip away into the night. At dawn, all the people gather by the ocean to wait for the men to bring the irooj, but he is nowhere to be found. They look out to sea and see his sail tacking off to the northeast.

"Waow! Older sister beats her *aje*. They change into a ravenous flock of terns that fly after them, but younger sister is ready. She has brought her mother's magic stick and points at them one by one."

At this, the old man grabbed his walking stick and began pointing here and there.

I point stick and chant,
I-tori-tori.[105]
Man Eb fly up — waow!
He falls over here.
Here shark go swallow!
I-tori-tori.
Man Eb fly up — waow!
He falls over there.
There shark go swallow!

---

[105] To diminish or shrink.

"Her magic proves stronger. The terns all fall into the ocean, and all are consumed by sharks. Last of all, her mother and father fly up and land on the outrigger. Their daughter puts down her stick. Her mother makes Abaratu promise: 'If you go to cut coconut — take her with you. If you go for pandanus — take her with you. If you go fishing — take her with you. Wherever you go. Whatever you do, take her along. Do not leave her alone.'

"When the irooj agrees to follow her instructions, the parents give the couple their blessings and fly by themselves back to Eb. So, the irooj and his mate tack on eastward back to Rongerik. They live there for many seasons, and Abaratu lives up to his promise. He takes her with him wherever he goes.

"Then, one morning, he wants to go trolling for tuna before dawn. He looks at her sleeping and feels sorry for her that morning. He says to himself, 'I'm always dragging her off fishing. She deserves her sleep.' So, he doesn't wake her and sails off by himself. He never returns, and nobody knows what happened to him or where his story ends. But to this day, if you sail to Rongerik and go too far east, you will see one kidid. She'll circle low to your boat and then fly up in a big circle and then come back down and look you over once again. She is looking for Abaratu."

The test

When the elder had finished his story, some of the children began running around, singing his chant and imitating him by pointing at each other, but the elder was quick to caution them.

"Children, remember we do not point at someone. It's disrespectful. What else do we not do?"

"Touch a person's head!" several replied at once, as they danced about in naughty form, pretending to point sticks at one another.

"That's correct," responded the elder. He tried to pose further questions and instructions to the rowdy circle, but Ijokelekel had stopped listening.

His thoughts turned to the jib in jowi that morning. He couldn't recall anyone hitting Anitok on his head. Could someone use such a custom to his advantage?" But just then, Limaalal interrupted his thoughts by clambering back down from above and circling busily among the children. Then she danced over to the elder, removed her flower head lei, and set it gently on top of the old man's head.

"*I-tori-tori* to you too, Abaratu!" At which point all the children laughed. The headband had cocked awkwardly to the side, making him look silly.

Ijokelekel noticed that all the adults in the group had turned toward the entrance to the irooj's loft. Limaalal, on the other hand, turned her back to the entrance from which she had come and boldly flopped down in front of him.

"I told Ļañinni about your plans to return to Pohnpei and revolt against the irooj there."

"You mean the Saudeleur," he said.

"Anyway, he agrees with me that you're the perfect leader for the Wōjjā boys of your clan. You might even end up carrying the coconut for them! He doesn't want to empower anyone obligated to provide more support for Taklur," she said.

Just then, Ļañinni stepped down from the ladder to his loft. He carried a coil of fishing line in one hand and was tossing a large lure up and down in the other, as though deliberating its weight.

"*Ej it ļañ?*"[106] he asked the group.

Ijokelekel had noticed several men duck outside into the square to observe the gathering clouds before returning to their work.

"*Eṃṃan*"[107] was the consensus among the group, though to Ijokelekel, it looked like the elder had been correct. The wind had switched, and a rainstorm was about to roll in from the south.

When Ijokelekel turned to the elder, he saw that the man's shoulders were moving up and down as though he was silently laughing at a joke no one had told. Was Ļañinni considering fishing in the teeth of a storm? To a man, Ļañinni's followers stepped out into the square with him.

"*Ajjeļọk eṃṃan in lañ ne ļe!*"[108] he heard several say, as though they were praising the finest weather a man could ask for.

"*Jen eọñōd!*"[109] announced Ļañinni, and the group headed down the shore of the passageway. Moments later, a conch sounded.

"Go, follow your irooj to Eb," teased Limaalal.

Haltingly, Ijokelekel rose. He glanced at the elder, who nodded abruptly in agreement.

"Go and stand by his craft. Do whatever he commands," Limaalal advised. "Don't be afraid of him. Remember, men will give away a lot just to prove they're not jealous."

As Ijokelekel walked down the shore, he mused over what she had just said. Had she lied to Ļañinni and told him that they had been lovers? Would

---

[106] "What is the forecast?"

[107] "Good."

[108] A saying: "The weather could not be better, boys."

[109] "Let's fish!"

she have done that to force Ļañinni to demonstrate magnanimity toward him? What if such a tactic caused an opposite response?

He noticed the string of small, thatched boathouses toward the ocean side of the shore passageway. He had also seen the large oceangoing craft of Ļañinni's followers nestled in the reef-protected harbor toward the end of the lagoon side of the island, so he was a little surprised they weren't heading in the opposite direction. "Why carry the small canoes down the strand when the larger ones lie anchored in the lagoon?" he thought. The larger were safer and more comfortable, especially in foul weather. But he followed the men south, down the shore of the passageway, and over his shoulder, he could see others coming with their lines and lures.

Ļañinni's canoe was the first they carried to the water's edge. Ļañinni was in the process of arranging the rigging he had carried himself from the rafters of his boathouse. He laid the sail, bundling its mast and two *rojak* lengthwise, down the length of his hull. The breeze circling the approaching storm had increased. Ijokelekel cautiously approached. The hastily tied bun on the irooj's head was unraveling in the wind.

Ļañinni began coiling his anchor line. "Like a careless boy, I left it all tangled," he said in an uncharacteristically self-deprecating way. "Can you raise the sail for me while I sort this out?" His face was nearly covered by his blowing hair.

Ijokelekel unwrapped the sheet that bundled the length of the sail. The mast, made of *ļọ*,[110] would be quite light, so he would be able to raise it easily, except the outrigger stay was still unattached.

"*To kubaak*,"[111] thought Ijokelekel, walking around the canoe, grabbing the thick mast stay, and securing it to the masthead. Returning to midcanoe, he raised the mast that was permanently attached to the sail's yard and simultaneously guided its *bal* below the tack of the sail into its grooved seat at the bow. Then he walked forward and secured the *bal* with the short line attached to it. The breeze had immediately caught the sail, and it was flapping uncontrollably. So, he sheeted in just enough to bring it under

[110] *Hibiscus tiliaceus* L. (Malvaceae); a large cordate-leaved, yellow-flowered tree with light but strong wood.
[111] The stay or stays between the outrigger and the masthead.

control. The small sail had no halyard. The mast had no stays other than the *to kubaak*. This was a much simpler canoe than the *tipñōl*[112] he had noticed anchored in the lagoon. Yes, such a small canoe was handier, but it was much more likely to swamp in a rough ocean.

Once the irooj had untangled the anchor line, he peered up and down the length of his open hull, perhaps taking inventory of its contents. He grabbed a forked hardwood stick and used it to prop and secure the sail boom by further tightening the sheet. Everything was set to launch. He gazed briefly northward at the lengthy line of canoes likewise being made ready by his men and apparently decided to bide his time by tying his lure to its line.

He stood to the water side of the waist-high outrigger platform, his face now so covered with hair that it kept tangling in the fishing knot he was attempting to tie. He was clearly annoyed yet careful, as though gently removing a plaything from a child. Turning his scarred face to the wind, he gathered and twisted his well-oiled locks into a properly organized bun and then speared it decisively with a stingray barb to fix it permanently in place. Having finished his knot, his first gaze was back toward the line of canoes and his second back into the wind toward the dark gray clouds billowing before them. His eyes finally turned to Ijokelekel. Without a flicker of apprehension at the cold-looking line of slanted rain across the horizon toward which they were headed, he nodded that it was time to launch. He turned his back, grabbing the outrigger platform between them, and before Ijokelekel had fully comprehended, he found himself at the helm as their craft glided across the mild current, steering as the wind permitted toward the opposite shore. The muffled sounds of conch shells announced their embarkation. Not a second statement passed between them.

It was midafternoon, and the incoming tide, now streaming to fill the lagoon, would flow against them as they attempted to exit the passageway. Needing as much momentum as possible to overcome the drift-provoking current, Ijokelekel removed the forked stick propping the boom and relaxed its sheet a bit more to fill the belly of their sail. The irooj nodded his approval before glancing behind them to see the remainder of his fishing fleet leave shore and follow. Ijokelekel had experienced the drift of the current from his

---

[112] Large outrigger sailing canoe, or proa.

swim firsthand and was now judging the gust required to exit the passageway against the incoming tide. Using these gusts could be why Ļañinni was known for leaving and arriving between the teeth of a storm. Ijokelekel began to feel a certain pride in his efforts, even as the first burst of storm wind began to lash their sail as they approached the opposite shore, shunted, and switched helms. He judged that, with both wind and current against them, it would take at least two more tacks to reach the ocean.

Now that Ļañinni was at the helm, his face affixed to the wind, Ijokelekel had the opportunity to interpret its features. The scar across his cheek that had at first appeared vengeful now seemed a symbol of pride. His face, if Ijokelekel were to guess, neither gave nor expected quarter from its enemy, nor indeed from the ocean at large. His features were handsome, yet his eyes were cold, like those of a fish. He had a knowing smile tinged with cynicism that would accept only truth. His teeth were wide apart and a bit scraggly, like those of a *jujukop*.[113] The lines on his face were vivid and well drawn yet fierce as a stonefish, and he cringed not as the first wave of rain slapped them with water cold from on high.

They shunted twice more without another word spoken. It was as though each man was taking the measure of the other, and Ijokelekel was silently doing his best not to come up short. His body seemed to be bearing the storm surprisingly well though he craved the touch of warm ocean water that periodically burst up at them and consistently needed bailing. That job he gladly took on himself regardless of his position, realizing that the exertion saved him the embarrassment of going pimple-skinned before Ļañinni's darting eyes.

As they exited the passageway, Ijokelekel would be the first to release lure and line, with the irooj studying him patiently. The ocean swells lifted and lowered their vessel at the same time as the wind-lashed waves slapped their bow from a different direction. After a period of cold anticipation, he felt his line meet the stubborn opposition of a hooked tuna. It was good sized, and he hauled patiently, afraid his line would break and the irooj's lure would disappear into the transparent blackness below. The others passed them by, facing the slanting rain, heading off under low, grey clouds toward the first

---

[113] A barracuda.

wūnaak swirling in the distance. The irooj, ultimately pleased with Ijokelekel's success, admired the fish even as he clubbed it to death and quickly slid it into the hull below.

Then they headed off again into the fray as he flopped their lure back into the sea and let out their thick fiber line, which had been tightly twisted and then braided. By that time, the fleet had broken into pandemonium as first one crew and then another stopped to draw their catch from the looming waves then shunt to join the flocks of white-and-black terns as they hovered low over panicking circlets of baitfish spiraling outside the passageway. They shunted, and this put Ijokelekel back at the helm. "No mistakes," he thought, intending to instill the greatest possible impression upon the irooj. There was much shouting, chanting, and heckling between the boat crews as proas passed by each other on opposite tacks, hauled in their catch, bailed bloody boat water back into the sea, and shunted back and forth as though mimicking the terns that swarmed and dived about them. Yet he concentrated not on the raucous human activity around them except to make sure he didn't collide with a crossing or oncoming craft. His ears attuned not to the screeching birds but rather to the surges of the wind in his ears, and his eyes fixed back and forth between the sail, the oncoming sea, and the dark clouds streaming around them. He knew their situation was precarious and changing by the instant. One overpowering gust, one miscreant wave, one lapse of concentration could cause their flying outrigger to rise vertical, flip turtle, and send the irooj sprawling into the sea. Such an experience, by its very nature, was destined to instill a bond between those who endured it.

Ijokelekel was so intensely concentrating on these immediate duties that he didn't see the sail of the boat ahead fall. Then, as the irooj encouraged him to approach the craft, out of nowhere appeared a man swimming in the water, forcing Ijokelekel to release his sheet to avoid sailing over him. The irooj immediately struck sail to slow their drift away from the man.

"Pako!" Ijokelekel heard the man warn as he struggled to stay afloat. Was he bitten? Had he been attacked? These were his first thoughts as his eyes turned instinctively toward the irooj, who nodded sharply as though to give him permission to retrieve the man. He came astern as though to take

Ijokelekel's place at the helm. There was no time for deliberation — the wind would soon carry them apart. So, he found himself flopping into the sea and swimming toward the struggling man. Who strangely, as though unharmed, began swimming back toward his own vessel, which was now drifting rapidly toward them. Bloodless, he hoisted himself out of the water and back into his boat, then motioned for Ijokelekel to swim back to the irooj's craft — shunning his obvious desire to board theirs. The men finished resetting their sail and resumed their fishing.

"How disrespectful," thought Ijokelekel. He had found himself nearly abandoned, anticipating the worst, as the *wūnaak* persisted about him. Was this all a ruse? Was Ļañinni jealously out to watch him drown between the jaws of the beasts that undoubtedly meandered around these feasts? Turning back to the irooj, whose boat had continued to drift in the wind and current, Ijokelekel felt relief that he was aggressively paddling upwind toward him, even as the man he had tried to help had long since raised sail and launched his craft into the storm. His impulse was to swim as fast as he could toward the irooj, who was struggling to reach him even as other craft, each trolling lines, sailed by at a distance from opposite directions. Yet, however misguided, Ijokelekel had already demonstrated his bravery. Why panic before these men and make a fool of himself now? Treading water was less likely to attract the attention of one of the circling beasts anyway.

With wind, wave, and current against him, the irooj's progress was slow. He had already stopped paddling once to arrange the struck sail, laying it diagonally across his outrigger platform. Ijokelekel imagined that the other craft were looking on as he bobbed up and down, as though moored in the swells and wind-caused waves. Yet he sensed that all — from a fish to a bird to a soul — had been caught up in an overwhelming current that was trying to sweep them into the midst of the passageway. As though the atoll itself, in its own moon-related cycle, was in the process of slowly inhaling, sucking life from the sea around it. He realized that, given this flux, if the irooj but held his own against the elements, the current would inevitably join the two. So, he did nothing, and in doing nothing, appeared all the braver while he bore whatever joke they had drawn him into.

When one reached the other, the irooj was taciturn as before and offered no insight into the why of what had happened. They fished with the others until their boats were too low to the sea to safely continue, and the headwinds of the storm broke as lightning flashed and Ijokelekel's father, Nahn Sapwe, spoke thunderously to them. Then, much to Ijokelekel's surprise, they headed not toward the Pikaajļā side of the passageway, but to Āne-piñ.

The tide was now high on the shores. Once there, surprising him further, Ļañinni ordered him to fetch his fellow initiates and to bring stake and coconut for a second jib in jowi. Ijokelekel stood there in the downpour, dumbfounded and about to ask him to repeat it all, until Ļañinni motioned with his head toward the path. So, he skirted the various irooj compounds and found his friends huddled by a fire at the clan's *m̧ōn kweiļọk*. Their various family members huddled beneath the broad eaves, protecting themselves from the downpour. He arrived amid distant flashes of lightning and the low transient rumble of his father's whispering approval. Without mention of where he had been all day, he simply announced that Ļañinni had commanded their presence at the passageway shore and asked Anitok to bring his husking stake. He grabbed the first fallen coconut he encountered along the path and followed the others as they rushed obediently through the persistent rainstorm toward the passageway.

When he arrived, his friends appeared to realize they were to get another jib in jowi. Some of Ļañinni's men were cutting *pap* while others had already formed a double line before the irooj. Still others were drawing their craft up on the shore of the passageway. Ļañinni motioned them to likewise cut *pap*, which — as they all knew — was a taboo thing to do so close to the homes of the irooj. But then the whole area they occupied was normally taboo, so most just shrugged, lowered their heads a bit to show respect, and cut the leaves they needed from the chiefs' trees. All of them were being naughty, which was part of their leader's mystique. The irooj were nowhere to be seen anyway. It was the middle of a rainstorm.

Anitok, realizing why Ijokelekel had asked for his hardwood stake, now turned to him with a look of confusion. Ijokelekel offered the nut to him, but Ḷañinni had marched between his lines and appeared before them, clearly rejecting the handoff. His eyes pierced into Ijokelekel's as though chastising him for his weakness. He must seize this opportunity for himself with no planning or advice from the others. Clearly, Ḷañinni was offering an opportunity of leadership to Ijokelekel and not the other, who had failed, and in that instant, all realized it. Still cradling the large coconut, he accepted the stake from his friend and stepped forward as Ḷañinni slowly retreated through the lines, carrying his aura of majesty to its distant end. There, he turned and nodded.

This was to be his chance and his alone. Ijokelekel took a moment to reflect on his life so far as he slowly gazed from one initiate to another. The rain was dripping from their hair and faces as he gazed into each set of determined eyes staring back at him. In turn, they exhibited hope, faith, loyalty, encouragement, and comradery. He recalled the morning he had stolen Lañinpo's proa and how, later that morning, he had fished out the bunch of water shells Lañinpo had tossed into the sea. He owed him for that one. He remembered the simple *kaṃōḷo* given by his new adopted family and all the preparations made by them and the families of all these young men standing before him with encouragement in their eyes. He recalled how he had lusted after Limaalal, who had given herself so willingly to the men around her, and he remembered the last things she had said to him — "He agrees with me that you're the perfect leader for the Wōjjā boys of your clan. Go, follow your irooj to Eb."

Ijokelekel bent his weight onto the stake as he twisted it forcefully into the sand. Not thinking of all the eyes upon him, he emphatically, both-handedly hammered the coconut down onto its beveled edge, speared through its upper husk, twisted and discarded the first loose quarter. His thoughts concentrated now on his mission to obtain his lines and seek out the man who would teach him everything.

He took another moment to gaze up the dual lines of his opponents and into the eyes of Ḷañinni. This was the man he had proved himself to, who had ordered him to jump into the middle of the *wūnaak*. He had survived the treacherous waters. He had not panicked. If this was his plan, how had he known Ijokelekel would survive the *wūnaak*? Obviously, he had not. It was fate. Or was it his very survival that had provoked this second chance? He stood there now before them all and forced a look of confidence onto his face. He didn't trust them, yet they no longer seemed like opponents. Hadn't he endured the brunt of their dangerous prank? Again, and once again, he hammered the coconut down onto the stake, and finally tore its shell free from the husk. Hadn't they had their fun? He had a plan that just might surprise them all.

In his mind, he transported himself back to the carefree antics of his childhood. Without further hesitation, as though once again recklessly casting his lot into the sea, he balanced the husked nut on his forehead and turned his eyes upward into the rain. Not waiting for the irooj's nod to begin, he stretched out his arms and began a slow balancing act between the first lines of the jib in jowi. To the gasps of his fellow initiates and the surprise of his supposed assailants, he maintained this exposed posture. Confused, the first men in the lines allowed him to pass unstruck. Undoubtedly, they expected the coconut to fall in the very next moment as he slowly continued to balance his way between the lines, managing to keep the coconut from falling by adjusting his head each instant as he passed them by. The group, obviously surprised at this never-tried tactic, seemed to glance at their leader for direction. What response they received Ijokelekel couldn't see, of course. He continued to focus all his concentration on the coconut he was balancing on his forehead.

When the men in the lines began to laugh at his caper, his confidence that they would allow him to pass grew and he began to proceed more quickly. Yes, he would prove himself the same fool who had fruitlessly risked his life for one of them, and now — perhaps out of respect or perhaps just confusion — might they refrain from striking him? It seemed so, but then a few finally did strike half-heartedly on his chest and then his back, but each time, he was miraculously able to adjust his head to keep his prize in balance. Would they know to slap his feet from beneath him? This was an obvious weakness of his strategy, and a strong blow would no doubt cause him to falter. There, someone tried — again not forcefully — and again, he was able to keep his balance. So, the blows were mild enough and staggered enough that he was able to overcome them all. It was as though the men were going along with his prank and not wanting him to fail. Finally, perhaps due to confusion, perhaps mercy, perhaps out of recognition for his balancing skill, he reached the end of their lines. To the glee of his fellow initiates, he thrust his neck forward and head-tossed the coconut into the irooj's waiting hands.

All eyes turned upon Ļañinni, and there was a moment of silence, as though to a man they had swallowed a large bite of food and were waiting for it to pass their throats. Then the subject of their attention slowly looked down into Ijokelekel's eyes, and an uncharacteristic expression almost like a smile, which quickly became more like a sarcastic smirk, appeared on his wet face. At any rate, he nodded in approval, and that was all it took for his men to break their lines and for Ijokelekel's fellow initiates to joyfully begin congratulating each other for the day's achievements.

Ļañinni later ordered the two largest tuna to be sent to the Irooj of Āne-piñ and divided the rest between his men and the initiates. Each initiate took his prize by the tail and headed in twos and threes back down the path from which they had come. Ļañinni's men reloaded their boats. And without saying another word, Ļañinni turned to his craft, raised sail, and drew it into the passageway, leaving Ijokelekel on the sand, holding his tuna by the tail in the rain. He wanted to thank him but knew not what to say. "*Koṃṃool,*" he said, gently placing it, unheard, on the wind against which the irooj launched his craft.

Exhausted from the day's exertions, Ijokelekel ambled with his tuna along the path behind the rest, who had scurried through the rain before him, no doubt hurrying for the shelter of the *ṃōn kweiḷọk*. Each young man who had rushed off depressed and empty handed from the first jib in jowi now returned elated, carrying a tuna to share with his family. They had achieved their goals. Of course, Ijokelekel felt good about this. He was proud that it was he who had been able to use his childhood talent to complete the jib in jowi for them, but strangely, now that all was over, he felt no sense of triumph, no elation to share with his family. His goals were far from achieved. He would get his lines and move on to the next challenge, confident that the voice behind the rumble in the sky would be there to guide his actions forward.

The story he had told of Jatokauai came to him as, alone, he dragged his feet along the path. He wondered, as he often did, about the moral of that story and recalled what Limaalal had said upon hearing it: "I don't like the ending."

"One day, when you two are older, you'll understand," his adopted father had said. "When a man completes a great task, he asks himself, 'What's left to accomplish?' If he has no answer, his story is over."

"Well, I have much more to accomplish, so my time hasn't yet come," he told himself in consolation. However, if he were to fulfill his destiny and conquer Pohnpei and depose the Saudeleur, he must find many followers. He looked despondently behind him at the lonely, rain-drenched pathway. All the boys had scurried ahead of him, leaving not one — not even his brother — to walk by his side. Leadership is a lonely task, he thought, one's followers thankless, fickle, and forgetful.

When at last Ijokelekel arrived at the *ṃōn kweiḷọk*, Lijāpe immediately brought him a fresh kilt and grated coconut for his bath and took his fish to the collective cookhouse for preparation. He hung the fresh kilt beneath the eaves and stepped back outside in the pouring rain. There, he squeezed the coconut gratings over his head and rubbed his skin with the surplus. Stepping back inside, he wrapped himself in the dry, fluffy kilt, dropped the old wet one at his feet, and joined the others by the fire. They politely separated, inviting him to move forward and dry himself before the fire. Once there, he was surprised to see the very same *aḷap*[114] storyteller who had directed the coconut cutting two days before on Wōjjā.

The elderly man smiled broadly at Ijokelekel and was the first to congratulate him on completing the jib in jowi. "They say you mesmerized the lot of them!" he said. "But you must have convinced Ḷañinni that you're the best man to lead your *jowi.*"[115]

"Nothing but a boyish antic," said Ijokelekel humbly, peeking at the many faces around him. "I guess it worked. I learned to balance a coconut on my forehead years ago."

[114] A paramount landholder who manages land on behalf of an irooj; a lineage head.

[115] Clan or tribe.

"No, it was more than a boyish antic. Ļañinni has no time for that. Somehow, you showed him you can lead your *jowi*. Who is your mother, boy?"

Ijokelekel named his adopted mother, Lijāpe.

"Well, it looks like she fed you well. You have the image of a natural, healthy leader. Have you ever heard the saying 'Your mother is always your mother, your father is the father of others?'"

Ijokelekel had heard this saying many times, but he played along with the hunchbacked *aļap* because he knew there was a story he was itching to tell.

"Yes, I've heard that saying before. What does that mean?" he replied, giving the *aļap* the lead-in he was looking for.

"The meaning here is that we follow our mother like Jebrọ did. Because we inherit our mother's land rights. The land our father works passes through his sister and her children." At this, the *aļap* looked at the children around them because this part of his story was meant for them to hear. He repeated himself. "In our custom, a daughter inherits land that she passes to her daughter. A son may work the land of his mother, but his children will inherit the land of his chosen one. That's why we say we follow our mother. If she dies, it's best to go to her sister or brother. They will look after us. Our father will take another woman and look after her and their children and may overlook us."

The *aļap*'s eyes were aglow with the reflection from the fire. His arms spread wide to include everyone when speaking of custom. He looked around to make sure he had everyone's attention. Then he began by singing the first lines of his story.

Ineril, what
fish do you eat?
Ineril — 'Ah!
Me and my papa
dive down and dive deep.
Dive so low.
Skin of one breadfruit,
bone of one fish.'
And what else?

'One tiny fish,
my food from my father.'
Why don't you come along?
You and I fly away!
'I'm afraid 'cause you are a spirit.'
Pinch him — crying, flying
off and away.

"Ineril's mother has died, and his father has taken another. But the new mate doesn't treat Ineril like he's her real son. She doesn't feed him well. So, when they go fishing and his father dives to check his trap, his real mother flies up as a bird and pesters him.

Ineril, what
fish do you eat?
Ineril — 'Ah!
Me and my papa
dive down and dive deep.
Dive so low.
Skin of one breadfruit,
bone of one fish.'
And what else?
'One tiny fish,
my food from my father.'
Why don't you come along?
You and I fly away!
'I'm afraid 'cause you are a spirit.'
Pinch him — crying, flying
off and away.

"She pecks at him. Pecks at him, waow! He starts to cry, and she flies away.

"When his father surfaces, he asks, 'Boy, why do you cry?'

"'I stuck myself on my fish.'

"'Why do you say your fish? Those fish are for the woman ashore.'

"When they beach their canoe, the woman comes to help his father lift the bow, leaving Ineril to carry the heavy stern by himself.

"The woman takes their catch and prepares supper. What does she give the boy to eat? The skin of a breadfruit, the scraps from fish already eaten, and a coconut husk to chew. The woman finishes the coconuts and eats all the fish and breadfruit.

"They sleep and the next day — same as before. The father takes his son fishing again. When the father dives to check his trap, his real mother flies up again and pesters him.

Ineril, what
fish do you eat?
Ineril — 'Ah!
Me and my papa
dive down and dive deep.
Dive so low.
Skin of one breadfruit,
bone of one fish.'
And what else?
'One tiny fish,
my food from my father.'
Why don't you come along?
You and I fly away!
'I'm afraid 'cause you are a spirit.'
Pinch him — crying, flying
off and away.

"She pecks at him. Pecks at him. Waow! He cries and she flies away.

"'Boy, why do you cry!'

"'I stuck myself on my fish.'

"'I told you before. These fish are food for the woman ashore.'

"They paddle back, and the woman comes down the beach and helps the father lift the bow of the boat, leaving the boy to strain alone with the stern. That evening, they eat as before, and when they finish, they give the boy a little of what they have left. The boy chews a bit of coconut husk and falls asleep.

"The next day goes the same as before. Only this time, the father decides to see why his son cries. He fakes his dive and comes up under the outrigger platform to watch. The mother flies up and sings as before, but when he won't fly away with her, she pecks at him until he cries.

"Surprised, the father dives and brings up his trap, but doesn't bother to ask his son why he cries. He understands now.

"The boy congratulates his father. 'Lots of fish for the woman ashore,' he says.

"Now his father begins to have pity for him. 'No boy, these fish are for you today! Come on. Let's paddle ashore, and I'll cut down coconuts and breadfruit for your supper.'

"When they reach shore, the father has his woman take the bow while he helps his son carry the stern. When supper is ready, he gives his son two breadfruit, two coconuts, and two fish. But the boy doesn't eat much 'cause he's not used to eating. He gives all the leftovers to the women saying, 'Here — for you to make me a new kilt.'

"While his father is in such a charitable mood, he also asks him to please make him a kite. The boy has asked for these things many times before, but this time, his father takes pity. And the next morning, he makes the kite. He orders the women to make the boy's new kilt. At supper that night, he presents these things to his son. He expects the boy to be happy, but Ineril has made up his mind to leave.

"Before daylight he is off — and on his way, singing,

Come rising, my kite,
and surprise all.
My people below,
my mother above.
All watching me sway
north, south — flying my way.
Then falling and
vanishing, sing...

"As the sun begins to rise, he runs with his kite down the shore of the village. People call after him and offer food. He stops to take a bit of husk from around the eye of a coconut and tells them to take the rest to the house of his father. He runs off again, chewing his bit of husk. Telling them he is on his way, singing his magic song:

Come rising, my kite,
and surprise all.
My people below,
my mother above.
All watching me sway
north, south — flying my way.
Then falling and
vanishing, sing…

"The villagers run to his father's house and wake him. 'Your son is running with his kite and calling after his mother.'

"The father jumps up and runs after his son, but he is too late. The boy becomes lighter and lighter as he sings, till the kite pulls him up into the sky."

Now that the *aḷap* had finished his story, he sat back as though he had nothing more to say.

There was a moment of silence. Then a voice broke into song. The parents and their sons stood, formed a line, and joined in as they slowly circled the fire and placed small gifts before Ijokelekel. The song was in his honor, and he felt bad he had doubted their appreciation.

The pledge

The jib in jowi represented the struggle each of the initiates would now endure alone, day by day, as one and then another had parallel lines engraved by mallet and bone on their ever-swelling skin. Ijokelekel heard some call his achievement "naive bravery" and others, "charisma." Whatever they thought about him, he — normally too young to take seriously — became their hero that day. His name, previously too long to say, now represented a series of rare events that had led to the group's unheard-of second chance. It was his name that crossed the lips of all who spoke that night as rumors spread around their fire about what they had heard from Ḷañinni's men.

Ijokelekel, on his part, had turned as silent as the taciturn irooj himself. He knew it was his father who had come to set things right. No one could deny the son of Nahn Sapwe the fine lines that would define him. He had shunted his story back to where it was supposed to be. No more disrupted lives. They would go forth with their clan's activities as previously planned, yet none of his fellow initiates, who now had their chance to become men, would ever forget what had happened or the man responsible. Under that very moon, once the women had sailed down the island to gather and prepare pandanus thatch and the men had successfully prepared their clan's gigantic pole house for thatching, they told him he would be first to have his lines drawn. He tried to pass this honor to Anitok, but Anitok rejected his offer.

The lines of the commoner's prow motif ran from shoulders to navel. It consisted of two triangles, the upper hull, and the lower waves through which it passed. The upper triangle ran from the tip of each shoulder and met at the breastbone. These were the first lines the artist drew with his *ak* tail feather, and according to legend, they would be the last ones seen. The hull they represented would carry him, even after his death, across the sea to his ancestral homeland. The black pigment used was made of burnt coconut husk mixed with water and brushed from a specially carved coconut shell. His tattooist had made the mallet from a length of dried *pap* and the tattoo chisel from the wing bone of an albatross captured long ago on Ānen-kio[116] and handed down to his tattooist by a great-uncle who had made the dangerous trip. The irooj treated a tattooist on Aelōn̄ļapļap, they said, like his first chosen woman — with profound respect to make up for the lack of attention. Tattooists attracted and drew islanders of various rank, clan, and sex from both ends of Rālik. Their skills brought all manner of tribute. The women, spared the indignity of the jib in jowi, had their own secret ceremonies, and female artists gave them their tattoos earlier in the season. Limaalal had confided that her clan's most painful motif was tattooed so low that she had to pluck her pubic hairs to keep it visible.

During the first season of his adoption, his mother had plaited two face mats for her sons' initiations. He had watched her make these with much curiosity and had grown up seeing them here and there around the house. He had bragged to his brother that he would bear the pain without one. The first day was relaxing. As it turned out, it ended up being the best time to get to know his tattooist. They called him Lanwe. He was a meticulous *likao*[117] from Bikini. Lijāpe had called him elegant, and he, too, had traveled to get his lines. A local woman had quickly taken him. She had more land than he wanted to cultivate, so he decided that tattooing interested him more. They said he had commissioned the construction of two canoes that he never personally used. He let them out to others who, by agreement, shared their catch with him.

Lanwe looked the part of a typical village rooster. He pulled his hair back into a bun. He filled his stretched ear lobes with freshly cut and rolled pandanus leaves two digits in girth. He perpetually placed a flower behind

---

[116] Present-day Wake Island.

[117] A young man.

each ear, and a bleached-white-coral necklace with six pendants hung round his neck. He strutted with a dignified manner, sat with good posture, and moved with careful deliberation. But once he opened his mouth, he set aside all outward pretense, talking and chuckling like everyone else and speaking in a friendly, if deliberate, manner. Yes, he would create quite a commotion with his mallet and chisel, seeming solely to satisfy himself, and then move on to the next of several initiates he was tattooing in sequence. Nevertheless, as the days passed, it became clear he was an artisan who was ultimately out to please his subjects.

Lanwe insisted that Ijokelekel wear his mother's mat on his face from day one, not wanting to have his concentration interrupted by him moving to look at what had just been drawn.

Day one was pleasant. Days two and three were annoying, and he was glad he had his mother's mat to cover his grimaces. Once the tattooist started chiseling lines parallel to those already swollen and painful, the agony suddenly became extreme.

Then one night, after the first few days of tapping, as he lay — already feverish — on his back, his arms folded beneath the mat covering him to prevent it from rubbing against his wounds, his father came to encourage him.

"The first strike is always the worst. He strikes its parallel farther from the infected area second." Ḷōkijdik went on. "The jib in jowi symbolized those parallel lines. Do you remember the determination on Anitok's face the morning he rushed the lines? Let his spirit be your guide. Just as he and all those other boys will keep your face in their thoughts as they, too, bear the first tap and anticipate the second."

Then he gently rubbed another layer of Lijāpe's waxy fermented *nen* fruit into Ijokelekel's wounds before moving on to his brother to provide, Ijokelekel supposed, similar advice and encouragement.

Was this the summation of their collective wisdom? This to hold deep in their throats and to cough up lovingly from father to son in preparation for manhood? "The first strike is always the worst." Was life truly to be like this? The first blow in battle, the first cold breath of rain from a storm, the first day adrift without water? Perhaps it was all Ḷōkijdik could think to say. Yet, from the tenor of his voice, Ijokelekel sensed he was fulfilling a mission he had waited all his life to complete. Was life something merely to be endured?

Perhaps Ḷañinni and his rebellious attitude had poisoned his thoughts? Ijokelekel was a little angry at them all. Why must everyone strive to have themselves tortured in this way? Was Ḷañinni's disaffection toward the Irooj of Aelōñḷapḷap justified? These chiefs' lives of comfort were based on convincing everyone they had to tattoo their bodies to appear like one another. Why? Where Ijokelekel had come from, one had a few lines, perhaps a turtle here or a dolphin there. This was also true of the men visiting from the western islands he had seen as a boy on Pohnpei. The motif seemed of little importance. Here, they took their meticulous designs to a level no one elsewhere had heard of. Were they wasting their time worshiping lines that would one day rot and decompose? His people spent their time placing takai that would endure forever. These Rālik Islanders constructed no temples to Nahn Sapwe. His clan members hadn't even noticed when Nahn Sapwe quieted the storm that subsequently turned the throat of Ḷañinni to provide them with their second chance. These people, like many in Pohnpei, were lacking the faith that could bring more certainty and glory to their lives. Where did they think his courage to walk the jib in jowi came from? They misunderstood so much it was tiring to go over it all.

On his part, these were only his thoughts. He didn't respond. Instead, he took Ḷōkijdik's timeworn advice and simply endured. On the other hand, his tattooist, whom his mother called "the rooster," never stopped talking. He commented repeatedly that her *jāānkun* was the best he had tasted, and even his woman, who was hard to please, agreed. In response, Ijokelekel simply stared up at her face mat, recalling the days and days they had spent harvesting, gathering, baking, smashing pulp from cores — and yes, drying it all in the sun. He recalled rushing back and forth to save it from the slightest rain cloud that appeared to windward. Thus, his strategy of endurance was to take himself back into his past and linger there until his tormentor passed on to his next victim.

Ijokelekel and his brother, Jorailik, had decided against identical tattoos, so they both chose Lanwe as their tattooist to avoid any happenstance. Though they would both exhibit the basic commoner's prow motif, they cast fish bones to determine which one would request oval clouds around the neck area and which would endure wavy clouds, and his brother won. His brother's oval clouds, which required fewer strikes, were less painful and carved later.

The period between the remaining half-moon and the beginning days of the next passed in feverish nightmares filled with walking between lines, lying down, swimming between the shores of the passageway with a shark at each shoulder, and drifting between walls at Nahn Madol, with his mother calling down to encourage him to fight on. Lijāpe's face mat became the peaked roof of his only refuge against the storm of repetitive, painful gashes.

The pattern of the prow motif Lanwe drew and then tattooed on Ijokelekel's chest was made of two triangles, an upper one pointing down into a V-shaped lower one called the keel. The lower triangle, which also pointed downward, was somewhat concave and blunt at the bottom, just above his navel, like the prow of a canoe. The base of the upper triangle extended between the shoulders, the imaginary point of which marked the exact center of his sternum. The triangular effect was created with two parallel rows of lines obliquely extending from each shoulder to the sternum. These two lines were themselves composed of a base of tiny, down-pointing triangles stamped so that their bases formed perfectly straight lines. Filling this upper triangle was a series of perfectly vertical columns made of oblique, inward-pointing slashes. Each slash was separated by perfectly uniform spacing. At the bottom of every other stroke were three dots separating these vertical columns. These dots gave the illusion of perfectly horizontal lines that filled the triangle and ran perpendicular to the vertically oblique slashes. The precision of the equal spacing separating these various elements, combined with the overall symmetry of Lanwe's design, gave the motif its overall charm.

At the center of this upper triangle, the horizontal dots were doubled, forming what Lanwe referred to as "the mast." He tattooed the upper portion of this mast directly down from below the neck to the sternum, where he switched this pattern of dots to four oblique, downward-slanting, inward-pointing slashes — the innermost of which formed a V. He tattooed about sixteen rows of these slashes all the way down the mast. This lower portion of his mast was outlined by two perfectly vertical lines that he tattooed upward from just above Ijokelekel's navel to meet the oblique lines that framed the upper triangle at the sternum.

Lanwe called the lower triangle into which the upper triangle notched "the keel." This he shaped from wavy lines, slanting downward from the bottom half of the upper triangle in consecutively longer patterns to the top of the lower mast. Then consecutively shorter patterns created the V-shaped prow design, ending just above the navel. This keel, or lower triangle, began at the armpits and ended above the navel. The lines stamped across Ijokelekel's back were more numerous but, for some reason, less painful. Except that he had to lie on his sore and swollen chest, so pain became the annoying visitor that never left. Finally, much to his surprise, on a day that started like any other, Lanwe declared his job completed and moved on without further comment, as he always did, to his next subject. At that moment, Ijokelekel realized the fight was over and he had won. Yet the nightmares continued for a few nights more until his body, tense from expecting extreme daily pain, gradually relaxed to normal.

"First man drawn" did not necessarily mean first chiseled or first completed. The tattooists had their own schedules dictated from above. During the period of his clan's confinement, several other clans — from still other places — completed their lines, congregated around other *ṃōn kweiḷọk*, rejoiced at their success, and embarked for their home islands. Other islanders from elsewhere were undergoing their jib in jowi. Still others were in the process of rethatching their shelters. It was a wonder that the irooj — there were several — could store all the tribute. Āne-piñ had become famous for its tattooists and the irooj had become powerful due to all the gifts they had to distribute.

When the chiefs' call for *kaṃōḷo* went out, the word spread throughout the atoll. It was on the outer islets where the food for the feast was prepared, then transported that same day to Āne-piñ for the celebration. In return, the irooj would distribute some of the tribute they had received to their outer-islet workers. On most islands, a *kaṃōḷo* was a rare event. On Āne-piñ, it was a never-ending celebration marking the arrival of one group and or departure of another.

The day of their *kaṃōḷo* arrived, and they planned to leave as a group the day after. That meant the men of his clan who had new lines were prime targets for women wanting to capture them. Matrilineages needed help tending their islets, and the chiefs wanted more workers. On the opposite tack, the men's mothers would maneuver to protect their sons in cunning ways.

Lijāpe, for her part, kept her sons busy by arranging for them to cut coconuts in preparation for their return voyage. Little did she realize what a crowd of thirsty young women would gather below the trees where the nuts fell. Ijokelekel had never seen older siblings so viciously dismiss away their younger brothers and sisters. These women were looking for men to take and wanted desperately to be alone with them. These newly tattooed girls, his friends would later disclose, had all plucked themselves and were eager to show the tattoos that adorned their little mounds of pleasure. Anitok, who had made himself Ijokelekel's constant companion, was the first to agree to peek and headed off with one of the women. Then, without further thought, Jorailik abandoned him there and headed off toward the oceanside with another. Was Ijokelekel supposed to keep appearances until the others returned? He busied himself husking coconuts for the other women, who sat not so politely before him.

"They say you are full of it, Ijokelekel?" one blurted out to provoke him.

"All the better to fill you up once my companions return," he thought to quip, but how could he lower himself to respond to such a stupid statement?

Another approached him from the side as he worked. "There, it looks like it's coming out your ears!"

He couldn't think of a good comeback for that one either. From childhood, he hadn't been the type of person who took well to teasing. There was an awkward silence. He kept working. The girls left, perhaps to try their luck elsewhere long before the others returned. Then he had to suffer the men's bragging about their exploits, then more teasing for having let the other girls fly away without snagging one. Perhaps Anitok sensed his frustration.

"Ijokelekel, you have a presence that we men envy and wish to follow. You need to develop the same confidence among women. Seize the moment!

Forget your work. Show you want them immediately, or they'll lose courage. They'll imagine rejection and vanish like Abaratu's kidid!"

They all laughed, but Ijokelekel recognized this as good advice, especially coming from a humble man who usually sought the advice of others.

"But isn't the whole point to pair up with someone you like?" he wondered. "How am I supposed to know if I like them? They appear so forward to me." Then, forgetting himself, he said out loud, "Somehow, I don't believe my father helps me with such things."

"Ijokelekel, you must be joking. You must be prepared to deal with such instances without your father's help. Who depends on their father for such things?" Anitok said. "Do what every man does in the face of these strange creatures — pretend! Stare them down! Don't avoid their eyes. Say anything. It doesn't matter. Women form circles of busy fish and listen more carefully to each other than to the men they speak to. Pretend you're talking to your mother. That always works for me. Just keep talking. If there's too much silence, they'll start thinking. Don't give them a chance to think. Women are good at thinking their way out of things."

Jorailik joined in, grabbing Ijokelekel around the waist and arching his head over his shoulder. "If you can't think of anything to say, do like this!" He puckered his lips like a *ūrōrmej*[118] and pretended to reach for Ijokelekel's cheek. They all laughed and then made puckered faces in turn. As they walked their coconuts back later, the two took turns puckering their lips at the girls they met along the path and invariably getting some sort of positive response.

"Ijokelekel, if you had a few more days on this island, you would definitely snare one of these pretty birds."

"Don't look at the bird. Look at the nest," said Ijokelekel without thinking, repeating something Lijāpe told her boys regularly.

"Those are the words of your mother," responded Anitok. "The nest will be what the nest will be! You have lines now. Look at those roosters over there. The rooster doesn't think about nesting when it clutches its beak onto the neck of one of his hens and grinds her down to the ground to have his moment on her."

---

[118] Damsel fish. A colorful fish with a somewhat-puckered mouth.

"Come on, now. Strut!" commanded Jorailik. He dropped his basket of husked coconuts to the pathway, lifted his shoulders back, and stepped slowly — his head cocked like a rooster, jutting forward slightly with each step.

Anitok laughed and then, imitating Jorailik and looking back at Ijokelekel, beckoned. "Come on, let's practice!"

Reluctantly, feeling silly, like a boy joining his playmates, Ijokelekel dropped his basket too and took a few steps mimicking the other pair of fools.

"Now, *ūrōrmej*!" ordered Jorailik, demonstrating in ridiculous fashion how he wanted him to pucker as he strutted.

The three laughed uncontrollably for a while until they began making a spectacle of themselves to passersby. They eventually returned to their previously discarded baskets and husking stake and resumed their walk back to the others. But every so often, they broke back into laughter as one or the other imitated a rooster or puckered like a *ūrōrmej*.

When the three arrived at the *m̧ōn kweiļo̧k*, Limaalal was there, sitting with Lijāpe and Ļōkijdik. She looked different. She had come early to the *kam̧ōļo* and had brought gifts she wanted Ļōkijdik to take home to her parents. Ijokelekel assumed she had already confirmed the story of how she had called to him from the opposite shore of the passageway, how he had swum to her and impressed Irooj Ļañinni. Rumors of his adventure had been circulating around his fellow initiates and their parents ever since the jib in jowi.

Now, speaking to the three of them, she came right out with her mission. "Ļañinni wants Ijokelekel and his fellow initiates to pledge never to take up arms against him," she blurted out.

"There is no way I'll make a pledge like that!" Anitok was still in a joking mood after their walk. "I love sticking my hand into the mouth of the barracuda. Why would I pledge never to do that?" he asked, to the laughter of several initiates who had gathered round.

However, she was insistent that the group discuss the proposal seriously. Truthfully, Ļañinni had them all so intimidated that none had ever even contemplated taking arms against him. So, if this was all he expected after granting them their lines, they — as a group — saw no harm in accepting the pledge. To a man, they and their families would have gladly given more. The gist of the pledge quietly passed from one initiate to another, and there were no objections. After all, they all wore the lines he had gifted them. It would be rude to reject such a friendly request.

Later, when Ijokelekel excused himself to take his bath, Limaalal insisted that she draw water from the well for him. She dropped the *jāpe*, with one of its two scoop-like ends pointed downward, into the water. Then she lifted its hoisting line, connected to one shell ring that slid upon a second, and slackened the handle line attached at each end. She hoisted the *jāpe*, showing her strong forearm strength. Something she had obviously learned at an early age was that allowing the ring to slide naturally to the exact middle of the slack line subsequently permitted her to raise the *jāpe*, now heavy with water, in balance. No water spilled from one end or the other. Finally, proudly, she entered the thatch-walled bathhouse — open to the sky — poured the water, and filled the large *kapwor* shell to its brim.

"Ļañinni wants us to sit together at the *kaṃōļo*," she informed him. "He'll sit with his other women in the chief's circle until just before the food is served. Then he'll come and sit with us to eat. This will signal to everyone that he has chosen me. Also, he wants to talk to you." She gazed approvingly at the little piles of grated coconut mixed with flower petals lying on banana leaves on a bench — one for each initiate. She left him to remove his kilt and scrub himself.

He wondered what Ļañinni would have to say. Then he heard others gathering and the *jāpe* plunging again in the distance. "So, Ļañinni is officially choosing her," he thought. "Everything is turning out the way she wanted."

The provisioned proas from Je were late arriving, so the *kaṃōļo* did not start until after sunset. The various clans were sitting in groups talking among themselves. The irooj and their families were sitting by the food, which was still in large baskets. Servers sat among them, wafting away insects with breadfruit leaves. Ļañinni left his group and came to sit with them as planned, but because it was dark by that time, whatever hubbub Maalal had anticipated seemed less than apparent now. No one could see whose eyes were glancing where — making it unlikely that he was successfully signaling anything to anyone other than those close by.

The irooj immediately began his inquiry. “So, who was your tattooist?”

“Lanwe.”

“Lucky again! He is one of the finest.”

“What does he mean by ‘again’?” Ijokelekel wondered.

Then Ļañinni got right into what he wanted. “Limaalal tells me you’re a rebel.”

“Why would she say that?”

“She says you hate the irooj on your home island.”

“They are called Saudeleurs and they are cannibals!”

“How do you plan to kill him?”

Ijokelekel had never thought about killing anyone. Nor about how he would lead a rebellion or cause the Saudeleur’s fall. He just supposed that, by the time he returned there, he would be wise enough to do whatever seemed necessary. “I figure the Saudeleur’s followers will just run off into the mountains once everyone turns against them,” he finally responded.

“It doesn’t happen that way,” Ļañinni replied.

Ijokelekel was intrigued. “How does it happen?” He needed to know such things.

“Nobody runs unless they are scared. Nobody becomes scared until they fear they’ll die. So, how do you plan to kill them?”

“Maybe I’ll just scare them to death! I’ll have so many followers that some of my opponents will just kill themselves rather than fight. The others will just run away.”

“Now that’s an interesting idea! Tell me, where will you get your followers?”

“Once everyone knows the truth, won’t they just appear?”

“It doesn’t happen that way either. First, no one is ever certain about the truth. Most people don’t care about truth. They’re simply repeating the lives of their parents. Each has their own mate, their own family, their own priorities. With all this distracting them, they find it easier to follow a group than strike out on their own.”

A flower-scented woman bowing low brought Ḷañinni a large basket of food and interrupted him. He grabbed a husked coconut from the basket and removed the last bit of husk about the eyes. After piercing the mouth, he put it up to his face, bent his neck skyward, and sucked loudly.

"They're like fish following the circle they grew up in," he continued. "They won't just appear out of nowhere, and if they do, they won't follow you. They'll keep following their circle no matter what."

Limaalal, on her part, seemed peeved that the woman hadn't placed the basket in front of her. Ijokelekel imagined she was also angry that Ḷañinni was ignoring her after she had arranged their meeting, and she was probably mad he had sat down on Ijokelekel's side rather than on hers or in between.

Ḷañinni continued. "You, on the other hand, are a leader. You know how to strike off on your own, but that doesn't mean the circle will follow. You must infiltrate that circle to take over its leadership. You must disguise yourself as one of them and wait for your moment to lead."

Limaalal quickly reached across Ijokelekel and snatched something to eat from the basket. This was something a commoner would never do. He supposed it was a sign to anybody watching that she had a special relationship with the irooj, but the moon was yet to rise, so if others were watching, she was missing the satisfaction of seeing who.

Ḷañinni continued, "Look at those chiefs up there." He pointed with his nose. "They don't inspire their followers. They're but shadows of their ancestors, who were true leaders of the people. All they know is how to collect tribute and distribute it to their workers. They're not leaders. They simply preside over a system created by their fathers. This ruler of Pohnpei you wish to overthrow is probably the same."

"You're correct. He is as you describe. Only now he has advisors who tell him to eat people as punishment when they break their agreements."

"Eat up his soul! Eat up his soul!" The irooj chanted ghoulishly from the story of Jibke.[119]

---

[119] Figure from the oral literature of the Marshall Islands who is given the impossible task of finding the source of the wind and lands in the mythical land of Eb.

"My mother taught me they used to use eels to enforce the law," continued Ijokelekel. "Until…" He had been about to go into the story of how Ḷōpako rose from the pit clutching the dead Nahn Samohl when he remembered the old man's admonition never to say the name "Pako."

"Until?"

"Until the little akebu came from the west and taught the Saudeleur it was better to eat people as punishment."

"Saudeleur. Yes, you mentioned that word. My father voyaged to Nahn Madol. He always said it was the best place in the ocean to trade. Then he stopped going there. I heard him say they had used up all their takai. What did he mean by that?"

"Mother told me they stopped worshiping Nahn Sapwe, so he stopped breaking the takai from the cliffs."

"If their great trading village was already built, why did they need more takai?"

"All I know is people got late delivering them. Kielua was late and they ate him. They made Paratak cook him like a turtle on Idedh. He didn't know I was there, but I watched him crying as he lifted parts of Kielua's cooked body and filled two baskets with him and paddled to deliver them to the Saudeleur. I swam all the way to Pahn Kadira just to see who would eat, but Lañinpo saw me. That's when I tore two limes from the Saudeleur's tree, which was taboo, and escaped."

"You should have cut a stalk from his banana patch. That would have gotten his attention."

"Oh, I got their attention all right. They followed me out to sea, but my boat was faster, and they couldn't catch me."

"You are a brave lad. You proved that to me three times. You're lucky. I'll give you that too, but are you smart?"

"About what?"

"Smart enough to seize your moment to lead when it comes."

"What will that moment look like?"

"It will rise as clear as that moon." With his nose, Ḷañinni pointed at the slightly oval moon that had recently broken above the pandanus trees amid the trunks of the palms. Suddenly, you'll notice that the people you need to get your revenge have been circling you all along. Eat!" commanded the irooj. Reaching for the basket, he scooted it in front of Ijokelekel and closer to Maalal. Ijokelekel obediently reached into the basket and began unwrapping something baked in a breadfruit leaf. He had been looking forward to this all day but had suddenly lost his appetite. He had never thought about getting revenge. His mother would not want it. Nahn Sapwe did not want it. According to his mother, Nahn Sapwe simply ignored those who ignored him. Yet, he admitted, the thought of revenge was enticing.

He looked around at his fellow initiates, some sitting with their families, others crowded in small groups of threes and fours. Some were already eating. Others — for whatever reason — were just sitting before their baskets, perhaps saving their contents for later. There were thirsty sounds of lips sucking coconuts. Dogs growling around the edges of the group as they fought for scraps thrown toward them by those already eating. Sweet-smelling women, shoulders oiled, talking, laughing, breasts jiggling as they lugged large baskets here and there. Men sitting proudly with flowers behind their ears, joking with the women as they walked between them modestly, gracefully, full of life.

Then, while the crowd was still eating, he noticed many initiates and other men of the Rilujien Naṃo clan stand and take their leave. Soon thereafter, the sound of a conch shell broke the distraction of the crowd. The rhythmic clacking of spears and methodic chanting ensued, these accompanied by the drum beat and responsive chanting of the *du*. The *jebwa*[120] lines began to fill the space between the irooj and the commoners seated below, and all turned, motionless and silent, out of respect for the dance. The men formed two lines segmented in groups of four whose spears clashed violently to the rhythm of the chant. Each foursome parried spears and rotated among themselves, but in unison with the other groups that made up the two lines. Their movements were mesmerizing.

[120] A battle dance; a fierce reenactment of a classic fighting style passed along from previous generations.

Ijokelekel didn't recognize many words in the chant. They were commonly used neither in Kajin Rālik[121] nor Pohnpeian. Were they perhaps of an ancient origin? Had this dance been brought to these islands by their original settlers? Why hadn't he seen it before? Perhaps they performed it only on special occasions and practiced only on the larger, more populated islets. There among the group were many of Ijokelekel's fellow initiates. He hadn't known that they possessed such talent.

Yes, he had heard talk of the dance previously but had no idea it was so captivating. Among all of Ijokelekel's adventures, the performance that evening stood out in his mind as the most inspiring thing he had witnessed so far. The tempo of the dance enthralled him. The meticulous parrying of spears, one against the other, had wakened his latent ambition to fulfill his destiny. These men and their ilk were the type needed to drive the success of his mission.

He turned to Ļañinni and asked, "How could a band of opponents ever defend themselves against such mesmerizing precision?"

Ļañinni answered with typical cynicism. "Your clansmen have trained to fight an opponent as honorable as they. What if their opponent chooses not to face them with spears but keeps their distance, circles, and throws rocks at them?"

For a first moment, Ijokelekel wondered how a man could show such contempt for the very way of life that allowed him to flourish. With one sentence, Ļañinni had defiled the mesmerizing beauty before them. Then sat there observing Ijokelekel's reaction. Ijokelekel responded by weakly nodding his head in agreement. But then he recognized the wisdom of Ļañinni's statement and, in doing so, came to realize what wisdom was. The ability to visualize outside his own circle of fish. Ijokelekel realized for the first time that coming from a different world gave him certain advantages. He came from another way of life so was able to look at the customs here from an outsider's perspective.

When would he become more than an onlooker? Suddenly, he realized the answer was never. He hadn't been born into Ļañinni's circle of fish and,

---

121 Language of the Rālik Islands, now the western chain of the Republic of the Marshall Islands.

therefore, had no right to judge his leadership. Perhaps the disrupter before him was right, perhaps no. It wasn't for Ijokelekel the onlooker to say. Just as the little akebu had been wrong to counsel the Saudeleur to amend the law of exchange, Ijokelekel must guard against interjecting his outside thoughts into their noble if imperfect way of life. Any change of direction would have to come from within their circle of life as they collectively faced the world and its challenges.

They sat through the extremely impressive performance, which ended abruptly. The audience followed with a respectful period of silence that was broken by Ļañinni, who — without another word — somewhat rudely stood and took his leave. Maalal, seeing the chance she was looking for to demonstrate their intimacy, grabbed the irooj's basket, squeezed Ijokelekel's arm, and followed.

That night, Ijokelekel went to his mat in the honored place assigned to his family before the fire in the *m̧ōn kweiļo̧k*. He lay there sleepless, with thoughts swirling around his head. He had accomplished much. Those were the good thoughts, and his lines, now healing, truly gave him a sense of accomplishment. However, the words that had come to him while he walked in the rain along the path after the jib in jowi haunted him. As he rolled within his sleeping mat, the words of his adopted father came back to him — "When a man completes a great task, he asks himself, 'What's left to accomplish?' If he has no answer, his story is over." Yes, Ijokelekel had accomplished this, but his earlier conversation with Ļañinni rolled with him as he turned from side to side.

"Tell me, where will you get your followers?"

"Once everyone knows the truth, won't they just appear?"

"It doesn't happen that way!"

How was he to attract followers? Was his destiny to return to Lijāpe's islet on Kwajalein Atoll? Would he find followers there? No, this didn't feel like his destiny. He still had to accomplish what, as a boy, he had set out to do. He still had to find the pali and learn everything. He concluded that, truly, the time to move on had arrived. He must quietly extract himself from his circumstance as an innocent, fluffy *koon*[122] would flop from its nest. He

[122] A baby bird.

was aware his brother knew he would eventually leave for Lae, because they had talked about it over the seasons. He hadn't mentioned it directly to Ḷōkijdik, but surely, he also knew that Ijokelekel hadn't changed his objectives and that he, Kijdik, had taught him all he could. They had pointed to Lae so many times under so many conditions that he had ingrained the direction into Ijokelekel and joked he could probably find it blindfolded.

Lijāpe was an entirely different story. She had adopted an outsider too independent to consider spending his life clearing her island. Though she would fight any woman who chose to entice him away, she was powerless to prevent him from one day following his own destiny. How could he possibly reconcile her love for him and her need to keep him close with these other plans pulling him away?

The next morning, it was time to say good-bye. He had come to know all the fellow initiates of his clan by now, and he saw only respect and loyalty in their eyes as, one by one, they came to him and wished him a safe journey. They didn't know he would soon leave for Lae, and he didn't tell them.

Under the very next moon, he would resolve the matter of his leaving with Lijāpe. They would agree to accept a simple lie they both pretended to believe. He would make a short visit to Lae to meet this Ḷōpako and return home before *añōneañ*.[123] The day he left, his mother cried, but she didn't wail. Holding back her tears, she took a step back to smile at the tattooed, muscular man who had blossomed overnight from the skinny, sun-battered child she had taken in and raised. She made him promise to return before the big winds arrived. He took his brother's advice and simply pretended to agree.

Ḷōkijdik, who had taught him well and guided him through his lines, lifted the stern of his canoe from the beach as Ijokelekel guided his boat from shore and nodded his last good-bye to his small and isolated family. His throat tightened as he remembered that first simple *kaṃōḷo* they had held for him on that very beach. He loved them all, but the time to leave had arrived. Suddenly remembering Ḷañinni's somewhat rude habit of quickly turning away and not looking back, he turned, saw them still watching after him, and nodded his good-byes a second time.

---

[123] "Call of the north"; the southern solstice, which annually coincides with winter in the northern hemisphere.

Ijokelekel sails to Lae

The day was clear, the weather mild and from the east. It was a day they had patiently awaited. Ijokelekel had left with the fisher birds, bulged his sail with wind, and wafted westward on the ever-growing swell from the east. In the light wind, he should reach Lae by dawn the next day, if not before. He was to follow the swell, point his prow to the setting sun, keep Liṃanṃan to his right, and watch the moon rise on his stern. The swell, initially blocked by the so-called "basket" of Kwajalein Atoll that protected him, would grow ever more pronounced as he left Kwajalein's shadow and approached his destination. It would be a simple journey where a young man could demonstrate his bravery before requesting apprenticeship of the pali. But he had learned that his plans, compared to the will of the ocean, were but so much oil floating on her surface. He was no longer an innocent boy enticed by her beauty but a lover experienced with her fickle temperament and outrageous tantrums.

So, for a second time, he sailed out into her vast expanse searching for a beach he had never seen and a man he had only heard of. Again, courage was his only companion and destiny his only reward. Would the pali agree to teach him everything? He hoped Ḷōpako would remember his mother. He had eaten the limes on his first voyage. Who wouldn't have? He had been starving. Should he mention that moment of weakness? Why would he? He was wiser now than to think such small tribute would be an adequate gift for a man so renowned. Had he not gotten the best of Ḷañinni? He planned to offer instead the fine kilt that Lijāpe had prepared for him. Why mention that his mother had told him to seek Ḷōpako out? What if by chance he had forgotten her? Hadn't she been but a mere servant of the Saudeleur? Why start by saying, "My mother told me to…"? Better to say "I am Ijokelekel, son of Nahn Sapwe. I heard you got the best of Ḷañinni, and I decided to learn how to do the same to those who bully others." He must show confidence.

He headed directly away from the rising sun, climbing the small waves as they pushed him along. When he looked back, as he'd been taught to do, he saw he was slowly drifting north amid the current beneath the westward-tilting basket. Lae was somewhat north of his islet of departure, so if he headed dead west this first day, that would point him right toward his destination. The sail of finely stripped pandanus leaves that Lijāpe had plaited for his trip bulged before him, catching the wind in its belly and magically transporting his craft over the rippling waves and gentle swell undulating beneath. The swell grew more predominant as the day passed, not because the wind had increased, but — as Ḷōkijdik had taught him — because it was reforming in the shadow of the basket as it converged around the atoll. Paratak had taught him how a stream swirling around a stepping-stone does the same. How much more would he learn from the pali himself? He was excited by the prospect.

There was no need to fish. Lijāpe had provisioned him for the last half of the moon and had given him gifts that she had implored him to offer, one by one, to whomever he met. Ijokelekel had made his brother promise to stay and take care of her. There wasn't much to do now except sit there at the helm, keep his eyes on his sail, and let his thoughts roam where they would. Limaalal had told him she was hoping to give Ḷañinni a boy because his other women had borne him girls. She seemed willing to throw away her mother's legacy to follow a man that others feared. He knew his brother felt jilted by her, and truthfully, he desired her too. You could see that Ḷañinni viewed her as a piece of ripe fruit. At least his brother had gotten the first bite.

He wished he had his brother's knack of going directly after what he wanted, regardless of the consequences. Women were strange fish pulled up from the depths. You never knew just what to expect or how to handle them. Are they edible or poisonous? Thinking of his mother, was that what the little akebu had meant when he told Lañinpo he wanted to eat her? Meaning she was friendly and compassionate and not like those who had mocked him? Lañinpo said he would know when he became a man. Was this what he meant? Perhaps the pali would teach him about women too.

It wasn't long before his craft fell into rhythm with the following sea. It inevitably wanted to yaw back toward the wind as it climbed after each trough of the passing swell. To tilt his prow off wind and prevent the craft from twisting broadside into the next, he had to apply increased pressure on his oar as the day passed and the swells grew more pronounced. Eventually, this task demanded so much of his concentration that it absorbed all his attention and he turned thoughtless, like the wind around him. He carried on like this, and he kept on carrying on until the sky before him turned red and wistful, and sleepiness overcame him. But he remembered from his previous voyage what could happen, so he stood and he sat. He ate, and he drank, and he splashed water on himself to distract from the desire to sleep. Then the sleepiness passed, as he became determined to brag to the pali that he had sailed the whole night through. He would show that conquering sleep was no problem for him.

So, the stars twirled westward on their separate paths. Those to the north and south rose and then sank into the horizon after completing their shorter arcs. Those to the east traveled on westward, and then the light of the moon rose from behind. The light of the stars dimmed, and both the moon and the sea rolled forward toward his destination. Then came the light of dawn, and very gradually, then suddenly, he recognized with certainty that he could see an island to his right, just as Ḷōkijdik had said he would. He sheeted in and headed north of east with much elation. Soon, after so many seasons, it would all come into perspective just as he had planned. If only a storm would ensue so his father could announce his arrival with a flash of light and the sound of thunder.

Ijokelekel approached the island as the sun was rising above the clouds to his right. Then he ventured westward again along the atoll's southern reef. When he approached the bird islets before the west-most one, he saw two women and two men walking on the reef. One of the women turned toward him, raised both her arms to acknowledge him, and began jumping up and down as though excited to see him. He knew from Paratak's many stories that the women of Lae were very friendly, of course, but this appeared almost silly and made him laugh.

He knew from Paratak that the only passageway into the atoll was on its west side, just north of the west-most islet he was approaching from the east. He even remembered the name of the irooj there. It was midmorning by the time he rounded the passageway and beached his canoe halfway down the islet's shore, amid the knee-high waves sloshing white foam that seethed up and then down its beach of white sand. It was his second day under the brilliant sun, and his eyes were exhausted. His frame ached from the repetitive movement of the sea.

As he approached, he watched a fisherman helped ashore by a group of four elders who carried his canoe all the way to his boathouse above the strand. So, Ijokelekel purposefully beached close to where he had observed the man land and began dragging his craft onto the sand as it emerged from the surf. As anticipated, the group, still hovering about, began ambling back down to assist him.

"*Iọkwe.*"[124] Their leader greeted him, raising his right arm straight into the air.

"*Iọkwe,*" Ijokelekel shouted, tilting his head back as he responded, rested, and waited for the elders to step casually down the beach.

"Where have you floated up from?" the leader bellowed back good-naturedly as they closed the distance between them.

"Kwajalein," he answered.

"Your lines are from Rālik, but you don't speak like you're from here," the leader observed.

"I'm originally from Pohnpei," Ijokelekel said, a bit surprised that he'd exposed himself with two words.

The men looked at one another as though surprised.

"Then have you ever heard of a man there called Paratak?"

"Yes, Paratak practically raised me."

The demeanor of the older men transformed, and — speechless — they looked at each other as though surprised by what he had said. They plopped

---

[124] "Aloha"; "hello (or good-bye)."

one after another onto the sand before him, not exhausted but clearly wanting to discuss something before proceeding. So, he sat with them there, a short distance in front his canoe. The sand was dry and warm, not yet hot. The sounds of the surf behind him washed in and out of his ears as they interrogated him in an accepting, friendly manner.

"The same Paratak who was among us before you were born? The father of Erwina?"

"Yes, he told me about this place, and pointed me in this direction. He told me about his daughter and her mother. What's her name?"

"Likōkkālọk."

"Yes, that's it," Ijokelekel said. "And he told me about the irooj here named Ḷōtokjān.[125] Is he still alive?"

"Yes," mumbled one. The others seemed preoccupied in thought.

"I'd like to speak with him."

"Is that Paratak's proa?"

"No. Paratak told me his proa could never sail here. He said it's a joke Ḷōpako played on him. It doesn't sail as close to the wind as it should."

All four smiled and continued to communicate to each other in nonverbal ways, as though one was saying, "I told you so" to the others who remained in disbelief.

"So Paratak isn't angry that Ḷōpako played that trick on him?"

Ijokelekel laughed. "All I know is he considers Ḷōpako a great friend and agrees I should become his *rūkkatak*."[126]

When they had first sat, Ijokelekel worried that he had said something wrong. Slowly, he began to realize he was providing information that resolved long-standing conjecture among them regarding Paratak's sudden disappearance. He quickly caught that, at minimum, they wouldn't have known if Paratak had survived his voyage back to Pohnpei because no one had come from there since.

"So, you came all this way to play anidep with Ḷōpako?" asked the leader.

"Paratak told me about that game. I want to become Ḷōpako's *rūkkatak*, whatever that takes."

---

[125] Liṃanṃan's uncle.

[126] Apprentice.

"A worthy goal, my friend, but that means you'll have to undertake one of his daughters!"

"One or the other," cried one.

"One way or the other!" said another.

"Two sisters from separate mothers. Like clams with precious pearls inside. One is easy to open, the other impossible. One a loyal friend. The other a fickle lover."

"Which one is which?" Ijokelekel asked.

The men looked at each other and smiled uniformly. Then one said, "That, my friend, will be for you alone to determine!"

"The one here is like catching a kidid without a trap. Impossible!" said another.

The leader said, "All the young men here who have tried to take her have failed."

"On Aelōn̄ļapļap," Ijokelekel added, "they say that one turned down Ļan̄inni."

"Called him a puffer fish to his face," continued the leader, revealing that they all knew the story.

"Speared him right through the neck," said another.

A third joked, "He's not likely to cough that out of his craw for a while."

"You're in for the surprise of your short life," the leader said.

"You better meet Ļōtokjān. He can teach you too, and he has three daughters himself!"

"As easy to pick as ripe breadfruit, they say. Your choices are many."

"My advice is to choose one and be loyal to her," said the leader, "or they'll pick you apart like an unfortunate insect caught amid a brood of hens."

Perhaps satisfied they had provided their best advice, they all rose to their feet and turned to Lañinpo's craft.

One man asked, "How do they call you, newcomer?"

"They call me Ijokelekel."

"We'll just shorten that to Paratak if you don't mind."

"Let's get Paratak's proa ashore. Ļōtokjān's spare boathouse by the big kiden," the leader directed, bracing himself to lift the lagoon side of the outrigger platform. Palms up on his shoulders, he chanted,

We are the men of this west-most place,

They paused after lifting the canoe a few steps over the sand, then —

Quick tack, then tack back.

They paused again before completing the chant in high-pitched voices on the last word.

They are they. Yet we are us!

The four elders carried Lañinpo's canoe like that. Two with their shoulders fore and aft beneath its outrigger platform lifted the weight of its hull, with the other two at the ends of the *kubaak*. Chanting, pausing, chanting repeatedly until they reached the boathouse, they placed it high and dry on two notched coconut logs. The thatch, made of stripped and plaited coconut fronds, provided such glorious shade it made Ijokelekel want to flop back on his outrigger platform and sleep in the breeze. However, with the clap-clap-pause, clap-clap-pause sound of anidep in the distance and his companions seemingly anxious to escort their discovery to the irooj, rest was not an option. Remembering Lijāpe's instructions, he first retrieved the food she had prepared for his voyage from where she had stowed it below and gave the baskets to the men. After thanking him graciously, they hung these in the same pandanus tree where they had hung the fish and led him off in the direction of the game.

Shortly, they reached a coral-stone pathway and then a large opening in a forest of pandanus trees. There, a circle of men was playing in the square on the oceanside beach stones surrounding Ļōtokjān's house. Ijokelekel marched with the elders right up to where the irooj was watching the men play.

As one, they sat on the stones before his mat. The elder announced, "It's Paratak back from Eb!"

The irooj raised his arm to quiet the commotion and silence the players. "Paratak?" he said uncertainly.

"Brought up and sent here by Paratak himself to apprentice under his old friend Ḷōpako."

"If that's true, it's a wonderful story," the irooj said, looking at Ijokelekel. "We all thought that rascal Pako had chopped a hole in his hull and set him adrift without a paddle."

"No," replied Ijokelekel. "Paratak says Ḷōpako taught him how to sail and pointed the way to Pohnpei. Then sent him off to follow his own destiny."

The players, too young to remember Paratak, mulled anxiously and took little interest in any of these revelations.

"Is it true that Ḷōpako gave him rights to an island among those in the stone village?" asked Ḷōtokjān.

"Idedh, the island of death, where Ḷōpako victoriously emerged from the lair of Nahn Samohl unscathed," Ijokelekel said.

"Now that's a story Ḷōpako hasn't spoken of," said the irooj. "You must tell us more before our modest relative gets his chance to use his influence to shush you up. His daughter Likāmeto should be back shortly. She's off to the bird islands to visit the latest nests. We have quite a flock of *ak* that has grown from a single pair that roosted here and attracted others. They almost disappeared because my ancestors were a desperate lot."

"He plans to ask Ḷōpako to take him as his *rūkkatak,*" offered one of the landing crew.

"Then you need your first lesson in anidep?"

Ijokelekel studied the game warily. Ten or so men, each facing inward, had formed a large circle. They resumed kicking a square object plaited from pandanus leaf between them and clapped their hands, which they never used to catch it. Clap, clap, clap, kick. Clap, clap, clap, kick. The timing of the first clap seemed to coordinate with the apex of the anidep being kicked from one to another, either with the side of the foot or with the instep. It was a game played only with feet.

"It looks hard," he said.

Ḷōtokjān grinned. "All it takes is practice. You might as well get started."

Ijokelekel joined the circle as the men rose. Some smiled in open invitation. Others appeared anxious to resume their game. Still others appeared happy for a break in an otherwise serious game. Everything proceeded as before, and as soon as he got into the clapping part of the game, someone kicked the anidep his way. His first counterkick was over everyone's head and his second too weak. The rest of his kicks were either too sharply angled and not high enough or kicked so directly above him that they required a second kick, which he missed. He followed each mistake, however, with a good-natured laugh, a short comment of self-deprecation that showed no embarrassment, or an enthusiastic plea for one more opportunity. Once he had achieved a single proper kick back, he soon retired from the group, thanked them for their patience, and sat back down next to Ļōtokjān.

"Thank you for that opportunity. I can't wait to be able to join such a circle. Where do the younger boys practice?"

"Now you're talking like Paratak," Ļōtokjān said. "Once they get their lines, most men around here think they're too good to associate with boys. I'd be happy to show you. They play at the island's end, where they can break and *bwilbwil*[127] as they wish. Do you want to go there now, or would you rather rest?"

"I was thinking about returning to my canoe and resting there in the shade of the boathouse."

"Nonsense, you'll climb that ladder and rest above." Ļōtokjān pointed to the single entrance in the exact middle of the floor above. Then he called to his woman, Lijitwa,[128] who was sitting beneath the home a short distance away, plaiting pandanus with her girls. "Give him one of your softest mats and show him his place to sleep."

Ijokelekel stooped below the house and followed her up the ladder, modestly grabbing hold of the fibers between his legs so as not to expose himself to the women below. The house was dark except for the indirect light coming through the open triangles beneath the eaves covering the roof peaks at each end. She unfurled a mat for him in a somewhat uncluttered area and retreated down the ladder, leaving him alone in the single sleeping room. The mat felt freshly plaited and had the smell of fresh pandanus leaves. Several additional mats cushioned the widely spaced floorboards below

[127] To make and race toy proas on reefs or along the shoreline.
[128] Her name literally means "point to the boat on the horizon."

him. He could hear the clapping and other commotion below, and the rhythmic sounds quickly coaxed him to sleep. His soul withdrew deep into his body, where it sailed on as he had the days before. He seemed to be searching for someone, though he knew not whom. Then someone invaded his private place and touched him there — where he had longed to be touched for as long as he could remember — while he struggled to pry himself out of his heavy slumber.

"Is it him?" asked a woman's voice.

"Limp as a rat's tail." Another giggled as she removed her toes from between the fibers of his kilt.

"Not a good sign," agreed her companion. They abandoned him to continue his voyage.

Finally, after falling back into the steep troughs of innumerable swells and climbing their back sides in hopes of seeing the island, he woke. The light had faded completely from the gables, and the room was filled with the comforting sound of others sleeping close by. Fading back in the comforting remembrance that he had, in fact, landed and was now safe ashore, he slept in anticipation of a great adventure to which he would awake after more much-needed rest. When he woke again, it was to the sound of a rooster crowing. Someone had lit a coconut-shell lamp. He managed to prop himself on his elbow and peer drowsily around the room, strewn with sleepers twisted in all directions, until his eyes settled on a glossy pair of eyes peering directly back. A black thicket of hair emerged slowly from beneath a mat and then, partially shaded from the lamplight, the two eyes gleamed at him. After a few awkward moments, he unpropped himself and turned toward her, but the sleeping bodies in between cut off his view, and sleep descended upon him once again.

Morning brought a flurry of activity. Children awakened and were hustled off to the square by mothers and aunts and older sisters to assist in the leaf pickup. Ijokelekel climbed down the ladder and sat there beneath the house, watching grandmothers starting fires, preparing earth ovens, and cleaning the fish brought back from the night's fishing by young men asking for coconut gratings for their baths. His eyes searched secretly to reunite with the pair from the night before. There was little doubt they must have been those of the one called Kāmeto, whose thick, unruly hair radiated in all directions above her slight frame, like coconut fronds at the apex of their skinny, graceful trunks. She rotated among these activities in a cheerful yet self-conscious manner, as though she realized he was there yet refused to acknowledge his stare. Finally, when the food was ready, she brought him his.

Without introduction and in a matter-of-fact way, she offered him an opportunity. "If you want to meet my father, we sail once we finish our morning meal." Then, for the first time, she acknowledged his eyes with hers, and nonverbal communication flashed like lightning between them. He realized she knew he would follow her anywhere, and that she would do the same.

But a short while later, he found himself presenting his mother's gifts to Ḷōtokjān and to Lijitwa, bidding them good-bye, and thanking them for their hospitality. Then he waited patiently, ready to launch his proa, which they had brought to shore for him.

He watched Likāmeto, close by, arguing heatedly with her younger brother[129] next to his craft. Then, her frowning face showing her displeasure, she turned from her brother in a pique and hustled back toward Ijokelekel, her pointy breasts jiggling. A heavy, coiled line of coir sennit hung from her shoulder. She clutched a shell knife in her hand deliberately, as though about to use it.

Taunting her brother, she told Ijokelekel, "Don't mind him. He is a stupid boy. The son of my shameless aunt." She turned back to her brother, saying, "I dropped him on his head when he was just a baby!"

Still smirking from her joke, she stepped into the water and placed both hands on Ijokelekel's outrigger platform, where she had tossed the coil and knife. Then she pulled his canoe into the water as she raised and turned herself and sat there facing him. Surprised, he hastened to push the stern lagoonward and scramble up onto the stern. Jumping up, she handed him his paddle, raised sail, and tied off the halyard. Flopping back down, she focused her jet-black eyes upon him.

[129] Technically, he is her cousin, but a matrilineal cousin is considered the same as a sibling.

"Don't you remember me from yesterday? I was the very first to greet you as you sailed up. I raised my arms and begged you to take me! Is it true you're the son of Paratak and you sailed all this way from Pohnpei?"

"I am the son of Nahn Sapwe. He is my protector and the voice of the thunder you hear."

"Okay, I had no idea you were the son of some high chief. Make it thunder then," she said.

He had been teased like this as far back as he could remember and knew from experience where it would lead. He would explain that he had no control over the thunder, but his father did. They would ask, how did he know? Had he seen him? He would answer that he just knew. They would ask how. Then he would eventually admit it was his mother who had told him, bringing the conversation around to her. Since he hated that, he had learned to just shut his mouth like a clam in its shell and stare off into the distance.

"Okay then, can you at least fart?"

That was a new one. He glanced back at her but, instead of condescension, he found a broad, understanding smile.

"You'll have to, at minimum, fart when you meet Erwina — chieftain to chiefess!"

"Who's Erwina?"

"Your sister, Paratak's daughter? She'll be the big fart around here when her mother decides it's time for her to take over, but just between you and me, her farts stink just like the rest of us."

"Paratak isn't my real father. He just took me aside and taught me. So, Erwina — if that's the daughter he talked about — isn't my real sister."

"He's not my real brother either," Kāmeto said, referring to the boy following in the other canoe. "He's my aunt's son. He wants to head straight home, but I want to gather shells on the reef there, ahead." She pointed to the submerged reef a little west of the apparent islet of their destination. "You don't mind helping me, do you?"

Ijokelekel was still wondering what her uncle and the others thought of her abandoning her brother's escort and climbing on board with him. The last thing he wanted to do was offend her father. He stared off at the horizon.

"Of course, I'll have to get out of these things." She pulled on the tabs of her mat skirts, which hung over the belt that bound them around her, as though they were a bird trap she wanted to rip away and free herself from. His response was to stare off again at the horizon.

"You won't mind seeing me naked, will you?" she asked, her eyes now staring into his.

She penetrated his soul as she had the night before — still trying to determine, he supposed, what type of man he was.

She took his wordless response as a *yes*. "Well, okay then. It's settled. Sail close to the reef. Unless you want to take me right out that passageway all the way to Ujae. That's where my freedom lies, if I ever get there to see it."

He spoke the words of the elder, seeing his chance to tease her back. "They say you're like a kidid, impossible to catch."

She split her skirt, reached down into the water with her foot, and splashed up water at him playfully. "It's not impossible to catch a kidid. Abaratu did it. The kidid must just want to get caught. It's a game we play." Now she was separating her broad toes on the bulwarks, nearly touching him where he was seated. The slit between her skirts naughtily separated to reveal the length of her leg.

"What?" she said, seeing him look at her leg and then look away, embarrassed. "We're *jeṃjerā*,[130] aren't we? Does that thing there ever get angry and stand up for itself?" She laughed, touching her toes to his thigh. "I'm the son of Nahn Sapwe!" She mocked him, laughing so hysterically that he couldn't help but laugh at himself as well.

Ijokelekel had laughed at himself among men, but this was new — a woman making him laugh at himself. Yes, of course he could feel himself stirring beneath the fibers of his kilt. Especially now that she had tucked her bare leg under her and the slit between her skirts had revealed a bit of light skin. Strangely, his thoughts turned to Maalal and the tattoo she had boasted adorned her private parts. He remembered that she'd told him he was too serious. But this woman was changing him. He liked this new person he was becoming, who could laugh at himself with her. *Jeṃjerā*? He liked this feeling of no longer being alone. Was this the way fate worked? Could it change a man instantly?

---

[130] Best friends.

The sky was still clear. The wind from the east. The tide weak and of little account. It would be a perfect day to explore the submerged western reef of an atoll he could see with one turn of his head. This passageway, the atoll's only one, wasn't as deep or as wide as the one he had swum across at Āne-pin̄. Here, the bottom was visible all the way across. It was but a notch at the edge of a half shell, where the water poured in to fill to its brim then poured out again as the surrounding sea ebbed all the faster. This must have been where Pako and Paratak had fished, parted ways, and sailed on to separate destinies.

"Stop explaining that you're not Paratak's real son. In our culture, when a man takes you in and teaches you like a son, out of respect, you treat his children as your brothers and sisters."

This made sense to him. Did he not consider Ļōkijdik his adopted father, Lijāpe his mother, and their son, his brother?

"Treat Erwina as a sister, but not her sister, who they call Jaki.[131] She's a man-eater just like her mother! She'll eat your soul and spit you out like a fishbone."

His thoughts turned to the men's warnings of the day before: "Two sisters… One a loyal friend. The other a fickle lover."

She pointed to the area up-reef along the atoll's light blue inner side, where the sandy bottom tapered before plunging into the dark blue depths of the lagoon. Eventually, she directed him to one of the many coral heads that spotted the reef's inner shoals. There, she struck sail, tossed his anchor stone to catch in the coral, and tied them off as his craft swung into the wind. Their chaperone continued to sail up-reef and likewise anchored himself off there in a similar location. Ijokelekel could see giant clams sitting about the sandy bottom, the green mouths between the interlocking teeth of their thick shells yawning as they sunned themselves in the clear water.

She sat dangling her feet, her back turned as she faced the wind. The waves rippled at them, bobbing their craft from peak to peak. She struggled with such annoyance to untie the multistranded belt around her waist that he half-expected her to take her knife to it. He glimpsed the crack of her buttocks as, free at last, she lowered herself with a plunge into the water below, and then he caught sight of the little beard of her between as she sculled and giggled

[131] Sleeping mat.

her way toward him from beneath the outrigger platform. The big hair had gone limp and now hung over her shoulders and down her back.

"What? You agreed we were *jeṃjerā*! Is the son of Nahn Sapwe standing up for himself yet?" She laughed. "Can you hand me my knife?"

He handed her the knife and watched her feet flutter her down to a midsized clam. There, she released bubbles that expanded as they rose, partially blocking his view of her as she slipped her knife inside and began cutting the clam's muscle away from its shell. Then she fluttered back up, apparently leaving her shell knife, with its hardwood handle, below.

"It's too deep for me," she blurted out quickly, in between gasps to catch her breath. She peered directly into his eyes. "Can you finish it for me?" When he didn't answer, she turned her naked body directly toward him and, clutching with both hands onto separate rungs of outrigger crosspieces, raised her pointy breasts out of the water to give him as good a look at her between as possible.

He stood, abandoning his old self in the knowledge that this was all a ruse to get him to drop his kilt. But he also knew that, if he glanced another moment at her between, he would pop out of his kilt anyway.

"Okay, but turn your head," he said in compromise.

Kāmeto turned her head for an instant until he dropped his kilt. Then she turned back naughtily just before he entered the chilly water and dove down, with the image of her excited eyes opened wide below her broad brow. She had left the knife deep within the right bivalve. He pressed the now-unattached half and cut through the muscle on the other side, behind the body of the colorful turquoise animal. He grabbed it through its gaping, female-looking orifice and swam the heavy, bulbaceous body to the surface.

Breathing heavily from his dive, he placed her knife on the outrigger platform next to her and clung to its boom with his free hand. The *kapwor*, freed from its shell, was too heavy to raise from the water. He needed her to pull it up from where she sat while he did his best to tread water and push it up and out of the water. Motioning down for him to lift the heavy, watery animal, she turned it until the gaping female part was just above his face.

"She wants you to kiss her good-bye." She laughed as she manipulated its oval orifice to appear lip-like.

Disregarding her silliness, Ijokelekel sculled as hard as he could with his feet to push the soft blob of water and flesh as high as possible as she braced herself and pulled it up next to her. When he looked up, she had one leg braced through the hatch against the inside of the hull, her knee braced on the outrigger platform, and her womanhood gaping before him, resembling the clam they had just raised from below.

He looked away politely, but she stubbornly held her position and commanded, "Look."

When he did, she had spread her legs and the lips of her womanhood for him to inspect what he, in all his seasons, had never seen. "You see! It's never been penetrated!" Looking at him now with an intriguing look of pride on her face, she said, "It's been waiting all this time for Nahn Sapwe to stand up and beg to enter. Come on, lift yourself and give it a kiss."

With one hand on his hull and the other grasping the outrigger boom below her knee, he readied to lift himself, but then came to his senses and recalled his purpose for coming.

"No, not yet. Not that I don't want to. This doesn't seem right. I don't want to feel like a thief when I meet your father. Once I took something that didn't belong to me, and to this day, it bothers me. I must follow custom and ask your father first."

"That's just what she said you would say." Kāmeto pulled her legs together and began arranging her skirts.

"Who?"

"My great-grandmother Taknam. She always said, 'A boy who borrows a toy will play carelessly until he breaks it. A man will cherish the toy and play carefully to preserve it.'" Handing him her rope, she said, "Here, dive back down and tie this to the *kapwor* shell, and we'll pull it up together."

When he surfaced this time, she was lying prone over the outrigger platform, chin resting on her crossed palms. "What happened to my Nahn Sapwe? He shrank a little in the cold water! Kiss me on the mouth then."

He had never kissed a woman. Could he trust her?

He sculled, lifted himself up, puckered his lips, and pressed them to hers. A feeling of elation overcame him as he backed slightly away and they focused on each other, face to face. She touched his cheek and pressed forward again, this time darting her tongue into his mouth and out again.

"What does Nahn Sapwe say to that?"

"He says he wants to try that again."

"Not, ask my father first?"

"Not wanting to bother him with every little thing."

"But you will ask him to bring me to you?"

"Yes."

"Okay then, one more kiss." She kissed him again as before, then reminded him that her brother was getting anxious waiting for them. When Ijokelekel looked over, he saw him sprawled as before, sleeping in the sun. She agreed to keep her back to him as he rose, manhood erect, into his hull and wrapped himself quickly with his kilt.

Then they worked together to raise the giant-clam shell from the bottom. He pulled, and she tailed the line around one of the cleat pegs he used to secure his sheet when sailing. The clam shell was very heavy and their progress, slow. Ijokelekel feared the peg would break, so they wrapped the line around the top and bottom of the outrigger platform and back up again, where she secured it, hand over hand, as she stood. She began waving to her brother for help, but he was either sleeping or, by custom, looking away from his sister with the newcomer. She shouted to no avail. Finally, he remembered the conch shell Lijāpe had insisted he take. One sound on that and her brother pulled anchor and sailed over to help.

In the interim, they had succeeded in raising the shell to the surface, where they realized it was just too heavy for two to lift. Her more experienced brother tied off to their craft, entered the water with a piece of file coral, and used it to file down the sharp, dangerous ridges on the shell's exterior. "This will prevent the men who transport the shell to her bathhouse from cutting themselves," he said before tying on a second line. Then he climbed onto the stern deck, and the two of them, with agile step, managed to cradle the shell and lift it onto the outrigger platform.

Then, without saying another word, the shy young man dove into the water and surfaced by his canoe, and before long, both boats were sailing across the lagoon toward the north-most islet of the atoll that they called home.

"So, what's our plan?" she asked once under way.

All of a sudden, he realized that, after so many seasons of journey, this was it. He was about to fulfill the promise he had made to his mother: meet the great pali and request the knowledge he needed to avenge her death. "Plan? I want him to teach me everything."

"Father teaches many men many things, but I've never known him to teach anybody everything."

"But I am the son of..."

"Nahn Sapwe. So, maybe he'll make an exception for you, but he's probably going to ask you for your plan anyway. Father loves plans. Right now, he's harvesting breadfruit and pandanus to preserve for the dry season, and he's cultivating his arrowroot plants so, when the dry season comes, he can dig up the roots to make *m̧akm̧ōk*. To Father, the essence of planning is making *jekaro*.[132] You climb the coconut tree and work just a little bit each morning and each evening to reap a benefit after a moon cycle or more. If we have a good plan, he'll respect that. He'll want to know where you intend to plant this knowledge and what it will grow into."

"I intend to return to Pohnpei, rally the workers against the cannibal Saudeleur, and with the help of Nahn Sapwe, avenge the death of my mother."

"Then I'll fight by your side, and when we win, I will be *lerooj* of the entire island."

"And I will rule wisely." Ijokelekel pretended to be a sagacious leader. "I'll set everyone free. Nobody should have to live under the rule of only one person."

"Father should respect that. I will be your kidid, and you will be my Abaratu. But you must never leave me alone, right? Tell my father that," she added excitedly.

---

132 Also called "tuba," "toddy," and various other names; the sap of the coconut palm tapped from the flower bud as it grows and continues to protrude between its mature frond leaf and the less-mature inner fronds of the palm's inner crown. The skill of making jekaro is practiced worldwide wherever palms grow.

The legends cross

Ijokelekel and Kāmeto planned their adolescent destinies, and thus, they strode hand in hand up to her mother's house as her brother-cousin gathered a group that first carried the *kapwor* shell with a pole and then carried the proas and beached them on the strand. A sweet smell of uncovered stone ovens and baked pandanus was in the air. A few children were playing with an anidep to the side, and a group of elders was sitting before a cookhouse, mashing the pulp of baked pandanus fruits from their cores against shell scrapers lashed to carved triangular stands. The sounds of their conversations quieted as Ijokelekel and Kāmeto approached. They stood together a man's length or so before this group.

Sitting somewhat apart, before a tripod pandanus scraper in the center of the elders, was a man of superior size, more fit and somewhat younger than they. Surprisingly, his handsome face was beardless and his earlobes unpunctured. Only a single bleached-shell necklace adorned his body, well maintained for his age. The bun in his hair had partially come loose and was left hanging to the side, due to the orange pandanus mash that covered both hands. Scars were visible on both forearms. He had the casual manner of a person in charge, and all eyes quickly turned to observe his reaction to their approach. His attention immediately focused on the hand Ijokelekel held in his. Then the man's eyes turned sharply to his, seemingly penetrating his thoughts as though attempting to visualize his intentions and gaze into his very soul.

Kāmeto dropped his hand like a hot stone and darted playfully behind her father. She drew the strands of his hair lovingly from his shoulder, twisted them the way she wanted, and secured the retied bun with his venerable stingray barb. His head remained motionless. His eyes continued to study Ijokelekel, like those of a moray eel before lunging at its prey.

Finally, the moment passed, and Kāmeto asked her father if he remembered a man named Paratak.

"No one here could ever forget Paratak!" He turned to the elders, who broke into laughter. "Does this newcomer bring news of him?" Still suspicious of Ijokelekel, he inspected him from head to foot, as if to say, "Who dares stand above me holding my daughter's hand?"

"He was raised by him."

"Raised by Paratak on Pohnpei? Then who tapped those lines?"

Afraid to appear forward, Ijokelekel spoke after a long, polite pause. "I escaped from Pohnpei as a boy and wayfared to Kwajalein, where I was adopted by Ļōkijdik and Lijāpe."

"Your lines are clearly from Āne-piñ. What do you mean by 'escaped'?"

"Pohnpei is different from when you left. Ever since the death of Raipuinlañ,[133] Nahn Madol has changed for the worse. His son, Raipuinloko,[134] eats the flesh of men who break the law."

"That's hard to believe. Where does Paratak live?"

"Nahn Paratak lives at Idedh. He keeps turtles in the pond and butchers them for the Saudeleur. That's the island you granted him with your symbol carved into his breast, correct?"

At this, Kāmeto's father dropped his inquiries, turned to the elders, and transformed into his usual comfortable self. Then he held his arms wide to accept the acclamation granted by the others as if he had just won a wager. The elders murmured among themselves at this news, some of them likewise seeming to congratulate themselves as though proved right as well. Others appeared puzzled.

"How lives my friend Paratak?" asked Ļōpako, speaking Pohnpeian now.

Ijokelekel responded in his native tongue. "Not so good. The day I escaped, the Saudeleur forced Paratak to cook and serve the body of one of

---

133 The prior, wealthy Saudeleur from *The Forbidden Man*; Raipuinloko's father.

134 Succeeded Raipuinlañ, his father, as Saudeleur. After Raipuinloko's death, his son, Sau-temoi, became Saudeleur.

his friends. I was watching him secretly from atop the wall behind him when he vomited while loading his rock oven."

"We must talk at length about Pohnpei tomorrow, after you've rested," her father said. "I'm very curious to hear about these developments." In Kajin Rālik, he spoke to a very lovely woman carrying another basket of pandanus kernels from the cookhouse. "Liṃanṃan, bring a mat for this son of Paratak."

Suddenly, the woman smiled at him and headed toward their pole house. She moved with such auspicious grace there was no doubt who she was.

"Paratak, Paratak. We thought we would never hear that name again, and now up drifts a third Pohnpeian-speaking man with whom we women can play anidep." This last was said by a second woman, younger than Kāmeto's mother, who had come chanting from the cookhouse with her empty basket and a plaited coconut-leaf mat and introduced herself as Kāmeto's aunt. "Girl, this is the handsomest fish you have netted so far." She flopped the mat down next to Ijokelekel and squatted beside him. "Better to club him now before he gets away. If I had only clubbed that shark father of yours when I first met him, I might be sharing his mat now instead of your mother."

She had the smell of smoke about her mussy hair. Her breasts, with dark elongated nipples, drooped. She was twice his age, so her children would be grown by now. She was shapely like Kāmeto's mother but, in contrast, exhibited an attractive ambience of unpredictability. She looked at him, feigning sympathy.

"Look at his eyes, Kāmeto." She spoke softly so as not to embarrass her father. "He's like a *jāpe* of *mokwaṇ* full to the brim. No way to handle without spilling!"

She released her joke privately and thus more tastefully than that of the young women on Āne-piñ, in such a way that it left Ijokelekel without embarrassment or anger. There was much discussion about Paratak among her father, some elders, and the rest of the group as she jovially popped up and continued bantering as she moved among the elderly workers, collecting the *mokwaṇ* from their *jāpe* into hers.

Still kneeling behind her father, Likāmeto made a face at Ijokelekel, then nodded abruptly. He panicked when he realized she expected him to ask for her right there and then. He hadn't prepared the right words. How was he to address her father without her father first addressing him? How to politely break into the ongoing conversation about Paratak? Yet, he couldn't let her down.

"I am the son of Nahn Sapwe!" Ijokelekel blurted out the words sternly in Pohnpeian. Then abruptly stopped as he watched Kāmeto's face cringe. The others stopped talking. Her aunt floated back toward the cookhouse. Her mother approached with a fine sitting mat that she placed next to him and motioned for him to slide onto. Not a word was spoken.

"I am the son of Nahn Sapwe," he repeated. "I came to ask you to teach me everything, and I want to take your daughter." His Pohnpeian speech hadn't masked the abruptness of his statements, and all had turned so quiet that the roar of *buñtokiōñ*[135] falling on the northern reef could be heard about them. Embarrassed, he added an afterthought. "With your permission, of course."

He had succeeded in turning the shark's attention. The half-smile on his handsome, strangely stubbled face slowly disappeared. His head moved slowly toward Ijokelekel until their eyes focused only on each other. A moment later, his face broke into levity, and he laughed before the group. "She's attracted another! This one more bewitched than the last."

Turning to Kāmeto's aunt in the cookhouse, he called, "Jo̧ļo̧k, have you been instructing her again? She's spearing their throats and filling their heads with sand."

"Don't accuse me!" she retorted, stepping outside again. "She's just like her father! Too preoccupied to take my advice. At least this one isn't an old man with a battle scar across his face, and not likely to attack us with his band of loyal miscreants." Then she turned to the men surrounding Kāmeto's father. "Look who's teasing another man about getting himself bewitched! One glance at my sister, and he renounced his ocean home, tossed his adventures to the wind, and relinquished his fortune. For what? To sit around and make baby poop?" She dipped her fingers into the *mokwaņ* and flung two fingers' worth of the orange mush his way, causing the group to roar with laughter.

---

[135] Swell that "falls from the north."

"Her aunt continues to defend me," thought Ijokelekel.

Kāmeto's mother, still stooping between Ijokelekel and the group of men, was also fighting on his behalf. She asked her daughter if he had passed the test.

Kāmeto, still hiding behind her father, casually confessed that she had offered herself to him and that he had.

"What test?" snapped the shark. He turned his head halfway back but expected the reply from her mother.

Yet continuing to demonstrate her independence, Kāmeto herself replied. "He said, out of respect for you, he had to ask first."

"And I told him we would talk at length after he had eaten and rested from his trip. Did I not, son?" He offered Ijokelekel a chance to politely end what he had inappropriately started.

Ijokelekel had no choice at that point but to confirm.

"Men!" Giving up, Kāmeto stood and, as though abandoning them, huffed off to the cookhouse to help her aunt.

"Don't worry. She's my only daughter. She always pouts like that until she gets her way," said the lovely woman, squatting now before him as she handed him a basket. "She has been taught to wait for the right man. You'll find that the women of this island have a history of showing weak knees to newcomers." She removed one of the husked soft-shell coconuts, punctured its mouth with a clean thumbnail, and handed it to him. She wore a bright, motherly expression on her face as though he was a baby she was about to feed.

"Women!" the shark repeated mockingly, laughing with the others.

"Don't mind him either," continued Kāmeto's mother. "He's just like that *kapwor* you and my daughter cut loose and hauled to the surface today — sharp and crusty on the outside, inflated with water like a puffer fish, but soft and harmless as an infant inside."

The shark tossed another glance at her before addressing Ijokelekel, lowering his brow and denying her words with a nearly imperceptible, condescending shake of his head.

Without looking at him, quick as a gecko, Kāmeto's mother picked up a few coral stones from where she sat and tossed them over her shoulder at him. "He's all puffed up now because his plan for our friend Paratak was successful," she said, a naughty look on her face. "Many thoughts hatched at his disappearance, and at least one among us wished him dead. As you know, you must slit a shark's belly to learn of its adventures. Tell us what they say about our Pako where you come from."

"He was granted the title of Jau Areu[136] because he caught eels for the Saudeleur," said Ijokelekel. "He spent a half day in the eel pit, bravely accepting the punishment for another, and when they raised him, he was clutching the carcass of Nahn Samohl. Some say he killed it. Others say that it died of the Saudeleur's mistreatment. Later, he became one of the Seekers who sailed to retrieve the trunks of large trees to build rafts to transport the big stones. One day, they left and were never heard from again until Paratak brought word of him and claimed his Jau Areu title."

"What I want to know is what the women say about him," she asked, snickering suggestively and glancing over her shoulder at Pako.

"I was a boy. I didn't speak to women." After a moment, he added, "But my mother always said he would return some day and teach me everything."

"Who is your mother?"

"She was killed a few days before I escaped."

That statement visibly drew the shark's immediate attention, as though Ijokelekel had pointed out a distant star on a cloudy night. It seemed he was about to question him when Liṃanṃan continued.

"What was her name?"

"Lipanmai, priestess of my father's temple and tender of his eternal fire."

At this, the man called Pako appeared visibly stunned, speechless as though from a blow to his nose. He stared at Ijokelekel in bewilderment.

"Who did you say your father was?" Liṃanṃan asked again.

"Nahn Sapwe, maker of thunder and lightning, quencher of storms, and he who breaks takai from the high cliffs."

"I mean your real father."

"Nahn Sapwe is my real father. My mother said it was so."

"But Nahn Sapwe is a spirit, right? Who is your real father?"

"Is the great Pedpedin still alive?" Ijokelekel asked.

---

[136] Pohnpeian title: master fisherman.

"No," Liṃanṃan said. "Father died several years ago."

"Do you not feel his presence from time to time? Do you not consult his spirit in times of trial?"

"Of course, but—"

"So, how do you think the young boy that was me when I left Pohnpei was able to sail in such a large proa across the ocean by himself, if not for the helping hand of his father spirit? How could I ever have reached the great pali in such a small place as this, and over such a great distance? And how do you think I could plan to return to the stone altar and set everything right without his help?"

"Stone altar?"

"Yes," answered Ḷōpako on his behalf. "That's what they call his island, but enough of your questions. Can't you see the young man is tired from his trip?" He stood as a man too close to a flaring fire would. He ordered Liṃanṃan to gather the women to make flower leis and prepare for a *kaṃōḷo* to welcome the newcomer.

He approached Ijokelekel and embraced him in Pohnpeian fashion. "If you had just announced from the onset that you were Lipanmai's son, our reception would have been more honorable."

"I was worried you would have forgotten who she was," Ijokelekel said. Then he remembered all she had told him to do and say. "Wait, I forgot the seeds."

Without further explanation, he left them standing in the coral-pebbled courtyard and went back to Lañinpo's proa to retrieve the lime seeds. As he emerged from the waist-high hull, he found that Pako and his daughter had followed him there.

"Here," he said, speaking in Pohnpeian and unwrapping the lime seeds from the *inpel*[137] he had wrapped them in. "She made me promise repeatedly and again to bring you limes. However, I was starving and ate them seasons ago, on the trip. But these seeds are still valuable, no?"

Ḷōpako, apparently lost in thought, reached forward and held the tiny seeds as though they were black pearls.

---

[137] The fibrous, cloth-like outer sheathing of the coconut flower buds found at the crowns of coconut trees; used to squeeze milk-like oil from coconut gratings.

"She made me promise over and over to tell you something once I gave them to you, but it doesn't make sense and she never told me the meaning."

"What was it?" Ḷōpako questioned him greedily in Pohnpeian.

"I go with you. You stay with me," he replied. "I warned you it doesn't make a lot of sense."

But the famous pali had lost his composure, had collapsed against the stern deck of Lañinpo's proa and was weeping like a child.

Likāmeto looked at Ijokelekel in astonishment, rushed behind her father, and put her arms around his neck. "I have never seen my father cry. What did you say to him?" she asked accusingly, peering at him from over her father's shoulder with a scowl on her face.

He spoke in her language. "Just what I was taught to say! She would never have meant to cause him sadness. He must have taken it the wrong way!"

"It's all right. The boy tells the truth," her father said. As he started to recover, he noticed the *wapepe*[138] symbol etched into the planks of the outrigger platform and pointed to it, looking for an explanation.

"It's not my proa," Ijokelekel explained, trying not to admit he stole it. "It belongs to one of your Seekers, one called Lañinpo. I sort of traded it for Paratak's. I mean, I tricked him."

The shark didn't appear convinced.

"Okay, I stole it, but I intend to give it back when I return to Pohnpei. I plan to let him escape because he gave me water for my trip, but with my father's help, I'll fight to free Paratak and the other islanders who cringe beneath the new Saudeleur's fist."

"Do you know that Lañinpo is a good friend of mine?"

"Yes, I know. When he gave up chasing me, he reminded me to tell you about the water for my trip, but he may no longer be the man you knew. He eats human flesh now. His brother, the little akebu, killed my mother."

This information seemed to shock Ḷōpako out of his remorse. "Okay, we'll learn more of your story later. Right now, we have your *kaṃōḷo* to prepare."

---

[138] Literally, "boat floating." The symbol represents the four swells, one from each quadrant, converging upon an island in mid-ocean.

They returned to the square, and Ijokelekel ate from his basket. Later, Ijokelekel joined the children at anidep, and then, as the afternoon ripened, he accepted a mat and napped under the house. He awakened to the sound of singing all around him. The great pali had gathered his workers and their families, and every woman and girl had made a flower lei for him. They began draping them around his neck one by one even as they pulled his mat from beneath the house onto another that they had prepared while he slept. One song led to another, and then a group of boys did a dance with pole nets, and then an elder woman told a story about men from islands south of Rālik coming to steal women. When the *kaṃōḷo* was over, they invited him to sleep above, and still exhausted from his trip, he slept even more soundly than the night before. During the night, Kāmeto crawled over to sleep next to him, and he was awakened by the sharp sound of her mother scolding her back to her mat on the opposite side of the house.

Ḷainjin sat before the cookhouse fire, feeding it an occasional coconut shell to smoke and then flame for a while before joining the glowing pile. Stunned by the events of the day, he had tried to sleep but could not. He had the son he had always wanted. But this lad was so odd. "I am the son of Nahn Sapwe." Those words, tattooed on the young man's soul like the lines on his chest, were his very reason to be alive. How was he to say to him, "No, I am your father!"? And why, after all these years, would the boy believe him? All the events of that stormy night returned to him so vividly now that he could hear the rain splashing on the altar of Nahn Sapwe and could feel her warmth as she twisted beneath him on the cold stones before the god's eternal fire. He could hear that clap of thunder at the very moment of his release. If his own mother had told him he was the son of Nahn Sapwe, who was he to say, "No, you are from my seed!"? Especially now, after all these years. If only Ijokelekel had come years ago as a boy. He could have been there to teach him to fish, to sail the lagoon, to walk the reefs. He hadn't been there to teach him to endure as he got his lines. It was too late. What would this mean? "You are my son." He has grown up. The time for a father is over. He has his own life to lead. And not a normal life at that.

Ḷainjin recalled Ijokelekel's words: "And how do you think I could plan to return to the stone altar and set everything right without his help?" He had this vision of himself as the son of a spirit, that Nahn Sapwe protected him. Why should he tell him that it wasn't so?

He heard Lipanmai's words again and remembered the very sound of her voice, "I go with you! You stay with me!" So contradictory at the time. He had taken it spiritually. Her memory would go with him. His memory would stay with her. That was the way he had always thought of those words. Even when he had sailed past her island, so tempted to rest there, his promise to his mother had won out. He had known that if he had lingered there even one night, Lipanmai might turn him from his destiny and his promise to a dying mother. They had already said their good-byes, and now this? Now, after the passage of so many years, to learn that her statement had meant that his seed would grow inside her. He had only her memory now, which was exactly what she had meant. He was ashamed that he hadn't returned to her. How could a man fight time and capture two destinies?

The soft sound of bare feet walking across the courtyard stones suddenly interrupted his thoughts. He turned just as his fire flared once again, lighting the smiling, knowing face of his loved one.

"What are you doing, Nahn Sapwe? Remembering your past, no doubt! I've let you mull long enough. What do you plan to do?"

Liṃanṃan entered his thoughts as she had a habit of doing. Over the years, she had grown to know him so well. There was nothing she missed from his facial reactions. Did she know this too?

"Are you going to tell him he's your son?" Getting right to the point that bothered her. Showing she wasn't angry he had fostered a child, or that he had cared for another before her. She bore that knowledge as given. But their daughter was about to crawl onto their son's sleeping mat. His reminiscences were fine, but some immediate action was necessary to prevent the unthinkable.

"Why should I tell him that? You heard him. He insists his father is Nahn Sapwe. Who am I to tell him that he's wrong, that I'm his father?"

"But someone must tell…"

"You tell Kāmeto. She's old enough to understand. This is something we'll keep between the three of us."

"Did you love her?"

"Well yes, I realize now more than ever that I did. But I turned my craft away from Pohnpei to follow my destiny here. That was what my mother wanted. She wanted me to turn to you!"

"And now she is dead. But you still have me! And Joḷọk! And Likōkkālọk," Liṃanṃan joked, laughing at him out loud.

He looked at her joyful face and at the fire reflected in her eyes, and he realized she could resolve his dilemma as she had resolved all that had come before. Had his mother foreseen all this? Did she really possess the ability to foresee his future? He thought about the poison from the akebu's little arrows. She had suffered his poison twice — once for each foot he had severed and eaten in front of her. Had the poison imparted the ability to see what no one else could? He thought again about that night and the house in that tree. He thought again of how Rojak's[139] mother knew it was her daughter about to open the window that horrid, fateful night. Did he possess this ability himself after the akebu's poison that he had suffered? He thought about his future and realized that this boy's destiny would somehow change everything.

[139] The female Seeker; Lañinpo's sister; aka Lirojak.

Anidep

During their morning meal the following day, the pali advised Ijokelekel that the best way to begin his apprenticeship would be to perfect his skills at anidep and the jebwa, but there weren't enough men on his island. The best place to train was, therefore, on Likōkkāḷọk's island. Later, he would introduce him to Ḷōbōkrōk, Liṃanṃan's brother, who would oversee this initial phase of his apprenticeship. They would sail together in separate boats that morning, but Ḷōpako needed to catch fart fish along the way for Likōkkāḷọk's tribute. So, the pali explained in detail where on Likōkkāḷọk's island he needed to beach in the interim and where her house was located. When her workers saw all the pandanus loaded on his boat, they would be sure to approach and help him. She would be grateful for the pandanus tribute and interested to hear what had happened to her long-ago lover Paratak.

Kāmeto came to Ijokelekel while the others were launching and loading his boat. She took his hand in both of hers. "Please disregard what my crazy aunt Lijoḷọk[140] had to say about us yesterday. She's always like that," she declared softly. "Everything to her is about … you know. She tells me to do it. Mother tells me to wait. That's my life so far. Above all, you must respect your apprenticeship. Father tells me he can't bring me to you and take you as an apprentice at the same time. It's about you two being on the boat together and you being able to observe him making ready when his stomach aches. It breaks custom. Then my mother says to wait some more before I give up my … you know. I get it now: 'I go with you, you

[140] Liṃanṃan's sister; aka "Joḷọk."

stay with me.' Ijokelekel, they cared for each other. My father cares for you too, and never doubt he'll teach you everything. You came to the right place. You did exactly as your mother wished, only..."

"Only what?"

"Things may not work out exactly as we talked about, but that's all right. I can promise you, no matter what, I'll be there beating my *aje* when you battle to win your island back."

As they crossed the beach to his proa, which Ḷainjin's *rijerbal*[141] had fully rigged and were holding at the water's edge for him, she placed her parting words — prophetically, as it turned out — in his ear. "Don't forget what I told you about Lijaki."

Ijokelekel embarked, and they nudged his proa out into the lagoon upon yet another adventure even before he'd had a chance to digest the meaning of her words. The headings of the two craft quickly split. The islet Ijokelekel targeted would take him away from the turquoise waters bordering the islets and the arch of contiguous reef stretching from the pali's islet all the way to Likōkkālọk's, along which the pali would fish. Ijokelekel's course would take him across the dark blue waters of the deep lagoon. The pali, on the other hand, began fishing almost immediately, closer to where the lagoon's edge rose to the shallows. Ijokelekel's objective was to enter the narrow passageway between Likōkkālọk's island and Lae before the lagoon's waters dropped too low to enter. Lañinpo's craft, so loaded with pandanus that he had little freeboard and little time to tarry, cut deep into the lagoon and close to the wind.

"I go with you. You stay with me." Once he had mentioned these words, he recalled, the tide in the pali's composure began to turn. His mother had always been right. How could he ever have doubted her?

The night before, Kāmeto had gently tugged the hair on his chin and then kissed him on the lips just before her mother had scolded her back to her sleeping mat. He remembered the smell of her breath. The taste she had left on his lips lingered even now. It was the taste of happiness. He had experienced desire for Maalal, but Kāmeto's promise, "I will be there when you battle," seemed even more reassuring than his faith that Nahn Sapwe himself would protect him.

[141] Workers with land rights to work the land.

The easterly breeze was good and lying to lee of the string of islets to the east, and the wave action was very moderate. He marveled again at the smallness of the atoll compared to Kwajalein or Aelōn̄ļapļap, and he almost wished the trip were longer. By midmorning, he had crossed the shallow sandbars that spread like underwater dunes before the mouth of the narrow passageway. There, by necessity, he'd had to strike sail and paddle. The tide was still moving lagoonward but had no doubt tapered as it approached its ebb. Still, he was taxed by its current as he approached Likōkkāļọk's large and stilted house, which sat high aback the strand.

Sauntering down the beach to greet him were three childless tattooed women leading a group of men that Ijokelekel hoped would help with the pandanus. Their leader, between the two, was an attractive woman with a welcoming smile. All three swayed with a careless swagger that appeared to show independence from the young men behind them.

The leader greeted him. "*Iọkwe*!"

"*Iọkwe*. Are you Erwina?" Ijokelekel asked.

"It's her sister, Lijaki," one of her companions exclaimed.

"I've brought tribute to your mother from Ļōpako."

"Well, thank you. Come into the shade with us," Lijaki said, then instructed the young men to start carrying the pandanus and to beach his canoe above the high-tide mark. The three women walked him up the strand and over to the shaded area beneath the pole house, which sheltered a profuse number of ground mats. The two young women sat down with him while Lijaki retrieved a freshly cut coconut from a hanging basket.

"Here, you must be thirsty. It's so warm out there," she said, sitting down in front of him and spreading her hands behind her on the mat. "Mother named me Jaki, and I grew up loving to make them. We made all these. I'll give you a special one. It's upstairs. I'll show you later," she said, as her friends snickered.

Was she flirting? If she was, he was too busy to dwell on it. He was enjoying the shaded breeze and looking out from the pleasant, sheltered area beneath the house at the young men toiling with the huge green-and-orange stalks of pandanus, over the glaring white sand and down at the clear bluish water flowing slowly through the narrow passageway from the ocean reef. The house seemed perfectly placed to enjoy the easterly breeze streaming through the narrow gap between the islets.

"I'm struck by the breezy openness of these islands compared to Pohnpei," Ijokelekel said.

"Oh, have you been to Pohnpei?" asked one of the women.

"I was born there."

"You don't look like you're from Pohnpei. You look like you're from Aelōn̄ļapļap," responded another.

"That's where I got my lines."

"Wasn't Erwina's father from Pohnpei?" asked a third.

"Do you know a man named Paratak?" Jaki asked.

"Yes, he was the one who pointed the direction here."

"Then be prepared. My mother will ask you a hundred questions."

"I have one for her," said Ijokelekel. "Paratak asked me to find out if you're his daughter."

"Anyone can answer that. I'm half shark!" The women all laughed.

"You mean Ļōpako is your father?"

"Well, he sent me all this pandanus, didn't he? He's probably fart fishing right now — that's my favorite fish."

"You're right. That's exactly what he said he would do."

"His way of acknowledging me is bringing food to my mother. They're both happy with their chosen ones" — Jaki looked over at her friends — "but when their eyes chance to meet, they could set a house on fire."

Her friends laughed their assent.

"So, that makes Kāmeto your sister."

"Yes, she is my sister," she said slowly, awkwardly looking not at him but at the other young women.

"Poor thing. Her situation is pathetic. Kāmeto has no land of her own," said one of the women.

"Her mother should have returned to Ujae seasons ago," offered another.

"Her family over there has a sandspit on a reef somewhere. She's like a bird flying around looking for a place to nest," continued the first.

"But she is a *rreo,*[142] so she does have that to brag about." The second woman smiled, enjoying their back and forth.

"Yes, and she has proved it to nearly every *likao* on the island!" They all laughed.

The two women kept gossiping. "She'd be better off following her aunt's example."

"When Lijoḷọk was still a young woman, shortly after her sister took Ḷōpako, she snuck off to Ujae and snagged the handsomest jebwa dancer of them all — right after practice."

"Brought him back to Lae, they say, before her reputation as a cavort caught up with her. Wrapped her legs tight around him and never let go."

"He's still here. Even though they say he has his own land there."

"He remains as crazy for her as the night she first laid her skirt down on the ground beneath her. He's still a head-turner too."

"She needed a story like that to compete with her sister's."

Jaki interrupted. "We'll leave her story for another day. Weren't you two going to draw water for Mother's bath?"

Then she addressed Ijokelekel. "Mother and Erwina should be returning from Lae when the tide is right. Tell me about this Paratak. He was gone before I was born."

The other two shut up but hesitated, perhaps interested in his answer.

"He's big and strong, but kind. He is much liked and respected by all. The problem is, he lingered so long here on Lae back then that his Pohnpeian woman took another. So, he lives by himself on Idedh, the island your father granted him with his title, Jau Areu. Now he must fish every day for the Saudeleur."

"He hasn't taken another?" Jaki asked excitedly. She quickly swung her legs behind her, lay on her stomach, and propped herself on her elbows before Ijokelekel. Then she raised her feet in the air behind her, showing the delicate pink soles of her feet.

"They say he could have taken any woman, but he has taken none. He and my mother became friends."

"What about your father?"

---

[142] A virgin.

"My father is Nahn Sapwe, the spirit of thunder."

"Okay…" She was skeptical and glanced at the others. "But are you sure Paratak didn't give her the old *wūdiddid*[143] when her back was turned?" She was joking, swaying her shoulders and breasts, perhaps in an attempt to center his attention on her.

"Paratak arrived back on Pohnpei long after I was born, so there was no *wūdiddid* while her back was turned. Besides, he's an honorable man and wouldn't do that to any woman!"

"Don't reject what you haven't tried!" argued one of her obstinate friends.

"Jaki likes it that way!" said the other.

Overlooking their jokes, he continued. "You are nonbelievers, so I don't expect you to accept my story." He was a little peeved at the group. "He and my mother both worked for the Saudeleur. She told me to call Paratak 'uncle.' They both had much respect for your father! They both referred to him as 'pali.' In Pohnpeian, that means 'great navigator.'"

"Speaking of Father, he should be here soon," Jaki said, looking across the passageway and distracted by something. "Let's go up the ladder, and I'll show you your *jaki.*"

Clouds of caution began to form on the horizon of his thoughts. Hadn't Kāmeto warned him about her? Yet he followed her up into the spacious, beautifully thatched room. There were no windows so it was dim, but light streamed through the gables at each end of the high, peaked roof. The room carried the scent of its occupants, but the mats were dry and crisp, probably from recent sun bleachings. She immediately covered the entrance with a mat. Suddenly, he felt the urge to scurry about like a cornered rat.

"There, we're alone now. Even if Mother or Father arrive, they will honor our privacy. Look at this beautiful *jaki* I'm giving to you. I made it myself." She unfurled the mat onto the floor and sat on a corner. "Scoot over and see how soft it is."

Once he had sat down cross-legged, she immediately lay on her back with her head on his thigh and stared up at his face with a look of absolute glee, as would a fisher who had just snagged one bigger than the last.

---

[143] A shiver.

What would Kāmeto have him do now? Here was her sister pretending she was his paramour, and she advanced this awkward moment of strained familiarity quickly.

"So, your tattoos are from Āne-piñ." Jaki touched the lines adorning his chest, extinguishing the silence with her voice and forcing him to politely respond.

He was busy wondering if she expected him to roll over on her right then and drill her like his brother would. Instead, he answered politely. "Yes, just this last season. I walked the jib in jowi for the Rilujien Naṃo clan." He was nervous, trying not to brag. His intention was to engage in conversation while he decided what to do.

"That must have hurt!"

"Not really," he responded anxiously.

"Did you see an irooj called Ḷañinni?"

"Yes, I went fishing with him once." He was ready to go on about that but got cut off by her next question.

"Did he mention my name? He went crazy for me!" she bragged, raising her knees and splitting her skirts to show them to him. "I wanted him to poke me before we left, just for story's sake," she said, looking up to get his reaction. "But he and Mother got into it about something, and I lost my chance. Dry your fish before it rains, I've heard them say." She concluded, swaying her knees back and forth playfully, then opened her eyes wide to command his attention. "It's never better to wait when you can get at it right now. Don't you agree?"

With that, she snatched his hand, isolated a finger, and touched it to the nipple of her closest breast. He could feel it harden under his touch as she tickled herself. She held his attention with her eyes, as though trying to catch his thoughts. "I'd like you to touch me someplace else, but you'd get your fingers wet. You're not afraid of a little clam juice, are you?"

"I heard Ḷañinni wanted your sister first." Ijokelekel blurted this out in a panic, his thoughts racing between the giant clam he had bonded with her sister over and the conversation at hand. He pulled his hand from hers.

That must have entered her throat like a fishbone. She playfully kneeled on the *jaki*, pushed his shoulders back onto it, then forced her erect nipple into his face. "*Ninnin*,"[144] she said, as he laughed and turned his head to one side.

"Why are young *rreo* so desirable to men? I'll tell you. It's because they prey on the weak and defenseless. That makes them feel bigger and stronger. They brag about being the first to make a girl squeal, the way they club an *ak* from the branch where it sleeps and then hang its tail feathers from the leech of their sail. Yes, Ḷañinni is that type of man. You're not that type of man, are you? Tell me you'd rather wrestle it from a woman who knows what she wants because she's had it before and knows how she wants it!"

Just then, the mat she had slid over the single entrance behind them was forcefully tugged through from below. Another woman rose into the room and violently grabbed Lijaki by the hair with both hands. She screamed as the woman yanked her backward off of him and, somehow, down through the hole as Jaki shouted, "Rape your mother! You … jealous hen! I found him first!" Others below must have caught and restrained her.

Ijokelekel thought he heard the pali's calm voice among the other more frantic tones. After much commotion and muffled contention — and repeated "jealous hen" accusations — the woman who had assaulted Jaki rose through the entrance again and sat politely before him.

He was sitting upright, stunned. He had never seen such violence among women in Rālik. He half-expected her to attack him too, at least until he saw a smile spread across her broad face.

"You have to excuse my younger sister. *E jaje mannit*."[145]

"So, you must be Erwina?" he said, immediately finding Paratak's features in her face. It was much broader and flatter than her sister's. She was physically larger. Her features were pleasant enough, but she wasn't the type that would catch Irooj Ḷañinni's eye. She answered by raising her eyebrows and wheezing audibly to the affirmative. He recalled that her father liked to answer him that same way.

"I can see your father in your manner."

"I'm excited to hear news of him. The morning I woke up and Mother told me he was gone was the saddest day of my life."

---

[144] Suckle.

[145] "She is ignorant of custom."

"You are constantly in his thoughts," Ijokelekel said. "He was the one who encouraged me to come here and bring you back if you wished."

"Thank you so much for saying that," she whispered, "but you must keep your voice low and never, ever say anything like that in front of my mother! Is it true that he received some sort of title that Ļōpako gave him?"

"Yes, his title is Jau Areu, and he was given the island of Idedh."

"So Ļōpako did tell me the truth all along. I've hated him so much for so long for what he did, and it turns out he's the only one who told me the truth about my father. Mother reminded me every chance she got that he's dead."

"Hardly. Ļōpako made your father a hero in the eyes of his family. Many even call him a pali. Of course, they don't know that his proa doesn't sail well into the wind. He says that's the result of a trick Ļōpako played on him."

"Has he taken another woman?"

"No, but the children from his woman before visit with him all the time. They're grown, and he has many grandchildren."

"What's all this the girls are saying about Nahn Sapwe?"

"He's my father, the one who got me here safely. He guided me through the jib in jowi. He's the one who, once my training is complete, will lead me back to Pohnpei to free my people from the tyranny of the Saudeleur, who has turned cannibal. He makes Paratak cook his victims!"

"That's terrible!" Then after a pause, she said, "But what do you mean when you say Nahn Sapwe is your father. He's a spirit, right?"

"No different from your father, Paratak. Your mother told you he was your father and you believed. You don't see him here, but when I say he lives in Pohnpei, you believe me. Belief is a powerful thing. My mother attended the eternal fire of Nahn Sapwe until the little akebu killed her. She told me who my father was. Why shouldn't I believe her? Especially when I see what he does for me. It's true. I am a lucky man. But to have luck you must risk, and to risk you need belief. With his help, I'll be ready to seize the moment to lead when it comes."

"My days with my father were the happiest of my life," she said. "He was with me more than my mother. If my father went fishing by himself, she would sneak off and abandon me. So, I always cried to accompany him. I would sit on his shoulders and fly over the reefs like a bird. We would catch lobsters and pole fish at the edge of the reef under the light of the moon. Later, we would hunt down Mother wherever she had gone and make her return to cook our catch. I loved him more than I have ever loved her. When you're ready to lead, I will follow. If there's a battle, I'll stand behind you and my father, beat my *aje*, and ululate like Likarwejoñ!"

As brother and sister, they bonded with that agreement as though she had granted him lands to attend and he had agreed to do so. But unlike the bond between Ḷōpako and her mother, theirs was based on something bigger than the day-to-day management of property. Their bond was based on something intangible — an idea and a common destiny that would bring it about.

When they climbed down the ladder, they found Ḷōpako sitting by himself. The women were cleaning fish by the passageway. The awkwardness of Ijokelekel's situation dawned on him. "Lijaki took me by surprise," he said, turning red and seating himself before the pali.

To his surprise, Ḷōpako laughed. "You have a lot to learn about women. Better to stay clear of them all — including this one — until you complete your training." He tickled Erwina's side. She giggled and scooted away.

"Ḷōpako, do you remember promising me something after you sent my father on his way home?" she asked in a serious tone.

"Yes, I told you that if you wanted to go and see him once you grew up, I would take you."

"Well, I want you to keep your promise. I can go with my brother Nahn Sapwe here, but you mustn't tell my mother our plans, and you must teach him the shortest way, so I don't get sick at sea."

"That's a difficult mission, but I owe it to you—"

"So, here is the baby shark my girls fight over," said Likōkkālọk. She had slowly crossed over the sand from the passageway, where she had been supervising the young women cleaning fish. She spoke from a distance as she trudged toward them. Her eyes shifted quickly from Ijokelekel to Ḷōpako, who for some reason seemed to disparage her comment without speaking, then back to Ijokelekel with a smile. "You must excuse my precocious daughter. We don't get many newly tattooed men arriving in this small, out-of-the-way place."

“I’m taking him as my brother,” announced Erwina. “He says he was raised by my father.”

“Paratak! Well, you are certainly a handsome young man, so it’s no wonder my girls are cackling like hens. But by the fine look of those lines, it appears that someone more than a fool raised you. Who sponsored your lines?” she asked.

“I was cast astray from Lae on my first attempt and landed on Kwajalein, where Lijāpe and Ļōkijdik took me in and adopted me. They sponsored my lines at Āne-piñ,” he responded.

“So, Paratak sent you, as a child, across the ocean to Lae in that huge canoe all by yourself?” Likōkkāļọk was speaking to Ijokelekel but looking at her daughter to emphasize her point.

“Well, not exactly—”

“You see, Erwina” — she cut off his attempt to answer — “Paratak is a fool. We tricked him adrift and thought him dead. Now this young man brings news that he survived. But he’s still the same fool he always was.” She turned back to Ijokelekel. “On Āne-piñ, you probably met another fool and heard a story with my name mentioned once or twice.”

“Yes, I met Ļañinni, but I wouldn’t call him a fool. Dangerous, yes,” he said.

“Dangerous like a puffer fish. Sharp bristles on the outside, poison on the inside. If he comes here, our warriors will spear his rear to a breadfruit tree, and I’ll launch his neck to the top myself… Although I might tease him a little first. But you’ll see. You will see. Ļōpako says you are to train with us, so you’ll see for yourself the quality of my defenders. We used to have but one shark. Now we’ll have two!” she declared, glancing toward a somewhat vexed Ļōpako teasingly. “Tell us your name.”

“They call me Ijokelekel.”

“Okay, Ijokelekel. You will stay here and train with my men, and I will treat you as my son. After all, if that fool who’s my daughter’s father indeed raised you for a brief time, then I can treat you like you’re mine. And I am a very annoying mother. Ask Erwina, and she’ll tell you all about me.”

Just as he was agreeing to accept her bargain, a single paddling canoe, apparently arriving from Lae, appeared in the sand shoals at the mouth of the passageway.

"That's Ļōetre,[146] my youthful *kubaak*," announced Likōkkālọk, still speaking to Ijokelekel. "He keeps me on course and prevents me from turning turtle in high winds." She continued glancing at Ļōpako with what appeared a naughty smile. "We have two children who spend their days across the passage being instructed by their elders. We come here mostly to practice our battle plans. There are too many curious birds on Lae who like to tattle to our competitor across the lagoon. Ļōetre has brought *jekaro* for our warriors, and they'll be along soon. You can start your practice today. Are you ready?"

"Yes, but I'm afraid I won't be much help at first."

"We have a place for you if you don't mind practicing with the untattooed."

"Not at all."

"You see, you are a young shark, carefully deliberating your own way, careless of what the capricious islanders have to say. You remind me of someone I knew once," she said, with the same naughty glance Ļōpako's way. "Come," she told Erwina. "We need to save those *jekaro* shells from the heat of the sun, or we'll all get drunk and sleep through our practice."

It was clear from the beginning that the man called Ļōetre, who had brought the *jekaro*, had a bond of long standing with Ļōpako. They respected each other as apprentice and mentor. The men whom Likōkkālọk had referred to as her "*jekaro* boys" showed up in twos and threes, formed several circles depending on their level of skill, and immediately began to play anidep. It seemed like child's play to Ijokelekel. He quickly found a place among the "untattooed boys," and even among this group, he was a standout poor player. Ļōetre was one of the best although Ļōbōkrōk was his equal and charged with leadership of the group. Ijokelekel would benefit from the one-on-one instruction by both, and no jealousy occurred among the other boys because the better he got, the better his group's performance. By the moon's next cycle, his first spear cured, his practice of the jebwa ensued.

Ijokelekel's skills grew, as had his footprints in the sand during his seasons on Kwajalein. Days passed quickly into moons as the cycles of island life gradually encompassed him. Moons passed into seasons. He studied

---

[146] Likōkkālọk's mate.

jekaro and practiced the patience it required. He took part in his first competitive jebwa "battle" his second season, and his performance skills continued to grow from there. Even their arch-competitor Ḷōtokjān made comment about him. Ḷainjin himself taught Ijokelekel the art of navigation by wave pattern. They circumnavigated the tiny atoll many times until he could recognize the four swells and, by process of elimination, tell which direction the islands lay. He taught him to troll and to fish long-line with sinker balls and to name a fish by its reaction once hooked. He learned proa lashings. How to right his canoe once it had flipped turtle and how to retie a *kubaak* in the open ocean. Finally, he had learned nearly everything, just as his mother had promised.

There remained, however, one problem the great pali was unable to discuss. The son of Nahn Sapwe was no closer to taking a woman than the day he arrived. The story of his sexual life was a feeble history of inexperience, poor timing, questionable judgement, and — most of all — inaction. His goals were aggressive and his accomplishments many and ongoing. But his love affairs, he had to admit, were mere figments of his imagination. Lijaki, though he fantasized about what might have happened, had disappeared from her mother's islet. She spent her days under the roof of her great-uncle Ḷōtokjān, across the lagoon. Erwina, on her part, became his best and most loyal friend. However, he suspected she refused to allow any other woman to cross his path, or at least he had heard comments to that effect from the few women he had approached.

On the occasion that his thoughts did turn to love, they always settled on Likāmeto, though, over these many seasons and after all these days of instruction, not a word concerning her had emerged from Ḷōpako. The once young woman he had fallen in love with had taken no man and was still rumored to be "as fresh as a *ut*"[147] and, he assumed, still waiting for her father's decision. In the brief moments that chance had allowed them together, he imagined he could see in her eyes her interest in him, which she silently concealed within her throat. Indeed, one way or another, she kept reminding him of her pledge to accompany him to Pohnpei, to seek their destiny there.

[147] Flower.

Likōkkālọk's curse

Now that Ijokelekel had learned almost everything, he knew the day that would mark his destiny must be approaching, like the islands the pali had taught him to find below the horizon. But where were the fellow warriors he had always supposed would surround him? He had felt out a few of his jebwa companions, but none had expressed excitement at the prospect of pulling up roots to battle on a distant shore — for what purpose? Surely, Likōkkālọk was a powerful influence who would stymie any such plans among her workers, who seemed happy enough where they were anyway. Did he dare ask his pali for help? He had no warriors of his own. He hardly had the workers he needed to finish brushing and planting his island, and these men owed their loyalty to Likōkkālọk as well. And again, ambitious woman that she was, he couldn't envision her sending men to invade foreign soil. Again, for what purpose? Sadly, his only actual hope rested in that distant conversation he'd had with the infamous Irooj Ḷañinni, who said that his moment would rise as clear as the moon. He had added, "Suddenly, you'll notice that the people you need to get your revenge have been circling you all along."

How long must he wait for this moment to come? Had he already missed his opportunity? Surely, these were the men of his circle, but why would they leave this pleasant haven to fight other men's battles over the islands of other men? As he had many times before, these were the thoughts Ijokelekel was pondering one bright afternoon while playing anidep with Ḷōbōkrōk's most advanced group. He was in the middle of teaching them to parry a particularly skillful move when he happened to glance out at the lagoon to see a proa advancing toward them. The wind had blown from the south all day. Not that a proa crossing the lagoon was in any way unusual, though they would usually be passing on their way north toward the small islets or returning south from there on their way back to Lae. But this proa wasn't headed toward Lae. It was coming from Ļōtokjān's island, and it was heading without waver directly at them.

During a short break, Ijokelekel asked Bōkrōk if he thought it was Ļōtokjān's canoe. He thought not. Then the others debated different suggestions as they played. They all seemed to agree that no one knew who it might be, and this became more conclusive as the proa closed the distance and the men observed a woman between two men, boldly raising her arm and acknowledging their group from afar. Could it be Maalal? The anidep players became too distracted by her to continue.

Ijokelekel couldn't comprehend the meaning of what he was seeing. Was he dreaming about his past? Had his story turned back upon itself? It looked like Maalal with his brother, Jorailik, and none other than Anitok. It was as though he had rounded an islet and come across his own footprints in the sand. The women were still stringing flower leis when Ijokelekel led his player companions down the beach to greet them. The travelers had lowered sail, and the two men were paddling across the unfamiliar sandy shallows at the mouth of the narrow passageway. Maalal was standing high on the outrigger platform, demonstrating her happiness to have found him, her arms outstretched as though to embrace the entire group of men. She was a woman now. Her breasts had grown large, dark nipples. She showed no remorse for the years, but where was her child? She jumped into the water as their prow touched the calm shore and ran to embrace him as though he were her father. The two men unloaded two baskets of salted fish then stood holding them, looking for direction from Ijokelekel. He nodded toward Erwina, who was leading a group of women down the shore.

Maalal, suddenly feigning humbleness, bowed slightly, offered the baskets to Erwina, and announced, "Greetings from Irooj Ļañinni."

Ijokelekel was sure the baskets of fish were from his father's island and not from Ļañinni but held any comment. Erwina and her companions responded by placing the flower leis around the necks of the three visitors and requesting that her anidep players beach their canoe high on the strand. Then she invited them up under the house for refreshments. He could hear Maalal, who had apparently heard the stories about how she had jilted Ḷañinni, inquiring about her mother, Likōkkālọk, as they headed back up the beach. Ijokelekel greeted his friend Anitok warmly. Anitok appeared distracted by Maalal and set off to follow the women.

Then Ijokelekel greeted and jostled with his brother as though they were boys again, on the shores of their mother's island. "Are the elders good?" he asked.

"Yes, they are good and send their love."

"You look good, brother," Ijokelekel said. "Have you chosen a woman yet?"

"Yes, and we have a son."

"How did you find me?"

"We stopped and made inquiry at the island across the lagoon."

"So, what's going on? Why the visit? Why Limaalal and Anitok?"

"They came to retrieve you. There is threat of war. They'll explain."

Limaalal sat next to Erwina. Anitok sat on her opposite side. Ijokelekel and his brother sat across and between them. The others crowded around, eager to hear.

"So, where is your famous teacher, Ijokelekel?" asked Limaalal.

"He stays up the reef mostly."

"And his timid daughter with the minor problem our Ḷañinni has pledged to solve?" Limaalal asked.

Her boldness took the group by surprise, leaving silence in its wake.

"Limaalal, tell us the purpose of your journey," said Erwina.

"I'd rather discuss Ijokelekel's love life while we wait for the elders to return. Who has he chosen?" She asked, feigning innocence but probably assuming there was no one yet. Was she trying to embarrass him? The players looked at one another as though they, too, were curious about how he would respond.

Erwina came to his aid. "We're still searching for the right match. I have taken him as my brother, and my standards for his choice are high. My mother comes and goes, and we don't know when to expect her. We're not expecting Ḷōpako today. I represent the next generation here. Why not go ahead and share the purpose of your visit with us?"

"Okay then, this new generation has a new paramount chief," said Limaalal. "Your mother and especially your brother Ijokelekel know him well. His name is Ḷañinni."

"You forgot to add 'self-appointed' to his title," added Anitok, demonstrating a certain tension between the two.

At this the players erupted into whispers and quiet discussion as she went on. "The paramount chiefs of the Rālik string to the south are gone."

This was followed by even louder comment among the group listening around them.

"Taklur has surrendered his island and taken to sea with his followers," continued Maalal.

"Ḷañinni acted despicably toward a peace-loving people," Anitok retorted.

"Anitok represents the only holdouts — the members of the Rilujien Naṃo clan," Limaalal said. "They are refusing to relinquish Wōjjā despite their pledge of allegiance to Ḷañinni, and even though they bear no history there."

"That's a lie. Taklur gave us our own *wāto*," Anitok said. "You know our history and so does Ḷañinni."

"He has offered them other lands more suitable to their numbers," said Maalal. "Through negotiation with Anitok and his clan, the irooj agreed to summon Ijokelekel to help settle the matter. They all agreed to postpone the battle to control the island until *jetñōl.*[148] That's three days away. So, we must leave tomorrow, and Ijokelekel must decide tonight whether he plans to depart with us. If he decides not to come, Ḷañinni will be very unhappy with the new alliance between his people and yours. He will drive the Rilujien Naṃo off his beaches and into the sea and might even make a visit here to confirm the loyalty of both your generations," she concluded.

"Now," Maalal continued, speaking to Erwina. "Is there a place where I can rest while Anitok continues to present his side of all this? I wouldn't want to interrupt your conversations."

---

[148] The night the moon rises at dusk upon the waves.

At that, Erwina led her to a small guesthouse along the ocean passageway. Ijokelekel, stunned at hearing all this, held his place and waited in silence for Erwina to return before asking any of the many questions he had.

"So that's it?" exclaimed Erwina upon her return. "She came all this way to talk to us, and that's all she has to say?"

"That's all she was told to say," said Anitok. "Don't forget, Ḷañinni is the father of her son. She can only offer what he has placed in her basket, and the lands she is offering are actually not even his to give."

"Anitok, what did she mean, 'Taklur has taken to sea'?" Ijokelekel asked. Suddenly, there was a hush among the surrounding men.

"They gathered provisions, boarded their proas, and left the island. A few elderlies and a few too sick to travel stayed, but nearly every family of workers left with the irooj."

"Well, what was their destination?" Ijokelekel asked.

"No one knows. Wherever they wash up, I guess. They didn't set their sails. They paddled across the ocean-side reef into the open sea and just drifted," said Anitok.

"Why would they leave with no destination?" asked Erwina.

Anitok answered. "For hundreds of years, they have known only peace. They thrived like children with no history of battle. No anidep, no jebwa — we brought those to them — no one taught them how to fight. So, Irooj Ḷañinni and his men sailed their shores day after day, from north to south, beating their war drums, brandishing their weapons, and taunting their men. The old Irooj Taklur, with his love of peace, had left his people unprepared for war. He was the one who first proposed it was better to just give up and drift away. The others had always followed him. They knew no better. It's just the Rilujien Naṃo clan, with our history of war, who have stayed to fight, but truthfully, we're hopelessly outnumbered and our situation appears grave." He now addressed Ijokelekel. "Can you help us?"

All eyes turned to him. The group became so silent that the terns returning from their daily feasts could be heard cawing in the distant trees. Yet he wasn't ready to speak. He was imagining hundreds of proas drifting in the evening sun, without destination or hope. Why would they just drift? Did they worry they were so many that, wherever they landed, they would have to fight or be turned away? Which island was large enough to accept that many? Plus, there were no islands west of Aelōn̄ļapļap — only days and days of open ocean except, of course… He seized his moment. "Yes, I can help!" he said, decisively addressing Anitok as though no time had passed since the jib in jowi. Since Anitok had passed the stake of leadership to him and had overcome the embarrassment he endured at the hands of Ļan̄inni. Then he turned to Erwina, who knew of his ambitions and shared his thoughts.

She nodded as decisively to the affirmative. "I'll inform Limaalal of our decision," she said, rising and turning toward the guesthouse.

"Men, who can offer us provisions?" Ijokelekel asked, and one by one, the anidep players offered what they could bring.

Erwina returned. "She's gone," she announced. "Perhaps she slipped off to the ocean side to make ready. After all, that was quite a trip she had. I'll give her some time."

"Don't trust her. She has her own plans," said Anitok, as the men began to take their leave and promised to return with their commitments.

"Where is her child?" asked Ijokelekel.

"Exactly my point," Anitok said. "Ļan̄inni has him hostage. Everything she says and does reflects that. He wants you to return with us. Ask yourself why. You can answer that better than I can. I've been trying to get her to tell, but she won't say. However, I promise you, whatever her strategy, her true goal is to fulfill whatever deal she struck with him to get her son back."

At this, Ijokelekel's brother spoke up. "She has changed. All she does now is make deals. You do this for her, she agrees to do that for you."

"Because of her relationship with Ļan̄inni, everyone thinks they are negotiating with him. But who knows? She's just desperate for her son if you ask me," said Anitok.

That evening, Erwina informed Ijokelekel that Maalal hadn't appeared. "She must have crossed the passageway to Lae. Perhaps she went to speak with Mother? You're planning to raise a circle of warriors among the drifting outcasts, aren't you?"

"I'd be lying if I told you I hadn't thought about it. I can't imagine all those people just giving up and committing themselves to the sea. I realize they're not warriors, but there must be some who would rather take their chances and join me in my quest."

"And the Rilujien Naṃo?"

"They must feel bad for Taklur and his people too. They were the very ones who took the Rilujien Naṃo in and gave them lands to work. Maybe they'll be willing to help me round up the drifters."

"Okay, I'm coming with you!" Erwina said. "Remember, you promised my father and you promised me, and so did your mentor. You heard him yourself. I'll hide in your hull. No one must know, or Mother will tie my leg like a sea bird."

"But I must say good-bye to Ḷōpako. I must thank him out of respect."

"You heard Maalal," argued Erwina. "The day after tomorrow. To do that we must leave at dawn, right? Ḷōpako, my mother… They're the old generation. Like the chant says, 'They are they, we are us.' If we give them too much deference, they may try to stop us. We are the new generation. We must take what they taught us and unapologetically apply that to our own destinies. We have our own stories to tell, perhaps our own mistakes to make."

Ijokelekel didn't sleep well. How could he leave without saying good-bye to Kāmeto? Hadn't she promised to accompany him as well? Would he be able to return for her? He rose before dawn to gather his *jekaro* shells and wash them among the coral pebbles lining the passage shore. It wouldn't be easy to leave these trees he had come to feel were his friends. The moments he had shared with the crown of each tree had grown into a cherished time for him. He had established a relationship with each. Or had the time alone simply strengthened his relationship with himself? Perhaps another of Likōkkālọk's men would climb and sit among their branches and talk to each bud as it protruded from above each stem. He had been remiss in not taking on an apprentice. Patiently, he removed the full, netted shells of *jekaro* and replaced them with clean empty ones after carefully cutting thin slices from the flat face of each bud. He whispered good-bye to each tree as he descended it and remorsefully turned to the next. Feeling that his destiny was calling, he had no choice but to answer.

Later, he found that Maalal still hadn't appeared. As they provisioned their boats with the things brought by Ijokelekel's anidep circle, Anitok confessed that she had told him, if she didn't return by morning, he was to search for her along the beaches of the islets to the north.

"What is she doing up there?" asked Ijokelekel.

"She mentioned something about collecting medicine. I don't know. She has been very mysterious."

So, they decided that if Anitok found her, he would head directly across the lagoon to the ocean passageway to the west. If not, he would return south, along the edge of the northern back reef. If he started to cross the lagoon, that would be his sign to Ijokelekel to sail and meet him there in the passageway. If she showed up in the meantime, Ijokelekel was to take her aboard his craft and sail first, and Anitok would turn and follow him across the lagoon. It was a solid plan, but why would she disappear like this, knowing that time was so important to her mission?

Ijokelekel, worried that Likōkkālọk would show up before they left, asked Erwina what she might do.

"Neither man nor your spirit Nahn Sapwe can keep a *koon* in its nest once it has reached its maturity. Ultimately, there's nothing she can do but tie me to a coconut trunk. If she didn't want me to know my father, she never should have matted him. Once she sees I'm dead set on leaving, she'll take solace in knowing you have promised to protect me. Besides, look. The tide is too high. She'll be unable to cross."

A few moments later, word spread that they had spotted Etre's canoe paddling from Lae. Then Likōkkālọk appeared on the opposite shore and, waiting for no man, plunged into the current at the mouth of the passage between the islands. Despite her strong strokes, the current caught her skirts and swept her lagoonward, where her abandoned partner intercepted her with his canoe and towed her toward the shore. Her less than graceful appearance was unusual at the least. If her awkward demeanor was any indication of her temperament, Erwina would have to summon considerable will to overcome her mother's obvious desperation. But how did she know of their plans? Perhaps one of the anidep circle had returned to Lae and informed her.

On her part, Erwina had apparently decided to meet her mother with resolution. She left Ijokelekel's side and walked deliberately down the shore to accost her. He wasn't about to interject himself between these equally willful women. Though he didn't care to hear what they said to each other, their words were so loud they were clear to all. Likōkkālọk reminded her she was her eldest daughter who would be *lerooj* someday. Why would she throw that away?

"I promise you, I will personally return her safely," shouted Ijokelekel.

"Your father was a fool. Ask anyone who knew him — and so is this so-called son of Nahn Sapwe. Look at him. He is a fish out of water flapping around on the shore, dead yet not knowing it. He can protect no one. Besides, Erwina, did you suddenly forget you suffer from seasickness?"

Erwina countered that Likōkkālọk had other more ambitious daughters. "I go with my brother, who will take me to meet my father, whose story is intertwined with mine by his selfless love during my childhood. You must now suffer the bloom of seeds planted long ago.

"There..." Erwina pointed to Anitok's canoe, crossing the lagoon toward the passageway on the opposite side of the atoll. "There is our sign of departure." Then she beckoned to Ijokelekel. "Come, let us be gone."

At that, Likōkkālọk, still dripping from head to skirts, threw herself down onto the dry sand before her daughter's feet and begged her to stay. But she had taught Erwina to be a woman of strong will, and she kicked her ankles free from her mother's hands. They boarded Lañinpo's canoe, and Ijokelekel and his brother began paddling them away.

He reflexively turned back when he heard Likōkkālọk shout at him. The dry sand had stuck to her wet face, hair, and arms. He imagined she was Likarwejoñ, about to swim after and eat him up.

"Ijokelekel, I curse the day you arrived on these shores. I curse the memory of your fool of a mother, who filled your head with the foolish belief you weren't born of the same lustful act as the rest of us! Yes, you who have convinced yourself you are superior! You return my kindness by stealing my daughter like a thief before dawn. I curse your destiny. May all men say you died like the fool you are — and a fool you shall thereby forever remain in their stories and chants."

Amid her tirade, his brother raised sail, and Ijokelekel set their heading toward the western passageway as planned. However, she continued to scream at him something about Ḷōpako even as her wind converged not on his ears but blew her words somewhat to the side. He had come to respect Likōkkāḷọk greatly, and her words had bit into his throat like the teeth of an angry dog. More so as he felt he had betrayed her. His loyalty was torn between the two of them, but he owed the greater allegiance to the daughter, as she was the one willing to stand behind him now that his time may have come.

Erwina, perhaps sensing his remorse, moved to the narrow bulwark to his left, took his free hand, and held it in both of hers. She managed to quiet his thoughts and distract him from her mother's foreboding curse. Consoling him, she said, "I have absolute faith that you and Nahn Sapwe will protect me."

Yet he wasn't a man to take such a curse lightly. However inadvertently, he had altered Likōkkāḷọk's willful expectations of him. He must now trust even more in his father's power to overcome this sense of encroaching doom she had cast upon him.

As they approached the ocean passageway, the headings of the two vessels began to converge. The first thing they noticed was that there appeared to be three aboard Anitok's vessel. But who was the third?

"Oh no! It looks like Likāmeto," said Erwina. "Now her father will be mad at us as well."

At the sound of her name, Ijokelekel's spirit immediately bounced back. Memories of their promise to each other flooded his thoughts. But how…

"Limaalal must have walked that reef last night and secreted her away somehow," continued Erwina. "I can imagine Limaalal telling her … either she goes to Ḷañinni willingly or he'll come here and burn her out. Why else would she leave her parents but to protect them?"

That showed him Erwina had no knowledge of their promise to each other. As the proas drew closer at the passageway and it became clearer that she was right, his throat burned for Kāmeto such that the cool morning air turned hot as noon and all thoughts of Likōkkāḷọk's curse dissipated like harmless bubbles in their wake. As the proas converged, Kāmeto raised her arms as she had on the morning of his first arrival how many seasons ago, and he recalled her flashing her between as he always did when he thought of her. Surely, Erwina could see the tears welling in his eyes.

"Ijokelekel..." Kāmeto said, but then nothing more, as though after further contemplation, she had decided to leave what she was about to say in her throat.

Suddenly, he realized he was in charge, and this would be his first voyage as *rijeḷā*. They were deep into the wet season. The winds were still variable but generally, like today, out of the east. The weather was fair. He planned to lead the two boats on a tack to the northeast, toward the northernmost islet of Kwajalein, and then southeast along the atoll's western reef to return his brother to Lijāpe's island. Yes, he could take a course southeast directly to Wōjjā, but he felt adamant that Jorailik, who had also promised to accompany him, must stay with the elders, his chosen one, and their son. The journey Ijokelekel was on had an uncertain ending, and the last thing he wanted to do was drag his older brother along with him. He must stay at home and take care of their elders.

His plan was simple: to beach on the ocean side of Wōjjā, emphasize the plight of those already adrift at sea, and convince his Rilujien Naṃo brothers to abandon the islet and round up as many of those they found at sea who seemed willing to join them in the vast, unclaimed valleys between the mountains of a new land. The only part he hadn't figured out was how to explain his plan to Ḷañinni — and now, how to dissuade him from demanding Kāmeto. How much time would they need to provision for such a trip? Could he reason with Ḷañinni? Could Ijokelekel arrange their departure from Wōjjā before Ḷañinni knew Kāmeto was there? If he found out he had missed her, would he chase them all the way to Pohnpei and risk fighting in unfamiliar terrain against uncertain numbers? Ijokelekel was hoping Limaalal might have answers to some of these questions.

As soon as two of the craft came into speaking distance, he began giving commands. "One person is always to rest below, and the crew member not at the tiller is responsible to keep their eyes on the other craft so as not to lose sight during the night or in a storm." Anitok nodded his agreement. Ijokelekel had much to ask of Limaalal and Kāmeto, and they both sat there facing him, ready for interrogation. Kāmeto was smiling at him ear to ear. Limaalal looked as guilty as a weather bird hovering before a storm. Yet what was he to ask or say? It was what it was. Limaalal had stolen her away during the night to appease some bargain she had drawn with Ļañinni. That was clear. The rest would be destiny.

Ijokelekel chanted, "*Emejjia wa iloṃeto*,"[149] and Anitok, who would remain in command of his vessel, repeated his words back to him. With that, the boats tacked and headed north from the passage outside the atoll's barrier reef. Each quickly caught a bonito for breakfast then rounded the ocean side of the atoll's north-most islet, which Likōkkāloķ had given to Kāmeto's father, Ļōpako. Ijokelekel expected the swell from the east that they now confronted would gradually diminish as they drew closer to Kwajalein and farther into the shadow of its basket.

Erwina and, of course, Maalal were the first to go below. Ijokelekel remembered from his first voyage as a boy the pitfall of sailing too close to sleep. He would keep his crew as fresh as possible. Erwina, however, could not sleep. Her head kept popping out of the forward hatch to vomit. Before noon, the last of Lae had sunk below their horizon, and the northernmost islet of Kwajalein appeared well before sunset, and that was when he gave the tiller to his brother and replaced Erwina below.

Lying on the floorboards below, he could feel his craft on its northeast tack periodically nodding to each wind-generated, westward-flowing wave. It would slap the starboard side of the bow and push its way along the flank of their starboard hull, which was held strong against it by his brother's oar. He imagined its force churned into their wake, trailing back toward the atoll they had left below the horizon. Then, ever so gently, he felt the force of *kāleptak* — still overwhelmed by its counterswell — roll beneath them from the opposite direction as it first teetered their stern, plunged the forward tip of their *kubaak* into the next wave, and then, just as smoothly, raised it again along with their bow as it passed beneath and rolled on toward the western periphery of the atoll ahead.

This was the level of awareness that his mentor, Ļōpako, had passed on to him, and never had he felt so conflicted. On the one hand, he felt incredible gratefulness toward a man who, as promised, had taught him everything. Following in the craft behind him was his daughter, who had

[149] "A boat dies slow in the open ocean."

been stolen away in the night. What a predicament he had fallen into. Surely, the *rijeḷā* was the type of man who would search the horizon for her, so Ijokelekel must assume that Ḷōpako was coming after them. He was sure to face him again someday, perhaps soon. How would he explain what had happened? He took comfort that at least he had asked for her.

These were his thoughts as they plunged forth into the night, as each wave they faced diminished imperceptibly. *Kāleptak*'s swell from the opposite direction grew until the waves became but ripples. Its swells slowly raised their craft high and, just as smoothly, lowered them sleepily into their troughs as they gradually passed beneath them. So, he knew by the feel of the sea around him that they were close to the atoll's western reef and wasn't startled by his brother's command to *diak*.[150]

He heard Erwina scrambling half an arm's length above him as she untied the spars and passed them back to his brother. This confirmed they were to lee of Ebadon,[151] the northwesternmost islet of Kwajalein Atoll. They would now have a straight course on port tack past the belly of the basket to their mother's islet near the southern tip of the atoll. Now he could sleep for good as his brother steered them parallel to the same lazy, east-flowing swells. They would rock him back to sleep as his brother gradually climbed up the side of one and then just as gently down the side of the following trough. However, long before Ijokelekel was fully rested, it was his brother's turn to replace him below, and before he was completely awake, he found himself back at the helm a second time.

The waning moon was still high in the western sky, and the ocean gleamed peacefully around them. His brother had kept them a good distance from shore, as there was no need to sail into the belly of the atoll's western periphery. A small wave had built up between them and the atoll now, and it was slapping their hull on its port side and providing a gentle rock to their sail. Erwina had wrapped herself in her pandanus mat and curled up on the outrigger platform. Their companion craft was clearly visible off their stern and a little to windward, so he completely understood why his

[150] To tack or, more specifically, shunt. The tack of the sail is transported from one end of the canoe to the other, keeping the outrigger to windward.

[151] The northwesternmost islet of Kwajalein Atoll.

brother had let Erwina rest instead of keeping watch as he had ordered. He sheeted in, their rigging tightened in the steady breeze, and they glided a bit more quickly toward their destination.

A moment later, Erwina erupted with a jerk as she vomited yet again. Ijokelekel gave her time to recover from her gagging and then asked her to sit up. After asking her to hand him the center of her mat, he made two cross cuts with a shark's tooth device he kept at the base of his mast as a precautionary tool to cut rigging. He asked her to slide her head through and then to bundle the mat around herself for warmth.

"Your mother cursed me yesterday, but she cursed you long ago by convincing you that your seasickness was inevitable. It is not. Seasickness occurs when you separate yourself from the sea around you. Once you become one with it, you will overcome your urge to vomit. You curled up in your mat to separate yourself, as though it could protect you. It can't. Have you ever taken the helm?"

"Of course not. The sail will fall down."

"No, it won't. Let's trade places." He released the sheet and moved forward, leaving his place for her. All bundled in her *jaki*, she reluctantly complied.

Once she was in place and tucked in, he asked her to point to the wind. "Turn your face until you hear her whisper equally in both ears." After a bit of testing, she could do so. "Now," he continued, "your objective on this heading is to steer our boat to the right of the wind as soon as I apply tension to the sail by retracting the sheet." He sheeted in slightly. "Do you see how the bow turns toward the wind?"

"Yes," she answered.

"Okay, now grab the handle of your oar tied there in the water and pull it toward you until the bow begins to turn a little off wind again."

Erwina did as Ijokelekel had requested, and the direction of the bow turned back downwind. Then he sheeted in a little more, and the bow retraced its direction back to windward.

"Now apply a little more pressure. The more I sheet in, the greater the pressure necessary to keep your direction off wind." He sheeted in a little more to demonstrate, and she applied more pressure, and their craft began moving. A moment later, he sheeted in some more, and they began to move faster. Soon they were sailing parallel to their companion craft, which had caught up to them.

"Now I want you to point the boat directly into the wind."

She did so, and the boat slowed, and the sail's boom hit the mast on its lee side. Just as the sail was about to backwind, he stood, pushed against the mast to stop its fall, and ordered her to turn the boat off wind again.

"So, your objective is to steer to the right of this wind. Otherwise, you lose momentum and allow your sail to backwind and then fall."

He was a patient teacher and she, a good learner. She seemed to enjoy the challenge. Best of all, there was no more vomiting.

After a period of further practice, she asked seriously, "So that's it?"

"No, that's it for this wind and this heading in these wave conditions. Each wind, every wave condition, and — depending on your destination — every point of sail will have its own unique set of challenges. But the concept is simple and never varies. The bow wants to drift into the wind, and by preventing it from doing so with your tiller, you use the force of the wind to create forward movement."

"If only I'd had a father to teach me such things. Etre is a good man and would have taught me if my mother had let him. She has him tied like a pet bird. My father, I guess, was a free man she couldn't control. When we came this way to get our lines, she told me where to lie down in the little hut they built there on the platform and where to vomit. She told me if I came out, I would either fall overboard or be in the way."

"Well, my father didn't teach me either. I've had to learn from my own mistakes and from others, but I feel he's always there supporting me against whatever adversities I face."

"But our mothers were very different," responded Erwina. "Yours taught you to rely on your own decisions. Mine taught me to rely on hers. I figured out how good she is at lying when her words wouldn't fit my throat. She tried to convince me my father never loved me, and I knew that to be false. She said Pako probably killed him, but Ļōpako himself told me no and that he would take me to see him when I got older if I asked. She claimed that, because he was from a big island, he would never be interested in caring for our lands in such a small place as Lae. But everyone told me he didn't want to go, so they had to trick him into leaving. Wouldn't it be something if I take a man from Pohnpei who sails me back to Lae and we prove her completely wrong?"

"There are men on Pohnpei who were raised on the surrounding atolls who have proas and could get you safely home. What do you think Ļōpako will do when he realizes Kāmeto is gone?"

"I've been wondering about that myself. He's likely to do whatever Mother tells him to do. I'm afraid she'll make him promise to bring me home as soon as he finds me."

"I agree. That sounds like something she would say, but it's not likely Ļōpako will follow her instructions and stand between you and your father. He's likely more concerned about the welfare of Kāmeto, and he also promised something to me."

She was pensive. "Ijokelekel..." Then she sort of sat there, watching the sail and the sea, and said no more than she had the last time she'd called attention to his name. He got the feeling there was something important she needed to say again but couldn't find the words to get it out.

"Whatever he decides to do, it will be very well thought through. It's not like him to rush up and disrupt all our plans," he concluded.

So, it went like that, she learning to sail and each confessing their fears and aspirations to the other. The seasickness passed like a cloud, and by the time the morning star appeared in the east over the atoll's western reef and the moon — still high in the western sky — began to reflect a shiny path westward on the rolling surface of the sea, he was sure that Erwina had adjusted to her rhythms. The gentle sounds as their vessel turned and twisted from the oar under her arm no doubt distracted her nausea as they beckoned her forward. The sway she experienced was no longer abstract motion but the result of her own reaction to the sea beneath her.

They arrived midmorning. The elders, standing behind their new daughter and grandson, were anxiously waiting by the shores of their little abode as their proas glided into their calm harbor. He was immediately overtaken by a flood of memories as he breathed in the smell of this distant place where he had found love and nurture. And there was Lijāpe, looking older, arms wide to embrace him as she had that first day so long ago, and he remembered how good her embrace had felt — despite his terrible sun sores. There she was, demanding he stay, and he responding that they needed to beach oceanside at Wōjjā by the morrow's high tide. Though her face turned from sunshine to cloud covered, she maintained the courage to allow him to seek his own destiny despite what misgivings she held deep in the wrinkled throat that overflowed with love for him. She ambled quickly to her cookhouse to bring a basket of his favorite snack — *mokwaņ* with coconut baked in breadfruit leaves. Then she called to Ļōkijdik, who had prepared to bid them farewell with enough *jāānkun*, dried fish, and fresh coconuts to get them twice to Pohnpei and back.

As they loaded the craft, Lijāpe began questioning Erwina, so Ijokelekel seized the opportunity to walk down the beach to Anitok's proa. There Kāmeto sat, looking excited, bright eyed, and as attractive to him as always, but it appeared Maalal was guarding her carefully.

"Does your father know you left with us?" Ijokelekel asked Kāmeto.

"No—"

But before she could elaborate, Limaalal completed her statement for her. "I told her that, if she stayed, Ļañinni was sure to come after her with all his men and probably kill her father and anyone else who tried to protect her."

"We are going to escape to Pohnpei, aren't we?" asked Likāmeto.

Limaalal added, "I told her you might agree to take her with you. I promised Ļañinni I would bring her to Wōjjā. It's a bargain I struck to get my son back. If you escape quickly, he's unlikely to chase you to Pohnpei."

Of course, Ijokelekel knew — though Kāmeto perhaps did not — that Maalal must have had a motive to walk the reef and steal her away.

"Okay," she continued, "I made a deal with Ļañinni only to bring her. But I never promised she would take him. That's up to her! If she wants to escape to Pohnpei with us, that's up to her."

"Us?"

"My son, my son!" called his mother, beckoning him to return to his craft. He turned reluctantly from one conniver to the other.

"Come spend your last moments here with your mother. That one over there has been after you since you were an untattooed boy, and she'll still be after you as you sail away. But I approve of this one! This one would be a catch to make your mother proud. She is next in line, you know, and she has—"

"And we have a tide to meet!" He pressed her hand softly between both of his and, in that manner, bid her farewell. "She has to see her father in Pohnpei! That's the reason she's with us." Then he repeated the well-practiced phrase she had previously accepted. "When I return, we'll catch up on all my adventures."

Then he turned away from the motherly concern in her eyes to the destiny he knew lay out there somewhere amid the uncertainty he now felt confident to face. He launched his boat from the sand, paddled out of their little harbor, and asked Erwina to hoist sail.

"Your mother is cute. She assumes we are sleeping together," she said, hoisting the heavy matted sail. "I didn't have the throat to tell her we've taken each other as brother and sister."

"It's just as well. Knowing you are Likōkkālọk's eldest daughter, destined to inherit all her islands, alleviates her sorrow and makes it easier to let me go."

"She did seem to warm up to me once she knew who my mother was."

"That was probably the first question she asked. She never tires of reminding me that, if I don't want to end up working for her younger sister, I better take a woman with islands of her own."

"Do you think it's true, Ijokelekel, that most men take a woman for her lands and not for love?"

"If they listen to their mothers, yes. Their mothers love them and, I guess, are a bit sorrowful they can't leave lands to them and their children. But from my experience, most men don't think that far ahead. The saying *ṃōṃaan ṃaj*[152] didn't come from nowhere. From my experience, men talk more about the holes than the reef attached to the land they might be invited to work."

"You mean that's the way men compare one woman to another? You mean they talk about that? How disgusting!"

---

[152] Literally, "a man is an eel," which means that he always develops a relationship with a hole. "Mōṃaan" means "man"; "ṃaj" means "eel."

"Maybe the real point of the saying is to describe men as the animals we are," he responded.

The two boats retraced their way back through the ocean passage and out to sea. Kāmeto seized his attention by taking command from Anitok. Small, agile, and spirited, she liked to stand at the helm, where most men sat on the stern decking, as though teasing each passing swell to toss her into the sea. She created such a striking sight that, though tempted to chastise her, Ijokelekel found his darting glance landing more often on her than on his own sail and riggings. She seemed not to tire, and by midafternoon, they were deep into the stream of swells rolling between the atolls.

The last of Kwajalein disappeared into their wake, and he knew, due to their late start, they wouldn't see the northernmost islet called Namu until well after sunset. So, they slowly climbed the side of each swell to its peak as they headed on their course to the southeast. The wind shifted slightly in their favor as the sun set, and they entered the lee of the atoll as the moon angled its reflection across its glistening lagoon to their left. As he had the night before, he turned his helm over to Erwina, whose job was simply to follow the atoll's western reef until dawn. He slept and periodically awakened, remembering the sadness in Lijāpe's eyes but taking refuge in the thought she must have felt gratitude that he had returned her other son safely to her.

The next morning, he returned to the helm for their final ocean crossing. They encountered *buñtokrear* swells identical to those they had the day before, and they steered their craft over them at nearly the same angle. Anitok was back at his helm. By noon, Wōjjā began to appear across the horizon. They arrived at the high tide late in the afternoon and crossed over its famously becalmed ocean reef as planned.

Having arrived safely, he paid little attention to the storm clouds that had appeared along the horizon to the southwest. Simply knowing that Wōjjā had been mostly abandoned left him unprepared for what he next experienced. Gone was the sound of a hundred children laughing as they played along the ocean's shore. Gone the graceful sauntering of young women, the chiding with young men, themselves joking and taunting one another. In their place were dogs and pigs set loose to fend for themselves.

Empty homes waiting pathetically for their owners' return. Belongings dropped or left abandoned close to shore. Traces of their hasty departure everywhere. The mindset of such desertion hovered like a ghost sensed but unseen.

"We all loved the old man, but it was as though he died, was let to sea, and they all followed him," said Anitok.

After a few seasons away, the islanders' absence — the almost empty village — shocked Ijokelekel, but their clansmen greeted them warmly and escorted them to a *m̧ōn kweiļo̧k* to meet. He recognized most of the men there, primarily the same circle of initiates from the jib in jowi, their parents, and a few other brave souls from their clan who hadn't followed Taklur to sea. The sun had completely clouded over, and the first gusts of the oncoming storm rustled the palms around the meeting place. There was a rush by all to enter its shelter before the first wave of rainfall splashed onto them.

Anitok, the first to speak, needed to raise his voice over the early sounds of the approaching storm. First, he asked what developments had taken place since his departure. They replied that Ļañinni kept informants hiding among the abandoned homes around them. That every day the same actions by Ļañinni's men occurred as they had the day before. His men would appear in their proas and sail by their *wāto* brandishing their spears and beating their war drums. But the irooj himself was absent, and his men didn't set foot on shore. These were the same tactics they had used to chase off Taklur and his workers. However, unlike Taklur, despite their pledge not to take up arms against Ļañinni, the clan had responded each day by lining the shore, flourishing their own spears, clashing them one against the other, forming jebwa lines, and dancing to the beat of the *du*'s *aje*. If negotiations were to take place, fine. But the clan intended to show him — pledge or no — that Ļañinni would have to fight to take the land Taklur had given them.

Anitok reminded all that Ļañinni had requested Ijokelekel's return to arbitrate the future of his clan. He thanked him for leaving his apprenticeship with the famous Pako and showing loyalty to his brothers and sisters. Anitok stated he was certain Ijokelekel hadn't come all this way without bringing an option for them to consider.

Such was the hush when Ijokelekel stood to speak that the only sounds heard were those of the storm raging over the quiet anticipation of his clansmen and their chosen ones. An immature breadfruit fell here. A mature coconut shorn from a swaying palm thumped over there. The sound of rustling breadfruit leaves filled the air. Those torn loose blew around the courtyard surrounding the well-built shelter.

Purposefully setting the fact of the pledge aside, Ijokelekel began his comments with a question. "Which of you," he shouted above the din of the storm, "is willing to accept Ḷañinni as their irooj?"

Unspoken words and murmurs prevailed.

He had to shout over the storm, which threatened to drown out the sound of his voice. "Then you find yourself facing the same options as your fellow islanders who deserted these shores — fight or flee!

"I offer you a third option. Retreat with me to Pohnpei and find new lands there within its very abundant mountains. They have so much land they have yet to settle their deep, fertile valleys. There's so much water it runs uncollected into the sea. The people will welcome you to their shores," he concluded, noting the nodding assents of those around him.

Then, in afterthought, he shouted, "And if not, wouldn't it be better to make your stand there, where — at worst — they chase you onto land they don't want? Here, even if you negotiate surrender, will Ḷañinni not eventually fight like a dog for every foot of your territory? Will he not push your backs across the reef into the sea anyway? Was this not the wise Taklur's conclusion? And thus, the reason he led his people to sea?"

The group received Ijokelekel's option well, and they reached a consensus to follow him. But how were they to provision for a week's journey on such short notice? They were expecting Ḷañinni's men to return the next day. So, they decided to have the boys and the girls assist the elderly with the provisioning once the storm had subsided. When the rain finally passed, they built fires on the shore and practiced the jebwa to demonstrate they were prepared for any confrontation. Their hope was that these continued tactics might delay Ḷañinni's decision to attack. Their hope was that, on hearing of Ijokelekel's participation in the provocations, the wily Ḷañinni might pause to assess this new development before risking his men in battle. How Kāmeto's arrival might affect such assessment, Ijokelekel didn't know. He did realize he might be forced to fight for her.

So, one development quickly led to another, and Ijokelekel found himself parrying spears for the first time with his brother clansmen and preparing for a battle he hoped wouldn't occur. They were impressed with his newly developed jebwa skills, but was he truly ready to face his ruthless mentor? He had honed his dancing skills to perfection with some of the best, but he was untried in actual battle and knew he couldn't match his opponent's savagery. Nevertheless, this was his moment. All the elements of his destiny were falling into place. If he stood up to Ḷañinni, these men would follow him anywhere. He had come too far and held his purpose for too long to look back. He had no time for fear, yet it lingered there amid the shadows within the abandoned homes surrounding them.

Ḷañinni and his men came with the morning sun in the expected numbers. Ijokelekel and his clansmen lined up before the surf that rolled in waves onto the shore. Erwina stood at his side and a little behind, beating an *aje* she had borrowed for the battle. His clansmen's spears were ready to face down these intruders with a level of determination they hadn't exhibited in the days prior. They had a plan. So did Ḷañinni, who was leading his fleet of some ten proas at full sail, drums beating and spears brandished as they approached.

For a moment, it looked like their strategy might work and that their adversaries would sail by without landing as they had in the past. Then, all of a sudden, Ḷañinni's arm rose as though acknowledging someone, and his proa bulged its sail and turned directly toward shore. Each proa likewise pivoted to target its separate space on the beach. The waves they were riding shoreward had built through the night as they crossed the lagoon and were sure to make each boat vulnerable for a brief period upon reaching the shallows before the shoreline. That would be when its crew would have to steady their hull and push it through the surf as it broke onto them from behind.

This is where the clansmen's practice dancing along the shore was to return reward. With a simultaneous clash of spears, the lines separated into groups of four. Each group was to concentrate its twirling attack on their opponents the moment they — hopefully preoccupied with their craft — plunged into the surf. Not surprisingly, Ļañinni was the first to launch himself into the water. Steadying his prow with one hand, he speared his hardwood weapon into the sand to steady himself with the other. Ijokelekel and his men had already twirled their way across the beach and into the surf to accost him. Had Ļañinni come to talk or to fight? All eyes glanced periodically at Ijokelekel even as the clansmen spun in turn and violently clashed their spears.

Then, much to his humiliation, Likāmeto appeared out of nowhere and raced across the shore toward Ļañinni. Those who saw her stopped in midmotion, captivated by the sight of her arms outstretched toward the irooj. Was she giving herself up to him? Quick as a *kōtkōt*,[153] her slight body moved so swiftly through the surf that her arms met those of the irooj before a stunned and motionless Ijokelekel could interject himself between the two. What was she doing? She had paused their confrontation at the worst possible moment. Then, as their arms met in the surf and she unexpectedly withdrew one of hers in a rapid, downward motion at Ļañinni's wrist, it quickly became clear to all what her intention had been. She had turned his foolish embrace into an attack and sliced his forearm with what looked to Ijokelekel like her father's shark tooth ring. Then she held her bloody hand high for all to see before darting back across the beach, outrunning the spears thrown her way by the irooj's dumbfounded crew. Meanwhile, holding his wounded wrist, Ļañinni had collapsed and was lifted back aboard. Then the entire fleet turned back into the wind from which it had come and sailed in mutual retreat.

The celebration started with the *du*, whose ululations had continued throughout the confrontation, but upon seeing their enemy retreat, the women reached an unheard-of strength that must have carried across the thud of the surf to reach the very ears of the fallen one. One and then another of the groups began to clash their spears again as their lines reformed back on the shore, and they danced as they had the night before, treading their steps like footprints into the memories of the defeated.

---

[153] Ruddy turnstone: *Arenaria interpres*. Marshall Islanders used to trap these small birds and train them to fight.

The little woman who had inspired Ijokelekel's bravery and single-handedly defeated his enemy was now dancing among the *du*, her arms held high. The thick blood of the irooj painted her palm and ring-strapped wrist down into the curly thicket of hair beneath her underarm. Truly, from youth, she had steeped in her parents' heroic ilk, and her cry — much to his veneration — was "Away to Pohnpei!"

The awakening

Ļainjin had been wide awake for a while by the time the first of the roosters crowed. There had been an unusual amount of dog barking the night before. Youthful trysting, he had assumed. "Where do they get the energy?" he pondered. His bones aching, yet his face smiling, he rose carefully to sip *nen* tea warmed by the still-hot rocks of the ground oven that had cooked their meal the evening prior. He liked to warm himself this way in the cool morning air. His body had been talking to him for many seasons now. His strategy? Simply ignore the pain as he did Liṃanṃan's words of caution every time he launched his proa off into the lagoon. She had risen from their mat, silently stared at him for a moment, and then dropped back into her dreams. Had she learned not to disturb his morning thoughts? She knew this was the time he cherished the most — when his head was clearest and his day lay before him like the fresh smell of the sky after a brief rainstorm.

His thoughts that morning, as they did so often, swirled around his son. "Yes, after all these seasons a son…" He pondered this as he made the rounds up and down his famous *jekaro* trees and watched from on high the two craft approaching outside the atoll along the western reef. Now lingering in the last tree, he continued to reflect on his relationship with Ijokelekel. Such was his obsession these days, he thought he could distinguish him out there trolling for tuna toward the northern point. His throat leaped for him. He had wondered often, "Was he, in fact, his son?" They were so different in makeup it hardly seemed possible. However, the words he had brought from his mother, Lipanmai, and especially the lime fruits she had instructed the boy to bring were the clearest messages she could possibly have sent. At this point in his reflections, his thoughts would turn alluringly to their very private night together in the rainstorm, beneath the shelter, amid the water splashing down from its low-hanging eaves onto the takai where they had lain. To their writhing next to the fire atop the altar of Nahn Sapwe — he recalled her very taste, with the remnants of lime juice in her mouth — to their moment of mutual ecstasy as the spirit himself thundered his pleasure, perhaps at the sight of his union with such a faithful servant.

Why did he have no control over the tears that welled up at the thought of Lipanmai? How could he explain this to himself if not as an indication that she had crept into his sky and was there even now, comforting him with her spirit's embrace? Now looking seaward, he thought he could see women on both vessels. For seasons now, he had no longer been able to trust his sight. Life had lost the sharpness of youth, yet he had learned to carry on by mustering the combination of his other senses and by thinking more and moving with more caution. Why would there be women on a trip to catch fish? One even resembled his daughter: such were the tricks his sight and his obsessions were now playing on him. Wasn't Kāmeto still resting in his village below? She, along with her mother, Liṃanṃan — as well as Likōkkālọk and her daughter Erwina… Those four were the only ones to whom he had acknowledged his possible parenthood of Ijokelekel. He had to warn Kāmeto of any potentially incestuous relationship, but how could he tell the cherished young man he had been living a lie? That his so-called "father" was an exaggeration, and it was none other than he, who had carelessly copulated with his mother on the altar of Nahn Sapwe, who had fathered him? If he must tell him, and tell him he must, why now, when Ijokelekel needed to muster the self-assurance to avenge her death and complete his self-appointed destiny to free his people?

It wasn't until sometime after their morning meal that Lijoḷọk, much like a small child who knew she had disappointed her parents, announced that Kāmeto had left the islet at low tide the night before to accompany Ijokelekel on his quest. And it wasn't until they had completed a thorough search of her sleeping area that the elder couple convinced themselves she had, in fact, deserted them. The souvenir ring Ḷainjin had given her long ago wasn't dangling from the corner post where she liked to keep it. To him, that proved she had left for good. What he thought he had seen that morning had been confirmed.

"And why not?" argued Lijoḷọk. "Let the girl find her own destiny out there as each of us before her has successfully done." Little did she know why her sister and her chosen one were so upset at this announcement and buried the comment in frustrated silence. "What?" she continued, in hopes of soliciting a response.

Ḷainjin had always viewed his partner, Liṃanṃan, as the youthful woman who had carelessly cast her life into the sea for him. Yet she turned to him now with the look of an old and desperate woman that surprised even her sister.

"Go. Bring her back, or I will wither and die like a leaf torn from its tree. This is a storm I can't endure."

As Ḷainjin prepared provisions for his journey, word came that Likōkkālọk had summoned him. What now? Did she have a foot in this as well? He wanted to find out what she knew as immediately as possible, but prudence had taught him to concentrate first on his boat's lashings. Like the hero in the story Mānnijepḷā,[154] he had to begin his long journey by patiently rolling coils of sennit. Luckily, he was able to solicit the help of his group of helpful elders. Some rolled coils while others cut and replaced the boat's weak, tired, or frayed lashings until, by nightfall, they had succeeded in replacing nearly all.

The morning next, Liṃanṃan was there on the beach beside him while he loaded the provisions. He knew he didn't have to assure her that he shared her concern. The birth of their only child had been so difficult that she had been unable to produce others. As he had once upon a time stowed his fortune below decks, they had cast their hopes, their aspirations for posterity, and their very story itself on the destiny of a somewhat difficult, unruly, and overly willful offspring, and they were simply incapable of letting go.

---

[154] A mythic bird that flew passengers from one island to another; the legendary bird that could not be satisfied.

They hadn't told Lijoḷọk, who was still known for her inability to keep a single secret, that Ḷainjin could be Ijokelekel's father. Not knowing about and thus not apologizing for the incestuous encouragement she had inadvertently provided her young niece, Lijoḷọk appeared genuinely confused as, together, the two sisters wetted their skirts and pushed Ḷainjin's stern away from the shore of their remote refuge to glide out onto the rippling blue waters and toward the horizon.

Ḷainjin recalled Taknam's words. "If you start with the younger sister, the older will honor that relationship and keep her distance from you. But if you start with the older, the younger will pursue you as long as the older allows." He hadn't revealed the lust for the younger but had buried it deep within his throat throughout these seasons. It was a daily chore he enjoyed more than most. Did Joḷọk know how often he had to smother these desirous coals? She had never stopped teasing. He had never let down his guard. He could have drilled her a little each day as he had the cross spars he had lashed to his outrigger platform. Yet he had remained true to the woman who had rolled her father's canoe at sea that night and submerged herself flat on her back despite her fear of circling sharks. Women, so inscrutable, were somehow usually right. He probably should have fostered children with the younger, but then a man has a right to cherish his pride.

When Ḷainjin finally arrived at Likōkkālọk's island near noon that day, he hoped she would provide details that might shed light on the undertaking that now lay before him. He would not leave her island disappointed. The intense jealousy between her and Liṃanṃan surfaced immediately as Likōkkālọk accused Lijoḷọk of preventing his journey the evening before, when she had requested his presence.

"Destiny forbid you spend a night here away from her clutches," she said seductively, spatting the words into his face. Long after the fires in their bellies had cooled, the jealous rhetoric between the two had continued unabated.

He pointed to the new lashings.

"As though we have no *ekkwaḷ* here! I would personally have twisted that rope of yours till she heard you scream from her island over there."

"And what about my good friend Etre?" Ḷainjin asked.

"Etre went fishing last night. He still sleeps there in the house."

"We both know you didn't ask me here to twist my rope."

"Now that your lashings are all repaired, I'm sending you on an errand of utmost importance to me," Likōkkālọk said. "Erwina left with that ridiculous son of yours. I want her back. I never thought anything would come of his preposterous plans, and I'm sure nothing will, but I want her back long before his imprudent destiny begins to unravel. He's off to challenge Ḷañinni, who has apparently appointed himself paramount chief of Rālik and has driven Taklur and his islanders to sea. If Ijokelekel stumbles into a battle with him, you and I both know he won't last the blink of an eye!"

"Kāmeto accompanied him as well," Ḷainjin informed her.

"So that's where that *pẹjpetok*[155] went off to. They say one of Ḷañinni's concubines arrived with Ijokelekel's brother and another from Wōjjā and that the woman disappeared before the incoming tide. She must have walked into the night all the way north to steal her away. Maybe she brought Ḷañinni's threat to sail here and take her if she didn't comply?"

"I doubt that Ijokelekel intends to challenge Ḷañinni. He's probably after Taklur's men. Maybe he hopes they will follow him to Pohnpei."

"What would he say that they would be compelled to follow?" asked Likōkkālọk.

"He speaks of changing the way of life on Pohnpei to make it better for his people."

"So, they throw caution to the wind and blow away with the first fool who promises them change. What's to change? Our ancestors suffered enough. Look around at what they gave us. Ḷōpako, what's to change? If we must fight, we fight to preserve what we already have. Who's calling them to fight for Pohnpei?"

"He is," Ḷainjin said. "Have you not noticed his charisma?"

"No, I have noticed only foolishness! Enough of this. Go chase them down and bring our daughters back before he gets them killed."

With that, she ordered his boat laden with more provisions and she, too, wetted her skirts as she personally shoved his proa on its mission away from

[155] The spent core of a pandanus kernel drifting about in the ocean or up on shore; a drifter.

her shores. As he plunged his paddle into the lagoon, first to port and then to starboard, his thoughts turned to Paratak. "We men spill our seed too casually, my friend," he thought, as though Paratak himself had joined him on his journey. "Now we spend our final seasons sorting out the results."

"You correct again." Ḷainjin heard his friend's imaginary voice respond in broken Kajin Rālik.

He paddled out into the lagoon until the breeze that had filtered through the palms began to form ripples on its calm surface. Then he stood and drew his halyard, opened his sail to the breeze's wondrous pressure, and steered himself toward the passageway in the middle of the bright blue horizon before him. Upon hearing Liṃanṃan's plea, he had resolved once more to leave the sheltered pool around him and cast his lot to sea. This time, however, his hope was that wisdom rather than luck would allow him to accomplish his mission. He entered the passageway by noon then rounded the atoll to the south, opposite the heading of his son the morning before, chanting:

We are the men of this west-most place,
Quick tack, then tack back.
They're they. Yet we are us!

The chant was more for his imaginary companion than for himself. Meaning that instead of devising a course of two long tacks toward his objective, he would multitack his way southeast to take advantage of potential variations in wind direction. He knew its direction was usually variable at this point in the season, and taking advantage of that was the only way he could hope to beat his son in their race to Wōjjā.

Now Ḷainjin spoke to his imaginary friend. "As the direction of the wind veers southward, we will tack eastward across it. Then, as it veers eastward, we will *diak* and tack back toward the south."

"You always correct!" was Paratak's imagined response.

By late afternoon, Lae had settled beneath the sea behind him, and he noticed the first sign of the approaching storm in the line of grey across the horizon to the southwest. A while later, he took solace in the dark grey clouds billowing above the lighter horizontal wind line. He interpreted these as more or less friendly rain clouds that would serve to dampen the force of the approaching gale. His craft and its all-important sail wouldn't be at risk provided he lower his halyard in a timely manner. In his younger days, he had loved to catch the foregusts of an oncoming storm and race across the still-unturbulent waters before striking his sail at the very onset of its preliminary gust. Today, he would forgo the excitement and take advantage of the interim by preparing his craft to drift well before the blow began.

By the time the storm arrived, he had lowered his sail and furled it around its two *rojak*. He had propped the resulting rigging to port and tightened the sheet to secure the streamlined assemblage. Finally, he had turned the *kubaak* to starboard, battened down his forward hatch, and seated himself in his hull, peering up at the clouds as they rushed overhead. The first wave of horizontal rain slapped and refreshed his sunburned face. Then he propped a pandanus mat between his back and the open hatch around him, letting the wind and the rain blow over him as he watched their torrent transform the sea, which rolled progressively more steeply beneath. While he sat there beneath this cover, scrutinizing the whitecaps looming about, he judged — from the feel of the underlying swell — that the wind had begun blowing him back in the general direction from whence he had come.

He showed his imaginary friend how to judge their drift by tossing a spent immature coconut into the water and watching it float back over the waves to windward. They conservatively agreed that, at minimum, they would fall another half day behind their progeny. There was no course of action left except to absorb, as best he could, the powerful presence of the storm. He had always loved to open his soul to its spirit, especially one like this, which growled but mildly, like an accepting dog that means only to remind an intruder that it's the master of its territory. He sat like that, enjoying his ride upon the ever-sharpening waves, until darkness settled upon him. Then he battened the rear hatch and braced himself as best he could amid the black wetness of his rocking hull.

Up to this point, luck had graced his life. Yet ever since Ijokelekel had told of Lipanmai's tragic ending, a certain sadness had crept into him. As it had before, upon the natural death of Ḷōpedpedin. As it had upon hearing the ill-fated news that Taknam had died as she searched through a storm for her visiting great-grandson from her sister's side. She had been struck by a falling coconut and found stiff, off the path, the next morning. The boy, as happenstance would have it, had taken shelter among the neighbor's children.

Ļainjin realized he hadn't treated Lipanmai well, and this saddened him. With Talupe[156] the callous trader, the inexperienced boy that he was had confused love with desire. With Lipanmai, he realized now, he had deluded himself the opposite way. Truly, she was the one deserving of his love.

He should have known she had borne him a son. He should have returned to Pohnpei and saved her from her unhappy end. The image of her vomiting as he had been hoisted from the well, gripping the putrid remains of Nahn Samohl, was vivid and more meaningful now. Of course, she had been with child. He had failed her, yet in her simple, unassuming manner, her only request in response had been to implore him to instruct their son, Ijokelekel. He thought back to their moment of separation, and tears flooded his eyes as he enunciated the many syllables of the young man's name off the roof of his mouth. Deep down in his throat, he knew he was ready now to sacrifice his life to protect him. If only he had stopped in Pohnpei upon his return from Sigaba.[157]

Now the sound of his mother's words, as though she were there in the ocean, on the outside of his convulsing hull, came to him once again. "Your calling is complete. You must remember to return now. There is a reason why the mother turtle returns to the island of her birth. Life preserves itself that way. Promise me now you will return to Rālik. Sink your roots into the clean coral sand. Lay your mat upon the ancient platform of coral stones brought forth from the beaches by your ancestors. There you will find your life's mate. Remember to love each other. You must come to know each other. Such is more likely to occur with a woman of your own kind. You must teach our *ikir*[158] to the next generation. Show them how to overcome

[156] The ambitious Pohnpeian woman who captures Ļainjin's attention.

[157] Later called Sio Island, a "place of mixing." A precontact trading center located off the Kunai coast of the Huon Peninsula of southeastern New Guinea.

[158] A navigational poem.

despair, and pass on the assurances that their ancestors sailed forth before them, survived their journeys, and prevailed to sing about them."

So, he had purposefully rested only among the outer atolls surrounding the stone altar. As soon as he heard Ijokelekel's story, it became clear to him that, had he returned, he would have lingered to raise his son there. Lipanmai was a creature of her environment. She and her altar were inseparable. He could never have successfully transplanted her like a banana cutting to his homeland. She would have ended up like a fish that had taken flight and landed on a shore somewhere, struggling for breath. Yes, he had abandoned his paramour Lipanmai, and after spending half his life finding her, committed himself to his mother's dying wish.

Yet the knowledge he had failed Lipanmai had brought a bleakness to his life. He wasn't one to fail those who depended on him, or had he just become numb to it? Had he not failed poor Lirojak[159] in one way or another? What about his ill-fated friends the palu and Ļōbwilñawa?[160] Wasn't it his plan that had failed them? Hadn't they given their lives to complete his mission? And what about Ngalen? Hadn't he left her to the devices of her Kingfisher?

"It is indeed a bleak night," he thought, "when a man finds himself trapped like this by circumstances beyond his control, leaving him to wonder, had he done this rather than that, about the difference it might have made to the lives of those he has admired and loved."

Thus, he pondered on into the night as the waves continued to steepen, and the rocking chafed his elbows and knees against the pandanus matting he had bundled himself in. True, he had been successful in teaching the *ikir* to a good many promising *rūkkatak* over the years. He had completed his mother's mission well, but was he ready — at this late stage of his life — to begin another journey, perhaps one more difficult than the last? He had to be. The two women with whom he shared his life were both insisting on it.

Relations had gone well enough between the two. Liṃanṃan had asked her sister Joļọk to spread her story of how she had seen Likōkkālọk cleaning Ļainjin's seed from his pandanus sleeping mat and impregnating

---

[159] Aka Rojak. Female Seeker; Lañinpo's sister.

[160] A Seeker; aka Bwilñawa; the rijeļā. Ļō: the male prefix, used to emphasize respect.

herself with it. By the time their daughter was born, Likōkkālọk blatantly acknowledged this truth to all by naming their daughter Jaki, and Ḷainjin participated in his daughter's *keemem* as would any father. He had heard rumors that, in private, she told false stories of torturing his mast as he had straddled her horizontal trysting tree beside the ocean. If his friend Etre had heard such nonsense, he showed no signs of jealousy. He and the young man were still the best of friends though their conversation did avoid certain topics. As for the rest of Ḷainjin's *jekaro* boys, they had all grown, raised families, and trained others to take their trees. Some had become his *rūkkatak*, learned his *ikir*, and followed him to sea to study the swell patterns first distinguished by their ancestors. He decided to tell one — and only one — his story and trust him to pass it on to only one *rūkkatak*. In this way, the story of his mother's end would become encapsulated in secrecy but not forever lost.

Thus, his thoughts came like the waves, one after the next though seemingly repeating themselves after a time as his hull slid down into the trough of each and his outrigger float climbed the following crest, culminating in an increasingly violent whitecap slap as the storm wore on and then peaked. From time to time, he overcame his desire to maintain his uneasy recline amid the torrent about him. Then he would burst up through his hatch into the fresh air and rain to quickly tighten his rigging, catch a glimpse of the storm's effects on the surface of the sea, and chant "Emejjia wa ilọmeto" before retreating and securing his hatch once again, like a hermit crab withdrawing to safety within his impenetrable shell. Then, after the rain had stopped and the worst had passed, he began asking himself whether it was time. But each time, the condition of the sea and the wind said *no*, though he had vowed to hoist his sail as soon as he was able.

Finally, he saw the morning star peeping through the still-rushing clouds. The sighting of a star gave him permission to raise his sail once again and brave the storm's tailwind. Even with the oncoming elements blowing strong against him, he sensed the temperament of the storm had ebbed such that he could now profitably challenge them. He had a lot of distance to recover and not much time before the eventual lull of the storm's aftermath would stall his pursuit. So, craft teetering frenziedly, sail fluttering wildly upon uphaul, he hauled sheet and headed as close to the oncoming elements as conditions allowed.

"This sea is different from the swells you rode upon on your way to back to Pohnpei," he thought, once again reaching out of his aloneness to his imaginary friend Paratak. "During that period, your craft rose high on their crests and dropped low into their wide troughs."

"Up down, up down like stick worm," replied the Paratak he knew and loved.

Ḷainjin responded in his thoughts. "You remember your lessons well, my friend."

"No friend to send another unprepared into sea without paddle," retorted Paratak.

"Well, look at you now. According to Ijokelekel, you sit fat on your island with my title there on your chest for all to see and admire. I'm told they even call you 'pali.' So, listen to your mentor. This portion of a storm's aftermath brings rough but short-period waves that rock our craft, undulate our bow, impede our progress, and sap the remainder of our energy. Yet we will press on even as our eyelids become heavy with the desire to sleep and even as our bodies ache from the trials of the storm past. Why? Because we know the wind will gradually subside as the damp morning turns dry by noon. Then, trying our patience even more, the sharp crests will eventually abate, the sky will change to wispy calm, and the last of its whispers will turn variable."

"So, then we sleep?" asked his imaginary friend.

"Then we sleep."

Once more, after all he had predicted eventually passed — this time, in the midst of the calm — Ḷainjin lowered and then secured his sail and, twice as exhausted as before, returned to his hull and slept.

At the first breath of fresh breeze, he woke to face a black, shimmering sea and a black yet bright starlit sky. Before taking time to eat, he again raised sail and headed off to the southeast. Although uncertain of his position, he would remain determined to hold this heading until he reached landfall. The lull that followed the storm's tailwind had calmed the sea, so though the breeze was light, there was no chop to impede his progress into the uncertain stretch of ocean before him. Nevertheless, *buñtokrear* had diminished enough to assure him that his position lay somewhere in Kwajalein's shadow but not close enough to the atoll for its counterswell *kāleptak* to become predominant. He ate, sucked coconut, and watched the moon — a quarter diminished — first brighten, then rise above the flat horizon surrounding him. He felt rested, cheered by the combination of breeze upon light seas, and ready to face the trials ahead.

He didn't sleep and watched the moon rise through a cloudless sky to outshine the stars beyond it. Then Jebrọ rose, and then the morning star that announced the dawning that was soon to come. He sailed on past the morning into the bright afternoon without sleep because the new day had brought a somewhat stiffened wind and, with it, the hope he might catch his progeny before disaster struck. Around dusk, he noticed *buñtokrear* building on his left and didn't fail to point it out to his imaginary companion.

"Feel the swell from the east building. We are passing from under the shadow of Kwajalein."

Then, halfway through the night, an island appeared in his path, and he knew exactly where he was. It wasn't an atoll islet. It was the single island of Lib, which marked the halfway point on the direct course between Lae and Wōjjā.

"It serves as a rock in the ocean stream between Kwajalein and Namu," he told himself, pointing through the pale moonlight of the diminished moon. "I felt it coming long before it came into view."

"Good, we go ashore now and eat hot food," he imagined his friend saying.

"No, we won't waste the time. We'll sail tight into her shadow, strike sail, lay to, sleep, and drift softly to lee of the stream. This will be much like a nap with Likōkkālọk's leg wrapped like a warm mat over you. When you wake, you'll quickly recover your position of the night before."

Ḷainjin imagined his friend looking quizzically at his face, not knowing if he was serious or if he should laugh. He had to admit it was a sick thing to say to a man who would probably never recover from the pain such a woman can inflict upon a man's life. It was no wonder that Ijokelekel had reported that Paratak hadn't taken another. She had taken his soul and left him a shell of his former self. And he, Ḷainjin, had been complicit and must eventually face his friend again. He would have to consider the right approach.

"Sorry if I touched an old wound, my friend," he thought, drifting off to sleep.

The next morning, he woke at dawn and, as promised, quickly recovered his position of the night before. He would sail all day, reaching Namu's shadow by midafternoon, reaching her southern tip early that evening, and repeating the tactic of the night before. The last thing Ḷainjin wanted to do was to face trouble on Wōjjā without the sleep he needed to replenish his stamina. Would he be fighting Ḷañinni the next day? This would be the second time he had entered the turtle's cave. Ḷañinni would be wary of his moves and not easily coaxed out into the open, where enemy-laid plans might foil his intentions. Yes, his young daughter had spurned Ḷañinni. True, but no man then attacks a girl's father. No, his predicament was because Likōkkālọk had then rubbed salt into Ḷañinni's wounds in a public performance before retreating into a storm, leaving Ḷañinni taunted, embarrassed, and vengeful.

Ḷainjin spent the night contemplating Taknam's response when he had asked her, before stepping foot on Lae, what his most difficult task would be.

"The most difficult will be resisting my niece, Likōkkālọk. She will do everything in her power to get onto your sleeping mat. She is very cunning, and she will not respect Liṃanṃan's choice or yours. If you're not careful, she'll pluck you out of the water like a fish and swallow you before you know what's happened!"

Now, years later, he could commend himself for countering many of her advances. He had fought and won many battles on her behalf, but as he had confessed to Paratak, she had successfully complicated his life to no end. Now, she had sent him once again — tired and no longer the spry man he once was — to battle against perhaps his greatest opponent with a more than likely chance of meeting his story's end.

"Then so be cast," he whispered into the morning's breeze, raising his halyard then setting his course on what he imagined would be the final leg of his journey.

Ḷainjin arrived off Wōjjā's ocean side midafternoon. *Kāleptak*'s deep blue swells were gently rolling over the edge of the colorful reef. The neap tide had already receded from its high point of flow, leaving his canoe unable to reach what appeared to be a recently abandoned beach. Whole, freshly cut pandanus fruits rolled in the calm surf, discarded mats lay on the bright sand, and newly made kilts and skirts hung from green branches along the strand, all as though ordered cast aside by someone other than their owner. He left his boat grounded on the reef in the sloshing tide and walked a well-worn path to the apparently abandoned village. His unsteady legs were happy for the exercise. Gone was the bustle of the village he had known. He half-expected to find dead bodies, the results of a vicious battle, and felt relieved when he saw none. The story he had heard was true. Taklur and his followers had deserted their island for parts unknown.

Somehow, he felt the presence of another as he approached one of many vacant homes about him. There in the doorway appeared a bent old man who had to turn sideways to peer back at him.

"Pako?" he asked.

Ḷainjin inhaled and wheezed his assent.

"Enter, but you come too late," the old man said. "The battle lasted but a moment. Your daughter wounded Ḷañinni as he disembarked there in the lagoon surf. She took the rest of the Rilujien Naṃo with her and sailed, they say, for Pohnpei. As it turned out, she didn't need the help of any man — cut the vain fool when he opened his arms to her. Stunned him quick as a stingray. What did you name that one? Kāmeto? You got what you asked for, one fierce *kōtkōt*!"

Ḷainjin, left stunned himself by the old man's words, stood speechless in the doorway.

"Hungry?" the old man asked. With the tip of his cane, he lifted a coconut-leaf basket by its handle from where it hung and flopped it into Ḷainjin's open hands.

"Chicken! I've been eating chicken for two days now. So few people are around to feed them, they rush right up — as unalarmed as poor Ḷañinni. I clubbed one of them on the nape of its foolish neck. Sit!" he ordered, laughing and wagging his cane as though about to strike him as well.

Ḷainjin did as commanded and obediently began to gnaw at the tough but tasty meat.

"She's following that Pohnpeian. The one with the long name and the charisma to go with it. I noticed him right off. Eager to climb to the top of my tallest trees and cut coconuts for others then sit like a child and listen to my stories. He was the only one of his *jowi* to impress Ḷañinni, who let him become the hero for his fellow initiates. Then, the other day, he was the one to lead this same group to stand up to the irooj. Crazy brave, that one. Just like that daughter of yours. Crazy pair there.

"Now he's got them off to Pohnpei to seek their destiny there. Thanks, I'll meet mine here. You'd think this village is empty, but trust me, plenty of others were smart enough to stay in their homes and wait for Ḷañinni to recover and take control. He'll let us be. He doesn't care who is *alap* or no, and neither do we. What's the purpose of a title anyway? 'Cut my coconuts up there. Harvest my pandanus there. Eat my breadfruit as you wish.' These are words, only words. Who cares who owns the fruit? An ancient saying comes to mind: '*Am wōt kwoj amine.*'[161] Ḷañinni and his followers can't possibly eat all the food that falls from these trees. So, what's the value of title when there's more food than people to eat it? Those young ones who followed the charismatic one should have gathered round and listened to me as they did when they were children. Instead, they grew up too smart to listen to an old man they consider too bent over to see what's in front of him."

With that, the old man speared another basket with his cane and smoothly set it in front of Ḷainjin. It contained a freshly baked breadfruit.

Later, after Ḷainjin had returned the old man's kindness by cutting loose a few bunches of coconuts for him, they gathered a few of the many freshly cut fronds discarded by the others and washed up along the shore. Then together, they used them as rollers to nudge his heavy canoe back into the slowly receding tide.

Venerable storyteller that he was, the old man released his last words immediately upon Ḷainjin's departure. "The way I see it, Ḷañinni's intention was to negotiate, but someone worked to turn his plan against him. A jealous woman would be my guess."

---

[161] "Yours is what you use."

Sau-temoi

Wading into the surf, Kāmeto, somewhat to Ijokelekel's surprise, approached his stern from its port side, braced herself upon its bulwarks, and climbed aboard to take his place before the tiller. No sooner had they crossed the reef, plied the breakers, and reached *kāleptak*'s rolling swells than she seized full command and ordered the crew to *diak* and head south along the reef, as though intending to chase her foe back to his lair at Āne-piñ. Stunned again by her boldness, Ijokelekel sat opposite her on his outrigger's deck, speechless and deposed. His back was to Erwina, who faced the bow and unselfishly allowed the younger woman to seize all the attention. Erwina leaned her back against his, and they sat there supported by each other.

They now had twenty-two families in scantily manned boats, ten in all. In turn, all of them flipped sail and followed her. Kāmeto stood upon his stern deck, Ļañinni's caked blood still splattered where it had spurted onto her, back shoulder braced against backstay. Her tiller in one hand, she shaded her eyes with the other. This was her moment. She seemed to be searching the shoreline for something or someone. What or who was she looking for?

They rounded Wōjjā's southernmost tip and headed southeast along a stretch of nearly islet-less reef. There, close to the end of that stretch of reef, she found them. Two diminutive figures — caught, no doubt, by the morning's incoming tide — stood grounded and hailing them from the tip of a wave-washed sandbank attached to a tiny islet that boasted but a single clump of growth too small to attract even a single flock of birds. Suddenly, Ijokelekel somehow recalled that, amid the recent excitement, he had lost track of Maalal. Was that her, perhaps accompanied by her toddling son? Had she walked the reef the night of the storm to steal him away during Ḷañinni's absence the next morning? Yes, a proud glance from Kāmeto was all he needed to confirm that she had promised not to leave Maalal if she was unable to make it back to Wōjjā with the child the following night. Had the two conspired to spurn the irooj and steal his son at the same time? The love, the trust, the respect that seemed to have developed between these two over such a brief period was beyond his comprehension, of course. The mysterious nature of women.

Kāmeto steered them diagonally over the *kāleptak* swells that broke gently onto the edge of the sand-strewn reef toward the stranded pair. Erwina lowered sail and then debarked with Kāmeto but stayed to steady their craft in the surf. The rest of their small fleet lowered sail and drifted in wait. The two women splashed through the gentle surf toward each other and embraced as long-lost sisters amid the ever-moving glistening blue around them. Maalal's son plunged bravely into the water by her side until Kāmeto picked him up and carried him on her hip the rest of the way. Ijokelekel had to admit it was an inspiring sight.

Back on board, Kāmeto was preoccupied and allowed Ijokelekel to reclaim control of his craft. The three women, chattering like night birds, had lost all interest in their bearings. Maalal's son was their center of attention. Nevertheless, Ijokelekel ordered them to flip sail and guided them back across the reef and out to sea, his followers in tow. Though he had regained the helm, he was clearly their leader in name only. He felt as if he had just pointed these three in the right direction. Their counsel would fashion their mutual fate.

They headed due west, mostly downwind, for over a day. He listened as best he could to the story of Maalal's successful quest to steal her son. As it turned out, she had no knowledge of Ḷañinni's condition, having long departed his village by the time of his untimely return, and she seemed surprisingly unsympathetic to his potential fate.

The winds were light and variable beneath a sky of few clouds. As previously planned, they began searching for Taklur's drifting fleet by zigzagging across a broad stretch of ocean, tacking to port then starboard then back to port in a timely manner at the sound of the conch from Ijokelekel's vessel. They fanned out in a line, each vessel staying within the sound of the conch to its right and left. He ordered the conch to sound as often as needed, depending on the strength of the wind, to ensure that they kept a steady view of the ocean around them. On the afternoon of the second day, someone on the left flank sounded an alarm. They had spotted at least one of the searched-for drifters.

By the time they reached the drifters' vessels, others from Ijokelekel's group had already begun to congregate. Most had struck sails. Some crews paddled. Some boats were sailing around the others, encouraging further gathering. A half-moon's passing of daily sun had devastated the drifters, such that upon taking water, their first request was to sound conches to summon together their group, as they had long lacked the initiative or reason to do so. So, all drifted together and passed their time locating sails here and there, creeping from all directions across the horizons. That was when Ijokelekel's confidence that his plan would get its chance for success grew. Everyone passed the word that they were to fend off their drifting crafts, one from another, yet form the tightest circle possible.

Luckily, the winds were so light that the gently rolling surface of the ocean's swells permitted such a gathering. A first concerted look at the survivors left an impression of the sun's relentless propensity to overwhelm. As any sailor can attest, its first appearance after a chilly night at sea is most welcomed. Its angled morning light inspires, and its warmth comforts. The dryness it brings is most useful to expel the night's dampness from kilt and skirt and matting. Yet by late morning, the sweat from its heat and its reflection off the sea begin to burn the eyes shut, and by noon, it is sucking water from the body as a spider does to prey caught in its net.

The green sea moss that had grown thick on the hulls and outrigger floats of these drifting craft had attracted an aggregation of colorful sea creatures that darted through the blue water below. Yet, upon the clear rippling water that thrived with life beneath them, the drifters appeared utterly defeated and disengaged. They were so unhungry they asked not for food but only water, so uninvolved they were not fishing. They were simply exhausted —

as though they, and not the fire above them, had daily tread the entire distance of the horizon. Sapped of their strength, they had, at some point, given up. They had accepted their fate and perhaps encouraged their children to do the same.

However, it appeared as though they had kept the children out of the sun's slow but effective torture, either by sending them below or into the small huts they had built on the outrigger platforms. The children immediately caught the attention of Ijokelekel's crew as they popped up here and there with a surprising spark of life amid the utter despondence around them. With some hesitation, one girl waved meekly at Erwina as she raised her head, covered by matting, above the bulwarks of an adjacent canoe. Perhaps touched by the girl's plea for hope, the motherless woman entered the water and swam to her side. Then, as the boats from both groups began to paddle and merge, others followed her example. Disregarding the sharks circling around them, the crews began to enter the water and, on occasion, lead a willing child or two from a boat filled with despair to one of hope. Surprisingly, such was their anguish that not a single mother complained or clung to her child. However, it was Ijokelekel's vision to rescue not only these few but the lot of them.

These boats, of course, were but a small portion of the original fleet that had set to drift. The storm and its aftermath had scattered their group everywhere. Some of the drifters, the rescuers heard, had shaded themselves from the sun by unfolding their sails, but they had drifted much faster than the others and were now long gone. They had caught fish and collected rain along the way, but the weather damage to those who had remained unprotected depleted their stamina and cracked their skin so severely that they could hardly move. When the last of the far-flung sails had finally arrived and lowered halyards and the last of the conches had fallen silent, the others' boats crowded around Ijokelekel. He ordered his clan to distribute their freshly husked coconuts from craft to craft, one to each survivor. The time for his message to them was at hand.

"Despond not my friends! We have come to release you from your commitment to follow the irooj that you love and have served well. Perhaps he still drifts to his destiny beyond the horizon, yet in your throats, you know that his glorious story has already ended. Let him drift forever in our memories as a great man who gave us generations of peace and prosperity.

"Our story's end, however, is yet to be told. There is an island due west from here with the great stone village you have heard of, its walls so tall your necks will ache as you bend backward to view their apex. This is an island so large that its vast interior lies yet unclaimed and has not been worked by any commoner. This island calls to you. Its name means "upon a stone altar." It is the altar of Nahn Sapwe, the spirit of thunder. My mother served that altar until her untimely death, and she calls to you now to raise your sails and follow us to your new destiny. Choose life, my friends. Choose your children and your children's children over your grandparents and their elders. You have completed your work for Taklur. Raise your sails now and claim a new life for yourselves."

This last he said with emphasis, as though expecting the group to follow his suggestion, chant their assent, and raise their rigging to points westward. Anticipating his command, his clan members had taughtened their halyards, as had Kāmeto. However, an awkward silence followed his words. There was no response from Taklur's workers, so he quickly stayed her hands from hoisting.

Then the voice of an elder shouted, "Ijokelekel, is it true you claim your father is this Nahn Sapwe, this spirit of thunder?" Much laughter from the crowd accompanied his question.

Maalal, her hands on her boy's shoulders, cringed at the blunt ridicule but recognized the voice. She shouted, "Pailañ, you are the son of Jeilañ, are you not?"

Pailañ did not respond, but enough heads raised and wheezed in assent that all knew she had gotten it right.

Finally, he responded. Standing, he said, "Yes, I am the son of Jeilañ, and I am proud to be called his son."

Maalal gazed over at Ijokelekel, tossing him the opportunity to respond.

"Why do they call you the son of Jeilañ?" Ijokelekel countered. "Because he acknowledged you as such. But what would you have done if you were acknowledged by no man? You might have done what I did: choose the most powerful one out there and claim him as your father."

At this, the whole group roared with laughter. Ijokelekel's self-deprecating remark had buoyed his prior speech and added the personality and levity needed to instill trust. He saw a proud sparkle in Maalal's eye. She, too, seemed to feel the tide turning in his favor.

Then a second voice from the crowd rang out. "So, according to your plan, the irooj of Pohnpei is supposed to look out and see a multitude of sails, and instead of ordering us killed as we set foot on his beaches, he'll give us lands to plant. What makes you so sure of this?"

"My plan is Taklur's plan, only my plan works faster. He no doubt anticipated that some of you would drift up on Pohnpei, some of you elsewhere. However, under his plan, some of you would have died and shriveled by the time you arrived. My idea is to lead you to the island more quickly. We will disguise our numbers. The most tired or sick will drift ashore first. Others later. Some on the east, some on the south, and so forth. The commoners of Pohnpei are kind. They will accept you, as newcomers generally are. You'll learn their language. When asked about your story, you'll simply tell the truth, and you won't fail to mention my name as the one who pointed you there. Tell whoever you meet that Ijokelekel is coming to avenge his mother's death. If you hear of a battle, you may join in or no, depending on your inclination at that time. That's it. That's your part. I expect nothing of you other than to live. Let us fish and eat and build strength for the voyage ahead."

He knew the men were dying to lower their lures because the drifted vessels had attracted a large circle of many types of sea life. So, they fished, and they ate, and they chummed, and they fished again until they had a large store of fish to dry. And one by one, the men from the boats with underlying sea moss entered the water with their adzes and began scraping themselves free of its grip. The next morning, they fanned out as they had before, only this time their line was all the longer. And as they sailed, they delayed often as they met others adrift and recruited them to their cause as well. After many days of formation but before the moon had waned to a sliver before dawn, they sighted the island. Ijokelekel filled vessels with the sickest and their families and sent them ashore first. However, he chose one of their stronger to accompany them ashore and assigned him the task of seeking out a man called Paratak.

"Tell him Ijokelekel is at sea and wishes to speak with him. Ask him to travel to Nahlap and, on a clear evening, to build a large fire on the beach. That will be my sign to come ashore that very night."

So, Ijokelekel hid his fleet below the horizon during the following days and crept toward the island's barrier reef toward dusk, when he would release a single vessel holding the weakest among them. Nahlap was an island on the reef fringing the Rontiki passageway. Unlike most islands within the barrier reef skirting most of the perimeter of Pohnpei, this islet, not overgrown with mangrove, offered direct access to the ocean. Perhaps it reminded Paratak of Lae, because he loved to visit there and often remarked that its beaches were "clean and not cluttered with mangrove." With much nostalgia, he had often talked of the Rālik atolls as open and airy and superior to his home island's obstructed view of the ocean. On a windless day, if you climbed a tree, you could see the outlying atoll of Ant[162] to the west. Ijokelekel had always wanted to sail on to see what it was like, but Paratak had always refused, explaining that it was too far or dangerous, or it would be dark before they could return.

On the night of the moon's first appearance, the fleet drifted in the open ocean off Pohnpei's southwestern edge, close to the Rontiki passage. Most of the crew slept as they rose on the black swells and then fell, watching the moon's thin crescent of dim light sink behind the mountains, beneath the backdrop of countless points of increasingly glowing starlight.

Though apprehensive, Erwina was excited about the prospect of meeting her father. "Ijokelekel, is it true my father is stupid?"

"No! Your father is not stupid."

"Well, that's what my mother told me every day."

That's when Ijokelekel realized, even after all the nasty words, he still had a sense of loyalty to Likōkkālọk. Was he still under her spell? He told Erwina, "Perhaps she meant to say that he is stubborn. He likes to make up his own mind, and he deliberates a long time before accepting an opinion. I'll say this for him: once he makes up his mind, there is no more thought of turning back. That probably wasn't the kind of reaction your mother wanted. She probably expected him to respond more … obediently."

---

[162] A coral atoll seven miles east of what is now called Pohnpei.

"You're right. She hates it when people don't do exactly what she wants. Ijokelekel, she is right most of the time. She has great faith in her powers to foresee what's best. Tell me again why you have to return your proa to… What's the name of that place?"

"Kelepwei. It's the islet for visitors across the channel from Pahn Kadira, the islet of the Saudeleur." Assuming things went well with Paratak, he was planning on taking Erwina with him as his single crew to return Lañinpo's proa. "This proa isn't mine. I borrowed it and must now return it to its owner, a man called Lañinpo."

"That's the one you said eats people. Why would you want to give his proa back?"

"Two reasons. One, it's the right thing to do. He was kind to me, even as I stole his canoe. Two, my plan is to anchor my name again in the stone village. When his canoe appears out of nowhere, it will be something to talk about, and the name Ijokelekel will circulate again. Hopefully, they will no longer speak of me as a thief, but as someone honorable enough to return Lañinpo's proa. The disenchanted among them may remember my mother's death and perhaps begin to think of me as their hope to set things right again. The Saudeleur will begin hearing my name — perhaps the rumor I'm at sea with warriors — and wonder when and where I'll come ashore. He'll think, 'Why has he returned?' I want him to suffer his defeat long before it occurs."

"*Jeej*![163] Ijokelekel, you are serious about all this, aren't you?"

But he was now concentrating on a light that had begun to flicker on shore.

"Ijokelekel, is that him?"

He provided no direct answer but instead released a low, muffled burst of air through his conch shell. This awakened the rest of his crew, who began executing his plan to move them and their belongings to Anitok's proa. According to plan, the fleet would fish the outer reef under cover of black night and then, under Anitok's command, retreat beneath the horizon before dawn. Ijokelekel and Erwina alone would sail into the broad mouth of the Rontiki channel, which eventually twists around the various reefs and

[163] An idiom used to express surprise. Translates roughly as "heck" or "darn it."

mangrove-lined channels to the village, out of sight and far ahead. But that wouldn't be their destination. There — close by, on the left side at the very entrance of the bay — lay Nahlap. When he was a boy, it was their favorite place to rest before returning home with their day's catch.

Erwina stood on the foredeck as they approached the islet's fringing reef, steadying herself there by clutching the forestay. Under the starlight, she directed him to the left or right, above the deepest crevice beneath the waves onto the flooded reef flat. All the while, they could see her father, blinded by the blaze of his fire, continuing to load timbers and oblivious to their approach, muffled as it was by the surf.

"Papa!" she cried, after releasing the halyard as Ijokelekel paddled vigorously through the surf toward shore. They saw Paratak, still blinded by the light, turn his ears to the sound of her voice in the darkness. Jumping prematurely into the waist-high water, she waded toward shore. On his part, Ijokelekel disembarked to steady his proa and guide it safely forward. Erwina halted her advance, set aside the mature leadership role she had assumed, and turned back into a vulnerable girl again. Standing in shin-deep water, she waited for her father's blank stare to eventually focus on her as he timidly advanced. His long arms spread wide when her feet took flight, until her breasts met with her father's chest and he twirled her in a circle — round and round again — as he had how many seasons ago when their lives were younger, more hopeful, and less complicated by the passing of time.

He spoke to her haltingly in a language he no longer used. "You understand I never abandon you!"

"Yes, I understand."

"Where Ijokelekel?"

No sooner had she pointed downshore than Paratak left her to rush toward Ijokelekel and likewise lift him above the sloshing surf, crying, "*Koṃṃool*! *Koṃṃool*!" Then he turned back to her, but still clutching Ijokelekel by the shoulders with his massive hands. "What a hero. What a hero. I don't recognize!"

Suddenly identifying Lañinpo's proa, perhaps by its characteristic pattern of *ak* feathers tied about the sail, he continued. "Returned! Returned! What a hero!"

Then, man with a plan that he was, Ijokelekel snatched the moment from his beloved mentor, and shot back, "Yes, Paratak, I must return to Kelepwei before dawn. Is there enough time?"

"No longer Paratak. My name Jau Areu," he reminded him, prideful of the symbol Ḷainjin had carved into his chest.

"I mean, before the sun rises. Do we have time to return Lañinpo's proa to Kelepwei before it gets light?"

At this, Paratak — still laughing — raised his gigantic wingspan, lifted his face upward, and spoke in Pohnpeian to the slowly creeping, star-strewn sky as though to Nahn Sapwe himself, the way Ijokelekel remembered his mother often had. "He return after many season and first question, 'Is there enough time?' Of course, enough time. You are home. You bring my beautiful daughter. There is time for everything now!"

Ijokelekel spoke again, wanting to make his plan as clear as possible. "I agree, from tomorrow, we will move as slowly as reef birds stalking our prey, but tonight, we must reach Kelepwei before the first rooster awakens the village."

Paratak pointed at his proa upshore. "I set my daughter at my boat's prow. I fly over water. Only one question: Can you keep up?" As he said this, he began laughing again. He spread his arms once more before his daughter, who again ran into them, and he twirled her as if she were a child again, trying to exhaust her father with play. He willingly accepting the challenge.

Then, as father and daughter headed hand in hand toward Paratak's proa, Ijokelekel returned to steady his at the surf's edge, where he had temporarily deserted it. While still beached, he watched them swiftly flip their sail from one end of Paratak's proa to the other. Then, demonstrating his commitment, the big man's hands clutched onto the forward outrigger boom beneath the deck of the heavy boat behind him and dragged its keel and parallel float seaward. He tugged the heavy craft down the beach with such speed that Erwina had to hustle to keep its rapidly departing prow from slipping through her hands and dragging through the sand.

Ijokelekel managed to flip his sail as well, but by the time he completed this task, the Jau Areu and his daughter had successfully overcome the surf, entered the channel, and begun their first of many tacks to the southeast.

As he sailed and paddled through the surf, he grew angry with himself for forgetting that Paratak liked people to use his title although few others obliged. He recalled avoiding the issue by following his mother's advice and calling him "uncle." In turn, this reflashed his often-recalled memory of the last time he had seen him. It was the Jau Areu's job to fish for the Saudeleur but also, at his request, to prepare the turtles they kept at Darong, the islet adjacent to his Idedh. He had heard they killed poor Kielua and were preparing to eat his soul for failing to deliver a stone he had been paid for. They had taken his body to Idedh for Paratak to cook like a turtle. The next morning, Ijokelekel had swum to the islet and climbed its north wall to find Paratak weeping as he loaded Kielua's cooked body parts into the basket he had to deliver to the Saudeleur. He would never forget the scent of cooked human flesh he experienced that morning for the first and last time. After that, he would have thought that Paratak would be ashamed of this title. He wished he had remembered to call him "uncle."

The night was black but clear, and the light from the stars tinted the gentle waves with a silver hue. Like the incoming tide, Ijokelekel's earliest memories of this dark, mountainous coast flooded his thoughts. The gigantic stones, so uniformly six sided and broken away, like those from the sharp cliffs… "Are they not proof that that my father exists? Who else had the power to break them off so perfectly?" His mother had tended Nahn Sapwe's fire atop his stone altar night after day. Was that not validation enough? Hadn't she testified upon his altar that Nahn Sapwe was, in fact, his father? True, his detractors had explained away his unlikely fatherhood so often that he could likewise play down his origin, as he recently had. Yet, back in the mysterious presence of these mountains, these thoughts from his youth came tumbling back like the strange reality of a waterfall. He didn't know where it had come from or how. Still, like the thunderous voice of Nahn Sapwe, there it was, immense and overpowering nonetheless. Wasn't the sightless thrill he felt through his ears — like feeling the direction of the wind — proof enough?

Paratak had begun their race against the sun on a seaward tack, but it wasn't long before he tacked back toward shore.

"Quick tack, then tack back!" Ijokelekel chanted to himself as he repeated the mantra, sure that Paratak was singing to his daughter. After all, hadn't they both been taught by the same pali?

"Feel the wind in your ears, Ijokelekel," Ḷōpako would say while instructing him. "Just as your head must sway to find it, so does the wind. It sways ever so slowly back and forth around the average direction it blows from at any given time. The wave the wind generates will show you this average direction. So, keep this sway in mind when you race into the wind. The end of each cycle will always be more favorable to the direction of one tack than the other. By doubling your tacks, you double your ability to sail longer on the more favorable tack. Watch the wave versus the direction your bow cuts into it. The sharper the cut, the more favorable the tack. Each wind has its own rhythm. Learn to anticipate the end points of its cycle and tack accordingly."

Ḷainjin would always end such instruction with the rest of the chant: "They are they, but we are us!" This last he would chant at a remarkably high pitch to emphasize the end of a cycle. Then he would explain, "The long tack is designed for the lazy navigator who doesn't want to disturb his crew or expend the energy to squeeze the maximum advantage from his rigging."

So, over the years, Paratak must have learned the importance of these teachings due to the purposefully flawed design of his craft, which Ḷōpako had hoped would discourage him from sailing back upwind to Lae. Even after such a short distance, Ijokelekel noticed he was gaining on his "uncle" to such an extent that he had to overpoint and spill wind to avoid overtaking him.

And so they tacked on against the light winds beneath the black starlit night. He noticed Erwina trolling and landing fish. Ever cognizant of his mission, however, Paratak seemed not to slow his craft to accommodate her haulings. They tacked repeatedly, keeping their heading as close as possible to the barrier reefs surrounding this stretch of the island's coast.

This may have been for fishing purposes, but more likely he was again listening to their pali's voice in his head: "Here is another reason to quick tack and tack back toward shore rather than continuing on a long-tack approach. When sailing around an island, be aware of the island's most windward visible point. Draw an imaginary line from that point parallel to the wind, and let that line mark the extreme of your seaward tack. When you keep your tacks landward of that line, you lessen your exposure to the wave action that streams downwind past that point. That wind-generated wave will always join with the quadrant swell from that direction and impede your progress to windward."

Finally, they passed the southeast corner of the island that marked the halfway point of their journey. From that point, they made their final tack and were then able to maintain a constant northeast heading. After a while, the lights from the village began to peek between the various breaks in its high walls. As Ijokelekel had anticipated, Paratak led them into the mangrove swamp west of the village to avoid the lookouts posted between its passageways. He recalled their words as he lowered his sail and paddled forth: "Ijokelekel, you are a sand crab!"

"Well," he thought. "The sand crab has reappeared though he scampers away from your sight for now. What report will you give to the Saudeleur? Once he hears rumors of my unreported entry, he'll wonder how I have returned — and to what end. Through which gate did I enter the village? He is unlikely to be amused by your answers."

Ijokelekel had hunted crabs with Paratak as a youth and was aware his uncle knew the twists and turns of the mangrove forest's labyrinth of channels. It bordered the Temwen coast, which faced the stone village they had built on its fringing reef. The many twists and turns of these channels were endemic to the forest, though their edges were often trimmed of overgrowth by passing islanders cutting loose some of the forest's many tool-shaped branches. They lowered their sails and paddled into the blackness of the narrow, often overgrown channels. Though they periodically came to a few starlit pools of open water, most of their journey was through such blackness it was a wonder that, after so many abrupt blind turns, they emerged from the canals just landward of Pahn Kadira.

Its gigantic walls of angled stone appeared loftier to him than they had before he left them. The stone village was the only life he had known. Now, having seen the outside world of coral atolls with tiny islets, the village seemed more magnificent than he had remembered. He recalled the difficulty he'd had describing them to those distant islanders, most of whom had never seen a real stone, let alone one shaped of six sharply angled sides. When they paddled past Pahn Kadira to Kelepwei, he was surprised no boats were moored there. He was easily able to anchor Lañinpo's proa in approximately the same spot he had taken it from so many seasons before. He glanced briefly up along the tops of the starlit walls to assure himself no guards were watching, then slipped into the water and breaststroked slowly away.

"His father is Nahn Sapwe! His father is Nahn Sapwe!" He bitterly recalled the children's teasing as he swam. Then he lifted himself in one powerful arm-pressing motion onto the outrigger platform of his uncle's proa. Clearing the water dripping down his face, he felt a sweet nostalgia for the craft that had been his constant companion for so many seasons past. Stealing away with her had been the best decision he could have made, and he was proud to have escaped at such a youthful age, before the nonbelieving keepers of this place had their chance to tie his leg to a branch and train him, like an innocent bird, to accept their impious ways. Then Paratak paddled quickly past Kelepwei's stone-walled southwest corner, motioned for his daughter to raise sail, and glided them the last short distance down the tide-flooded canal to the similarly walled man-made islet called Idedh.

No alarms had sounded, so other than the sudden appearance of Lañinpo's proa, nothing unusual had occurred. He had launched his plan in flawless fashion. Now he must stay out of sight, as any passing villager might notice the foreign tattoos on his or Erwina's bodies and perhaps relate their observations through a web of contacts leading to the merciless, ever-informed cannibal at its center. So, after washing in Paratak's saltwater pool, veiled by the slowly departing darkness before dawn, they retreated to his humble thatch hut at the corner of his takai-walled compound.

Exhausted, Ijokelekel slept through the quiet morning and woke in midafternoon, in the heat of a bright day. Erwina and her father were gone. They had risen much earlier after waking him several times with laughter. He rinsed his face with water from one of the netted coconut containers that hung about the hearth of the pole-framed hut and cautiously exited the open door that led to the courtyard of the empty compound.

"Siss." Erwina alerted him from a corner of the walls above. There she sat, in the corner shaded by the crown of a coconut tree planted many seasons ago, casually peering out at the village before her.

"Don't let anyone see you," he cautioned, whispering as he climbed toward her.

"Don't worry, Ijokelekel. I haven't let anyone see me. I know your plan. You've told us a hundred times: 'Let the drifters come ashore first, here and then there. Over a period of several moons, they will all tell the same story about how Ḷañinni chased the peaceful people of Wōjjā into the sea.'"

"Okay, good."

"This has already happened. My father told me they all say they were rescued by Ijokelekel, who lives at sea and is accompanied by many warriors."

"Where is your father?"

"He went with the incoming tide to take my fish to the Saudeleur. Wait here, I'll bring yours."

With that, she carefully stepped down from the wall, entered her father's hut, and returned with a freshly husked coconut and Ijokelekel's fish in a leaf-covered basket. She bore the look of a woman proudly offering food to one of her own.

"She's happy here and has already settled in and taken Idedh as her home," he thought.

"It's better here in the breeze. The beauty of this village takes my breath away." Erwina gazed east and north at the many stone-walled, man-made islets and canals, and at the gigantic stone walls that bordered the village and separated it on three sides from the sea and surrounding reef. "But you were born here, so such a sight is part of who you are. I have only imagined what it would be like from my father's stories, and it has surpassed my expectations. Who could have imagined?"

Ijokelekel sucked sweet juice from the coconut and, while he ate, cautiously peered at the sight before them. She was right. The village was more impressive now that he perceived it as unique among the surrounding islands. However, something had changed, though he wasn't sure what.

"How long has Paratak been gone?"

"You mean my father, the Jau Areu," she joked, laughing at them both.

"I don't understand why he still prizes that title. The last time I saw him, it was from the other side of that wall, and he was loading a man's body parts like they were turtle, except he was crying like a woman."

"He told me about that, but that's no more. Ijokelekel, there's a new Saudeleur. He's just as mean as the last, but this one is weak. The last person the old Saudeleur tried to punish was Kosraean,[164] and the Kosraeans all over the island threatened revolt. So, he discontinued the practice. The new Saudeleur is afraid of the Kosraeans too and has given up enforcing the law. So, the Jau Areu is back to fishing and baking turtles just like before."

"Well, you know our plan. We're not staying. I'm going to ask your father to take us back to the fleet tonight."

He missed watching Kāmeto standing at the helm, her eyes darting from rigging to wave to sail as she gripped the tiller with all her might, allowing him to view every movement of her slight body unnoticed. Not that she hadn't already shown him everything, but he imagined that too — unseen at the center of his desire for her.

"There he is now," Erwina replied, scrambling down to meet him as he approached and taking the basket from his hand.

"What's this, Father?"

"Breadfruit," he responded in her language. "Reciprocity from the Saudeleur."

"Look, Ijokelekel." She handed the basket up to him. "Something to eat with your fish."

Then she followed her father into his hut as she would have as a little girl, and their soft laughter once again echoed about the corner of Idedh. Ijokelekel finished his meal in silent pleasure, enjoying the breeze, the shade, his thoughts of Kāmeto, and the wonder of having returned with a solid plan and circumstances ripe to execute it.

He wasn't eager to return to the stale air in Paratak's hut and was relieved when the two reappeared and climbed toward him. "Father has agreed to take us," she said, as she sat on a takai below him.

---

[164] Kosrae, an island about 300 miles southeast of Pohnpei, is now one of the Federated States of Micronesia.

"Uncle, something about the village seems to have changed, but I can't figure out what."

Though questioned in Pohnpeian, Paratak responded in the same broken Rālik his daughter was used to hearing, perhaps in deference to her. "No coming, going."

Ijokelekel nodded. That was it. With an incoming tide, there should have been a lot more comings and goings between the village's many islets. The structures appeared the same, but with less activity. "But why?" he asked.

"Long story. Part you know already, but I repeat for Erwina."

"Well, I'm always glad to hear a good story a second time. We have a long wait before darkness falls."

"As you know, I'm very hurt by Ḷōpako," Paratak said.

"He hurt me too, Father. I always thought he was your friend. Then we found out Mother was carrying his baby, and that explained it all."

Paratak appeared stunned by her words. Perhaps he had assumed all this time that Ḷōpako, in tricking him and sending him home to Pohnpei, had Paratak's best interest at heart. Now he appeared stunned to learn about Ḷōpako's ulterior motive.

"Why you no tell me last night? Why you tell me now before my nephew?"

Now Erwina looked hurt. "Father, we were having such fun. Why would I spoil it by bringing up something like that? If that was on your mind" — she became defensive — "why didn't you ask me about her?"

Then, strangely, Paratak began nodding his head and laughing at their surprised faces.

"Everyone thinks me fool, but no! I already know about seed Likōkkālọk steal from Ḷōpako. Lijoḷọk tell me long time ago. Him no pleasure my woman. She pleasure herself. Him my friend. But trick me bad that day. Show me path over swell. Yes, but that is it! All the way to Pohnpei? I am scared. I sail all night not to forget that cut into swell. Then I remember he tell me, 'Take down sail and sleep.' So, I stop, sleep, but remember path over swell all the time. Then sail again, then stop again, then sail again. Always the same path."

Paratak spread five fingers wide, stretching his arm in front of them. "That is how many days before I see beautiful mountain," he said, using the other arm to point behind him. "That small" — he illustrated with his finger and thumb — "when I first see above water. But that happy!" He stretched both arms wide with fingers spread, as when he had first embraced his daughter.

"That's when I thank him. Yes, just like he said I would. I am happy to find Mother and Father alive." He hugged himself, twisting and showing pleasure on his face. Then he abruptly changed tone. "But as you know, I'm sad my woman takes another man to fish for her."

"How are your children?" asked Ijokelekel, offering to break him away from that unhappy thought.

"Children fine. They come to visit me here. I have four grandbabies now," he said, his eyes lighting up again.

"Erwina tells me there is a new Saudeleur."

"You remember the good one, Raipuinlañ. As soon as he sees scar on chest, he knows mark of Ḷōpako. He gives me my title and my Idedh. As you perhaps remember, he die after that. Then Raipuinloko takes over. But Nahn Samohl is dead, so still no law to enforce agreement. Islet building and trade slow, and village life is not good like before. Then your friend the great pali Lañinpo arrive with that Rālik proa no one here knows how to make. He brings a companion they call the little akebu from western island. They come but Lañinpo is very disappointing. They say no strong like before.

"We have our own story of *liet*," Paratak said. "Cannibals long ago banished into mountain. That little one like them, but he has many things to trade and give away, so he stay popular with new Saudeleur and many women also. They eat people where he is from. So, he says to Raipuinloko, 'Why not let me poison the transgressor? Then we'll eat him as punishment.'

"That how eating people come back to Pohnpei after how many season of *liet* banish to mountain. Then like crazy, it work because people afraid to lose soul. Building start again, and Lañinpo and little akebu get rich from trade. That when my life change to bad. My title require me to cook turtle for Saudeleur, so he tell me to cook one lawbreaker to eat. That when you steal canoe and leave island. But one problem. The people no like new law. When they kill first Kosraean, people get mad to revolt. Saudeleur renounce new law, little akebu no longer poison anyone."

Paratak then switched into Pohnpeian and, turning to Ijokelekel, said more softly, "I'm embarrassed to say this in front of my daughter. He teaches his boys to seek semen from older boys. He claims this is good custom."

Then he spoke again in Rālik. "Lañinpo is then disfavored. No proa, no trade. He live in dishonor. His big mistake to bring western custom to Pohnpei. No one call him 'pali.' He live with little akebu on Temwen.

"Prestige of Raipuinloko never recover. His death big mystery, and his son, Sau-temoi[165] become Saudeleur and change back to old law called *kauat*.[166] When someone default on agreement, Saudeleur tell them to bring feather from Tiripeijo bird.[167] Impossible task. Transgressor must hide away, landless, on mountain — cut off from family."

"Is that serving to enforce the law?" asked Ijokelekel.

"Yes, somewhat. But you see for yourself, not much coming and going. Not like before. But people still required to bring tribute to Saudeleur though he has little to give back. So, reciprocity uneven. Stone worker from Kosrae not fed like before. Saulikin Ant,[168] he know how to raise eel. He say, 'Bring back the day of Nahn Samohl.'"

"Who is Saulikin Ant?"

"He rule over long island Ant Atoll," Paratak said. "Remember, you always want to go, but I always say too danger? Then I meet Saulikin Ant. He come here to trade, and he tell me Jau Areu has property over there at a place called Pontip. So, I must go and see for myself this place where there is a pool of water named Areu in Ant. He say that is one good place to raise eel."

"So, he wants to raise eels again to enforce the law like before."

"Yes, he want turn back our ways to please Nahn Sapwe again to break stone from mountain again. Last two Saudeleur turned away from our past. He say it's time to turn back."

"I'd like to meet Saulikin Ant," said Ijokelekel.

"Father says he can take us there!" said Erwina excitedly.

---

[165] As the son of Raipuinloko, succeeded him as Saudeleur.

[166] Term for something difficult or impossible to accomplish, as presented in *The Book of Luelen*.

[167] A legendary bird in the story of Lamuak and Lapanmor, as told in *The Book of Luelen*.

[168] The chief of Ant Atoll.

"Better to rest at Ant than stay at sea," Paratak said. "Much danger at sea. You can lose warrior if drift off into storm. We can leave tonight. That your plan, right?"

"Right," Ijokelekel said. "I don't want to get caught and be told to bring the feather of… What bird did you say?"

"Tiripeijo bird from an old story."

"Tell us, Father. We need to hear," said Erwina.

Paratak, proud that his daughter had asked him to tell a story, promptly filled his chest with air as though about to dive for fish, gave a quick obligatory look toward Ijokelekel to assure himself that he, too, wanted to hear, and began telling the story.

"Lapanmor is chief of Madolenihmw.[169] He gives land to one of his workers, man named Lamauk. Man knows how to make one beautiful garden. Plant banana from Paniep. Take first stalk and bake in ground oven. Bring chief food to Lapanmor on rainy day. His mistake to throw banana stalk into stream.

"Now firstfruit must always go to Saudeleur. When stalk wash up on steps of Pahn Kadira, the Saudeleur is angry. Ask whose oven stalk comes from. They know it must come from beautiful garden of Lamauk. So Saudeleur command Lapanmor to appear before him. He scold him for not bringing firstfruit to Saudeleur. So, he punish him. Must bring feather of Tiripeijo bird.

"But this bird no live on Pohnpei. Live only on islands they call Palikapi, many day west. So, Lapanmor set out on long voyage. His crew — one cockroach, one mudskipper, and one Kusaie eel basket called Kemeui. He travel under many moon to find island of Tiripeijo bird. Then one problem. Bird nest high in tree. They wait long time for feather to fall, but then cockroach say, 'Let me and basket get it.'

"So, cockroach climb up to nest and crawl onto head of bird to cause itch, and bird scratch loose one feather that drift down into basket. Then they return to Pohnpei, and that how Lapanmor prove to Saudeleur he can trust, and that how custom of *kauat* first begin," Paratak concluded in his broken Kajin Rālik.

---

[169] One of the five municipalities of Pohnpei.

"It's a story about teamwork," thought Ijokelekel with a chuckle.

Lying back to nap, he surmised, "Paratak will be Lapanmor, and Erwina will be Kemeui. I'll be the cockroach who saves the day. But what will the feather of the Tiripeijo bird look like, and what will be the Saudeleur's response? What does it feel like to be a cockroach, anyway?" he thought. That was when he realized that heroes in Pohnpeian stories don't get much respect.

They left that night as they had come, not through the guarded breaks in the walls facing the ocean, but by way of a maze of twisted canals through the mangrove forests on the reef bordering the beachless coast of Temwen. They retraced their course and found their fleet drifting where they had left it, far off the coast to the south and west of Pohnpei. They decided that Paratak and Erwina would sail to Ant by themselves, to meet Saulikin Ant and ask permission for the fleet to come ashore. Then Maalal insisted that Ijokelekel allow her and her son to accompany them. What was he to say?

Lañinpo's story

"How long since I last viewed these intriguing walls of Nahn Madol?" thought Ḷainjin, as he approached the stone village. He had veered north of his target, where he noticed that *buñtokiōñ* had grown so predominant he had no choice but to turn his back to it until the tips of the mountains appeared from beneath the horizon in front of him. A day later, he entered one of the northern passageways through the barrier reef and retraced the familiar path through the lagoons between the barrier and fringing reefs to the village's so-called "back door." He had been surprised to find no guards along the northern wall. No alarms had sounded, and at first, he hardly noticed the scarcity of boats coming and going in the low but passable half-moon tide. He headed directly for Pahn Kadira as he had, under similar circumstances, how many seasons ago. Now he needed to deliver the two large tuna he caught that morning to the Saudeleur while they were still fresh and tasty.

Lowering his sail while he approached the entrance to the Saudeleur's great compound, he was surprised to see no craft anchored across the canal at Kelepwei. Had his son and his Rilujien Naṃo contingent not yet arrived? Had there been a battle? He was confused by the absence of the Rālik proas he had expected to see. The guards at the entrance were surprisingly unconcerned at his arrival. One questioned the purpose of his visit to Pahn Kadira. The other stared off into the distance as though indifferent to his response that he had come to speak with the Saudeleur.

Through the open entranceway, he caught a glimpse of the altar of Nahn Sapwe. No fire was burning there. His thoughts turned to their last moment together, how many seasons past. "I go with you. You stay with me," she had said prophetically.

"Nice fish," the guard commented, as though planning to eat them himself.

"I caught these off the passageway as firstfruits for the Saudeleur."

"Who do we say brought these?"

"They call me Pako."

"We'll see that he gets them. You from Rālik?"

"Yes."

"You can stay across the way."

"*Kalahngan*,"[170] he said.

The guards unloaded the fish, set them on the steps of takai, and called to others to tend to them.

Instead of anchoring at Kelepwei, Ḷainjin paddled past, turned the corner, and headed down a second canal toward Idedh. He was anxious to meet his old friend Paratak and thought he might be invited to stay with him. It was obvious from first glance that someone was living there and tending the grounds, which were immaculately kept. There was a neatly trimmed thatched house on what had been the raised, open mound where the crowd stood next to the well the day they lowered him into it. A neat railing, perhaps constructed from the very scaffold that had lowered him into the well, now bordered it. He couldn't resist looking down into it, but the sun wasn't high enough to see its bottom. He thought not of the cold night he had spent there but of the untold numbers who'd had their manhood violently torn from them by the first bite of Nahn Samohl. Again, he felt their spirits silently calling out to him as they had that day so long ago.

Yet Paratak was gone, and more revealing, his proa was absent as well. Perhaps he had gone fishing. If so, he should appear shortly. The tide was slowly receding, making a later return problematic if not impossible.

Ḷainjin entered his humble abode. The artfully arranged quarters further endeared him to the memory of his old friend. His sleeping mat was furled in one corner. His drinking cup of coconut shell stood on his shelf, snugly placed within the hollowed, upside-down base of another. The rafters held

---

[170] Pohnpeian for "thank you."

his thin mangrove fishing pole. Everything was set just so, just as he had purposefully left it. These surroundings spoke of a Paratak who had become a man with purpose and dignity as opposed to the frustrated and confused man he had been on Lae. Ḷainjin could hardly wait to meet him, but alas, the tide was seeping away.

Ḷainjin tried to paddle back to Kelepwei but scraped bottom with his oar. He ended up subtracting his weight, wading back down the canal with his proa in tow, and anchoring at the very spot where Rojak had confronted the palu and made the huge man cry. The past welled up around him as he entered the open entrance to the compound. But the facilities appeared in disarray and long since abandoned. The cookhouse, gathering places, and sleeping huts were all in need of rethatching. He recalled the evening, how many seasons ago, when he had first entered the same compound with his new companion Talupe to the sounds of pounding kava, the lively din of dozens of simultaneous conversations, the view of workers' comings and goings, and the smell of open ground ovens and cooked foods of all types. He had arrived hoping to either reestablish friendships or be challenged by a fight but now expected neither. What had caused such a change of atmosphere? He was too exhausted by his trip to speculate.

Too tired of his craft to return to it, he lay down on the raised platform where he and Talupe — he full of excitement and anticipation, she full of scheme and ambition — had sat among the Saudeleur's contingent that first night. The tides of time had swept all that away.

He slept in the still, quiet atmosphere as the water in the village canals receded slightly more and then, toward evening, began to flood somewhat again. He woke under the half-moon. The night was clear, and that was good because the poor condition of the thatch above him couldn't safeguard his sleep in the rain. He was hungry. Surprised that no one had reciprocated his gift by bringing a meal at low tide, he returned to his craft to retrieve the provisions Liṃanṃan had prepared for his voyage. The taste reminded him of her and took him back to the decision his mother had encouraged him to make amid the listless, vast *kāleptak* to press on to his homeland.

But was he now using his mother's advice as an excuse for having abandoned poor Lipanmai? Hadn't that selfless statement from Lipanmai's throat inspired his life and taught him to pass on her selfless love to another? His determination to save the son of Lipanmai and the daughter of Limanman hardened like the very takai around him. "Each one of these stones must have its own individual story now, though without doubt long lost," he thought. He must do whatever he found necessary to avoid a similar fate for his children. His son's passion to make his own mark, to avenge his mother's death, and to set things right must not pass unfulfilled. His daughter, however misguided, must fulfill her destiny here and then return to fulfill her mother's last wishes. He resolved to avoid reckless behavior, proceed with utmost caution, and seek what advice he might find along the way.

The slight breeze that channeled through the canal was so welcoming he spread his sleeping mat across the outrigger platform and slept there until the light of the morning sky gently awakened him. He felt rested and fortunate his arrival had lacked the commotion he feared. At least he had recovered some of the energy drained by the long voyage and felt readier to face the challenges ahead. With no guards visible on the walls, his eyes turned to the action at the entrance of Pahn Kadira. He saw three figures from the group step down into the ankle-high water of the reef. Were they finally bringing him food? The two on either side carried baskets. The figure in the center, somewhat familiar, seemed to be stepping out of his past.

As they approached, he realized it was none other than his good friend Ewalt.[171] "Just the person," he thought happily, rising in recognition of their friendship and singing the proverbial greeting down the channel at them. "*Kaselehlie*!"[172]

Ewalt approached with a broad smile. "*Kaselehlie*!" Soon they clasped arms and embraced.

In Kajin Rālik, Ļainjin softly asked, "How are the elders?"

"Both gone," Ewalt said, speaking Pohnpeian. "Mother went last. Gone for two seasons now. Mother was adamant that you were still alive and spoke of you often. She is one who never doubted your success in locating

---

[171] Ļainjin's interpreter in *The Forbidden Man.*

[172] Pohnpeian for "hello."

your mother despite having discouraged your departure. We heard from Lañinpo all about the deadly rescue. Then, when Paratak returned from Rālik, he told us you had washed ashore on a small atoll there."

"I was able to reunite with my mother for a brief time only. She perished amid the travails of *kāleptak*." He spoke in Kajin Rālik again.

"I've always hoped for your return" — Ewalt was still speaking in Pohnpeian — "but Mother just said, 'An *ak* returns to its island of birth when it's time to nest.'"

"To return to Rālik was my mother's last wish for me." Ḷainjin responded again in Kajin Rālik.

Ewalt appeared eager to ask another question but then stopped himself, turning instead to his two companions. They had both come close, as though listening intently to their conversation.

"Please place Pako's baskets over there at the entrance." He spoke abruptly, dismissing them.

They waded to the entrance, placed the baskets, and then returned. Ewalt pointed to Pahn Kadira, indicating that he wanted them to leave.

Once they were on their way, Ewalt began speaking in Ḷainjin's language for the first time. "The Saudeleur has insisted I speak only in Pohnpeian. The reason, I'm sure, is so those two can report back to him what they learn."

"About what? That doesn't sound like the Saudeleur I knew. Come, let's sit while I examine the contents of those baskets and find something to snuff my hunger."

Ewalt sat down beside him. "Raipuinlañ is dead," he announced.

"I know. Ijokelekel told me. I assume the whole island showed up for his *pehdinpwong*.[173] Where lies his *lolong*?[174] Nahn Dowas?"

Ewalt raised his eyebrows and wheezed loudly in assent. "Our way of life died with him. Pako, you must understand, nothing has been the same since you emerged from that pit, dragging up the putrid remains of Nahn Samohl."

"I was sorry to hear about Raipuinlañ. Ijokelekel told me about his death. I had much respect for him." Inspecting the baskets, Ḷainjin quickly

---

[173] A Pohnpeian wake.

[174] A stone burial chamber.

plucked out a freshly husked coconut, removed its eye cap, and began to suck its contents. "We talked about Nahn Samohl at the time. Obviously, it wasn't me who killed him."

"No matter, you marked the turning point. Now, after all these years, you show up again while Ijokelekel is rumored to have returned with a contingent of Rālik warriors. The season is repeating, and it all seems to rotate around you. Can you see why this latest Saudeleur is so suspicious?"

Ḷainjin answered with a question. "Where is Ijokelekel now?"

"We thought you would know. That's what the Saudeleur is trying to find out. Rumor has it Ijokelekel has a large fleet of followers and they're drifting at sea. Perhaps waiting for their opportunity to attack."

"If so, then why no guards?"

"The Saudeleur is having trouble feeding his workers. Some have left for the outer atolls. Others claim to be sick. Truth is that reciprocity has broken down between the Saudeleur and the people. The Kosraeans are hungry! The reign of Sau-temoi is an even bigger failure than that of his father and predecessor, Raipuinloko."

"The one who ate people?"

"Only a very few who broke the law were ordered eaten. He adopted the akebu's customs, but they were so abhorrent the people rebelled."

"Customs?" Ḷainjin began munching on a chunk of roasted taro.

"That's the way the little akebu describes it. He brags that the cause of his virility is the amount of enemy flesh he has eaten as an adult and how much semen he ate as a child."

"Did he tell you his father raped his mother repeatedly, enslaved her, ate her feet in front of her, and ordered him to kill his sister? That's not custom. There are as many customs as islands out there. It's true, some eat the flesh of their enemies," Ḷainjin said, "but they don't eat their fellow villagers as punishment." He sucked again at the mouth of his coconut to wash down the taro. "Customs encourage life, not death. He's teaching the *tuwe*[175] he learned from his father. I told Lañinpo to kill him too. I should have killed him myself and destroyed the akebu's favorite seed out of revenge for enslaving my mother. That was the biggest mistake of my life. But I deferred

---

[175] Another word for "magic."

the decision to Lañinpo, and the little *ṇakṇōk*[176] was quick to emphasize their brotherly bonds, so I guess he kept putting it off. Still, I fail to imagine why he would bring him here."

"They're like brothers now," said Ewalt. "The older excuses the faults of the younger."

"I have no younger brother, so I don't understand such tolerance."

"Remember Talupe?"

Ḷainjin had thought of her often — the sweet memory of her sexuality and the incredible desire he had held for her mixed with the bitter way she left him that eventful day, accusing him of copulating like a rooster.

"She thought she could manipulate the little westerner like the rest," Ewalt said. "That was her mistake. When she repeatedly defaulted on her agreements to deliver takai, the Saudeleur gave the akebu an order to poison her. They ate her up, got drunk on her poisoned meat, and extinguished her story. Under the new law, she was the first. Now she's gone forever. No grave. No ceremonial letting to sea. Even her children, I'm told, can't bring themselves to mention her name."

That news shocked and disgusted Ḷainjin. What a terrible mistake Lañinpo had made bringing the little akebu here. "How many have been eaten under this new law?"

"You mean the old new law. Raipuinloko revoked it, and Sau-temoi, his son, has likewise renounced it. Under Raipuinloko, only a few were eaten. But ever since, the story of their deaths follows the akebu wherever he goes. So, he starts with the gifts, then — I'm guessing — reminds the women coyishly what happened to Talupe, then out pops his baby. He is supportive of these children. I can say that for him. You should see them running around or being carried all over the villages, but not among the Kosraeans. They'll have nothing to do with him because of Lipanmai, and they're bound together like strands of coir sennit too strong to break. Their hunger is a big problem for Sau-temoi because he's no longer getting enough tribute to feed them. You're probably wondering why it took so long to reciprocate the fish you gave him? Raipuinlañ would have had baskets of food at his feet, but Sau-temoi had to wait to feed you. It's sad."

---

[176] Witch doctor; shaman; expert.

"Ijokelekel would say times are bad because the Saudeleur has turned his back to Nahn Sapwe. I noticed there's no fire atop his altar, and we can thank the akebu for that. But why has no one replaced Ijokelekel's mother?" asked Ḷainjin.

"I don't know the answer to that, but his followers have been washing ashore over these past days and telling a story that he has hundreds of warriors out there drifting and waiting for the right time to attack. How did the young Ijokelekel ever find you?"

"He showed up as a tattooed man one day, told me the akebu had killed his mother, and asked to be my apprentice."

"Not everyone around here believed Lipanmai when she claimed that Nahn Sapwe is father to the boy," said Ewalt. "Are you aware of the rumors that he's your son? Before you answer, let me tell you that the Saudeleur has heard this rumor as well and you would be wise to deny it. Lipanmai never acknowledged you or anyone else. If the Saudeleur thinks you're the boy's father, word has it he's prepared to capture you as a hostage."

Ḷainjin understood his old friend was advising him to lie, so he quickly complied. "Then tell him I deny the rumor. Tell him I'm the boy's tutor and nothing more. And tell him Ijokelekel is a religious man, like his mother, who only wants to restore faith and hope to his people. The only one who has cause to fear is the little akebu because Ijokelekel is convinced he was the cause of his mother's death."

"That might alleviate his worst fears," Ewalt said, "but he's likely to remain suspicious because you can't deny that he's of Kosraean blood. The Saudeleur fears a Kosraean rebellion. They have been serving Nahn Sapwe for generations. Now there's no work for them. They're landless, like the clouds that hover in the valleys threatening rain. He would return them all to their homeland if he could. Though many Kosraeans gave their lives to build this village, the Pohnpeians treat them like foreigners.

"As for the akebu, he retains a strange influence over the Saudeleur. The akebu knows how to poison people. However, he has one good trait — he's consistently honorable in his personal affairs. He is very loyal to his brother and his local mates. I suspect the Saudeleur fears him yet trusts his loyalty. I doubt he cares what happens to the akebu. Though he clearly humors him, treats him honorably, and gives him no cause to seek revenge."

They sat on the steps of Kelepwei for the rest of that morning, reminiscing over their shared past and catching up on each other's stories from the point that Ḷainjin had departed. As they spoke, the tide rose sluggishly in the canal next to them. With its ebb, the same two attendants who had brought the baskets earlier that morning paddled over in a small canoe they had launched from Pahn Kadira and announced that the Saudeleur commanded their presence. Much discussion ensued between the men and Ewalt, who was upset they hadn't brought a larger craft to transport them down the canal. Uncharacteristically angry, he rudely removed his kilt, presented it to them, and began wading down the canal. On his part, Ḷainjin repeated his friend's actions. The two attendants paddled beside them and returned their kilts so they could cover themselves as they climbed the steps of the Saudeleur's compound.

"This Saudeleur lacks the grace of his ancestors," Ewalt said quietly.

They entered the enormous compound, and Ḷainjin once again found himself struck by the lack of activity. He recalled the festivities on the day he had received his title — the din of the crowd, the power of the storm that engulfed them. Then he looked up and over at the place where Lipanmai had taught him to talk to her and then at the spot where she was given his necklace. Finally, he looked a second time at the apex of the temple, where the smoke of her fire had always wafted skyward to show the direction of the wind. There was no sign of life there, or hardly anywhere else now.

The dwelling of the Saudeleur, on the other hand, stood out among the others. It alone was recently thatched and well kept. Ḷainjin smelled fish cooking on an open hearth and saw attendants carrying food to the Saudeleur's living quarters. Suddenly, he felt hungry again. No one else appeared before them, so they sat in the adjoining meeting house for a long time in silence. He spent the time reminiscing about his first arrival here and how Raipuinlañ had made him feel that his arrival was of great import and his surroundings were the center of their ocean world. Now he felt watched by someone wishing to undermine his fate.

When Sau-temoi appeared, such were his adornments that, at first glance, Ḷainjin mistook him for a woman. He wore several attractive necklaces, an elaborate belt surrounding his fluffy hibiscus kilt, trochus-shell arm bracelets, and a sweet-smelling flowered headband. His tattoos, however, were sparse and crudely drawn. He welcomed Ḷainjin with a short smile and a brief nod of the head. His voice lacked tenor, and he sat on a platform raised slightly higher than theirs. Ḷainjin membered Raipuinlañ sitting at that same spot, magnanimously engaging with genuine interest in the affairs of those before him. This man seemed more preoccupied with himself.

"Thank you for the tuna. I love raw tuna. You must have come to take your title back. Your namesake hasn't brought fish for several days. Does anyone know what happened to Paratak?"

He looked around the empty meeting house as though used to speaking before a group of advisors — though none were there. The two attendants looked at each other. Neither Ḷainjin nor Ewalt responded.

"Where is the food I ordered for the famous pali who has returned to visit us?"

Again, the two attendants looked at each other with confusion in their eyes. One began to saunter away.

"Hurry! Move like a man! If I wanted women attendants, I'd have them," he said, looking around as if an audience was laughing at his joke. Then he glanced back toward Ewalt. "I sent command that Lañinpo and his akebu appear as well! Where are those two when I need them? The tide, they say," he said, as though his remaining attendant had answered. He had not.

"Always the tide," he repeated, seemingly disgusted that it didn't respond to his whim. It was clear that he considered himself in charge of everything.

"He's an insect," thought Ḷainjin, viewing him with condescension and immediate dislike. "He is but a spider meticulously commanding its web, oblivious to the gathering storm that will soon wash it away." He wished he had his ring, ready to slice the Saudeleur's throat before he screeched another order.

The Saudeleur turned his gaze from Ewalt, who was lowering his head, perhaps to avoid the ruler's rambling, unanswerable inquiries. Ḷainjin, disgusted by his manner, steadfastly returned his gaze.

"I've been told you are another of these pali who sailed to Katau[177] and back."

Ḷainjin didn't respond to his indirect question but continued staring straight into Sau-temoi's eyes to take the measure of the man.

The coward immediately retreated behind closed eyelids, then busted forth with a question Ḷainjin couldn't avoid. "Is it true you killed the akebu's father? Cut off his head and hung it to rot in the men's house?"

"I wanted to kill him, but another beat me to it."

"Lañinpo? So, he was the one who killed his brother's father and hung his head to rot?"

"It's true the little akebu claims to be his brother," Ḷainjin said. "I have no knowledge of the rest."

"This eating semen that the akebu brags about. Is it true it makes a boy more virile when he grows up?"

"Better to ask the akebu. I have no knowledge or belief in such things."

"This Ijokelekel, the son of Lipanmai. I am told you knew them both?"

Again, Ḷainjin chose not to offer a response.

"Does he have markings on his skin?"

"Yes."

"Are they of the same design as yours?" asked the Saudeleur. "Anything different?"

"Per our custom, we each share the markings of a common man."

"Yet they tell me you are not a common man, and neither seems he. What is your relationship?"

"His mother sent him to me to tutor in the ways of the navigator."

"Why was he sent to you specifically?"

"As you say, I am known here as a pali," responded Ḷainjin, cunningly closing the circle and leaving the Saudeleur back where he had started.

"What if I told you Ijokelekel may have been captured and killed?"

"Then I would say you've lost an opportunity to maintain peace on your island. He is a charismatic, religious man with many followers who only wants to turn your people back to the faith of their forefathers. He wants to light the flame of Nahn Sapwe again to cause the cliffs to crumble, more takai to fall, the village to grow, and your wealth to increase."

---

177 An island in the west frequented by legendary Pohnpeian heroes.

Ḷainjin's speech was interrupted by a third attendant, who stood before the Saudeleur and said something in his ear.

"The tides? Don't bother me with the tides. Yes, of course they can shore their proa within the walls! Then, he spoke to Ewalt and Ḷainjin, "Tides! Your fellow reef-speaking islander has arrived at Kelepwei with his little Black brother."

Without notice, Ḷainjin impolitely stood and left the meeting house. He crossed the compound and arrived just as the two men were disembarking at the entrance steps.

Lañinpo had the unexpected appearance of a much older man. He looked thin, hunched, sickly. His eyes had sunk somewhat into his skull. His Black brother had paddled them across the channel from Kelepwei. Ḷainjin's question had been answered. Lañinpo hadn't brought the little akebu to Pohnpei. His assumption had been wrong. The Black one leaping the steps to catch Ḷainjin off guard with his western embrace had brought the now-frail Lañinpo back.

"I'm sorry I killed my sister Rojak," the little man said. As he apologized in broken Pohnpeian with seeming sincerity, Lañinpo waved his hand and sat down on the steps of takai. The little man then spoke in broken Pohnpeian to the guards, who called for additional help to carry the heavy proa inside the entranceway and place it next to Ewalt's.

Ḷainjin recognized the proa as belonging to Ijokelekel. Had he returned it? Ḷainjin sat next to his once tall friend, who glanced at him, shook his head in defeat, and looked down as if too fragile to hold his head high.

"I should have left with you," Lañinpo admitted, as though mumbling to himself. "I stayed there too long. I'm better here. That place has bad air."

The akebu arrived with Lañinpo's cane and helped him to his feet. Then, while Ḷainjin looked on in disbelief, he took his free hand and led him forward. Time had defeated his once vibrant hero. Now he was dependent on the care of the very one who had killed his twin sister. It was all too much to immediately absorb. Ḷainjin wanted to ask about Ijokelekel but decided to put it off till later.

When they reached the meeting house, Lañinpo dropped down next to Ewalt and, as they acknowledged each other, the akebu surprised Ḷainjin again by flopping up on the Saudeleur's platform. This was taboo in Pohnpeian culture and elicited a negative response from the attendants, who moved toward him to address the transgression. Laughing, the Saudeleur glanced at Ḷainjin, then stayed them with a wave of his hand. The little akebu thanked him with the broad smile of a forward child.

Lañinpo chastised his brother angrily in his own language. "What am I to do with this naughty westerner who does not follow our customs?"

The Saudeleur was evidently humored by the charisma of the little man, but Ḷainjin noticed the guards' uncomfortable, silent responses. Apparently wanting an interpretation of Lañinpo's words, the Saudeleur asked, "What says Lañinpo?"

"He means well. In his homeland, the men all sit at the same level, the women below. The biggest among them is simply the one who feeds others the most. He is higher than you in that regard, and his followers very loyal."

"Yes, I have heard he feeds many families by trading this for that and poking our women as they bend to admire his wares. He does not follow our customs or speak our language. Yet he has no trouble communicating with our women. Waow, how he communicates with them! They end up carrying his seed, and every other moon, they announce the birth of a new kinky-haired infant. How does he do it? Look at those teeth — how far apart? That must be so no human flesh catches between. He looks like he'd just as soon eat my arm as embrace it," the Saudeleur concluded, rattling the bracelets on his arm as though taunting him, looking over at Ḷainjin as though to catch his reaction. "Lañinpo, do they all look like that?"

"No, his father came from the interior, where their skin is dark. Along the coast, many are taller and lighter. And as you know, they only eat their enemies, never their friends. It's a point of honor among them."

"A point of honor, Ḷainjin. Did you hear that?" questioned the Saudeleur. "A point of honor lost upon the Kosraeans! He nearly caused a battle for Raipuinloko."

If the akebu understood fully their conversations about him, it didn't show in his manner, which exuded a naive amicability. He seemed happy to let his brother speak for him.

"Lañinpo, we've been over this before, but for the benefit of our friend here" — again, the Saudeleur glanced toward Ḷainjin — "can you once more describe the circumstances, long ago now, surrounding the death of Ijokelekel's mother, Lipanmai?"

Upon hearing her name, the akebu's eyes turned with concern toward his brother Lañinpo.

Ḷainjin immediately saw through the Saudeleur's question. It was an obvious ploy to see if his reaction might reveal a past relationship with her. However, he couldn't disguise his interest in hearing his friend's comments about what had happened. Of one thing he was certain. The akebu would have been a young man, and Lipanmai would have been much older than he, and certainly not one of his easy triumphs.

"As I have always said" — began Lañinpo with a cough — "it is a short and simple story. Lipanmai treated my brother like he was her nephew, and the akebu was attracted to her religion. He wanted to learn how to make thunder. If he wanted more from the relationship, he didn't show it. He showed her respect and she taught him chants."

He spoke slowly, coughing so hard that the attendant brought him a coconut, which he opened and sipped from. Then he continued. "He was carrying firewood with her when it happened. It was raining. She slipped and broke her neck on the temple takai. That's it. He was responsible only for helping her. Had he been guilty of anything, he would have run away, hidden himself, and left her in the rain. But no, he carried her home."

Ḷainjin felt the Saudeleur's eyes upon him, so remembering Ewalt's warning, he was careful to show no emotion. The little akebu nodded from time to time, as if affirming Lañinpo's explanation. Perhaps his ears understood more than his mouth could speak.

"How do we know the little philanderer didn't try to rape her?" asked the Saudeleur.

"That was a long time ago," Lañinpo said. "Has any woman come forth since, accusing him of such a thing? Has any father of his many paramours come to the Saudeleur with complaint? As I have said, I didn't witness this event, but my brother's story seemed credible at the time, and you must admit his actions since haven't proved inconsistent with it."

"If he is so innocent, why do the Kosraeans hate him?"

"The Kosraeans are poor, landless, and hungry," responded Lañinpo. "It isn't your fault they blame you, and it isn't his fault they blame him."

"I have said it before. I will say it again," commented the Saudeleur. "They are all of one mind. If one is lazy and his family is hungry, they all claim they're hungry. Drive them into the mountains and let them eat leaves. That's what my people say!"

Ḷainjin and Ewalt turned to each other, apparently with the same idea. Ewalt spoke first. "If I may remind the Saudeleur of Pako's suggestion to allow Lipanmai's son — if he isn't already dead — to revive the faith in Nahn Sapwe. Might that not avoid commanding the lot of them to retrieve Tiripeijo feathers? If they don't go into the mountains peacefully, or even if they do, we risk starting a war that could be long and costly and might not result in your favor."

"Lañinpo, what do you know about this Ijokelekel?"

The conversation now turned risky. Would Lañinpo reveal his relationship with Lipanmai?

"As I told you the last time you asked. After his mother was laid to rest at Nahn Dowas, we lost track of him. This was when we all lived here at Pahn Kadira, close to Raipuinloko. One morning, Ijokelekel came rushing among us using the word *liet,* stealing from the Saudeleur's lime tree, and then making off with my proa. When I tried to catch him in Paratak's proa, he claimed the Saudeleur had turned away from the religion of Nahn Sapwe and that he would return one day as a learned man, once he found the pali who would teach him everything."

"Did he tell you how he knew of this pali's whereabouts?"

"He said Paratak told him."

"Where is Paratak when I need him? I find this all very suspicious! Ijokelekel suddenly returns your canoe! His followers wash up like stinking fishes. Paratak disappears!"

The Saudeleur turned to Ḷainjin, "Now you, after all these years! All right! Everyone stays at Kelepwei until Paratak returns. My informants will confirm the whereabouts of your Ijokelekel and his followers. I, too, command men of the sea, and I will make my decision — alive or dead, religious man or rebel — based on my wisdom, and their advice."

When they left Pahn Kadira, the tide was lower still, so they left Ewalt's canoe and Lañinpo's proa there and splashed into the shin-high water of the canal. Lañinpo trailed behind, grasping his cane with one hand and his brother's shoulder with the other. Their food had finally been prepared, and the Saudeleur's attendants carried it alongside them. They entered the compound and sat around the food baskets on the raised platform of the tattered thatched meeting house. Again, Ewalt dismissed the attendants.

Ḷainjin was the first to speak, in Kajin Rālik. "Do you think he believed me?"

"Never mind if he believed you," answered Ewalt. "You were successful in planting a fertile thought in his head."

"What thought?" asked Lañinpo.

"He's trying to avoid a war when Ijokelekel comes ashore with his followers," said Ewalt.

Ḷainjin noticed the akebu turning his attention to Ewalt as soon as he mentioned Ijokelekel's name. "How much of our language does that one understand?" he asked.

"A lot," Lañinpo said. "But don't worry. He won't betray our confidence."

"Speak," said the akebu in their language, indicating a small amount with his fingers. Then he demonstrated a larger amount by spreading his hands. "Understand."

"At least he's not pretending to be ignorant," thought Ḷainjin. "But how can such a man be trusted?"

"He listens. He decides. He doesn't speak — but his actions show you he understands," explained Lañinpo.

"I'm sure the Saudeleur will accept your idea," said Ewalt. "Truth be known, he's a coward and doesn't know how to fight. He has but a few widely scattered warriors. It's not as it was in the past, when there was wealth here to protect. His rule is all he is trying to protect now, and he protects himself mostly by treachery rather than outward violence — by manipulation rather than generosity. If Ijokelekel comes ashore, he's more likely to welcome him … and then command your brother to poison him."

At this, the akebu held up the palm of his hand with a smile and waved it back and forth to assure them he wouldn't do such a thing.

"He always consults with me now before he poisons someone," Lañinpo said.

Ḷainjin and Ewalt shared a look of amusement that Lañinpo would say such a thing. Truly, he had lived so long among westerners he had adopted some of their less civilized traits as his own.

"Lañinpo, you better tell us your story so we…" Ḷainjin paused, searching for the right words. "So we…"

"So you understand why I didn't kill my brother like you told me to?"

At this, the akebu grinned from ear to ear, folded his legs beneath him, and — showing no interest in the food — sat straight backed, as if eager to hear his brother's story.

"Well, you obviously found reasons not to," Ḷainjin said.

"It's a long story that, yes, goes back to the years after our bearings parted." Lañinpo spoke in a weak, hoarse voice — worn, perhaps, from his persistent coughing.

"You headed home with your mother. We returned with Kanari[178] to Murik to live among the mangrove people. Kanari hung the akebu's head on the outrigger stay and the smell of its slowly salting flesh permeated the breeze we sailed upon. The little akebu was clearly despondent. Recall that, in the blink of an eye, he had speared our sister as she climbed through the window of their treehouse and, consequently, watched our footless mother fall to her death trying to save her. Then he had watched me, his brother, decapitate his father. It was a lot for both of us to come to grips with, and Kanari's antics were not helpful."

Continued coughing interrupted his words such that his story was pathetic to the ear. It was his brother who thought to crack open one of the fresh coconuts discarded by the others and offer him some of its soft, oily contents to lubricate the raspy sounds coming from his throat.

"Each time one of us looked at the other" — Lañinpo nodded back toward his brother — "the deaths came back like ghosts between us. It was Kanari who began learning enough of the akebu's language to find out why

[178] A Bar Nor man who accompanied Ḷainjin to Sigaba.

he wanted to leave the Kunai.[179] He was his father's favorite son, so he had no name. He was to carry on the name of the akebu. Everyone hated but feared his father. Many wanted revenge for those he had poisoned. Not yet initiated, the little akebu was unable to kill, so no one there would be afraid of him. He had no idea how many people his father mistreated. Once he was dead, his favorite seed would surely be a target for revenge. My brother was running for his life, and I knew it would never be easy. He wasn't much, but he was the only blood I had left. So, I couldn't bring myself to kill him. At first, I simply ignored him. Kanari recognized my predicament, took him under his wings, and began to teach him the ways of the mangrove man. Then it was Kanari who began the discussion about Sarakena,[180] the woman I loved. She had killed herself after her older brother had beaten her. You remember the situation, right?"

Each phrase sounded as though it had been coughed up from the throes of death rather than spoken by a strong pali who had traversed *kāleptak*. Gone completely was the strong, authoritative voice he had apparently used up on the Saudeleur. Lañinpo asked this last question with such obvious struggle it sounded like it could be his last.

"Yes, I was supposed to watch over her the night she killed herself. Alas, I betrayed your sister's trust, fell asleep, and allowed the woman Sarakena to slip away unnoticed," Ḷainjin said.

"You betrayed no one," said Lañinpo. "According to Kanari, it was her selfish, jealous brother who betrayed her love. I thought she killed herself out of shame. I thought it was my fault for being too open too soon with our relationship. But Kanari taught me that she killed herself to end her servitude to her brother, and to shame him for his greed. She wouldn't live any longer as his property, so she took herself away. He said it was my duty to avenge her death and that no one could fault me for it. That was why her brother ran away. Not because he was ashamed. Rojak had beaten him terribly for what he did. But because he worried that, if my sister did that to

---

[179] "Grass men"; also, the New Guinea pidgin English term for "grass," or *imperata cylindrica*. It catches fire easily during the dry season, when it is between two and ten feet high.

[180] A Bar Nor woman who killed herself in *The Forbidden Man*.

him, I would do worse. He convinced me in my vulnerability that Sarakena's spirit was reaching out to me — crying out for revenge."

"So, what happened?" Ḷainjin asked.

"What happened is too long a story," Lañinpo continued. "The tide will fill the canals, you will fall asleep, and it will still be in the telling."

Ḷainjin looked at Ewalt. "I won't sleep. I wait for the tide to return. Tell your story. I love to hear tales about our home islands of long ago, to see how our way of life changed as they sailed out into our part of the ocean."

"Here is the first tale that Kanari taught me," Lañinpo said. "It's supposed to explain the meaning of *kakar*."[181]

"Good!" Ḷainjin said. "That, I believe, was his word for 'bravery,' and I remember him as a brave and happy warrior."

"That's the point," said Lañinpo. "All warriors are supposed to attain the state of *kakar*. It's the result of their initiation process. But first, the tale of Sendam, the spirit man, the father of warfare. His mother was a wild pig and his father, a lowly villager. When the men of his village hunted down, killed, and ate his mother, Sendam retaliated by destroying them and moving his sister and her children to Murik,[182] where he found the villagers fighting with much chaos and without weapons. He introduced the spear and sling — and the concepts of hunter and prey, victory, and death — to the battlefield."

Lañinpo coughed and cleared his throat. "The villagers of Kopar were under attack by two sea-eagle spirits that nightly copulated in a tree above the village. Sendam climbed up and killed them there. The villagers below wanted to honor him with a great feast, but Sendam refused their offer and instead insisted each man bring his woman to copulate with him. But the husband of the woman Sendam wanted the most refused him. That's when Sendam turned himself into a tree. The men coveted the trunk for the center post of their cult house. When they tried to carry the trunk back to their

[181] Small ceremonial spears kept in the Bar Nor men's house that can be touched only by those men who have successfully been initiated into the kakar cult; bravery in battle.

[182] The Murik Lakes lie just north of the mouth of the Sepik River. The Bar Nor live in five or so villages along the banks of its mangrove swamp. This area was a precontact maritime trading center similar to Sigaba.

village, it suddenly became too heavy to carry. It wasn't until their women came once more to copulate with the spirit man that they were able to carry it closer. The story repeated itself several times before the men of the village found success."

"I don't understand the story," said Ḷainjin. "Kanari used that word *kakar* as though he was proud of it. What's to be proud of in that story?"

"You must learn to think like a man of the west," Lañinpo said, coughing again. "The men had to overcome their jealousy to become successful. Kanari would say, 'A victorious warrior must be free of all ties.' A mangrove man cuts loose his ties to his woman during the initiation process. That was the goal Kanari had for me. First, to complete the initiation process, then to culminate my initiation into the *kakar* cult by avenging Sarakena's death by killing the brother who demeaned her.

"By the time we arrived back in the Lakes, I was ready to begin the process." Lañinpo paused again to clear his throat. "Kanari gave me one of his cross cousin's daughters. A mangrove man's only path into the cult lies between the legs of a woman. Her name was Bwakama, and Kanari held her in the highest regard. Her charm was such that she was sure to raise my status in his *kakar* cult immediately. She seemed to have an insatiable desire to copulate with me, and she seduced me into it repeatedly. We did it during the night as her sisters giggled at the noises we made. We did it in the afternoon behind bushes, watching the villagers pass by. I began to think of nothing else and hardened at the very thought or sight of her."

Wheezing, Lañinpo continued. "The initiation process is led by the *pokanog*, otherwise referred to as 'the knot.' This is a leader selected for his ability to concentrate solely on his job. His job is to untie the knot in the string that binds the *kakar* spears after they've been taken down for display, then to retie and rewrap them and put them away in the loft of the cult house, where they're stored. He must accomplish this without touching the spears. They're not real spears but small decorated images of spears. It's taboo to touch them. Their power lies with the *kakar* spirits that inhabit them. These spirits are deadly to the unpure and uninitiated.

"The knot appoints his successor based on a single measure: he should find the rare man who is 'hard' and strong enough to control his desires.

When a woman enters the cult house, she is bent on one thing only — seducing her husband's sponsor. The knot must remain chaste in the face of desire. He must coordinate this copulation. The cult house is distinguished from other structures by a roof ridge, or 'nose,' at each end to allow smoke to escape from its dual hearths. It has a dimly lit center where the erotic ceremony is to take place. Bwakama was to enter the cult house from its 'anus' or rear 'nose,' and Kanari was to enter from the other by crawling beneath a curtain, symbolic of their mothers' skirts, made of pounded sago palm midribs. The knot was to oversee their copulation amid the dim light of the firepits at each end.

"I was to wait for them in our house," Lañinpo said, coughing again. "After Kanari 'shot' her with his spear in the presence of the knot and the *kakar* spirits, he was to escort her home. She was to return unwashed and prepare my supper of sago pudding while Kanari lingered outside to listen for any anger in my voice. Tradition required me to absorb these otherwise humiliating acts with complete composure. I remained as calm as lagoon waters to lee of a storm and passed my right of initiation. However, not finished enhancing my prestige, the very next day, she flirted with another in the senior cult, who also demanded his right to shoot her. Then so forth each night, she returned with a new achievement until she had seduced the entire membership. Finally, she culminated my initiation with the most prestigious act possible — she seduced the knot himself, which forced him to step down in disgrace.

"Kanari was ecstatic at her success. Outwardly, I kept my composure, but inwardly, I was shamefaced. My mistake was to confide in the little akebu. Understanding little of my objective other than coveting the death of my Sarakena's brother, the akebu poisoned him and brought me his head. Such a rogue act by an uninitiated man was taboo and sure to be answered with retaliation, so we sailed for our lives that night and never returned to Murik. It was only after we arrived in Pohnpei and met with Raipuinloko that the akebu presented the *kakar* spears as a gift to the Saudeleur and I became aware he had stolen them!"

"But you said those spirits are deadly to the uninitiated?" said Ewalt.

"Or so they say," replied Lañinpo.

"Well, what if Raipuinlañ touched them? Could that have been the cause of his death?"

Lañinpo had no answer forthcoming, and after a few moments of each looking at the others, all ended up looking to the akebu for an answer.

"No! I tell do not touch. Very much power. No need to touch! I tell."

Ewalt, visibly shaken, looked at Ḷainjin, who turned again to Lañinpo, who — in turn — inhaled and wheezed his assent.

"What? He was old man," exclaimed the akebu, with a smile that appeared not as innocent as before.

"Yes, he was old, but he seemed to get old very fast at the end." Ewalt said. He left to check the tide level.

The tide turns

The moon was rising round and tranquil against multishades of transparent blue as their small contingent of overloaded proas cruised within the shelter of the Ant lagoon to lee of its string of southmost islets. They beached in the high tide just east of a narrow passageway on the reef between two of them. The women found dry spots along the shore, flopped down on the sand, and chatted like birds at nest. The men cut and split fresh coconut fronds they had gathered up and down the strand. They passed these to the women, who then plaited and strung them together into a long barrier, or *ok*,[183] that they planned to fence between the islets to trap circles of fish as they swam lagoonward in the receding tide. Likewise, they plaited baskets for their catch, working rapidly in good humor. All were happy to be ashore, and the night was perfect for their mission. The tide had begun to ebb, and the moon was rising rapidly through the palms to further light their work from behind. All manner of fish had no doubt crept out of the lagoon to feed on the flooded ocean-side reef, and they would eventually return through the passageway they planned to fence.

"Who would have thought?" said Anitok, as he and Ijokelekel lowered the sails and trimmed the decks of his craft. "The women have done more to further your plans than us men."

How could he disagree? Kāmeto had single-handedly won the battle with Ļañinni. Erwina had arranged for them to take refuge on her father's island.

---

[183] A barrier made of coconut-palm leaves stripped from their fronds, tied together, and plaited into a barrier to trap fish.

The previous night, Maalal had caressed the throat of Saulikin Ant and announced he had agreed, against his better judgement, to allow them temporary refuge. They had only brought three proas. All the others they had left back at Areu in Ant, where their contingent had camped. After fishing, they were planning to walk back because they hoped to fill all three proas with fish. They all needed to exercise their legs after so many days at sea.

"The men will have their chance when the battle begins," Ijokelekel responded.

"No man could do better than any one of them, but they wait patiently for your decision," continued Anitok, still concentrating upon the women. "All three seem to revere you. They're like ripe fruits hanging on a tree outside your house. Why not pluck one and offer the rest to the others?"

"It looks like Saulikin Ant has already chosen one of them," said Ijokelekel.

"He chose the evening star that comes and then quickly disappears," Anitok said. "He'll search for her one night and find her coupled with another below the horizon."

"Paratak is like a father to me. That makes Erwina my sister, and to sleep with her taboo."

"That leaves the one who captivates your eyes? And not just yours. What does your throat say about that one?" asked Anitok.

"Her eyes shy away from mine."

"Not just yours," Anitok said. "That's her way with us all. Trust me, her eyes are kind to all, but they follow none of us."

The moon broke above the brush and shone through the palm trunks to light their faces as they talked. The men continued to bustle about with their adzes, cutting and then tearing strips of leaflets from each side of the sapling coconut fronds.

"I asked her father for her once and he never responded," admitted Ijokelekel.

"That means he awaits his daughter's decision. He's a man acclaimed for his fairness," Anitok said. "You don't have to take your adze to the stalk. Just thump it a little to see if it's ripe for the picking. The men await your decision and so might she."

"Soon our sailors' eyes will be surrounded by so many beautiful Pohnpeian porpoises they won't know which way to turn."

"True perhaps. But in the interim, the nights are cold, and that one has a fire in her belly that would last till dawn."

"Her mother's name is Liṃanṃan," Ijokelekel said.

"And her father is the shark that never sleeps — a combination for the ages. Don't allow such fruit to be wasted or mistreated in the hands of another."

"How many days will Saulikin Ant allow us to stay and prepare our attack?"

"That's a question for our evening star," joked Anitok.

"How many days of anidep will you need to train the men?"

"If we fish at night and practice every day, it will take the rest of this moon and at least half of the next just to get their lines straight and make a show of strength."

"Have you counted the men?" asked Ijokelekel.

"We are three hundred and thirty-three to a man. That's either a lucky number or a cursed one."

"And the jebwa?"

"Many of these men have no spears," said Anitok.

"We must use what we have in shifts. What about *kōņņat*? Can we straighten those with fire?"

"We'll try everything. But will we have enough time?"

"We have plenty of time," responded Ijokelekel. "The Saudeleur has no fleet. He can't touch us as long as Saulikin Ant provides us refuge."

"The Saudeleur seems to share your faith that, if your people turn back to the beliefs of their ancestors, their god of thunder will restore them to their former prosperity," Anitok said.

"The trader in him said that. The prosperity of his people depends upon trade, so he's in favor of anything that renews construction in the village. Saulikin Ant wants to provide items of trade again, especially the eels to rehabilitate the islets of Idedh and Darong. But it may take many seasons for another Nahn Samohl to re-emerge — if ever.

"His words still linger in my ears," added Anitok. "'A man is less afraid of having his soul eaten than of losing his private parts to a hungry eel!'"

"But I doubt he believes in the temple of Nahn Sapwe or the necessity to revolt — or even believes my story."

"Your story is incredible. When I saw those men take their families and drift off from Wōjjā, I looked upon them as principled but foolish for their willingness to die out of loyalty to a feeble old man. Now you have given them a chance for life, and they look to you as their irooj. You are Ijokelekel. When you say you are the son of thunder, they don't snicker!"

"But does Saulikin Ant snicker?"

"Maybe his women do! But not when Maalal wraps her legs around the old fool, pounds his back with her heels, then squeezes him like a lime until he cries out like a night bird ready to empty his gullet. Not these men who follow you like a line of *m̧ọle*[184] on the reef, and not their women, who thought their men cowards until they raised sail and abandoned Taklur's feebleminded drift to nowhere!"

Thus, they sat. And thus, they strategized as the moon continued its upward climb, the tide continued to recede, and the women continued the crisscross plaiting and tying together of their *ok*. Once the tide had dropped to waist deep and the length was deemed adequate to span the passage, the whole group gathered, grabbed hold of the *ok*, and strung it out along the shore. The first in line waded into the water. Ijokelekel saw his opportunity and seized it. Looking back at Anitok with a smile, he rushed to cut in line and took the spot next to Kāmeto. He raised the *ok* where it dragged at the shoreline and followed her into the water.

"*Wōt jej*!"[185] he exclaimed loudly. Hoping to initiate a conversation with her, he added softly, "That's cold."

"Your own fault," she replied loudly, as the group waded slowly across the reef. "You men grew those appendages, and now you're complaining you've got no way to warm them up. We women are warm inside, aren't we, sisters?"

"That's right! We have no sympathy for your problems!" shouted a woman up ahead. The water was now up to his waist and getting deeper as he approached the midway point between the islets.

---

[184] Rabbitfish: *Siganus rostratus*; also called "ellōk." This fish schools in a straight line.

[185] A more emphatic expression of surprise than "Jeej."

"Maybe a passing shark will relieve him of his big problem!" said another, to much laughter.

Yet another woman chanted, "*Kook, kook, kook, kook! Wōde im ajoḷe*![186] There was even more laughter.

"Maybe a shark ate yours when you were little, and you just don't remember," retorted one of the men.

"You must be right!" another woman answered. "I still have this little stub that stands up in anger now and again! Come, I'll show you! But no warming up. That's reserved for my man. It's where he likes to store his little fishing pole. His last chore before he falls asleep!"

This hilarious exchange, the sort of merriment that brings serendipitous good luck, brought laughter to the line. They waded until the first of them reached the far shore. The round moon was now blazing at them, reflecting up into their eyes off the water in the passageway and lighting their expectant faces. Yet they all knew nothing was likely to occur for a long, long time.

Jurōk[187] was the most boring of all fishing methods. It was a waiting game where the determination of the fishers to stand their ground as human posts behind their leaf barrier would inevitably scare their prey to death, trapping them in shallow pools as the tide receded to naught. Based on what they had heard from the local villagers, they were expecting a large catch. The small surface fish would pass over the *ok*, and the small bottom fish would eventually skitter under. The larger the fish, the timider they were, and the more ingrained they were in their lagoonward passage. These were lagoon fish — crossing the reef into the ocean when the tide retreated would never occur to them.

Such a large variety of fish would make excellent tribute to the Saudeleur from Saulikin Ant. This, as repeatedly pointed out by Maalal, would demonstrate his ongoing loyalty to the Saudeleur and alleviate any fear that he intended to side with Ijokelekel in a rebellion. Per their plan, Paratak and Erwina were resting back at camp, waiting to fill his canoe and return upwind, back across the ocean passage to Nahn Madol.

---

[186] "Chew it and gnaw at it!" (As if it were a pandanus nodule.)

[187] Placing a barrier between islets to strand fish on the reef as the tide recedes.

"How many fish can we catch like this?" asked Kāmeto casually, no longer speaking loudly to the group but rather in the same hushed tone Ijokelekel had used when he first spoke. This was the first question she had asked him since their journey began. He was ecstatic.

"We did this once for Likōkkālọk last season and filled, as I recall, eight or ten *kilōk*."[188]

"Doesn't it depend on how often the fishers do this?" she asked.

"I suppose so, but it doesn't seem like the islanders come down this way very much. It doesn't look like anybody's living over here."

"How are we going to get our catch back to the stone village before they spoil?"

"The group back at camp is preparing to salt the fish as soon as our proas deliver them," said Ijokelekel.

"So, we walk back? Uhh! My legs are sore."

His thoughts turned to the beautiful skinny ankles popping below her mat skirt that fixated his stare every time he stood behind her, and his mind flashed back to the image of her innocently revealing her most private parts for his inspection the very first day they were together. What had intervened to spoil their plans to unite?

Suddenly, a ruckus in the line back toward the middle of the passageway caused several fishers to abandon their stations. A woman cried, "Pako! Pako!" Then, in a calm, laughing tone, a man's voice declared, "*Jaab*[189] *boraañ, boraañ*."[190] They had allowed a stingray to pass through the line and had accidently broken the *ok* in the process. Several rushed to the area to reconnect it.

"*Boraañ*! What was he doing up on the reef?" Kāmeto asked, resuming the conversation. "They usually spear those in the lagoon, right?"

"Right, and from the protection of a canoe. It must have been fishing here in the deep water of the passage when we arrived and scared it up onto the reef. It will either bring us luck or the opposite," he replied.

---

[188] A strong, trapezoid-shaped basket plaited from the central portion of a coconut leaf. It features braided handles.

[189] "No. (It's not a shark, it's a…)"

[190] Stingray.

"I just hope that's the last of them. I hate those ugly things. *Mādepep*[191] of the sea!"

"I wouldn't fear them. I've heard they're only dangerous if you spear them."

"Or step on them! But Papa taught me to believe in myself and not fear anything. So here I am."

He turned to her, about to make a joke at that last remark, but hesitated. They both knew she was still unpenetrated. He hated it when people teased him so decided to let it pass.

"I can hear what you're thinking, Ijokelekel" she said quietly. "You're not a crude man, but you can't stop longing for me, can you? I have felt your eyes caressing my body like a persistent breeze. Caught you staring at me like a hungry dog watching its master's every move. You can't stop thinking about my between because I'm guilty of *kapāl*![192] It's my grandmother Litaknam's fault. She taught me the woman's weapon of love magic: 'Set the hook hard, then give your catch plenty of line to run until he thinks you have set him free. Then ever so slowly squeeze the line and pull him in.' I'm sorry for what I did to you. It was wrong. You're a nice man, Ijokelekel. Most men are crude and they disgust me."

"You mean Ḷañinni," he said, changing an uncomfortable subject. "Well, you got your revenge on him. He's probably dead!"

"I sought no revenge! Yes, he scared me when I was young, but to tell you the truth, I enjoyed the attention. I hurt him because I feared he would kill you in battle. If I wanted him dead, I could have swiped his throat. Father taught me the best way for a woman to stop a man was to swipe his wrist."

"You didn't believe Nahn Sapwe would protect me in battle?" Ijokelekel asked her.

"I didn't grow up with your religion. I decided to take things in my own hands," she said.

"To tell you the truth, even I wasn't sure who I was. Now I'm certain who I am because my destiny is right here before me. This Saudeleur seems weak and vulnerable." He lowered his voice. "The season seems ripe for my plan

---

[191] Butterfly.

[192] Magic; as used in this context, love magic.

to come to fruition. We're both here as we planned. The only thing lacking is your father's permission. Why hasn't he spoken?" Now he was speaking in an even more hushed tone.

"Father has warned me not to do or say anything to diminish your faith in your mission. We both believe in you and want you to succeed."

"If you give yourself to me, you'll make me the most successful man alive. I find myself living for only two things, and you are one of them."

"And I'm trying to tell you that's the *kapāl* talking. You have only one mission!"

Kāmeto suddenly screamed and jumped to Ijokelekel's side. He felt her foot on his and her leg against his as her arm reached around his back and her hand clutched onto his shoulder. He saw a dark shadow nose its way through the coconut-leaf barrier. A reef shark had apparently rubbed against her.

"He felt like sand rubbing against my thigh," she exclaimed. "I'd rather fish some other way!"

"And you said your father taught you to fear nothing."

"He also taught me to think about what I'm doing," Kāmeto said, moving back to her post along the *ok*.

"Okay, let's do that. You saw a passing shark and said 'Hi!' to him."

"I'm pretty sure it was a girl shark because it didn't bite me."

"Even if it had been a man shark, it wouldn't have bitten you, and you know it," said Ijokelekel. "Why not? Because you know you don't smell or move like a fish. She only bumped your leg because she nosed through where you stood, and she took advantage of that to say good-bye. Would you have rather caught her on a hook? In that case, she might have taken your hook and all your line. At best, you would have had to struggle with her half the night just to cut her loose. Or would you have rather met her underwater with a fish at the end of your spear? In that case, your sister would have taken your catch faster than a *pejwak*[193] gobbles a baitfish. And don't think she would have bothered to say thanks. Or would you have rather—"

"Enough, I get it! So, we just stand here like shark bait for the rest of the night?" said Kāmeto.

[193] Brown noddy: *Anous stolidus*.

"They don't call this *kijen pako*."[194] They call it *jurōk*. We stand like posts."

"Pretty dumb if you ask me."

"The point is, the fish are dumber. Even the big ones can easily pass between the leaves of our *ok*, but they won't. Why? Because just like you, they're afraid of something they aren't used to and don't expect."

"You sound just like my father. I suppose he taught you all this."

"He taught me to look around, study things, and see them for what they are. For instance, where is the wind coming from?" Ijokelekel asked.

She pointed her head toward the islet to their left, where their craft were beached.

"Right. The wind is coming from the east, as usual. Then why are swells coming from the south and breaking on the ocean reef ahead of us?" he said, pointing and raising his head toward the passage between the islands ahead of them. "And why is there a faint swell sweeping across the lagoon reef behind us, entering the passageway and clashing with the oncoming current and causing these little ripples around us to stand high?"

"I know all that. You're talking about the *wapepe* now," said Kāmeto. "He started pointing out the four swells about the time I started to walk." She laughed. "I couldn't get him to shut up about them."

"Well, that was his life. He traced those swells to their beginnings. He traveled back in time to the far islands of our ancestors. He's probably told me things man-to-man that he would never tell a daughter."

"Like what? Tell me what!" she begged.

"The ways of the women out there for one."

"What ways?"

"Ask your sisters. You women hold hands when you walk. So do us men. You have your sister talk. We men have our talk as well."

They bantered on like this for some time, but Ijokelekel didn't reveal her father's tales of western women and their peculiarities. How was he to tell her about the women from Truk,[195] who enlarged their womanhood to increase their pleasure and required a man to rub them as though polishing

[194] Shark food.

[195] The next island and language group west of Pohnpei.

an adze? He told of the dark-skinned Manus,[196] who shave their heads but nevertheless remained, at least to him, the most desirable women out there, and the Black women of the far west, who turn their backsides to their men and pinch them with shells to prolong their intercourse. He hadn't been told of such things personally by Pako, as they called him, but by others who had relayed his tales. His apprenticeship had been different than that of the others, almost as if Pako treated him as a son. Ijokelekel assumed this was because he had asked for his daughter. Since he had heard these tales thirdhand, he had found some easy to understand. Others not so.

He had grown up under the cloud of telling his story to deaf, unbelieving ears. But once he had proved himself, others started to listen. Lately, he had tasted the gratification of being both heard and believed. He went on to tell Kāmeto about his growing up. How he had come to know Maalal and Anitok. He knew she had heard his story from their throats, but he needed her to hear it from his. He needed her to hear him this night — this auspicious night that had started so favorably — beneath this round moon that rose slowly amid the clearest of dark blue skies, casting its light momentarily upon the gleaming, rippling waters as they retreated from the reef beneath them.

She broke into his story often, revealing that she was listening with interest, adding parts of her story in short anecdotes and in such a simple, self-deprecating way that he respected her more for her innocent honesty. This was how they passed their time, and the fishers on either side grew closer as the tide withdrew and the passageway narrowed to the point where others could listen to their chatter. He often felt her foot on his and felt pleasure as his manhood stirred and she appeared to look straight into his eyes now, even as he peered deep into hers. In a little while, they would be ready to drop their barrier onto the reef.

But then, by happenstance, an *aolōk*[197] passed between the leaflets of their *ok* and stung him above the ankle. "Waow! Aaah! *Aolōk*!" he cried, watching the offensive blue bubble drift away. Splashing and writhing in agony, he

---

[196] Part of Manus province, and the biggest Admiralty Island, Manus lies in the Bismarck Sea north of Papua New Guinea.

[197] A Portuguese man-of-war; genus *Physalia*.

dropped the *ok* and limped off to the far islet, which was the closest shore. He didn't speak to the surprised fishers as he passed. Strangely flooding his thoughts was Lijāpe's admonition seasons ago when she had proudly handed him the face mat he was to use when his lines were chiseled. "*Kinjin emman*![198] Don't make the others feel your pain."

Kāmeto followed, imploring him to explain what was wrong. "An *aolōk* stung me!" he said, as she crept beneath his arm to support his limp and walked him up the shore to the dry sand. He collapsed there, feeling the poison creeping up into his groin as though it was an evil spirit taking revenge on the happiness he had felt but moments before. He fought the urge to enunciate his pain. He twisted his body and turned his head, refusing to let her see the agony he knew his face reflected.

He called to the two fishers approaching, saying he was okay and asking them to return to their stations.

"Aren't you supposed to pee on it?" said Kāmeto.

"I don't think I can stand right now."

They inspected his injured leg, where the assailant had whipped its lashing marks around his lower calf.

"All right, I've been waiting to do this all night anyway." She upfolded her mat skirts and squatted so low over his leg that he could feel her womanhood. "Is that where it stung you?"

"No, a little higher. That's it … right there," he said. As their eyes met, he felt the warm urine gushing against his leg as her body kissed his wound. She held the position — one she had exercised from youth, no doubt, from her daily gathering of fallen breadfruit leaves from the courtyard outside her parents' house — for some time. He imagined her strong legs squatting like that, imagined her hovering above his erect manhood, which he understood was the preferred position of Rālik women. As their eyes met, each of them seemed to read the other's thoughts, which neither cared to hide. But then the airway in his throat began to narrow, and he began to struggle for breath. His remembrance of that night — or rather, its remainder — would be clouded forever in pain, in struggling to walk and simply catch his breath.

---

198 "Scratch of a man."

The fishing trip, he gathered later, was successful and ended with baskets of fish being sailed back to their camp. His followers salted these and loaded a portion for the Saudeleur. Paratak and Erwina then sailed as immediately as possible for the stone village.

Ijokelekel did recall refusing transport by both boat and dragged litter, professing that he was okay to walk. Then he remembered he and Kāmeto falling so far behind their companions that they were unable to cross the final, wide passageway across the reef with them to rejoin the encampment on the other side. They arrived at the passage a little too late and were caught by the tide.

He recalled Kāmeto naked in the moonlight, watching the tide-engulfed reef to the east as the moon drifted deep into the western sky. She would have piled *kōņņat* leaves to pad their nest on the islet and then removed her wet skirts. He would have removed his wet kilt and then implored her to lie down on top of him, to cushion herself against the still-sharp coral stones at the islet's end. Long before the approach of dawn, the need to clutch at each other's warmth — the desire to embrace the sweet sleep they required — would have necessitated that they first relieve the constantly swelling obstacle between their naked bodies. He imagined in his unsullied mind all the ways they could have done so. Yet truth be told, the single most painful event he did remember from that night was her abrupt retreat before penetration as she said, "Make ready," and then her belated return at daylight, offering the excuse that she had found a warm pool of water in which to bathe on the ocean side.

By morning, the poison from the *aolōk* lashing had subsided. Yet this pain from Kāmeto's rejection was fresh and disconcerting in his throat, though he didn't speak of it as they crossed the final stretch of open reef together. He slept again on the other side before a visit by Saulikin Ant, who — in his polite manner — congratulated and thanked him for the enormous catch.

Maalal, who had become Saulikin Ant's constant companion, had crowned him with a sweet-smelling head lei.

"I wanted to go fishing with you too." She spoke softly in Kajin Rālik. "However" — she raised her eyebrows in fake pomposity — "I take my obligations to the chief very seriously."

Maalal spoke no Pohnpeian, so it was a mystery to all how she had gained influence over him so quickly. Saulikin Ant, of course, spoke no Kajin Rālik. He was a modestly adorned trader with grey-streaked hair who stood out merely by the confident way he carried himself. So, her little joke was private — except she had glanced over at him and emphasized the "obligations" part with a funny face and an almost imperceptible jerk of her hips.

"I never know what she says," admitted Saulikin Ant in Pohnpeian, "but the spirited way she says it makes me laugh! She knows how to make an old man feel young again."

"This young man is actually quite virile," Maalal continued, still joking and showing she did understand some of what he said. "One of his women had a son last season. I get along well with them. Trust me, they're happy to get a break from this beast."

"Thank you also for all the help," said Saulikin Ant. "The Rālik Islanders you have brought us are hard working. They have already cleaned away the islet's brush and brought up stones from the beaches to pave the settlement area. This encourages me to plead you stay longer," he concluded.

Maalal flashed another of her "look what I'm accomplishing" faces before dragging him off to complete their tour.

The stones have ears

Back at Kelepwei, Lañinpo had completed his story and appeared exhausted by the task. Ḷainjin watched Ewalt wade back to Pahn Kadira, retrieve his canoe with the help of the guards, and paddle toward home. Lañinpo and his brother spent the night and disappeared the next day.

Ḷainjin then spent a few days resting from his voyage. He kept trying to imagine the details of his friend's incredible story. Lañinpo seemed so sick. How had he ever managed his return? The surprising thing was how Ḷainjin's impression of the little akebu had changed so quickly. What a contradiction he was. Half western man, half Rālik. Half good, half *tuwe.* How was Ḷainjin ever to trust such an enigma? Should he consider him a friend, an enemy, or something in between?

Such were Ḷainjin's thoughts as he sat atop the south wall of Kelepwei, enjoying the faint breeze in the early evening moonlight and watching the transparent color of the cloudless sky turn from light to dark blue. A rare proa approached from the south. The craft had entered the break in the south village wall to the sounding of a conch shell. This was the first warning sound he had heard though he had noticed that the guards were back. As the heavily loaded proa closed the distance in the light wind, he gradually began to suspect it was his friend Paratak returning home. Ḷainjin held up his arm to the craft as it approached the west wall of Kelepwei. Then he climbed down, crossed the courtyard, and reappeared through the north opening, where his proa was anchored.

He signaled again just as the craft turned the corner, headed into the wind, and stalled. He recognized the passenger as Erwina, who busied herself lowering the halyard as her father began paddling toward him with powerful strokes.

"*Kaselehlie kompoakapah*!"[199]

"*Kaselehlie*! You trick me big! All day to sail from Ant!" complained Paratak, good-humoredly bringing up the flaw in his boat's design. His daughter tossed Ḷainjin their painter, and Paratak dropped a stern anchor stone behind him.

"All right, I promise to fix that for you now," offered Ḷainjin, as he tied their craft to one of several vertical takai along the wharf. The moon had risen above the walls, casting a shadow where they stood and glaring off the calm waters of the canal. The smell of undried, salted fish hung heavy in the still air of the lee shore.

"Jau Areu bring fish for Saudeleur," boasted Paratak. He followed Erwina and jumped ashore, then reached out to clasp Ḷainjin's already extended arm.

They each repeated, "*Kaselehlie meing*,"[200] as they had that day long ago when the *jekaro* boys expected blood to blot the sand upon their meeting. But this was no formal expression of love. This, to Erwina's amazement, was an expression of true friendship. The men tugged and tugged again at each other's arms, looking into the other's eyes, not wanting to let go.

"The Saudeleur," joked Ḷainjin, "told me he wants me to take the Jau Areu title back. He says you fish too slow. 'Too many days now without fish!' he mentioned yesterday."

"Saudeleur just like pet *kasap*.[201] At least wild bird will lead you to island. Pet *kasap* useless. No point your way. No do anything but wait for fish, preen, poop, and complain."

Then, in a sign of great intimacy, he touched the side of Ḷainjin's head and, with his thumb, rubbed away a tear of happiness from his cheek. "You want title back? Where is knife? I carve it here." He laughed, stepped back into the water, and tugged on his painter. Removing a salted mullet from one of his baskets, he rinsed it in the clear water of the canal, then handed it to Ḷainjin.

---

199 "Hello, old friend."

200 A formal greeting in Pohnpeian.

201 Pohnpeian for "frigate bird."

It was well scaled and had a good smell, so Ļainjin tore a strip of sliced flesh from the skin with his teeth, chewed, and savored the excellent taste. "Your pet *kasap* should be very happy."

"Pleased yes. Happy no. This one never happy. This one like Mānnijepļā — never satisfied."

"Come, I have food from Mānnijepļā for you. I know Erwina has you caught up on our stories. Now you must tell me yours."

Ļainjin led them behind the walls to the tattered shelter where he had rolled his sleeping mat. He placed a large basket of food from the Saudeleur and another filled with freshly husked coconuts before them. They sat on the coral pebbles close to the great *sakau*[202] stones that had sung out in years past. Something there reminded him of the hundreds of previous tales told by countless seafarers who had visited from afar and met and sat in this very place.

There, the mercurial Pohnpeian related the story Ļainjin had waited patiently for so many seasons to hear. Because it was partly the same story Erwina had heard him tell Ijokelekel, she added carefully placed clarifications that served to punctuate the singsong of her father's broken Kajin Rālik. He told of the five lonely nights and days he had experienced after Ļainjin tricked him into sailing home that evening. Told how he had taken Ļainjin's advice and hove to and lay below in his cramped hull as night fell. How his body had begun to ache from the constant strain of just holding his position in the rolling seas. At last, on the fifth morning, he sighted the mountains and told of the joy he felt at seeing them — and later, at seeing his parents. Then he told of the sadness he had felt at hearing that his woman had taken another, as well as the pride of receiving the Jau Areu title from Raipuinlañ. Then he spoke of the admiration he held for the man who had the wisdom to trick him and the foresight to predict his thankfulness. Finally, he spoke about the fear and real danger of his trip: "It cooked, with this gratitude, beneath cover of earth oven into mixture as sweet and rich as ripe breadfruit with coconut milk baked into center."

This latter phrase eventually caused much laughter. It began with an unexpected burst of air from Ļainjin's mouth, followed by a giggle from

---

[202] Kava; a drink with anesthetic properties made from the mashed roots of the propagated *Piper methysticum*, or pepper plant.

Erwina, and finally, a laugh all around as even Paratak joined in, poking fun at the way he had connected it all to his stomach in typical Paratak-speak.

"You must be hungry, Father," said Erwina, extending their laugh. She reached into the food basket, produced something baked in a leaf, and handed it to her father, who accepted it in a similar self-deprecating manner as their laugh at his cooked-breadfruit analogy.

Of course, they were tired from their voyage, but they stayed up late because of the unexpected excitement of seeing their friend. At some point during the night, Paratak brought up Lipanmai. When Ļainjin had asked him if Ļōbwedi[203] was still alive, he said that he had died a few years past. But Ļōbwedi had suggested in passing that he thought Ijokelekel might be the son of Ļōpako. Paratak had asked Lipanmai about this but was told that Nahn Sapwe was the boy's father. Then Paratak had heard rumors that Ijokelekel was familiar with Kāmeto, so he was asking for clarification.

Just then, they heard a sound outside the entranceway, and Ļainjin rose to investigate. He thought he might have seen someone disappear around the corner of the wall but was too tired to pursue them.

When he returned, he found that Erwina had discreetly answered Paratak's question to his satisfaction. He turned quiet and, perhaps exhausted from his trip, soon began to snore.

Erwina took the opportunity to talk to Ļainjin privately. "I explained to Father. He'll keep it to himself."

"Has Kāmeto told Ijokelekel yet?" Ļainjin asked.

"No, she's waiting for later. Perhaps after the battle. Mother implored you to come fetch me, didn't she?"

"Yes, I'm here to take both of you home as soon as possible. Your mothers are so worried, they're hysterical."

"I know," said Erwina. "She was eating sand when I left. It was pathetic, but you promised you would bring me here, and I've just arrived. He's just like I remembered. Big, strong, and gentle. That's the way he always seemed to me at least. I know Mother didn't treat him well, and then you had to chase him away."

---

[203] A Seeker; aka Bwedi.

"He and your mother weren't happy together. He's better off here although I see now that circumstance might turn against him."

"How can I tell him I'm leaving as soon as I get here? Don't you plan to help Ijokelekel win his battle?"

"Erwina, this isn't a safe place for any of us. This Saudeleur is dangerous. I don't trust him."

"Well, I'm meeting him tomorrow. I have a message for him from Ijokelekel."

"I'm not sure how to say this, Erwina. Don't you think Ijokelekel is being a little naive about all this? It's true this Saudeleur is weaker than his predecessors, and trade has stagnated for some reason. So, the Saudeleur receives less tribute, but he'll fight like a cornered boar for this village!"

"Of course, he's naive! Anybody can see that. That's why everybody loves him. He's going to win! You should have seen him stand up to Ḷañinni before Kāmeto cut his arm."

"With my shark tooth, I suppose," said Ḷainjin.

"Yes, so you've heard?"

"Yes, I followed you to Wōjjā. But what if he doesn't win? Battles are often won by the most treacherous. Are you willing to die with him?"

Erwina didn't answer. Perhaps he had given her something to consider. He decided to let her digest it.

"Well, all I can say is that this trip has liberated me from the confinements of Lae," she finally said. "For the first time in my life, I feel like I'm myself and not a mat my mother is plaiting."

That next morning, the Saudeleur's guards showed up to summon the three of them, and they set out to take him the salted fish, yet to be dried. Ḷainjin noticed that the number of guards at his compound had increased. As before, Sau-temoi entered his meeting house from his adjacent quarters. Adorned as before, he sat above the seated trio on his raised platform.

He politely expressed gratitude for the gifts from Saulikin Ant but seemed indignant that Paratak had been absent for so long.

"Who is this lovely Rālik woman you have brought for me?"

From the tone of his voice, Ḷainjin knew it had been a mistake to present Erwina to the Saudeleur. Paratak explained that she was his daughter from Rālik and she brought word from Ijokelekel.

"Then, by all means, present these words from Ijokelekel," the Saudeleur told Erwina. "No, wait. I think I've heard them before, from his father. He is a religious man who plans only to light a fire at the temple and worship Nahn Sapwe. Is that not correct?"

As best he could, Paratak interpreted the Saudeleur's words for his daughter.

"Yes, that is correct," said Erwina. "He wants to turn the island back to the way it was before his mother was killed or rather ... died." Paratak again interpreted.

"Very helpful! How lucky we are that Ijokelekel has sent such a beautiful, truthful, and innocent emissary. Paratak, you can now leave her here with me while you kindly fetch me the feathers of the Tiripeijo bird. Or perhaps you would rather bring this Ijokelekel and his new friend Saulikin Ant to appear before me with due haste?" he continued in his condescending and overly witty way. "To ensure your speedy return, she will remain at Pahn Kadira under my close observation."

He uttered these last words with sly insinuation and a lewd glance at Erwina, coupled with an enigmatic rise of his eyebrows.

Ḷainjin began to seethe at the Saudeleur's arrogant demands and insisted he, too, would stay at Pahn Kadira to personally guard her from mistreatment. He soon realized that, by losing his temper, he had fallen headlong into the trap set for him. Before he had a chance to prepare for a fight, the Saudeleur's guards had seized him and bound his arms from behind.

"Absolutely, I'd like that. You can watch as I exercise my right to pluck firstfruits."

At this, Paratak stood and walked over to the Saudeleur. He loomed over Sau-temoi, who showed no fear, and his attendants soon overcame the concerned father with violent clubs of their spears.

"Go now! Complete your mission swiftly and return to find your lovely daughter unharmed. So, promised. Don't forget to tell Ijokelekel that his father awaits his return. This useless *kasap,* as you refer to me, will have him placed in our ancestor's treasure vault at Kariahn.[204] There, he'll be sealed without food and water in his *lolong* with some of the largest stones that pave the old market."

At this, Ļainjin signaled *no* to his friend. Further struggle on his behalf would be useless. He was unceremoniously dragged from the Saudeleur's house and out through the courtyard, where he was stunned and sickened by what he saw next. Apparently, the Saudeleur had had his proa filled with tinder, and his guards were in the process of setting it on fire. They placed him into a paddling canoe even as he abraded his wrists in an unsuccessful attempt to free his hands from their bind behind his back. Looking back as he was paddled away, he saw them light his most valuable possession on fire.

He turned his head, deciding not to watch. Enraged, he then got an unexpected tour of the same flooded canals that had once bustled with energetic trade. The attendants paddled him to Kariahn, where he had traded in prior years. It now appeared abandoned. Where, long ago, he had gained much wealth, they placed him into the very takai-walled vault that they had once guarded night and day, that had been the depository for the village's items of trade. Observing the large man-force necessary to move the large takai to seal him in the vault, Ļainjin realized that his host must have been planning for days to encage him.

That scorpion fish! Sau-temoi must have received critical information from someone who had overheard his various conversations. The odd relationship between the Saudeleur and the akebu came to mind. Had the little akebu betrayed them? What now? The sounds of heavy takai levered on rollers, slid, and wedged into place filled his little chamber as they sealed its entrance with long, six-sided stones the thickness of his forearm from hand to elbow. He slowly began to face a suffocating darkness, only here and there illuminated by streams of light seeping through small spaces between the takai now surrounding him. No sleeping mat — no food — no water. Perhaps he could dig his way out? No, somewhere in the depths of his memory was the knowledge they had built the vault on a base of takai. He

[204] A Pohnpeian islet where trading takes place.

was entombed alive within a dense structure built to withstand the onslaught of *buñtokrear*'s fiercest slap as it entered a passage through the fringing reef, crossed the intervening lagoon, and collided with the walls surrounding the vault.

Ḷainjin had promised himself that he would proceed with caution, yet he had dropped his caution at first match and let Sau-temoi get the better of him. Now he sat trapped like a well-concealed trinket, so well encased it would take a large team of men just to release him. He felt cramped, isolated, and too disgusted with himself to think. Was his story to end this way, with his stupidity finally catching up with him? He was already cold, and the night had just begun. He lay down then curled into a corner. Sleep would be his only companion.

Yet there was someone who cared. Ḷainjin was awakened sometime during that night by the sound of water being poured.

"Find water. Open mouth," came a strange voice in what sounded like broken Pohnpeian.

Water dripped onto his shoulder. Turning his face upward in the dark, he raised his hand and searched to find the stream of water. The trickle was being poured from somewhere through the takai above. He opened his mouth first to taste it and then to quench a thirst that, in the cold, he had almost forgotten he had. Someone was giving him water to drink. Who? One of the guards perhaps? He overheard someone, almost certainly a guard, giving abrupt orders to the one pouring. Before he'd had his fill, the pouring stopped. Then all was silent save the gradually diminishing drips off the takai above him.

Ḷainjin felt relieved by the hope that Sau-temoi wasn't planning to let him die of thirst — not immediately at least. Yet he was a hostage. Who would know if he was alive or dead? Only the guards. Then he remembered Sau-temoi telling Paratak where he would be kept. Why would he mention where a hostage would be kept? Because he was bait for a trap. Kariahn was the most defensible place in the entire village. If Ijokelekel were to attack this place with his fleet, he would surely fail.

Ḷainjin had had a premonition about all this the night before, after speaking with Erwina. It was as though he was reliving a tragedy he had been through once before, when they had freed his mother. The only question now? Would it all be over in one terrible burst of death as before, or would the battle unwind slowly with the resultant death prolonged and the consequences more terrible than he could imagine? He had been like a *kōtkōt* pecking from one crumb to another, oblivious to the basket he was gradually creeping under. He envisioned the overly adorned Sau-temoi gleefully hiding, peeking, clutching the string to pull the stick out from beneath the basket.

Too many tides of good fortune had passed in and out, lulling him into treating life as a game constantly won. He had gotten careless, and now he was about to lose. He had already lost his boat, his most prized possession. He had awakened suddenly to realize it was no game at all. Life and death were in equal balance. How had he forgotten that? He must assume that the Saudeleur had miscalculated. Ijokelekel held him in high regard but wouldn't toss aside his plans to turn Pohnpei back to the past. He was unlikely to waste his chance for success by attacking here, where he was surely expected.

Of course, Ijokelekel didn't know Ḷainjin was his father, and he had warned Paratak not to tell him. He had traveled here to save his son and daughter. Now, due to his sluggish reaction, he had let the tide turn on him, and it was he that needed saving. He felt for a dry spot, curled up once more in the darkness, and returned to sleep.

He woke the next morning to remembrances of days past, when he had sat here counting his treasures with grand expectations for his life ahead. He had eventually traded these items for experiences. Now he had to figure out how to utilize these experiences somehow, to save his son and daughter from an unhappy end.

As the day progressed, it sounded as though more men were arriving. Ijokelekel wouldn't know from outside the walls how many were waiting inside. They had left only one small square space the size of a fist in the middle of where the entrance used to be. However, Ḷainjin found several additional spots between the takai where he could peer through and see the courtyard and two spots on the top of the eastern wall. Eventually, he got an idea of what was happening, and yes, it seemed that more men were slowly gathering. Many had spears, and he thought he saw pairs of men carrying heavy baskets to the tops of the walls. These would be rocks.

So, he spent the morning spying through one tiny window or another. He got quite thirsty, and then someone came again to pour water that splashed and then dripped down from the takai above him. He got the impression this person wasn't a guard, but he wasn't visible from any of his peepholes, and Ḷainjin was too busy gulping water to speak out. He vowed to better control himself the next time.

That night, he had his chance when he was again awakened by water splashing down from above. Pale light shone from a smaller moon.

"Who is this?" he shouted, just before opening his mouth to catch the water.

"No speaking!" A guard reprimanded him through the wall as though he had some way of stopping him.

There came no answer. Only slowly poured water and then nothing.

"Thank you!" he said to the quiet, empty vault.

The next day was a repeat of the day before. Again, Ḷainjin spent his time spying, through his small window and various peepholes, on the gathering throng of men in the courtyard. If they were preparing a surprise defense of the structure, what were they doing with all the canoes that had transported them there? Wouldn't these boats be a giveaway of the numbers inside? Canoes would normally be tied along the long eastern wall leading up to the main entrance of the central structure. However, these vessels wouldn't be visible to anyone approaching through the lagoon from the ocean-side passage or even to anyone who had successfully crossed the reef that fronted the wall until they reached its top. And by then, the forces on the other side would be there to quiet them. But surely, Ijokelekel would somehow get spies into the village who would see the paddling canoes lined up against him. Unless, of course, there were none to be seen. Perhaps the men were gathering so slowly because the wily Saudeleur was transporting them in successive trips, using a limited number of transport vessels. This was the more likely case, but was he making a strategic error by isolating his forces? What if Ijokelekel overran Pahn Kadira instead? But how was Ḷainjin to warn and advise?

This was his third day without food. He used to be good at fasting. Not so much anymore. But what he really needed was water. When it came again, he was quick to ask who was pouring.

Softly, in broken Kajin Rālik, came a response. "No safe to talk. Small water. Drink to live," the voice whispered.

This was a mystery as it wasn't Paratak's voice. Where had he heard that voice before?

Then the guard on the ground again admonished them in Pohnpeian. "No talking."

"It sounded like the akebu!" Ḷainjin thought. But he had only heard him speak a few words. It could have been any Pohnpeian, a guard even, who had but limited knowledge of his language. Then came a thought-provoked flash of fear. What if it was the akebu, and the Saudeleur had sent him there to poison him? Ḷainjin immediately checked his senses. Why was he so cold in the middle of the day? He started to breathe heavily. Then wondered if this was a symptom of the poison he had just drunk for the fourth time. He caught himself. Why would the Saudeleur go to all this trouble to encage him as a hostage and then kill him there? He began concentrating on the bits and pieces of conversations he could hear amid the comings and goings outside his vault and thought he heard several words that supported his suspicions. But was his mind playing tricks on him? He had to admit that it would be an ingenious form of slow torture. Would he prefer to die of thirst or poison?

By evening, he had resolved to stow his thirst and, instead of lapping up water like a dog, to get serious with whoever was pouring. He was determined to find out if it was the akebu. And if so, whether he was poisoning him.

"Are you akebu? Are you poisoning me?" he demanded.

"Yes, I am akebu. Yes, Sau-temoi sent me slow poison you," he said in broken Kajin Rālik.

"I knew it!" he thought.

Then he heard several thumps, as though the akebu was being clubbed. What seemed like the remainder of the water splashed down, wasted. "I trick Saudeleur. I no poison my brother friend. Take him home with you!"

His words became fainter as the guards continued to beat him and drag him off into the night.

What had Ḷainjin done now? Had he just exposed the single soul willing to help him? Did the guards know enough of his language to understand what he had said? Had his self-centered stupidity again gotten the best of him? When would he get the grip on himself necessary to further his cause? His every action so far had proved counterproductive. The remainder of that night proved the worst yet. He felt strangely unsettled and in despair. He thought about Likōkkālọk and Liṃanṃan and the smoldering grief that would burn them to death over the seasons ahead should he fail to save their daughters.

By midafternoon the next day, he had become desperately thirsty. Then, with no warning or indication, the Saudeleur arrived. A guard came to Ḷainjin's window for the first time and ordered him to stand for Sau-temoi. He stood peering through the little window, and the face of the Saudeleur soon appeared from the other side of the wall, their faces but the length of a forearm from each other. He appeared joyful, almost giddy. Ḷainjin felt a pang in the pit of his throat.

"I have someone here who is dying to talk to you," the Saudeleur said. Stepping aside, he held up his disgusting surprise, the severed head of the akebu. From his last expression, he hadn't suffered a painless death. It wasn't a joke by any means, but the Saudeleur, still holding the akebu's hair, laughed as though it was. However, his cruel mirth found no companionship among his followers. Only obedient silence hung in the air about him.

"He is my present to the Kosraeans! I'll hang his head upon the altar of Nahn Sapwe. I have avenged the death of Ijokelekel's mother. I can hardly wait to show him. Waow, where is Paratak when we need him? Hopefully, Ijokelekel will now accept my offering and land in peace upon our shores. In which case, I will release you without further harm, and you can swim to your islands and spread the news that the stone village has recast itself as a great center for trade again. Waow, I almost forgot to remind you. An adage among those of us who have lived in this village a long time: 'The stones have ears, and the Saudeleur hears everything!'"

Paratak's return

Paratak returned to Ant a few days later, visibly upset. He brought unexpected news.

"Sau-temoi must be killed," he announced in Pohnpeian. "He will never agree to allow Ijokelekel to bring his followers to enter the village in peace. He will not allow the fire at the temple to be relit or discuss the process of turning island life back to the way it was. He demands that Ijokelekel and Saulikin Ant both agree to come to Kariahn with me, where he has entombed Ḷōpako without food and water."

"Where is Erwina?" Ijokelekel asked.

"Sau-temoi has kept her till I return. Everybody is a hostage now!"

"Ḷōpako has arrived?"

"Yes, we met him at Kelepwei. Someone told Sau-temoi I called him ungrateful *kasap*. My fault I anger him. That spoil your tribute and chance for peace."

Ijokelekel's first thought was hopeful, that he could once again ask Ḷōpako's permission to take Kāmeto. She remained on his mind constantly even as she was frustrating him again by keeping her distance.

"When can we depart?" Paratak was anxious.

That was when Ijokelekel became afflicted by second thoughts. No, he wasn't ready. It seemed obvious to him that the turn of events Sau-temoi had initiated now isolated him from Pako's assessment of the Saudeleur's battle preparedness and from any advice he might have for him. Separating Paratak from his daughter encouraged haste. Did the well-informed Saudeleur know that Ijokelekel needed further time to prepare his men for battle? Was he setting a trap for him? Of course, he was. He had taken a hostage but wasn't leveraging his advantage by keeping Ḷainjin's location secret. By revealing the location, Sau-temoi was inviting an attack. But what ransom did the Saudeleur want? What was he after that Ijokelekel's appearance at Kariahn would further? He decided to leave Paratak's question unanswered. He needed to discuss all this with Saulikin Ant.

"I must discuss this with Saulikin Ant tomorrow," Ijokelekel replied. "You get some rest. You look like you haven't slept for days."

When he approached Saulikin Ant with Paratak's news the next day, he was happy to have found him with Maalal. He knew he could trust her to be supportive although he would be speaking in Pohnpeian. Saulikin Ant paused at the suggestion that he appear personally before Sau-temoi.

"I don't want to enter the turtle's cave if he isn't sleeping. Any Saudeleur would have been anxious about inviting you into the village, given your numbers. So, he invites you to a very defensible position with a very narrow entrance. He may say, 'If you're truly a religious man, then enter in peace and yield to my authority.' If you enter by yourself or with a small group of men, he will surely have you killed. He may feel his supply lines are strong enough to fend off the remainder of your warriors from there for seasons on end."

"Be wise, Ijokelekel. You don't want to walk into a trap now that we've come so far to seek our destiny." Maalal spoke in Kajin Rālik, demonstrating how quickly she had tuned her ear to her new language.

Ijokelekel must have looked surprised. "Yes, she is learning Pohnpeian quickly, but she has a good teacher," said Saulikin Ant. "Actually, we've been discussing your problem together for days now. If you try to attack the village, they can hurl stones down on you and your craft. They can even lever takai from the tops of the walls."

"I know. I don't like that course," said Ijokelekel. "My idea was to arrive peacefully and seek rebellion from within."

"Then let me present another plan. You surprise him and enter the lagoon off Metalanim and anchor at Auankap. Metalanim is the current center of unrest between the Kosraeans and Pohnpeians. To the rest of the islanders, the Kosraeans don't present a problem because they are few, and many have taken Pohnpeian spouses. But in Metalanim, they are many and they are hungry. At Auankap, you'll find all the room you need to maneuver your craft and develop your relationship with the Kosraeans. If you can, let the dogs chase the pig until he tires. Let the Kosraeans start the battle, and you immediately double your numbers. The Saudeleur will have to walk his men over land to attack you, and he'll have to catch you ashore. If he's foolish enough to divide his forces like that, anyone could sail into the stone village and take control — even someone as ill prepared as our valued counselor here!"

At this, Maalal punched the older man in his still-toned bicep. Then laughed as he feigned pain.

"These women of yours are brutal!" said Saulikin Ant.

"Pohnpeian men just can't take it!" She spoke in Kajin Rālik, wiggling her hips to amuse him. "But he's right, Ijokelekel! Don't forget that you're Kosraean! You can be their leader too!"

"If you maneuver correctly, you can confront Sau-temoi on two fronts at once," added Saulikin Ant.

"I like your plan better. We would be close to the ocean if we needed to escape his clutches," Ijokelekel said. But if we anchor at Auankap, won't Sau-temoi be furious? What about Ļainjin, and even Erwina?"

"Ijokelekel, I have watched this weed grow within the stone village since he was a boy. He'll hang on to your friends like a spoiled child hangs on to toys until they break. I'm sorry to say, Paratak's daughter and this Pako are gone unless you tempt the Saudeleur into dividing his forces. You can try to save them immediately, but they're bait for a trap, and you know what happens to bait. It's cut, fished, or discarded. The best you can hope for is that they get discarded at some point. Better he gets furious, and you live for another day."

Ijokelekel started wondering how Paratak would view this plan. He knew that Paratak's inclination was to rush an attack and simply overwhelm Sau-temoi with their numbers. "How do you see your part in all this?" Ijokelekel asked Saulikin Ant.

He replied with a confident laugh, "I remain here — wealthy, isolated, and protected by my people. If you lose, I was never part of your rebellion. If you win, you'll remember my hospitality and wise counsel and allow me to help you allocate a land you're unprepared to rule. Who better than a lowly trader to assist a religious man like yourself to divide the bounty you may take possession of?"

Ijokelekel found himself returning to camp with his head spinning. He would spend the rest of that day by himself, in thought. He had planned a jebwa-style attack that would astonish and discourage his opponents, but the drifters weren't ready for that. He recalled his day-after-day practices and realized it would take seasons to prepare them. They still lacked agility and discipline. He was afraid things were spiraling out of control. Would he have to confront the Saudeleur on his terms rather than his own? But the recent turn of events required him to do something, so he decided to move forward. He saw merit in the plan proposed by Saulikin Ant.

The next morning, Ijokelekel told Kāmeto to go among the women and have them prepare provisions. Paratak had already informed her that the Saudeleur had taken her father hostage. It was time for her to gather the women, who would prepare their drums and join their men in battle.

Paratak was as distraught as the moment they had last spoken. Ijokelekel asked him to accompany Anitok and ask each family to decide who in their group would sail into battle and who had better stay in camp. As soon as the drums started beating, the men cut coconuts and gathered the provisions provided by Saulikin Ant, and Ant came to life.

Adding to the excitement that day, clouds rose across the lagoon and filled the western horizon. As the breeze began to shift in that direction, it became obvious to the sailors among them that such a shift was optimal to exiting the atoll through the Tauenai passage, crossing the sea between Ant and the island, and skirting its eastern shore to Nahn Madol. Was this a sign from Nahn Sapwe that he would bless such a spirited voyage with good luck? Ijokelekel had been uncertain about his decision earlier that day, but as the storm brewed in the west and its dark clouds flashed and gurgled intermittently, he became even more certain he was making the right choice. He encouraged his followers to load their crafts ever more quickly. Then, with the windswept surf now pounding onto what had been calm leeward shores, and the dark clouds spitting down upon them, he decided to harvest the moment by launching and leading the fleet toward the passage.

They launched to the beat of Kāmeto's drum. She sat on the outrigger platform in the downpour even as they chanted and rolled the heavy craft down the shore and into the waves. Their eyes met for the first time since she had urinated on his leg. She so elated his spirit that she extinguished the cold from the rain falling about them.

Some fifty proas sailed into the teeth of the westerly that evening. In single file, they followed Ijokelekel out into the middle of the lagoon, then tacked south to twist their way through the Tauenai passage just before dark. In line, they set to sea through the howling storm to the tip of the west coast of Pohnpei and followed its southern coast eastward as the storm tapered and then cleared. They rounded the island's southeast corner as the tailwind from the storm turned gradually southward, continuing to allow them to bulge their sails as they skipped like flying fish from one following wave to the next. Then the moon rose. From the cloud-mottled eastern horizon, it periodically lit their way until the storm's aftermath swept the sky clear — just before they passed the eastern walls of the stone village and approached the passage into the lagoon that fronted the structure called Kariahn.

Ijokelekel watched the marvel of the village capture the attention of his crew, who were seeing its megalithic structures for the first time. As planned, he intended to sail north and enter the many times larger lagoon off Metalanim at Auankap. However, as they reached the village built on the reef, he recalled the terror that Ḷañinni's men must have inflicted on Taklur's village and began to consider a similar approach. They had instilled this fear simply by sailing up as though about to attack and then sailing past as though promising to return.

So, he steered his proa into the passage, sailed to the lagoon's end, tacked, and approached the great walls of Kariahn, careful to remain just outside the boundary of hurled spears or stones. His line of proas followed in his wake, many carrying their ululating *du* of drum-beating females, each trying to outdo the others, and all carrying his warriors. As he passed them, sailing in the opposite direction, he ordered them to brandish what hardwood spears they had. The others shouted, taunting their adversaries, who — in gathering and tossing stones — inadvertently revealed their large defensive numbers. Then, just as quickly as he had appeared in the moonlight, Ijokelekel led his line of proas back out through the passage to sea, tacked a second time, and headed on north toward his destination.

In truth, he wasn't sure if this little demonstration of strength helped or hindered his objective to depose Sau-temoi, but it seemed to fall in line with the night's prior stormy adventure. And it was one way to alert his mentor that help had arrived though, as they entered the lagoon off Metalanim at Auankap, he had no idea whatsoever what to do next. The storm had been harsh on those families who had refused to break up and leave members on Ant. They were cold and wet, but at least they had plenty to eat. Maalal and Saulikin Ant had presented them with hundreds of baskets of breadfruit seeds to provision their journey.

The following morning, Ijokelekel decided to let these families go ashore in Paratak's company, carrying baskets with some of the seeds to test the hospitality of the villagers. Ijokelekel accompanied them as well, for several reasons, not the least of which was wanting to keep close to Paratak. He was worried about his daughter and kept talking about rescuing her by himself. Ijokelekel refused to accept his plan due to the high chance of failure and because he needed his knowledge of the area and its various leadership personalities. Ijokelekel spread word among his followers that they were to treat him as a commoner with no deference paid. He didn't want to fall victim to one of Sau-temoi's informers. Henceforth, he was to be a nobody.

It was an after-the-storm morning with lots of breadfruit leaves to pick up. He amused himself by approaching people and asking if they had heard the name "Ijokelekel." Some weren't familiar with the name, but one said, "He is a Kosraean rat." Most pointed to the fleet at anchor. Some said he was at sea, planning his attack against the Saudeleur. Only a few — mostly the elderly — had it right: he was the son of Lipanmai, come to avenge her death.

"No one fights on behalf of a vague memory," he thought. Only a few knew his purpose, and none had expressed interest in joining his cause. However, when he had asked how they felt about the Saudeleur, the response was uniformly negative or indifferent at best. Finally, he found a young Kosraean man who knew the story, hated the Saudeleur, and — most important — knew the place on the slope of Temwen mountain where the man called Ewalt lived.

All night, Paratak had been questioning him about how he planned to rescue Erwina from the clutches of the Saudeleur. Ijokelekel had already decided that Sau-temoi was probably in wait with his followers behind the walls at Kariahn. The events of the previous night, when they had surprised his guards by appearing so soon after the storm, seemed to confirm this. Had the Saudeleur perhaps left Erwina at Pahn Kadira, relatively unguarded? This seemed plausible, but did he really want to risk sending a small group to rescue her and perhaps give him more key members of his group to take hostage?

These were the reasons Ijokelekel had thought of asking this man called Ewalt to first take measure of the situation. He didn't remember meeting Ewalt in his youth but had listened to Ḷainjin's stories about him. He gathered they had been good friends, and Paratak also knew him well and trusted him. He gathered that Ewalt had been a confidant of the previous Saudeleur and had translated for his traders from the Rālik islands, but Ijokelekel knew that no more trading was going on these days. Perhaps Ewalt would be willing to help.

So, Ijokelekel asked this young Kosraean, "Can you find Ewalt and tell him that Ijokelekel wants him to visit a woman called Erwina at Pahn Kadira?" Then, remembering Pako's stories about Ewalt's gardening, he added, "Then tell him Ijokelekel says you are to be rewarded with one of his prized yams."

The young man smiled and thanked him for the opportunity to help.

Later, Ijokelekel came across a group of boys playing *bwilbwil* along the shore of the lagoon. He had always loved *bwilbwil* as a youth. What child doesn't love to play with a toy boat? Kosraean boys and a few girls were playing in teams set up on both sides of a narrow inlet, racing their model canoes from one side to the other. A child's teammate was to *diak* their canoe when it reached the other side and set it on its course back across the inlet to the opposite shore. He watched a winner hold his boat high above his head as he performed a little victory dance for his less successful companions. The only children at loss in such a game, he thought, would be the ones whose fathers neglected to make a model for them.

Suddenly, in the middle of the next round, a second group of older boys — no doubt Pohnpeian — emerged along the path. As though by premeditated design, they began hurling stones at the boats as they sailed. The bullies didn't stop until they had toppled the sails of the lot of them, and then they laughed their way down the path.

Ijokelekel was livid at the injustice. He didn't like to see one group belittle another in such a way. He was sensitive to the children's plight as he had been relentlessly teased as a child. A few of the Kosraean boys cried. Others simply bore the injustice like men who had learned to accommodate such mistreatment. He followed one child back along the path that bordered the inlet to his Kosraean village and saw him run crying to his father, sitting amid a group busy preparing breadfruit, presumably felled by the storm. Ijokelekel politely sat, addressed the boy's father, and confirmed what he had seen. The village was well laid out, with a broad courtyard at its center and takai used here and there to favorable effect.

He was surprised to find the group unfazed by the incident. Only the boy's mother, who emerged from their tidy house, seemed to share Ijokelekel's outrage. Had they resigned themselves to such ill-treatment? This wasn't their homeland. The very breadfruit they were preparing were probably not solely theirs to eat. They would undoubtedly have to give some to their Pohnpeian overlords, who might even have to share a portion with the Saudeleur. Such was their lot in life, but to resign themselves and their families to this senseless cruelty seemed wrong, so he confronted them over their complacency.

As others gathered around, Ijokelekel couldn't help but question their odd restraint in the face of such unfairness. He spoke in Pohnpeian, carefully interjecting a recalled Kosraean word now and then out of respect for their language. "Clearly, fate has cast you into an unfortunate situation. I understand that, but can you explain your history? Tell me how your people got here and why?"

"Our ancestors were stone fitters too," replied the boy's father. "They crossed the sea to Nahn Madol in their great proa from their similar village of Lelu."

Ijokelekel remembered his mother's tales of a much smaller sister village on Kosrae called Lelu. It was made of similar takai. "You share a similar fate with Ijokelekel, whose mother was the daughter of a stone fitter."

"Our ancestors heard tales of the construction of the new village and its need for workers," the boy's father said. "They came here to earn their fortunes by lending their hands to its building. Their proas have long since rotted into dust. Construction is now finished for lack of takai, and here we sit on the Pohnpeians' soil. A few of our ancestors were given land, but the rest no."

"So, at least part of the knowledge to build the stone walls to such heights came directly from your ancestors?"

The boy's father looked around at the men surrounding them. They all agreed that that was their history.

"Now tell me this." Ijokelekel asked. "Did the Pohnpeians throw stones at them and tell them return to Lelu?"

In unison, the answer was *no*. "They ate before the Saudeleurs," said one.

"They were granted adornments and allowed to trade at Kariahn," said another. "They were allotted land to plant."

With each response, the group's verbal agreement grew louder, and this drew the attention of others who had stopped to listen to the words of this Kosraean-looking, Pohnpeian-speaking man from the fleet anchored offshore.

"They threw no rocks at your ancestors, so why do they throw rocks at your children? What has changed?"

"The takai no longer break away from the cliffs," the boy's father said. "They've used up all the stones."

"And this is your fault? That's why they throw stones at your children as they play in the lagoon?"

"No, this isn't our fault," answered one.

"It's the fault of the Saudeleurs who have turned their backs on Nahn Sapwe," added another.

"Those were just boys being mean," suggested the mother of the crying child.

"Do their Pohnpeian fathers not teach their sons to respect the children of those who lent their hands to the construction of the great villages?" asked Ijokelekel. "And do you have no older sons to protect their younger siblings?"

"You encourage us to rebel against this maltreatment?" questioned an onlooker. "You sound like you have an objective in all this."

"As you know, I am from Ijokelekel's fleet, there in the lagoon. I am but a passerby, but our leader has come to avenge the death of his mother, Lipanmai."

"Then your chief has come too late," the man said. "The Saudeleur has already killed the little akebu. They say that he severed his head and it hangs from the entrance of Kariahn. It's said this was done to appease her death."

The turn of events surprised Ijokelekel, who had always assumed the little man had somehow permanently captured the Saudeleur's good graces and always thought of the cannibals going down together.

"Yet the unjustness continues, does it not?" he responded.

It soon became obvious to all that Ijokelekel had a larger purpose for his words.

"Maybe you are Ijokelekel!" The accusation of one man was followed by much laughter.

"They say he can talk a sand crab from its hole," joked another, to more laughter.

"I'm not here to confirm yes or no to anything, but I can tell you this. Ijokelekel has well-trained warriors, and if he sees his brother Kosraeans fighting, he will protect their backs. I can promise you that, and you can spread that word to your fellow villagers."

With that, Ijokelekel felt like a fisherman with a full basket and decided to return to the fleet.

That evening, Paratak continued arguing his plan to take a small party of men through the back door to Pahn Kadira, perhaps even as Ijokelekel led the fleet back into the Kariahn lagoon to repeat the events of the night before. But Ijokelekel didn't want to repeat anything so regularly. "That was Ļañinni's mistake," he thought, remembering how Kāmeto had waited in the brush until he waded ashore. They would wait a few days and carefully watch the developments before he responded.

The next morning, a group of vessels from the fleet exited the lagoon and went trolling for tuna in the sea outside the passageway. They caught more than enough tuna to feed the fleet, so Ijokelekel had a few delivered to the village where he had stopped the day before, the village of the boys whose canoes had been broken by the Pohnpeian youths. Word came back later that morning that a stone fight had broken out when Pohnpeian boys again destroyed a few of the Kosraean boys' model canoes. When the Kosraean boys had retaliated with a flight of stones, they hurt several of the Pohnpeian boys. Their fathers then came into the Kosraean villages and fist fights and more rock throwing ensued. That was when Ijokelekel decided to make a show of force. He went ashore with a group of his jebwa fighters and performed in the Kosraean village that evening. The message he intended to send to the Pohnpeians was that he supported the Kosraeans in the *bwilbwil* dispute.

There was more heavy rain that night, but Ijokelekel sent his fishing crew onto the ocean for tuna the next morning nonetheless, and their catch was even larger than the morning before. Again, he fed the Kosraean village. However, his men heard remarks from Pohnpeians on shore. His gifts to their village were stirring anger among the Pohnpeian elders, who felt slighted by not sharing in firstfruits before the Kosraeans. He also heard word that, due to the continuing Pohnpeian aggression against them, Kosraeans from outlying areas had begun migrating to the relative safety of their stronghold in the Metalanim village. Word spread that they were suffering injuries along the way.

"Such injuries on each side should eventually lead to even more retaliation and escalation of hostilities that only the continued rain would be able to dampen. What is likely to occur once the weather clears?" Ijokelekel wondered.

Late that afternoon, as he was resting in the shelter of his hull, Paratak awakened him. "Ijokelekel, come see! You were right! Always right!"

He rose and peered out from beneath the pandanus-mat sail they had hung like a tent to protect themselves from the rain. There was no wind. The lagoon was still, flat, and dull beneath the grey, cloud-filled sky. Paratak pointed to a canoe, there in the distance, paddling toward the fleet. As Ijokelekel's eyes adjusted to the light, he began to discern what Paratak had already concluded. It was his daughter, Erwina, in the middle of a canoe paddled by two men. Perhaps one was the man called Ewalt.

Paratak was a man whose thoughts appeared clearly on his face, and it beamed with happiness now he knew for certain that his daughter was safe. He held his hand high until she saw him and acknowledged back, and her craft pointed their way. The oarsman steered his hull parallel to theirs, and Ijokelekel invited them aboard. The man was indeed Ewalt, and he had much to tell them. The other man in the canoe was old and appeared infirm. Ewalt did not introduce him.

Ewalt had had no problem entering Pahn Kadira because Sau-temoi had left for Kariahn, where they expected the battle to take place, and taken all his guards with him. Ewalt had found Erwina unharmed, and his biggest problem was convincing her to leave. She had worried that her father wouldn't know where she had gone. At this point in his story, Paratak had to break in and explain that he would have armed himself with a hardwood spear and battled as many guards as the Saudeleur threw at him, but luckily, Ijokelekel came up with a better plan.

"I know you would have, Father, and that was why I was so worried — and at first, unwilling to leave the exact spot you left me."

"I no abandon. You know. Right?"

"Yes, of course, Father."

Once Ewalt was able to finish, he informed them that the Saudeleur and all his men were very vulnerable at Kariahn and couldn't hold that position much longer.

Ijokelekel was curious. "Why not?"

Ewalt responded, "Because the Saudeleur depends on a constant flow of provisions flowing from the mainland through the canals at high tide. These supplies are likely to dwindle because the Saudeleur is counting on loyalty alone to obtain these provisions. He provides no actual reciprocity."

As Ewalt spoke, Ijokelekel envisioned his men taking over these provisioning vessels, sneaking up to the backside of Kariahn, and attacking through the inside entrance. Then he looked down at his chest and realized his men couldn't be mistaken for Pohnpeians due to their distinctive lines.

Ewalt continued, "It wouldn't take much force to stop these lines of supply. Within a half day, his men would be thirsty and, within a day, hungry."

Was this wise man Ewalt providing a solution to his problem? Only time would tell. Ijokelekel lay confidently snuggled in the hull that night, listening to the rain drain off their tented vessel into the lagoon. He envisioned time passing like the water of the streams trickling down from the mountains. During days of no rain, the streams slowed down. At other times, they rushed rapidly to the sea. Was this one of those times — something he had envisioned since childhood — when hundreds of years of tradition would suddenly run to an end and a new way of life would rush into place?

The next morning, word came that the inevitable had occurred. Men on both sides had started using slings to hurl stones, and a young Kosraean girl had gotten caught in the middle and now lay unconscious. Her Pohnpeian assailant had been chased down, speared in the leg, and then smashed in the head until dead. The Kosraean villagers were asking Ijokelekel to again intervene. So, he sent the same jebwa fighters he had the day before. Later that day, however, word came back that the first wave of men he had sent ashore had been likewise attacked with stones on their way to the village. There, they had formed their circle and handily defeated the first Pohnpeians who attacked. Later, the Pohnpeians had come in such large numbers that they overran the village, and Ijokelekel's men — along with their Kosraean cohorts — retreated to the shore before them.

The rush was on. Ijokelekel's time had come. Kāmeto and her *du* thundered on their drums. He ordered the fleet ashore. Any children, along with two adults per vessel, were to return all craft to the safety of anchorage. All others were to join in the attack. The Pohnpeians who fought with spears were quickly defeated by his jebwa fighters. Then the *du* set aside their drums and plaited baskets for fist-sized stones they gathered here and there for their men to hurl with their slings. Now it was the Pohnpeians who were driven back, flanked, and then herded onto a peninsula and surrounded directly south of their village at Metalanim.

Ijokelekel rested among his lines before the final attack. There was little doubt his warriors could wipe out the lot of them, and he was giddy at the thought of winning his first battle. He remembered his conversation with Ļañinni that last night, while watching the jebwa. "Nobody runs unless they are scared," he had said. "Nobody becomes scared until they fear they'll die. So, how do you plan to kill them?"

Just then, Ewalt appeared with the old man who had helped him paddle. They sat down next to Ijokelekel and asked how things were progressing. He told them the Pohnpeians appeared to be cut off from their village and that he planned to attack them as soon as his men had rested. They would have the battle won before dark. They sat in silence for a while. Ijokelekel and his men were winded from their successful flanking movement. The air was thick, and sweat poured down his face.

"How will you know when you have won? The battle, I mean," asked the old man. He spoke in Pohnpeian but had a vaguely familiar accent.

Ijokelekel, about to answer, became caught up in thought. Finally, he said, "I guess when Sau-temoi is dead."

Suddenly, he saw the situation in a new light. Was this his opportunity to form an alliance with the Pohnpeians? They were in a dispute with the Kosraeans, but he knew they were unhappy with the Saudeleur and his untraditional ways.

It was almost as if the old man had seen Ijokelekel's thoughts on his face. He suggested, "Why not talk to them?"

Ijokelekel worked his way through the front lines of stone throwers, spreading his arms wide as he entered the area held by his Pohnpeian adversaries, and solicited their attention.

"You face two choices," he declared in Pohnpeian. "First choice: you can kill me now or take me hostage. But in either case, you face certain death from Ijokelekel, his warriors, and his Kosraean cohorts who surround you. Second choice: you can live under his protection, listen to my words, and carry them back in safety along the estuary to your village. Which do you prefer?"

"He's trying to talk us to death!" someone shouted.

"Let him speak," yelled another. Others agreed.

"Our women wait to polish our spears!" shouted another, and much light-throated laughter followed.

"Then I promise not to delay your return to them," Ijokelekel said. "I have only one question. You suffer from a lack of reciprocity with the Saudeleur, do you not?"

Another Pohnpeian spoke up. "He's as poor as a clown fish dodging around his house of coral. Who knows what he eats? He shares with no one!"

"So, if your problem is with the Saudeleur because he demands firstfruits but doesn't reciprocate, why throw stones at your Kosraean brothers?"

"The Saudeleur is an insignificant sucker fish. The Kosraeans are many. They have big bellies, they never stop eating, and they defecate all over the mangrove swamps," came the answer, followed by more laughter.

"And then the crabs eat up their defecations, and then they eat the crabs!" shouted still another man, to even more laughter.

"Yes, but you both suffer the same problem, don't you? They are stone fitters. The building has stopped. They have no takai to fit. The Saudeleur doesn't feed them — but not because you no longer offer tribute to him. You know he has nothing to reciprocate. Why? Because the trading has stopped. Why? Because the takai no longer break from the cliffs. Why? Because the Saudeleur has turned away from Nahn Sapwe. Did you not hear him rumbling in the night? Ijokelekel has returned to turn you back to the faith of your forefathers. Join in alliance with the Kosraeans against your common enemy, or continue to be shunned by the great voice about you."

"He forgot to say 'why.'" This came from a new voice.

"The Rālik Islanders speak in circles just like their insignificant atolls that Nahn Sapwe will one day cover with waves," said yet another.

A third man, with a tone of authority, said, "Enough talk. Lead us to safety. Don't worry. We won't fail to bore our children to sleep with your fable."

Ijokelekel motioned for two of his men to come forward. He told them to pass the word ahead to allow the Pohnpeians to retreat along the path beside the mangrove swamps that bordered the estuary north to their village.

Accepting his verbal defeat with dignity as he always had, Ijokelekel greeted each man who passed, looked him in the eyes, and said, "Until next time." Many greeted him back with a cold nod. Others offered a grateful repeat of his own words. The very last man, however, stopped with an aura of command and explained, "We Pohnpeians pride ourselves on not speaking or agreeing as one. As for myself, I will be sure your words are passed to others."

Ijokelekel and his men returned to the Kosraean village in the rain, everyone elated over the victory. It was the Kosraeans' turn to feed his warriors, and they did so with extreme generosity. Rumors of what Ijokelekel had said to the Pohnpeians was spreading among them. The Kosraeans all spoke of the man called Ijokelekel and wanted him pointed out, but his people knew his identity should be kept secret and didn't reveal it. His markings were the same as the others', and he sat among the commoners as though he were one of them. Some of the unpaired men and a few of the unpaired women slept in the village while the others returned with Ijokelekel to the anchorage.

That night, the clouds crept down onto the water, the sky wept, and the sounds of his father's deliberations echoed across the water and reminded all of what Ijokelekel had said the day before. Morning brought a breeze that cleared away the mist, and he sent his fishers out for provisions. When they returned with their catch, he sent two boats up the estuary toward Metalanim. But the crews reported upon their return that, as they had approached the village, the mangrove forests on either side narrowed to the extent that they became exposed to sling stones and had to stop and anchor midway there. Then they ended up unloading the tuna onto small canoes that approached them warily, and their gifts went unreciprocated. The Pohnpeians, Ijokelekel decided, were a difficult and undisciplined bunch to deal with. In his mind, they required a decisive defeat, but that wasn't likely to happen until the Saudeleur's men added to their numbers and provoked a second attack.

From Ijokelekel's sources, he gathered that just about everyone expected a conclusive battle to be at hand. He had consolidated his relationship with the Kosraeans, who were temporarily free from Pohnpeian harassment and no longer providing them firstfruits. The Pohnpeian commoners of Metalanim had been roundly defeated and then wooed by Ijokelekel, so their overlords were no doubt pleading for the Saudeleur's help. The stream of provisions to Kariahn had probably backed up by now, so the Saudeleur was likely to comply. At least his warriors could eat their way along the trail by requisitioning food as they traveled. Ijokelekel had considered ambushing them before they met up with the Metalanim villagers but, remembering

Saulikin Ant's advice, decided the better course was to stay put at his anchorage, where he could always escape to the sea if events turned against him.

The day dawned pregnant with such anticipation. Both sides seemed balanced on the edge of battle. Ijokelekel's men had cut hardwood spears and sharpened them for all. Drum skins were stretched and ready. Baskets of breadfruit seeds were likewise ready to off-load to provision the hungry. Coconut-shell containers were filled with fresh water. Ijokelekel had six proas manned and ready to transport a group of Kosraean stone fitters. They would sail to Kariahn under the command of the man called Ewalt to recover Pako from Sau-temoi's entrapment.

Finally, word arrived that fighting had begun between the Kosraean villagers and some of the same Pohnpeians they had previously defeated. Ijokelekel had to assume that the Saudeleur's men had now arrived and emboldened them to attempt to overrun the Kosraean villages once again. So, he sent Ewalt and the six proas off to Kariahn. Then, except for those needed to preserve the fleet, he ordered all the others to line up for battle. For the most part, the men moved forward in jebwa formation with the *du* behind, carrying baskets of stones and, of course, their *aje*, which they beat with incessant fervor. Kāmeto stayed close to Ijokelekel and Erwina, close behind her father. Because Paratak spoke Kosraean, he was one of the first to enter the village.

Ijokelekel found the Pohnpeians hurling rocks over the mangrove forests between the village and the lagoon and into the village with their slings — undoubtedly using stones transported to their positions by canoe. The barrage of stones was so heavy the Kosraeans had all taken shelter within their homes. So, Ijokelekel ordered his men to rush through the forests with their spears, to route the Pohnpeians from their wading positions along the edge of the lagoon. Their spears were more appropriate to that environment anyway. Unfortunately, unbeknownst to Ḷainjin, the forest was filled with their enemies, waiting to attack the village once the bombardment had finished. His men were surprised by a fierce counterattack all along the periphery of the forest and were driven back out. There, safe from the stones hurled overhead into the village, Ijokelekel ordered them to form their jebwa lines and await the attack that was sure to come.

They didn't have long to wait. A few of the Pohnpeians entered the clearing to throw their spears at Ijokelekel's men, who easily sidestepped them or batted them down. Ijokelekel ordered the fallen spears to be carried to safety so they couldn't be picked up again by their enemies. When the attack came, his lines — even though greatly outnumbered — held and delivered a punishing rebuke to the Pohnpeians.

Then someone directed the rock throwers to sling their shots just over the mangrove stands to land them where Ijokelekel's men had their lines. So, he had them scatter in groups of four throughout the village. Then he sent a contingent of his men to the fleet, to return with enough canoes to wipe out those storing the stones and those slinging them from the shallows fronting the swamp. His goal was to prevent further bombardment and force his opponents into the open, giving his more disciplined fighting forces the chance to decisively defeat them.

Paratak, with his limited ability to speak Kosraean, oversaw the villagers who were withstanding the worst of the attack. They were huddled in their thatch homes. The thatch broke the momentum of the stones, but their weight penetrated it nonetheless and the stones were pelting the cowering villagers. Suddenly, the pelting increased. Had more men in the forest joined those slinging stones from the lagoon, or had more attackers joined the fray? The answer was soon apparent. Pohnpeians stepped from the forest in greater numbers than before and confidently lined up for a second attack against them.

Ijokelekel watched as Paratak, standing in the middle of the village square, flaunted his leadership. Behind him and to one side, his daughter, Erwina, moved cautiously — beating her *aje* energetically and goading him on as he reprimanded his cringing Kosraean colleagues. Whether it was a particularly vindictive, well-aimed shot from a sling or just part of the Pohnpeians' random bombardment of the village, Ijokelekel could only hope she hadn't seen death coming. The stone struck Erwina's forehead and felled her instantly.

Kāmeto had just sprung toward the corner of the cookhouse where they had taken temporary shelter, her eyes glancing skyward at the barrage of stones as though she were about to jaunt toward her stricken sister, when Ijokelekel dissuaded her with a hopeless sway of his head.

Eyes ahead on his enemies, Paratak must have noticed her drumming had ceased. He turned, saw she had fallen, and rushed toward her lifeless body. Now oblivious to the battle around him, he sat weeping as he cradled her head in his lap. Ijokelekel looked upon the two with deep sorrow. Had Likōkkālọk envisioned just such a calamity? He suddenly recalled her curse. Then, recognizing Paratak's vulnerability, he leaped forward to his defense, only to be struck himself. He saw the face of a Pohnpeian man who had bravely entered the square just as the sharp, dense stone he had thrown struck Ijokelekel's mouth, smashed the teeth from one side of his face, and left him stunned, more helpless than Paratak, whom he had attempted to defend.

Lying face to the sky, Ijokelekel opened his eyes and saw a second, handsome Pohnpeian man with a raised polished spear, its stingray point looking deadly sharp, standing above him. Instinctively turning a shoulder, he twisted his body to absorb a blow that curiously never came. When he twisted back, he saw Kāmeto pleading with a young man, apparently to spare his life. She whispered something in the Pohnpeian's ear as she stayed his arm by enticing his free hand between her legs with both her hands. Then she led the surprised man reluctantly away, and his spear fell harmlessly down next to Ijokelekel. "Where was she taking him?" he thought, as the taste of blood filled his mouth and the desire to sleep overcame him.

Perhaps it was Ijokelekel's vulnerability as he lay there dazed and bleeding. More likely, it was anger that the aggressors had killed his daughter. With posterity now his witness, screaming with the entire force of his powerful lungs, Paratak plunged the fallen spear through his foot and staked himself to the middle of the square next to Ijokelekel. Thus, refusing to retreat, he challenged the Kosraeans to defend their own village, and he called to the scattered Rālik Islanders to reinforce his position. Whether his men rallied to Ijokelekel's aid or to Paratak's heroic stance, Ijokelekel would never know. Later, he was told that the canoe contingent had successfully overcome the stone throwers at the lagoon's edge, but ultimately, the winning of the day was granted to Nahn Paratak and his stubborn show of sheer will and refusal to retreat.

Yes, Nahn Paratak would gain yet another title that day for making his historic stand above the fallen leader, but the renown granted would rest worthless now that he had lost the daughter he loved so dearly.

To Ijokelekel, the rest of the day seemed like the *aolōk* attack he had experienced while *jurōk* fishing a few days before. He was engrossed with pain and missed Kāmeto's warm presence. He stayed in the Kosraean village for many days, mourning the loss of Erwina and recovering from the terrible wound, which had disabled his eating and permanently marred his face. Likewise, Paratak was engrossed in a fit of mourning and did not appear before him.

When Ijokelekel came to his full senses many days later, Anitok told him the battle had been won. Sau-temoi had been chased into the mountains, and Pahn Kadira had been taken by the recently freed Pako, who himself had disappeared into the hinterland and was yet to return. There was nothing left for Ijokelekel to do but sail into the stone village in triumph and take his place there as the new Saudeleur.

Ḷainjin's revenge

Ḷainjin had quenched a desperate thirst during the storm's first downpour by frantically navigating his open mouth above the sounds of water splashing. Thus, he had rounded his dark, leaky cave, leaving his face, curly hair, and kilt drenched and his hungry body cold, disoriented, and exposed. Folding his arms and curling himself into the driest corner he could find, he rested there as best he could. Then, after the thunder burst, after the rain ceased, and the light of the risen waning moon crept into his cage, he fell into a deep sleep as though he lay safe but cold in a crypt with the ages passing about him.

Before dawn, he woke to the sounds of imminent attack. Now aroused from their shelters, the Saudeleur's men were moving around, apparently transporting stones to the top of the seaward wall. All supposedly directed by the shrill, despised voice he could now distinguish amid the din of any crowd. At first, he seemed to be lining his men up as reinforcements. Then he seemed to be calling them back, once the attack had begun.

"No! Do not throw stones yet! Do not show yourselves!" Ḷainjin heard the Saudeleur shouting from the wall above what would be a shining, rippling lagoon, where Ijokelekel's fleet of canoes must be approaching. When no attack came, he heard Sau-temoi's shrill voice berating those who had prematurely revealed themselves and thrown the very stones he'd had hauled up to them. Ḷainjin laughed aloud at the Saudeleur and his failed surprise attack, then snickered as he returned to sleep, hearing the shrill voice repeating the same belittling speech. Ḷainjin realized Sau-temoi's dilemma at this point. Although he had congregated his forces in this isolated post, it must be difficult to supply, given the breakdown of trade and reciprocity that his forefathers had enjoyed. The fool was following ancient plans. No doubt, they would have worked quite well for his ancestors but were now hopelessly dated, given the current circumstance. All Ijokelekel had to do now was to wait, but did he know that?

The next morning, Ļainjin was wakened by the prod of a spear. As he had slept, somehow — probably trial and error — someone had found the perfect crack in the surrounding takai to take a straight poke at him. He quickly grabbed onto it, pushing it aside as he scrambled to his knees, and engaged his assailant in a match for the spear that he had so easily won. Then he heard the hated voice laughing from outside.

"You see how vulnerable you are. Like a mosquito waiting for my swat!"

A second spear poked through from a different direction. Ļainjin levered it with his foot and attempted to stab back with the spear he had just taken. But he missed his tormentor. "No, you are the vulnerable one! You are the mosquito that has sucked the blood of your hosts, and they see your greedy belly turned red, leaving you too heavy to fly. You are the one who is doomed. Why would Ijokelekel attack when all he must do is wait for your supply lines to continue to thin? I can go for days without eating. I hear your men complain when their morning meal is late or if there is too much of this or not enough of that. They follow you like dogs wishing to be fed. As sure as dusk follows the evening sky, they will fade away, and that's when I will come after you and shove this very spear down your throat until it pokes through the skin on the back of your neck."

"Continue to dream if you like, but don't sleep or the next time you feel my spear, it will be poking through *your* skin!" menaced the Saudeleur. His laugh sounded less confident.

Ļainjin may have gotten the best of Sau-temoi in their latest spat, but the thought that he shouldn't sleep acted like a weight on his eyelids and made him struggle to stay awake. The takai were so large, the sound penetration was so thin, and the angles to view the outside were so varied that he really had no idea who might be watching when or from where. As darkness set in, he became confident he could no longer be seen though he knew, of course, that any snoring might give away his position. So, his sleep was fitful. Then, sometime before dawn, he heard something slide through his small window and drop on the ground. He edged forward in the dim light of the waning moon that had somehow crept through the cracks of his vault. Someone had dropped a quarter slice of baked breadfruit for him. Dare he eat?

He crawled back to his nesting place in the corner, set the food next to him, and began the discussion. If he weren't dying of thirst, there would be no debate. Eat it or continue to starve. Yet he hadn't eaten for such a long time his stomach had shrunk to the point where it was quiet as the moonlight. Not so his thirst. His mouth was so dry that his lips were cracked. How was he to eat such a dry substance anyway? He put the food to his nose. It had obviously been baked, and its burnt skin scraped away, that very evening. Had Sau-temoi gotten hold of the little akebu's poison? From Ḷainjin's own experience with such things, he knew there was little chance of that. There was no smell of any foreign substance. To have a fatal impact, such a substance would have to be freshly mixed. Who would give him such a thing? A sympathetic guard perhaps? Was this the ration of someone who, like himself, was too thirsty to eat it? In either case, clearly someone was trying to either help him or poison him. Which was it? Out of all the men at Kariahn, how many were likely sympathetic to his cause or to Ijokelekel's? Reason would have it that there should be at least one.

He broke off a small piece and placed it in his dry mouth to slowly absorb what water might come, then lay back and rested with the food tucked inside his cheek like a rat that has stuffed a bit of food in its pouch for later.

By morning, the food had dissolved, and so, feeling no ill effects, he popped another piece into his mouth. By afternoon, the sky had clouded over, so his misery had hopes of rain. By evening, the rain was coming slowly, and he knew a slow rain would last. He stood where the dripping was consistent and opened his large mouth. Over time, he managed to quench his terrible thirst and, at the same time, finish his breadfruit meal. The rain continued the whole night into the next morning. He was now so wet and so cold and his thirst was so quenched that he wished the rain to stop. Then it did, and he noticed the outside had become quiet. So quiet that suddenly, he realized he was all alone. He shouted through his window.

"Anyone there?"

No response.

Though the water and food had provided nourishment against the cold, the elements continued to weigh heavily upon his frail body, causing it to begin spiraling down the abyss into which it was sinking. He shivered himself to sleep again and slept through the evening, the night, the next day, and the next night. And by the following day, he must have been near death when, as though in a dream, he heard friendly voices crying from the outside and then the sound of the giant takai being levered away. He felt himself being raised somehow and heard kind though unfamiliar voices. His head was raised somehow, and water put to his lips. When he opened his eyes, so delirious was he that he expected to see Ngalen, the Mwanus[205] woman who had nursed him on the other side of the *kāleptak*. Such were his thoughts before they covered him in a warm, luxurious mat and allowed him to bake within it as they transported him to Kelepwei. They put more water in his mouth, and then they placed him before a fire and gave him breadfruit soup with coconut milk. Soup! He craved it. Who would want to be fed anything else? Finally, he realized that Ewalt — and of course not Ngalen — was directing his rebirth.

Ewalt told him, "You must lie like a yam buried in the warm soil of my garden and concentrate your thoughts on climbing upward toward the light."

Gradually, as Ḷainjin came to his senses, he remembered the important thing he had forgotten to do, and his first request was for the spear he had left in the vault. Surprisingly, whoever had raised him from the crypt had also raised his only possession. They had transported it with him, and there it lay next to him. He ate and drank and slept and fingered the spear without talking or questioning. Slowly, over a period of how many days, he felt himself growing in spirit like one of Ewalt's prized yams, creeping his vine higher and higher into the light.

As he recovered, his friend Lañinpo visited him daily. First, he told him of Ijokelekel's victory. Then of his injury, and his convalescence in the

[205] The people living in villages who build on the reefs of Manus and the other islands of what is now called the Admiralty group.

Kosraean village. When Lañinpo told Ḷainjin about Erwina's unfortunate death, he suffered the knowledge in silence, fingered again for his spear, and clutched onto it tightly.

Kāmeto, accompanied by her quiet yet dignified Pohnpeian man, came to Kelepwei to pay their respects to Ḷainjin. He listened with curiosity to how their union had come to be and realized how quickly his spunky daughter had trained the handsome young man to follow her lead when he promised to return her to him if requested. Speaking alone, she assured her father that she had found the hero she was looking for. Ḷainjin clasped his spear and blessed the union. Although he knew this would be hard for Ijokelekel to accept, it should be easier now, with his victory. He would have women crawling all over him by now and would have his pick of the best of them, he thought.

Ḷainjin had always assumed the lad's fiery love for his sister would burn itself out without harm. He told the couple before him that their destiny was their own, but they had to promise him they would first accompany him on a visit to her mother on Lae. They promised, and thus, he had but one mission left to accomplish.

As soon as he had recovered enough strength to walk — not waiting for Ijokelekel's triumphant entrance to the stone village and despite Ewalt's protests and plea to accompany him — he set off alone with nothing but his spear. He would locate Sau-temoi or expire trying. From experience, he knew that the pathways through the Pohnpeian jungle were well worn and easy to follow. He also knew the Saudeleur cut an unmistakable image that would leave a broad wake and be easy to find and follow. His biggest problem would be the persistent rain, but he knew the people to be generous. He would find food and shelter along the way, especially once he revealed his mission, which was to locate the Saudeleur and require him to eat the tip of his spear. He walked and, given his weakened condition, rested in short intervals. He stopped at homes in even the smallest villages along the way. Yes, he met many who had returned from battle with mixed feelings toward Ijokelekel. None had experienced any recrimination at battle's end, though, so they seemed content to wait and see what demands, if any, were to come. None, however, expressed any loyalty to Sau-temoi.

The generous Pohnpeians offered much food and many coconuts, and this nourishment strengthened Ḷainjin as he searched leisurely from day to day. As time passed, he heard tales and rumors of some sightings. Slowly, the story of the Saudeleur's whereabouts began to coalesce. At battle's end, he had retreated with a few loyal followers down the same path he had taken to Metalanim. Then, hearing that Pahn Kadira had fallen, his followers abandoned him one by one as he fled along the river of Janipan, farther and farther up into the mountains. The Pohnpeians had settled here and there along the river, so the Saudeleur had stopped to demand food as he advanced. Perhaps he sought to hide at the river's source. His manner of flight, of course, would leave his trail easy to follow. If he had been a different man, capable of gathering his own food, he might have been more difficult to locate. Alas, this man was only capable of sitting and eating from the hands of others. His feet were tender, and Ḷainjin came to recognize his tracks along the often muddy trail. The Saudeleur's progress was slow and halting while Ḷainjin, on the other hand, grew stronger by the day. And remembering his promise, he sharpened his spear as he climbed into the island's interior.

One day, the Saudeleur had apparently climbed up one of the stream's tributaries and, having gotten stranded against a cliff, had to turn around and head back down. And that was when they met suddenly in close quarters, face to face. Ḷainjin, in no hurry to attack now that he had perhaps trapped his quarry, stood motionless at first. He had never seen such a person so out of place with their surroundings.

What had been a clean and fluffy hibiscus kilt was now dingy with the mud that covered the slippery path. Sau-temoi's trochus-shell arm bands were likewise muddied by falls. His necklaces, vestiges of lost authority, had broken and were hanging from his belt. His eyes darted fruitlessly for any way of escape, then his throat cringed one last swallow when he realized there was none.

Ḷainjin held out the spear as though to offer it to him as a reminder of the promise he had made after pulling it through the crack back in his enclosure. A false grin crossed Sau-temoi's face like a brief ray of sunlight streaking through a cloud-covered sky, until he realized he wouldn't know what to do if he grabbed onto it. At that moment, Ḷainjin realized there was no need to repeat his recent threat: "That's when I will come after you and shove this very spear down your throat until it pokes through the skin on the back of your neck." He slowly approached the terrified soul, his determined eyes veering not from the other's. Before Ḷainjin had a chance to even raise his spear, the frightened little man jumped for his life, down into the rapidly flowing, boulder-strewn river below.

The oral traditions were kinder to the fallen Saudeleur than Ḷainjin's account would have been. They say he turned into a small, lowly fish that still thrives in the river to this day.

* * *

When Ijokelekel entered the walled compound of Pahn Kadira, he felt no sense of triumph. How was he to revive the prosperity the village had brought during the building years? There weren't enough takai left to build a single new structure, and Nahn Sapwe no longer broke new ones from the cliffs. He felt overcome with despair. Yes, he had defeated the Saudeleur's meager forces. In hindsight, that had been the easy part. Now what had always seemed simple and inevitable appeared impossible. He realized, unexpectedly, that he had no real plan. He had no idea what to do next. Or what to say. Or who to ask. The constant rain depressed him. He longed for his Kāmeto. In all honesty, he had traded her away for his life. What life? A life once characterized by hope had turned morose and pointless. His face still throbbed despite all attempts to heal it.

As he rifled through the many possessions of the fallen Saudeleur, he found the old miniature *kakar* spears that the little akebu had given Raipuinloko. Ijokelekel discarded their coconut-cloth wrappings and displayed them as a curiosity for his visitors to admire. Yet visitors were slow to come. He found leadership in such a compound to be a lonely affair. But soon after, the old man who had paddled Erwina to the lagoon off Metalanim at Auankap requested permission to meet with him. Ijokelekel was glad for the company and showed him one of the little spears.

The old man was taken aback. "Did you unwrap them?" he asked.

"Yes, why not? They were sitting here all wrapped up. The cloth was hiding their beauty. They're unusual, are they not?"

"They are *kakar*! They have powerful magic and are not to be touched."

"*Koṃṃool*!" cried Ijokelekel, putting the little spear down with the rest.

"The little akebu probably gave those spears away because he had no ceremonial place to store them," the old man said.

"Who are you, by the way? Where are you from?"

"You know me, but I've grown old and sick from my time in the land of the little akebu. I gave you water to save your life once."

"Lañinpo?"

The man raised his eyebrows and inhaled sharply. "Thank you for returning my proa."

"Thank you for…" Ijokelekel had been about to say "lending it to me," then recalled he had stolen it.

Lañinpo broke in. "Never mind. I'm sure you made better use of it than I could have. Where was I going to go? The little akebu brought me back here to die. It was just…" He paused to cough. "It had sentimental value. I had spent my whole life in that canoe!" More coughing. "But I must tell you, watching you sail away… I had a surprisingly good feeling about it. Now look at all that came from it." He spread his arms and looked around, as if to use the house of Pahn Kadira as a metaphor for having conquered the island. "You must have felt the same way when you returned it. It became a part of you, didn't it?"

"Well, yes. It did."

"So, I want to gift it to you. On behalf of the little akebu. Yes, he was responsible for your mother's death, but it was an accident. He didn't expect her to slip and fall. What I told you out there that day was true."

Ijokelekel looked at him skeptically.

"He was killed by Sau-temoi. Doesn't that convince you he was on your side? He knew you probably hated him, but he smiled when he heard you had returned. He said he was glad you hadn't died out there."

"He was a cannibal!"

"There are worse things a man can be. You'd be surprised how many honorable cannibals are out there."

"He was responsible for changing the law and making it customary."

"No, Sau-temoi made it lawful. The little akebu only suggested it. To solve the problem after Nahn Samohl died. It was part of his background. To him, it was an obvious solution. We eat a tuna, and the tuna has eaten other fish, but what do we care! It's a complicated issue, but more than anything, it depends on how you look at it."

Ijokelekel was uncomfortable with this subject and wanted to get back to the *kakar* spears. "You said I wasn't supposed to touch the spears?" There was a long pause. "He's not going to tell me the truth," he thought.

Lañinpo's answer was abstract. "Magic is in the throat of the believer. If you don't believe, you have nothing to worry about."

"But I wasn't supposed to touch them?"

"No. But that's their custom, not yours." At that, he went into a fit of coughing, had to excuse himself, and went outside.

He didn't return. Later, Ijokelekel found him gone, but the canoe was there — pulled into the courtyard just like Lañinpo had said. He couldn't help but go over to it and run his hand along its side. It brought back years of memories that swirled in his mind for the rest of the day.

The arrival of his friend Saulikin Ant cheered him temporarily. Maalal rekindled a fire atop the temple of Nahn Sapwe, but she wasn't persistent and didn't believe in its power, and the fire soon petered out in the intermittent rains. As Ijokelekel lost his faith, he lost his will to live. As Maalal brought forth one idea after another to revitalize the village, he would say, "Have I not accomplished enough?"

Finally, it was Maalal, perhaps disgusted with his despondence and lack of interest in life and knowing the reason for it, who disclosed what he should have known all along. "Kāmeto is your sister. Stop coveting her like she's your lover! Yes, Ḷainjin is your father, which is probably why your mother sent you to Lae to begin with. Ijokelekel, things have worked out for the best. Make the most of it. Stop feeling depressed about everything. You'll age yourself with worry before your time!"

Her words stunned him and made him more pensive still. Suddenly, it all became clear. Kāmeto had exposed herself to him and shown him the most intimate part of herself, but that, as he recalled, was before he had told

Ḷainjin who his mother was. Truly, she had captured his throat, and she had followed and battled with him as promised. Then she surrendered her cleanliness to his enemy out of love for him as a brother. True, she had peed on his wound and lain with him. Yet she had remembered herself before the point of penetration. His mother had lied to him about his father, who had continued his adventures not knowing she was pregnant. He remembered how Ḷainjin had broken down when he gave him those seeds and how he had never addressed his request for Kāmeto. How could he?

Had Ijokelekel crossed the ocean, gathered a host of warriors, and won the battle without the help of Nahn Sapwe? Was Nahn Sapwe just a figment of his mother's imagination? Perhaps Nahn Sapwe was just a tale made up by ignorant Islanders to explain the takai. If he had been watching, why was there was no thunder during the battle? Did this explain why Nahn Sapwe hadn't welcomed him back by breaking takai from the cliffs? Who, then, had broken the stones in ages past? For the first time in his life, reality crept around him, and what he saw was unbearable. There was only him. He was alone now. How could he make the most of a life based on a lie? How could he lead his people without Nahn Sapwe? Hadn't he promised that Nahn Sapwe would deliver more takai? It was suddenly clear that this, too, may have been a lie of his own making.

He had befouled his honor by breaking the customs of the Pohnpeian, Kosraean, and Rālik Islanders by lusting after his sister. He was ashamed of himself. Yet, did the people not treat him as Saudeleur? Wasn't it his responsibility to make the law? Couldn't he command Kāmeto be his chiefess? Couldn't he buy her by offering lands to her Pohnpeian chosen one? Taking her would be even more shameful than lusting after her. But who was to say no? Lawmaking was up to him now.

No, that would be just like something Sau-temoi would do. Why would she accept him now, with his mouth broken? He recalled the horrible reflection of his face he had seen in the calm canal as he was paddled to Pahn Kadira. Why would she want to commit acts that break all custom with someone so ugly? What would her father, Ḷainjin, say?

Had Ijokelekel, in fact, been speared that day by the handsome Pohnpeian? Had he been killed that day? Perhaps he was dead already and everything since but a nightmare. Perhaps his appointed time had come. He remembered the story of Jatokauai and realized he had told his own story back then. He took solace in thinking that perhaps hearing that story from his mouth might lighten the grieving throats of his true mother and father back on Kwajalein, should they hear of his end. But his story must be humble. Unlike Jatokauai, he would take only his own life and make such a statement so that all those hearing his story would understand why he had done what he did.

On his behalf, Saulikin Ant began the work of reuniting the Pohnpeians and Kosraeans under common leadership. Lands were allocated to the Rālik Islanders who had fought beside the Kosraeans. Saulikin Ant was instrumental in locating a tree for Ḷainjin's replacement proa in Nanjokala, in the section of Airika. From that point on, Ḷainjin busied himself hacking daily to fell the tree with his adze. Ijokelekel missed his father's counsel but felt embarrassment in his presence and no longer had anything to ask him anyway.

Two moons later, word came that the tree, which was at the edge of the jungle, would not fall. Later, Saulikin Ant reported that, when he went to inspect the tree, he was as surprised as Ḷainjin to see that a series of vines was preventing it from toppling. The tree became such a spectacle that it became a sign to the people, and the meaning they took from it was the importance of uniting under this principle of diverse leadership. The five major vines Ḷainjin had to cut to topple the tree represented the regions into which Saulikin Ant and the elders divided the island. This pleased Ijokelekel, who, unlike the island's previous leaders, lacked any inclination to amass personal power, wealth, or prestige.

One day, Anitok brought into Ijokelekel's presence a man called Taukir, who had fought on the side of Sau-temoi. Ijokelekel recognized him as the man who had thrown the stone that ruined his face. It was clear the little man expected punishment and feared for his life. However, to his amazement, Ijokelekel congratulated him on fighting with so much loyalty on behalf of an obviously bad leader.

"Leadership," he said, "is not easy. It is only men like you who make it possible." He told Saulikin Ant to reward the man generously for his courage.

Then Ijokelekel took his proa and paddled and put ashore a short distance from Metalanim. He beached it with the help of some local boys and rubbed his hand along its length as he had seen his adopted father do the morning he had found him washed ashore. Its length had grown shorter as Ijokelekel grew. He had heard about Ḷainjin's pursuit of Sau-temoi from the people and how he found kindness and generosity wherever he went. So, Ijokelekel had decided to take only a shell knife as though he were a worker and walk as incognito as possible among them, as he had before, to again hear for himself what the people he had freed had to say. On the way to shore, he was mesmerized by his own image on the surface of the calm swamp. He no longer recognized himself. His appearance was that of an ugly old man with a torn lip. Baring his teeth and seeing those broken by the stone, he thought he would never smile again. That much was clear.

Poor Erwina — her life cut short. So full of love for her father and, one day, struck down by a hasty stone. The coward who had thrown it disappeared into the battle.

In his ear, Ijokelekel could hear the downhill rush of the stream and realized that it must start with just a trickle. Perhaps a lazy pool of rain that overflows and pours a bit into another, like his former life, with all the time necessary for every pursuit. How they had idled all those years away, expecting life to proceed at the same pace. But the pace changes forever once the trickle enters the stream and picks up direction and momentum. From that point onward, its direction is down and, very gradually, it picks up speed. But this is the trick — it can never turn back. Youth can no longer languish. It has tasted the thrill of the downward rush and must rush on now to its story's end. No one expects a wind so strong, a wave so large, or a haphazard stone to fall where it does.

As before, the people were kind and very direct as he passed among them, but most were disappointed that life hadn't improved more quickly under the new Saudeleur. Ijokelekel hated to hear this for two reasons. First, he didn't think of himself as a Saudeleur and wasn't pleased when people referred to him as such. The whole concept of a single ruler had to be extinguished. Second, he had begun to realize it wasn't fair to lay all the blame for Nahn Sapwe's passivity upon him. Yes, the Saudeleurs had turned from the faith, but the people themselves had also turned away. Why was this his fault?

He knew now that his mistake had been to assume a change in leadership would awaken Nahn Sapwe from his inertia. It was an even bigger mistake to promise this to his followers. Wherever he roamed, he asked all why Nahn Sapwe no longer broke stones from the cliffs. Most said it was because the rulers had turned away from their religion. He couldn't resist asking them if they had heard rumors that Ijokelekel had matted his sister. Most had heard these rumors but thought it was no great matter. Was the Saudeleur not above the law? Then, curiously, he asked each one for lengths of coconut-fiber twine of whatever length or thickness they could spare. He took these with him in a basket as he kept the rush of the river in his ear. Later, he twisted the lengths together into a strong rope. He began looking for young coconut trees of just the right size so he could make a loop with the rope. Then he would bend the crown and tie it off to the trunk of another so that when the line was cut, the crown would snap back with great force. After a long search, he found the perfect setup next to the rushing stream.

Although his mistakes were many, overall, he had accomplished much. It wasn't the kind of life most men aspire to, but hadn't he saved many lives? Inspired others? Granted the precious gift of freedom to all? Rather, couldn't this be but the beginning of his next adventure? Wasn't he still a young man? The image of his broken face told him no. But yes, he regretted not finding a mate to share the good and the bad, to procreate and while away the ages to come as most men do. Yet he had loved. He had been loved. He had fought the gale, tasted the cold rain, braved the ocean, and seen her surface calm and shimmering as far as the eye could see in the light of the great circle around the moon that some said destined a man to the best of luck.

True, after all this time, he still wasn't sure who he was — good or bad. But he hadn't cringed in battle and had seen what he had seen. He had chosen his words carefully, said what he had said, and done what he had done. He had even come to understand why Jatokauai, who had retrieved the malpur shell and won his life back, was too exhausted and disappointed in the Saudeleur to accept his reward, instead setting fire to his home to end his story.

It was this call of rushing water that brought all stories to their end. He had seen death and it wasn't too bad. Poor Maalal, he knew, would now understand. He had failed to return Erwina to Lae. He had defaulted on his promise to return her to her mother. All would see this as his duly accepted punishment and the rightful result of Likōkkālọk's curse.

Then, with his painful memories as clear as yesterday and ripe for harvest, he tied a second line, waist high, to the tightly drawn rope that bent the crown. He lifted his kilt and tied this line into a loop tight around his manhood and breadfruit nuts. Bracing himself, he sawed through the taut rope and was pulled off his feet and onto his back as the coconut sapling swung upright, tearing his organs from between his legs and leaving him to lie there, where he had tied off the tree. He turned cold, but luckily, the sun warmed him where he lay. Turning onto his side, he drew up his legs and covered himself with an imaginary *jaki*. He bled out that way until he slept and dreamed again of that day he had dived for clams with his sister and, together, they promised to conquer the great stone village. His blood trickled down into the stream and disappeared into the rush, headed toward the ocean below.

* * *

It wasn't long thereafter that Ḷainjin completed his great proa from the famous tree that had refused to fall. It was even larger and even better than the one he had taken across *kāleptak* and back. As promised, he took his daughter Kāmeto and her Pohnpeian man and set off on their return voyage to Lae. He had said good-bye to Ewalt and his family and to the now-famous Nahn Paratak, who, despite his limp, had become hard to find amid all his comings and goings around the island.

Then Ḷainjin said good-bye to Maalal and to the lucky Saulikin Ant. After Ijokelekel's death, Maalal had retrieved his canoe, had all the lashings replaced, and kept it for herself. Ḷainjin found it endearing to watch his daughter and Maalal part for perhaps the last time. They had known each other for but a fleeting period, yet his son, Ijokelekel, had touched them both during his short life, and they shared admiration for his inspiring soul.

Ḷainjin insisted on taking Lañinpo, who was getting sicker by the day. Perhaps the coming dry season in northern Rālik would prove better for his health. Ḷainjin had decided to give the tiller to Kāmeto, who had never sailed such a large proa before, so he could quietly reminisce for the last time with his friend about their adventures before they slipped forever from memory. Eventually, alas, the once uniquely energetic Lañinpo would meet his story's end, wrapped in Ḷainjin's arms, before they reached their destination. Yet again, Ḷainjin would let the body of another loyal friend slip from his hands into the forever moving sea.

But before all this, they would commence their voyage home on a happier note. He would chant the first line of their mothers' famous *ikir* before repeatedly beginning it again, until all had memorized the words and the rhythm, the way their mothers had wanted them chanted.

We sail. We look back.
We see mountain. We beat sharkskin.
We embark on a course to death.
Our final task, our last cast: 'Do we die today?'

"No!" All would learn to whisper this silently as Ḷainjin had. He dipped his toes into the sea below as Lañinpo — his friend for life — rested his head on his lap. "Not today."

A thoughtful review is the greatest compliment a writer receives.

Amazon US:
https://www.amazon.com/dp/B0B9ZR5N71#customerReviews

Amazon Canada:
https://www.amazon.ca/dp/B0B9ZR5N71#customerReviews

Interested in more of The Legends of Ḷainjin? Here's where you can purchase my other books:

Amazon:
https://www.amazon.com/dp/B0B9ZLMVCV

Iguana Books:
https://www.iguanabooks.ca/books/man-shark
https://www.iguanabooks.ca/books/the-forbidden-man
https://www.iguanabooks.ca/books/the-legend-is-born

Glossary

Aelōn̄ļapļap — Aka Ailinglaplap Atoll.

aje — An hourglass-shaped sharkskin drum carried by women when they accompany their men to a battle.

Ajjeļǫk eṃṃan in lan̄ ne ļe! — A saying: "The weather could not be better, boys!"

ak — The frigate bird: *Fregata magnificens.*

akebu — Komba word for a lineage leader who served as the priest or "forbidden man" of Lāpio cult worship and practiced the medicinal and magical arts.

aļap — A paramount landholder who manages land on behalf of an irooj; a lineage head.

Am wōt kwoj amine — "Yours is what you use."

Ānen-kio — Present-day Wake Island.

Āne-pin̄ — An islet of Aelōn̄ļapļap where tattooing was done.

anidep — A game in which a foot-sized cube of woven pandanus leaves is kicked back and forth within a circle by clapping participants.

Anitok — The one chosen by his clan to undergo the "jib in jowi" test by carrying the coconut through the lines of Ļan̄inni's men.

an̄ōnean̄ — "Call of the north"; the southern solstice, which annually coincides with winter in the northern hemisphere.

Ant — A coral atoll seven miles east of what is now called Pohnpei.

aolōk — A Portuguese man-of-war; genus *Physalia.*

atat — A plant with small, thin leaves; the stems of this plant, *Triumfetta procumbens*, were processed to make skirts and kilts.

bal — The foot beneath the clew of the lateen sail where its vertical gaff and horizontal yard join.

Bar Nor — Melanesian peoples inhabiting the Murik Lakes region of what is now Papua New Guinea; a coastal, intertidal area characterized by connected inland lagoons seasonally flooded with overflow from the Sepik River.

boraañ —Stingray.

bunbunbun — "Bunbun" means "to count"; in the chant, the syllables are repeated for alliterative purposes.

buñtokiōñ — Swell that "falls from the north."

buñtokrear — Swell that "falls from the east."

būtti — Wart; projection from skin; slang for "clitoris."

bwilbwil — To make and race toy proas on reefs or along the shoreline.

diak — To tack or, more specifically, shunt. The tack of the sail is transported from one end of the canoe to the other, keeping the outrigger to windward.

du — Women beating drums and accompanying their loved ones to a battle or supporting their chant as they dance the jebwa.

Eb — Mythical cannibal isle far to the west.

Ebadon — The northwesternmost islet of Kwajalein Atoll.

E jaje mannit — "She is ignorant of custom."

Ej it ļañ? — "What is the forecast?"

ekkwaļ — Sennit; coir fiber line made from processed coconut-husk fibers.

Emejjia wa ilọmeto — "A boat dies slow in the open ocean."

Eṃṃan — "Good."

Ennylabegan — An islet of Kwajalein Atoll.

Enrā lale rārā — A saying: "A basket to take care of those close to us."

Ewalt — Ļainjin's interpreter in *The Forbidden Man.*

Idedh — One of many man-made islets on the reef off the coast of eastern Pohnpei.

Ijokelekel — Ļainjin's son with Lipanmai.

ikir — A navigational poem.

inpel — The fibrous, cloth-like outer sheathing of the coconut flower buds found at the crowns of coconut trees; used to squeeze milk-like oil from coconut gratings.

iọkwe — "Aloha"; "hello (or good-bye)."

irooj — Chief.

Irooj Rilik — A mythical chief of the west side of the ocean.

i-tori-tori — To diminish or shrink.

jaab — "No. (It's not a shark. It's a...)"

jāānkun — Sun-dried sheets of pandanus pulp rolled into a log and wrapped in a sheath of pandanus leaves.

jaki — Sleeping mat.

jāpe — A wooden, trapezoid-shaped vessel carved from breadfruit wood and used to knead breadfruit; the constellation Delphinus, the dolphin.

Jau Areu — Pohnpeian title: master fisherman.

Jebrọ — Aka Pleiades; constellation. Also, the youngest son of Ḷōktañūr, who allowed his mother to board his canoe. Jebrọ first appears just before dawn and disappears in the sunrise. Later in the season, he appears earlier in the night and thus higher in the sky.

jebwa — A battle dance; a fierce reenactment of a classic fighting style passed along from previous generations.

Jeej — An idiom used to express surprise. Translates roughly as "heck" or "darn it."

jekaro — Also called "tuba," "toddy," and various other names; the sap of the coconut palm tapped from the flower bud as it grows and continues to protrude between its mature frond leaf and the less-mature inner fronds of the palm's inner crown. The skill of making jekaro is practiced worldwide wherever palms grow.

jekḷaj — The day after tomorrow.

jeṃjerā — Best friends.

jen — Kajin Rālik word for "from."

Jen eọñōd! — "Let's fish!"

jetñōl — The night the moon rises at dusk upon the waves.

jib in jowi — A rite or trial of passage that must be successfully completed for clan initiates to receive their tattoos.

Jibke — Figure from the oral literature of the Marshall Islands who is given the impossible task of finding the source of the wind and lands in the mythical land of Eb.

Joḷọk — Liṃanṃan's sister; aka Lijoḷọk.

Jorailik — Ijokelekel's adopted brother.

jowi — Clan or tribe.

jujukop — A barracuda.

jukkwe — Sand clam; a bivalve; word used to refer to one's vagina.

juon, ruo, jilu — One, two, three.

jurōk — Placing a barrier between islets to strand fish on the reef as the tide recedes.

kabwebwe — Pole fishing.

Kajin Rālik — Language of the Rālik Islands, now the western chain of the Republic of the Marshall Islands.

kajjeor — A boys' game, the objective of which is to ricochet a dried and somewhat flexible aerial-pandanus-root spear off the ground and into the air. The spear's throwing end is notched like an arrow.

kakar — Small ceremonial spears kept in the Bar Nor men's house that can be touched only by those men who have successfully been initiated into the kakar cult; bravery in battle.

Kalahngan — Pohnpeian for "thank you."

Kalahngan en komwi — Pohnpeian; "Kalahngan" means "thanks." "Komwi" means "honorific you."

kāleptak — Swell that "slaps from the west"; the countercurrent of the Intertropical Convergence Zone, which periodically streams through the islands just north and south of the equator.

kallep — Trap-jaw ant: *Odontomachus simillimus.*

Kāmeto — A name: "Fly the ocean"; Ḷainjin's daughter.

kaṃōḷo — A newcomer celebration.

Kanari — A Bar Nor man who accompanied Ḷainjin to Sigaba.

kapāl — Magic; as used in this context, love magic.

kapin meto — Literally, "back side of ocean"; the westernmost atolls of the Rālik Chain.

kapwor — Giant clam: *Tridacna gigas.*

Kariahn — A Pohnpeian islet where trading takes place.

kasap — Pohnpeian for "frigate bird."

Kaselehlie — Pohnpeian for "hello."

Kaselehlie kompoakapah — "Hello, old friend."

Kasalehlie meing — A formal greeting in Pohnpeian.

Katau — An island in the west frequented by legendary Pohnpeian heroes.

kauat — Term for something difficult or impossible to accomplish, as presented in *The Book of Luelen.*

kawko — The penis of a small boy; the term "child" is used until a boy dons a fiber kilt.

keemem — The first birthday feast after the passing of two seasons or thirteen cycles of the moon.

Kelepwei — A man-made islet across from Pahn Kadira used to house visitors.

kiden — Soldierbush tree: *Tournefortia argentea.*

kiden ta kiden — The words "Kiden, what's kiden?" are also part of the chant in the fable *Labibat.* A live branch of the soldierbush tree (*Tournefortia argentea*) is used to tenderize the octopus's otherwise tough flesh.

kidid — Wandering tattler: *Tringa incana.*

Kielua — The man who failed to deliver his stone as agreed and was sacrificially eaten.

kijen pako — Shark food.

kilōk — A strong, trapezoid-shaped basket plaited from the central portion of a coconut leaf. It features braided handles.

Kinjin emman — "Scratch of a man."

koṃṃool — Thank you.

kōņņat — A short, sprawling tree that grows next to the shore; beach cabbage: *Scaevola taccada*; "naupaka" in Hawaiian.

koon — A baby bird.

Kosrae — An island about 300 miles southeast of Pohnpei that is now one of the Federated States of Micronesia.

kōtkōt — Ruddy turnstone: *Arenaria interpres.* Marshall Islanders used to trap these small birds and train them to fight.

kubaak — Outrigger float.

Kunai — "Grass men"; also, the New Guinea pidgin English term for "grass," or *imperata cylindrica.* It catches fire easily during the dry season, when it is between two and ten feet high.

Kwajalein — The largest atoll in the Rālik chain.

kwarlin — A magic chant; no translation is available.

kweet — Octopus.

Ļainjin — Tarmālu's son, left behind shortly after birth when she led her fleet to sea in the face of a typhoon; Liṃanṃan's chosen one and Kāmeto's father.

Ļañinni — A name: "weather strong enough to blow coconuts from the trees."

Lañinpo — A name: "heavy weather requiring the striking of sails." A Seeker; Rojak's brother.

lerooj — Literally, "woman chief."

Li — Female prefix, used to emphasize respect.

liele — Trigger fish.

liet — Pohnpeian for "cannibal" or "cannibal peoples."

Lijāpe — Literally, "woman container of breadfruit"; Ijokelekel's adopted mother. A jāpe is a wooden, trapezoid-shaped vessel carved from breadfruit wood and used to knead breadfruit.

Lijitwa — Her name literally means "point to the boat on the horizon."

Lijoļọk — Liṃanṃan's sister; aka "Joļọk."

likao — A young man.

Likarwejoñ — Legendary monster who lives in a kiden tree on Karwe, an islet of Ailinginae Atoll.

Likōkkālọk — Character introduced in *Man Shark*; Erwina's mother.

Limaalal — Literally, "woman evening star."

Liṃanṃan — Irooj's daughter; Ļainjin's chosen one. A name: "woman beautiful." "Li": the female prefix; "ṃanṃan": "very beautiful." The north star, Polaris.

Lipanmai — Ijokelekel's mother; a Pohnpeian name meaning "woman under the breadfruit tree."

Lirojak — Aka Rojak. Female Seeker; Lañinpo's sister.

Ļō — Male prefix, used to emphasize respect.

ļọ — *Hibiscus tiliaceus* L. (Malvaceae); a large cordate-leaved, yellow-flowered tree with light but strong wood.

Ļōbwedi — A Seeker; aka Bwedi.

Ļōbwilñawa — A Seeker; aka Bwilñawa; the rijeļā. Ļō: the male prefix, used to emphasize respect.

Ḷōetre — Likōkkāḷọk's mate.

Ḷōjourur — Literally, "man thunder"; Ijokelekel's nickname.

Ḷōkijdik — Ijokelekel's adopted father; literally, "man rat."

lolong — A stone burial chamber.

Ḷōpako — Aka Pako; Ḷainjin's nickname. Literally, "man shark." "Ḷō": the male prefix; "pako": "shark."

Ḷōtokjān — Liṃanṃan's uncle.

Maalal — Evening star; Venus (evenings only).

mādepep — Butterfly.

Madolenihmw — One of the five municipalities of Pohnpei.

ṃakṃōk — Arrowroot; a nutritious starch processed from the rhizomes of the dryland, knee-high plant *Tacca leontopetaloides*.

Mānnijepḷā — A mythic bird that flew passengers from one island to another; the legendary bird that could not be satisfied.

Manus — Part of Manus province, and the biggest Admiralty Island, Manus lies in the Bismarck Sea north of Papua New Guinea.

mokwaṇ — The atoll dwellers, especially the Marshall Islanders, cultivated numerous varieties of edible pandanus. Some had flavorful juice they sucked from the fibrous nodules. Other pulpier varieties were chewed like fibrous carrots or baked, and the pulp was subsequently scraped from the softened nodules. This mash, or mokwaṇ, was either dried into jāānkun or mixed with arrowroot starch and coconut milk and rebaked in a breadfruit leaf.

ṃọle — Rabbitfish: *Siganus rostratus*; also called "ellōk." This fish schools in a straight line.

ṃōṃaan ṃaj — Literally, "a man is an eel," which means that he always develops a relationship with a hole. "Mōṃaan" means "man"; "ṃaj" means "eel."

ṃōn kweiḷọk — A meeting house.

ṃōñā — Kajin Rālik for "eat."

Murik — The Murik Lakes lie just north of the mouth of the Sepik River. The Bar Nor live in five or so villages along the banks of its mangrove swamp. This area was a precontact maritime trading center similar to Sigaba.

Mwanus — The people living in villages who build on the reefs of Manus and the other islands of what is now called the Admiralty group.

Nahn Madol — A Pohnpeian village on the reef.

Nahn Samohl — The sacred eel used to arbitrate disputes between trading partners.

Nahn Sapwe — Pohnpeian spirit of thunder; he cracked the megalithic basaltic crystals from the cliffs with his voice.

ṇakṇōk — Witch doctor; shaman; expert.

Naṃo Atoll — Aka Namu Atoll.

nen — Fruit from *Morinda citrifolia*, a small tree prized throughout the islands for its medicinal properties; a tonic thought to promote health. Also called "noni."

Ngehi sang Pohnpei — Pohnpeian for "I'm from Pohnpei."

ninnin — Suckle.

n̄n̄ūr — Growl.

noni — See "nen."

ok — A barrier made of coconut-palm leaves stripped from their fronds, tied together, and plaited into a fish barrier to catch fish.

Onolan — "Onolan" is Luelen's spelling; this region of Pohnpei is now known as "Onohnleng."

O-wa-tak-li — These ancient words are a chant repeated in the fable of the giant octopus, the mother of Labibat. They translate roughly as "come east, or appear from west."

Pahn Kadira — The man-made islet of the Saudeleur.

Pako — Shark. Ḷainjin's nickname: "man shark." Aka Ḷōpako.

pali — Pohnpeian for "palu." "Traditional navigator" in the languages of what are now the Western Caroline Islands of the Federated States of Micronesia.

pap — A coconut-leaf stem from the first leaflets after its base forward a few feet.

Papa Ḷōetao — A legendary trickster.

Paratak — Ḷainjin's Pohnpeian friend and the father of Likōkkāḷọk's daughter, Erwina.

pehdinpwong — A Pohnpeian wake.

pẹjpetok — The spent core of a pandanus kernel drifting about in the ocean or up on shore; a drifter.

pejwak — Brown noddy: *Anous stolidus.*

Pohnpei — Currently one of the principal island groups that make up the Federated States of Micronesia, located in the Eastern Caroline Islands.

proa — An outrigger canoe rigged with a sail.

Raipuinlañ — The prior, wealthy Saudeleur from *The Forbidden Man*; Raipuinloko's father.

Raipuinloko — Succeeded Raipuinlañ, his father, as Saudeleur. After Raipuinloko's death, his son, Sau-temoi, became Saudeleur.

Rālik — The western chain of atolls of what is now known as the Republic of the Marshall Islands.

Ratak — The eastern chain of atolls of what is now known as the Republic of the Marshall Islands.

rijeḷā — Literally, "bones that know"; navigator; captain; pali; palu.

rijerbal — Workers with land rights to work the land.

Rilujien Naṃo — "Ri" currently translates as "people" but may originally have referred to bones. "Lujien Naṃo" means "those who lost from Namu."

rojak — The individual booms of the lateen sail. Vertical boom: rojak ṃaan; lateral boom: rojak kōrā.

Rojak — The female Seeker; Lañinpo's sister; aka Lirojak.

rreo — A virgin.

rūkkatak — Apprentice.

sakau — Kava; a drink with anesthetic properties made from the mashed roots of the propagated *Piper methysticum*, or pepper plant.

Sarakena — A Bar Nor woman who killed herself in *The Forbidden Man.*

Saudeleur — The highest titled one of Nahn Madol. The ruler of Pohnpei.

Saulikin Ant — The chief of Ant Atoll.

Sau-temoi — As the son of Raipuinloko, succeeded him as Saudeleur.

Sigaba — Later called Sio Island, a "place of mixing." A precontact trading center located off the Kunai coast of the Huon Peninsula of southeastern New Guinea.

takai — Pohnpeian for "stones"; essentially the same as the Kajin Rālik word "dekā." The hexagonal basaltic crystals used to construct the pre-historic city of Nahn Madol upon a reef flat off the eastern shore of Pohnpei. These megalithic crystals date back to the volcanic origin of the island.

Taklur — Paramount chief of Wōjjā.

Talupe — The ambitious Pohnpeian woman who captures Ḷainjin's attention.

tipñōl — Large outrigger sailing canoe, or proa.

Tiripeijo bird — A legendary bird in the story of Lamuak and Lapanmor, as told in *The Book of Luelen.*

to kubaak — The stay or stays between the outrigger and the masthead.

Truk — The next island and language group west of Pohnpei.

tuwe — Another word for "magic."

ūrōrmej — Damselfish. A colorful fish with a somewhat-puckered mouth.

ut — Flower.

wapepe — Literally, "boat floating." The symbol represents the four swells, one from each quadrant, converging upon an island in mid-ocean.

water shells — Mature coconut shells, their meat hollowed out by tiny crabs, filled with water and their mouths stuffed tight with a plug.

wāto — A tract of land from the ocean side to the lagoon side.

Wōde im ajoḷe — "Chew it and gnaw at it!" (As if it were a pandanus nodule.)

Wōjjā — Aka Woja Atoll; the easternmost islet of Aelōñḷapḷap Atoll.

Wōjjej — An idiom used to express surprise.

Wōt jeej — The same as "jeej." An idiom used to express surprise that translates as "heck" or "darn it." Demonstrates more deliberation than "wōjjej."

Wōt jej — A more emphatic expression of surprise than "jeej."

wūdiddid — A shiver.

wūnaak — Flocks of seabirds diving for baitfish driven to the surface by tuna or other large fish.

Bibliography

Abo, Takaji, Byron W. Bender, Alfred Capelle, Tony DeBrum. *Marshallese-English Dictionary*. Honolulu: University of Hawaii Press, 1976

Athens, John Stephen. "The Discovery and Archaeological Investigation of Nan Madol." *Micronesian Archaeological Survey reports*. Saipan: Historic Preservation Office, 1981

Bernart, Luelen. *The Book of Luelen*. John L. Fischer, Saul H. Riesenberg, Marjorie G. Whiting, Eds. Canberra: Australian National University Press, 1977

Lipset, David. *Mangrove Man*. Cambridge University Press, 1997

Petersen, Glenn. "Lost in the Weeds: Theme and Variation in Pohnpei Political Mythology." *Occasional Paper Series 35*. Honolulu: Center for Pacific Islands Studies, University of Hawai'i at Mānoa, 1990

Rehg, Kenneth L., Damian G. Sohl. *Ponapean-English Dictionary*. Honolulu: University of Hawaii Press, 1979

Spennemann, Dirk H.R. *Tattooing in the Marshall Islands*. Honolulu: Bess Press, 2009

www.ingramcontent.com/pod-product-compliance
Lightning Source LLC
Chambersburg PA
CBHW020842020726
47497CB00005B/1216
9781771806350